"You have _____

_____"

"I have since I was twelve years old," Jenna replied.

"You have five seconds to produce whatever you have hidden in your dress or, I swear by all that is holy, I will rip your bodice in half and retrieve it for you," said the Duke of Worth.

"Ah. Is this your area of expertise?"

That stopped him short. "What the hell is that supposed to mean?"

Jenna smirked at him and cocked a brow. "I thought bodice ripping might be part of your overwhelming charm."

Worth's eyes darkened even further. "Very well, Miss Hughes, have it your way."

God's teeth, he was calling her bluff.

She watched as the duke's hands went first to her shoulders, then to the edges of her bodice. She felt the backs of his fingers brush against her bare skin as he curled them around the seam. Jenna remained perfectly still, her breath caught in her chest and her heart thundering against her ribs.

The air around her had thickened. Every muscle in her body had clenched, and it wasn't in fear. It was in anticipation.

ALSO BY KELLY BOWEN

I've Got My Duke to Keep Me Warm

KELLY BOWEN

A Good Rogue Is Hard to Find

FOREVER

NEW YORK   BOSTON

Copyright © 2015 by Kelly Bowen
Excerpt from *You're the Earl That I Want* © 2015 by Kelly Bowen
All rights reserved. In accordance with the U.S. Copyright Act of 1976, the scanning, uploading, and electronic sharing of any part of this book without the permission of the publisher constitute unlawful piracy and theft of the author's intellectual property. If you would like to use material from the book (other than for review purposes), prior written permission must be obtained by contacting the publisher at permissions@hbgusa.com. Thank you for your support of the author's rights.

Forever
Hachette Book Group
1290 Avenue of the Americas
New York, NY 10104

HachetteBookGroup.com

Printed in the United States of America

First Edition: April 2015
10 9 8 7 6 5 4 3 2 1

OPM

Forever is an imprint of Grand Central Publishing.
The Forever name and logo are trademarks of Hachette Book Group, Inc.

The Hachette Speakers Bureau provides a wide range of authors for speaking events. To find out more, go to www.hachettespeakersbureau.com or call (866) 376-6591.

The publisher is not responsible for websites (or their content) that are not owned by the publisher.

*In memory of the late Elizabeth Thornton,
who first suggested that England might
be a good place to start.*

Acknowledgments

Once again, thanks to my wonderful agent, Stefanie Lieberman, and to my very patient and hardworking editor Alex Logan. And a sincere thank-you to all the incredible romance authors I've been lucky enough to meet this past year who have generously offered their encouragement, support, and wisdom.

Chapter 1 ——————

London, England, June 1817

William Somerhall, Duke of Worth, glared at the clock on the mantel.

It was a terrifically horrid piece, cast in some sort of heavy metal that he supposed was meant to look like bronze. Robust chickens pranced their way across the top of it, spindly legs interspersed with leafy vines that ended in pumpkins. Or turnips. From where he sat, it was hard to tell which.

The hands of the clock were in the shape of feathers and painted a garish red, and they marched around in circles, ticking incessantly. Bits of red paint had been applied to the combs of the cast roosters above the face, and the entire thing looked positively ghoulish in the glowing firelight.

"If you like the clock so much, Worth, you can take it with you."

Will tore his gaze from the hands relentlessly creeping around the face. "Have I ever mentioned how much I hate chickens?"

"Repeatedly," the Earl of Boden drawled, though not without some sympathy.

The minute hand reached half past and the clock chimed, reminding Will he should leave. Leave the warmth of the fire roaring in the hearth. Leave the company of a dear friend, the pursuit of a good card game, and the bliss of a truly superb brandy, to ride the mile and a half to his mother's dower house. To be tortured.

"Dear God, but I don't want to go. Please don't make me."

The Earl of Boden raised his palms in defense. "I've never succeeded in making you do anything. In fact, I'm quite happy to have you drinking in my drawing room, donating your money to my coffers. Another three rounds of cards and I believe I will have won enough from you to buy a new clock."

Will grinned at his friend despite himself. "It is the ugliest clock I've ever seen."

"It came with the title and house. Like everything else I never wanted." Boden fixed his bright-blue eyes on the duke. "But you really should go. It's only a dinner party, for Christ's sake. And she's your *mother*."

Will glanced again at the offending timepiece and made a face. "If my mother had her way, I'd suffer through every single one of her weekly dinner parties."

"How bad can they possibly be?"

"Which part? The part where she will skewer me with questions about my life I have no intention of answering? Or leaves me with whey-faced virgins who are calculating my net worth and testing my title on their tongues? Or parks me in front of stuffy peers who pressure me to adopt whatever cause they are currently championing?"

"She has good intentions, Worth. Any mother who cared about her son would do the same." The earl gave him a long look. "And it wouldn't kill you to find a girl to marry and a cause to champion. You're a duke, in case you've forgotten."

"I've already found the girl I want to marry."

Boden snorted. "Ah, yes, the mysterious woman who disappeared from your ball last year like an enchanted princess."

"I'm quite certain she wasn't actually a princess. But she was utterly enchanting."

"Did you ever stop to think, Worth, that the idea of marriage to this woman appeals to you because she doesn't exist? I'm sure marriage to an imaginary woman would be sublime." The earl rolled his eyes. "An imaginary cause would be just as good."

"Harsh words from my unmarried, cause-less friend."

Boden sighed patiently. "I have a cause, Worth. It's called a business. Something I've been managing on my own for a long while. And if I could find time to unearth a woman who doesn't care my title was accidental and my fortune was made in trade, and could multiply six-digit numbers in her head on demand, I'd marry her on the spot."

Will scoffed. "Say the word, my friend, and I'll find you one who likes money. I trip over them everywhere I go. The mathematical requirement might be more difficult."

The earl smiled a rare smile and waved his hand. "Go to your mother's, Worth. Before she just plain skewers you for missing another one of her dinners. Or worse, blames me. You can't avoid her indefinitely."

Boden was right. Will had ducked the last half dozen invitations she'd sent him, and the guilt was starting to nag at him. He'd successfully avoided the dower house for more years than he could count off the top of his head. He supposed he should go, if only to verify the house still stood and was in good repair. Will employed staff who dealt with that sort of thing, but still. He really should make an effort.

Sighing, Will reluctantly heaved himself to his feet. With luck he would arrive at the very end of the party, after the gentlemen had already debated their passions well into the depths of their port and the women had come to terms with the fact that the duke would not be available to dance attendance on their unmarried daughters. He had no idea why his mother insisted on these parties. All she accomplished was providing the ton with a week's worth of gossip.

He wondered if the duchess even realized just how peculiar everyone believed her to be.

"How is the duchess these days?" Boden asked carefully, as if reading his mind.

"Oh, God," Will groaned. "What have you heard now?"

The earl made a tactful noise somewhere in his throat. "Nothing of import." He paused. "Does she still keep... ah, birds?"

"The chickens, you mean? The ones she insists on carting around everywhere like ugly avian lapdogs to balls and musicales and garden parties?"

The earl winced.

"Yes." Will scowled. And all that stood between his eccentric mother and outright ridicule from the whole of London society was the fact that she was a duchess. And that her son was a duke who wouldn't stand for it. "Have I mentioned recently how much I hate chickens?"

"Have you tried talking to her about it?"

"She doesn't want to hear anything I have to say. Though I suppose I can't really blame her, for nothing I have to say on that particular topic is pleasant." Will yanked on his coat, his mood souring more with every passing minute.

"Try again."

Will's jaw clenched.

"Take her the clock as a peace offering." The earl gestured at the poultry-covered clock.

"Are you trying to be funny, Boden?"

"No." The earl sighed. "I'm trying to be helpful. You're going to have to have a conversation with your mother, and you're going to have to have it soon, whether you want to or not."

Will grumbled under his breath. His mother's eccentricity was accelerating, and everyone knew it. "I will." He stabbed his fingers into his gloves.

"I appreciated your company tonight, Worth," the earl said, and Will was relieved that Boden had let the subject drop. "It was a welcome distraction from, well, everything as of late."

"Of course." Will turned back to his oldest and dearest friend. "If I recall, you did the same for me after my father died. The only difference being, of course, that you actually liked your father."

"Will, your father might not have been perfect—"

"My father was cruel and used everyone around him to achieve his own ends, including his family. There has never been any point in pretending otherwise." Will took a deep breath. "Your father wasn't perfect either, but he was a good man and I'm sorry that he's gone. He was always kind to me and my sister."

Boden suddenly looked tired.

Impulsively Will clasped him on the shoulder. "I'm here to help, you know that, right? I promise, whatever you need, you just have to ask."

"Thank you." The earl smiled faintly. "Now go, so that you might live long enough to make good on that promise. It's getting late."

Will took one last look at the clock and sighed again. It wasn't nearly late enough.

⁓

The dower house was situated on the far western side of his Breckenridge estate, closer to the Earl of Boden's ancient manor house than to his own mansion. Twilight was settling comfortably over the land, deepening the shadows on the sides of the path that connected the two properties and illuminating the leaves and grassy ridges with silver. Will allowed his mare to wander along the narrow path, in no hurry to arrive at his mother's and in no hurry to risk his mare's legs in rabbit holes.

Idly he wondered if anyone would believe he'd fallen from his horse if he dismounted and rolled around in the leaves and mud. A purported tumble would make him quite late, or better yet, unable to attend at all. It would, however, also ruin the new coat of black superfine he'd just purchased, and he couldn't bring himself to do that to such a splendid garment. The tailor who had crafted the coat was a true artist and to purposefully destroy such a creation would be something approaching sacrilege.

His mare scrambled up out of the trees and onto the road, and Will sighed. Up ahead the lights of the dower house were just coming into view, a soft glow winking through the multi-paned windows. Once he was closer, he knew the sounds of the pianoforte would become audible if the windows were open. His mother would be dressed to perfection, the meal would have been splendid, and everyone would be lingering over the fine wines and liquors that would be flowing freely, and pretending to ignore the chicken clutched under the duchess's arm.

Will was tired of pretending. But he didn't have the smallest idea how to fix it.

He'd suggested to his mother just a few weeks ago that she hire a companion. A capable soul who would be the perfect answer to his mother's escalating unpredictability, unerringly guiding the duchess back from the edge of eccentricity. His mother had informed him she already had a companion—in fact, had had one for years. Another stab of guilt had pierced him, with the realization that he hadn't even been aware. And perhaps therein was the problem.

Absently Will guided his mare to the side of the road, still mulling over the problem that was his mother as a carriage clattered by in the opposite direction, the horses moving at a rapid clip. Even as a child, Will had never been close with the duchess. He knew she'd done the best she could, but all her energy and efforts had seemed to go into managing his father's angry moods. She'd spent her entire life trying to love the only person who wasn't capable of loving her back. Of loving anyone, for that matter. Perhaps Will should have spent more time with her once his father had died. Perhaps that would have bridged this chasm that seemed to have opened up, filled with ignorance and lack of understanding.

Another carriage was barreling up the road. Will

frowned at the speed of it. He'd never drive his horses like that in the dark. The equipage rumbled past him, and his mare tossed its head at the pebbles that were scattered from beneath the wheels. A horse and rider were galloping behind the carriage, the man's coattails flapping in the wind, making him look like an oversize bat in the darkness. Will stared as the rider thundered by, not even acknowledging his presence.

Will urged his mare into a trot. Up ahead a third carriage threaded the stone posts that flanked the driveway and turned in the direction of town, its lanterns swinging wildly. From the house a shout reached his ears on the breeze, then another. Alarm began to clamor. Something was wrong. His mare broke into a canter, and Will allowed it to lengthen its stride, less fearful of the footing on the road.

Another carriage lurched up the driveway. The mare veered around it, Will's focus on the house ahead. Nothing appeared to have collapsed or to be in imminent danger of burning to the ground, which offered a small measure of relief, but did not bode well for what he might find inside. He had visions of his mother lying hurt or worse, and by the time he reached the circular drive leading up to the wide stone steps, his horse was at a full gallop.

The last carriage remaining was being brought around hurriedly by a harried coachman he didn't recognize. Will ignored them all, desperate only to reach his mother and whatever disaster had befallen her within. Whatever her eccentricities, no matter her peculiarities, he loved her and couldn't bear the thought of her suffering.

Coming to a skidding halt in front of the wide stone steps, Will leaped from the saddle and took the steps two at a time, the rush of flight and fear making his legs unsteady. He reached for the handles of the heavy doors, but they crashed open before he could touch them, narrowly missing his face. A matronly woman tumbled out, squealing in distress and with her face flushed an alarming color. She made a desperate beeline for the waiting carriage. On her heels a white missile followed, careening into the night amid a flurry of wings and loud squawking. Will ducked instinctively.

"Lady Gainsey? What— Gack!" A second hen hit Will square in the chest in an explosion of feathers before he could finish his sentence. He stumbled backward, landing hard on his rear.

"God almighty," he wheezed, swatting frantically at the chicken that seemed to have become temporarily entangled in his cravat. The bird screeched its displeasure before flapping away after its comrade, and Will was left flat on his back, staring up at tiny bits of down floating around his ears. A deafening crash came from somewhere inside the house.

Will swore before shoving himself to his feet, only to be nearly mowed down again by a burly man, wide eyes peering at him from under a disheveled wig that had been fashionable fifty years earlier.

"Your Grace," the older man spluttered, hurrying after his wife into the waiting carriage. "Thank God you're here!"

A wave of panic once again assailed Will. "Is my mother all right?"

The man paused at the door of the carriage long enough to give Will a look of utter disbelief. "All right? Your mother is a menace!"

Will felt his mouth drop open. "I beg your pardon?"

"Er, that is to say," the man spluttered at Will's expression, "I—" He didn't get to finish before he was yanked into the interior of the carriage with enough force to knock his wig from his head and into the dust. The carriage door snapped shut, and the vehicle lurched off down the drive.

Will gaped after it for a half second before turning toward the house, his heart in his throat. He dashed through the doors left hanging ajar and staggered to an abrupt halt as he laid eyes on the tableau before him.

His mother's hall looked as though it had been plundered and pillaged by a horde of barbarian invaders. The chairs nearest the fireplace had been overturned and with them a small end table. A large vase lay victim at its side, a thousand pieces of blue-and-white porcelain strewn across the gleaming floor amid a puddle of water and scattered roses. At his feet a glove lay forlorn and forgotten, and the remnants of a lady's hat sat crushed in a corner. On the richly papered walls, a cracked mirror hung crooked, and as he stared in disbelief, a piece fell from the frame with a resounding crash.

And everything, everywhere, was covered with a fine scattering of white feathers.

"There you are, you little bastard."

The voice was low and vicious, and Will jerked in alarm, instinctively dropping to a crouch and backing out of the hall, groping for a weapon he didn't have. His heart was pounding, and he was breathing hard. What manner of outlaw was stalking the hall? And had he been seen? And where was his mother?

"Come to momma now," the voice crooned, and Will

felt a bead of cold sweat slide down his back. He snatched a parasol from where it had been abandoned near the door and crept back out into the night, pressing himself flat against the wall. It wasn't much but it was better than nothing if he needed to defend himself.

Cautiously he peered around the doorframe.

A behemoth of a woman was stalking across the hall, the sleeves of her dress shoved to her elbows and her apron covered in blood. A massive butcher knife was tucked into the apron strings against her hip, and her eyes held the promise of murder. Will swallowed with difficulty, tightening his grip on the parasol.

Except she wasn't looking at him. Her slitted eyes were trained instead on the ornate mantelpiece, where another chicken flapped in disgruntlement.

The leviathan crept closer to the wall and stopped, wiping a forearm the size of an oak across her forehead. "I got yer friends," she murmured, holding up her left hand, in which two other birds dangled and struggled. "Let's just make this easy, hmmm?"

The chicken on the mantel spread its wings in defiance, but with a speed that belied her size, the woman's arm shot out and seized the hen before the bird could make good on its escape. The chicken screeched, and Will flinched.

"I got 'em all, Your Grace," she bellowed at the top of her considerable lungs.

A second later a door opened at the rear of the hall, and his mother swept in.

"Thank you, Margaret," she said pleasantly. "Well done."

Will put a hand out to steady himself, relief making him feel a little wobbly. The duchess was safe. She wasn't lying hurt or bleeding or dying. In fact, not a strand of her carefully coiffed white hair was out of place, nor was a stitch askew in her fashionable dinner gown. She did not seem unduly distressed or even upset. And Will suddenly recalled that Margaret, the Amazon brandishing the knife, was only his mother's oversize cook.

Will's panic and fear started a rapid descent down the slippery slope of irritation and anger.

The Earl of Boden had been right. Will needed to have a conversation with his mother, and he needed to have it soon. A dozen of the most distinguished aristocrats had just been driven out of his mother's home by a flock of pampered poultry. Not to mention the demolition of the hall. And the destruction of the reputation and credibility of his mother. And by association himself.

God, but he hated chickens.

Will began to straighten, but his mother's voice checked him.

"Did you find Phillip?" The duchess had moved to the bottom of the stairs and was peering up into the empty space, still oblivious to his presence.

Phillip? Who the hell was Phillip?

"Yes." A disembodied female voice floated down faintly from the first floor. "He was in your bed again."

Will felt his eyes bulge.

"Thank goodness." His mother put a hand to her chest in obvious relief. "How is he?"

"He seems a little stiff. Do you think I should give him a rub or just try to warm him up?"

Will sucked in a breath in an attempt to dispel the black spots that had begun to dance in front of his eyes. A mental image of a naked man sprawled across his mother's bed popped unbidden into his mind. And then the duchess entered the sordid scene, and Will ruthlessly stomped on the vision before his imaginary mother could discard any imaginary clothing.

The duchess tipped her head in consideration. "Bring him here and we'll put him in the kitchens. It will be easier to set him to rights there. It's warmer."

"Very good. I'll be right down with him."

Oh, dear God. Whatever was going on in his mother's household was far, far worse than he had originally thought. Will mentally girded himself for the conflict he was about to charge into, knowing it was unavoidable.

A woman was now descending the main stairs, presumably preceding Phillip, and as Will's gaze fell on her a strange, inexplicable frisson of awareness skittered through him.

The woman was tall and lithe, her plain gown of insipid blue serge doing absolutely nothing to disguise the fluid grace with which she moved. Her hair was dark as pitch, pulled back in an unadorned knot at the back of her head, yet the simplicity only served to display the elegance of her neck and the striking angles of her face. Will felt the floor tilt beneath his feet.

It was *she*.

He recognized her instantly as his enchanting, mysterious princess. He'd spoken to her only once, at the ball he'd hosted at Breckenridge a year ago. He'd not had the chance to learn her name, and in the chaos that had ensued that evening, she'd simply disappeared. Though certainly not from his memory. He'd been captivated that night, enthralled by her beauty and her poise, but no amount of inquiry in the assembly halls, the clubs, or the drawing rooms of London had given him the gift of her identity. Yet somehow, impossibly, the woman who had haunted his imaginings stood in his mother's ruined hall, even more breathtaking than he remembered.

"He's not injured, is he?" his mother asked, and Will could hear the concern in her voice.

"No, he seems quite all right." The woman had reached the bottom of the stairs, and her voice was warm and throaty. Will sucked in his breath at the evocative familiarity of it. Just the sound made his blood heat and his pulse skip. She exuded heat and vitality, and Will found himself shamelessly spellbound.

Until he became aware she was holding something in her hands.

The thing was at least as thick as his arm and the length of his leg, its skin a smooth, glistening patchwork of rich mahogany and black. Every once in a while, a forked tongue would flick out to test the air as its head swiveled. Gently, like a pagan goddess, the woman lifted the snake and settled it about her shoulders, where it curled, to all appearances sublimely content. His mother clucked in approval.

William thought he might have made a strangled noise somewhere in the back of his throat. Breathing seemed to have become a chore. Revulsion warred with awe.

The forgotten chickens, still clutched in Margaret's hands, seemed to catch sight of reptilian death and suddenly renewed their frantic struggling and squawking.

"You want I should put these back in the drawing room, Your Grace?" Margaret asked his mother, holding up the birds.

"Yes, please. The two that got out will likely find their

way to the stables sometime tonight. You can check in the morning and bring them back then."

"Very good, Your Grace." The cook bobbed her head and disappeared through a doorway on one side of the hall.

The duchess looked around the hall and put her hands on her ample hips. "So unnecessary," she said with a faint hint of disgust. "Clearly I did not secure the latch on the cage properly this afternoon."

The goddess shrugged, unconcerned, though there was amusement in her gesture. "I thought the crystal might implode, the way Lady Wilston was screaming."

"*Hmph.*" The duchess's lips twitched. "She certainly ruined a perfectly good dinner. And Margaret had gone to such work, what with the soup and the stuffed fish."

"The soup was quite delicious," the goddess agreed.

"She even made lemon tarts for dessert," the duchess said regretfully.

"More for us now, though."

"True."

"Did she use lemon in the fish as well, do you suppose?"

"Indeed. Mixed with pepper in the most pleasing manner."

"I wonder if she would make it again?"

"I'm sure she would. With biscuits and butter, perhaps. Now that would be delightful."

Will was aware his mouth had fallen open again, and he made an effort to close it. There had been chickens in the drawing room and there was a beautiful woman with a snake around her neck, and his mother was standing there, idly discussing the menu.

Will shut his eyes, wondering if he was the only sane one left.

"I believe Lady Wilston thought Lord Gainsey was taking liberties under the dinner table," his goddess was saying in that throaty voice of hers, laughter bubbling just below the surface.

Will's eyes popped open. Her words and her tone made him wonder if his princess might be a courtesan. But her clothing in no way supported that supposition. Her dress was proper to the point of being prudish, and the fabric sat more like sacking than silk. And why the hell would his mother be entertaining a courtesan? Then again, why did his mother do anything she did?

"Ah. I was wondering why she was blushing and squirming like that." The duchess snickered.

Will blinked in alarm. This was not a suitable—

"I do suppose it would have been a bit of a surprise. 'Tis not every day one finds a python up one's skirts," the goddess said.

A line of sweat broke out along Will's forehead as comprehension dawned, along with horror. Was she saying that . . . thing had crawled up Lady Wilston's skirts?

Good Christ, but he would have screamed too.

"Just looking for a warm place, I imagine," she continued.

"Probably the first to have that view in years," the duchess drawled, chuckling. "Don't know how warm it would have been."

Will choked and felt himself blush to the roots of his hair, something he hadn't done since he was fourteen.

The dark-haired woman only laughed.

"We might have made it to dessert had Lord Gainsey not left the table then," his mother mused.

"Lady Wilston certainly would have," the goddess murmured with smoky innuendo.

The duchess guffawed, and William lost his balance where he was crouched, falling into the open doorway and landing hard on his backside for the second time that night.

Both women whirled in surprise.

The duchess froze until she caught sight of William. Shock shadowed her features so quickly that Will was certain he had imagined it. He blinked, and his mother's face creased into her customary expression of vapid delight.

"Worth, darling, whatever are you doing on your hands and knees in my hall? Have you lost something?"

An unwelcome embarrassment pricked, and Will scrambled to his feet with as much ducal dignity as he could muster. "No, Mother, I have not lost anything." Like his temper. Yet.

She gave him a puzzled look. "If you've come for dinner, you've missed it." She sniffed accusingly. "Again."

Will strode forward into the wreckage of the room, porcelain crunching beneath his boots, and eyed his mother. He ignored the snake and the goddess it was draped over with incredible effort. For now.

One thing at a time.

"I thought you were hurt. Or sick. Or dying."

"Good heavens. Why would you think such a thing?" The duchess looked mystified now.

"Because I was nearly run down by a great number of carriages fleeing your home. Because I arrived here to find *this*." He gestured at the wreckage of their surroundings.

"*Pssht*." She shrugged indifferently as though this were all a regular occurrence.

With a horrible sinking feeling, Will began to suspect that it was.

The duchess pulled out a quizzing glass and was peering closely at him. "Good heavens, Worth darling, but you look a state. Your hair is a mess and what on earth happened to your cravat? And is that a parasol you're holding? Please tell me you didn't go out looking like this tonight."

Will looked down at the lacy parasol still clutched in his hand and threw it to the side as though it had burned him. "I thought you were dying, Mother," he gritted. He could feel a muscle working along his jaw.

"I'm quite fine, as you can see." She waved her hand airily, dislodging a feather from Will's shoulder.

"Tell me you're not still keeping chickens in the house," he said, trying to keep his voice even.

"Why, I like chickens, dear. What harm is there in it?"

Will stared at the duchess and counted to ten silently before he answered. "No one else likes chickens in the house unless they are on a plate served with wine."

"*Pssht*," the duchess scoffed again.

"Mother," Will started, "your chickens just chased your dinner guests out of your house and down the drive."

"Oh, that wasn't the chickens, darling. That was Phillip." She stepped back and gestured at the goddess with the snake, and Will was finally forced to face both.

He was relatively pleased that he managed to hold his ground, even as the serpent extended itself toward him, probing the air with its flicking tongue. He wrenched his gaze away from the unholy creature and focused instead on the woman, meeting a pair of enigmatic ice-blue eyes, nearly level with his own. Awareness flared once again, and his heart hammered against his ribs. She smiled at him—a smile lingering somewhere between amusement and mockery, as though her surroundings and the people within were for her a form of constant private entertainment.

"A pleasure to see you again, Your Grace." The dimple creased in her cheek, and her eyes continued to hold his.

All the air in the room seemed to have suddenly been sucked out. He searched his repertoire of witty comments for a clever remark that would impress and charm. Yet his thoughts had scattered. Her single smile had reduced him to a simpleton.

Inbred manners finally saved him from himself and made his mouth move. "No, my lady, the pleasure is mine. I regret that I did not get a chance to further our conversation under more pleasant circumstances. You disappeared before I had the chance to thank you for your graciousness under duress."

His goddess smiled fully at him then, and it was a little like looking at the sun.

"Oh, have you already met Miss Hughes, dear?" the duchess asked. "My hired companion?"

Will blinked, alarm slicing through the fog of fascination that had addled his brain.

"Companion?" he croaked. That couldn't possibly be right. Miss Hughes had been dancing at his ball, dressed in a glorious gown, looking for all the world like the glittering princess he had fancied her to be. Not a companion.

Hired companions were demure and genteel. Paragons of discretion and diplomacy, models of flawless politesse and social restraint. Hired companions tended to be invisible. Reserved. Plain.

None of which even remotely applied to the woman who now dropped into an improbable curtsy more suited to court than a country hall.

"Indeed, Your Grace," Miss Hughes murmured quietly, the sound of her voice once again sending heated thrills zinging through his veins.

"You live here?" Will demanded, unable to help himself, and the duchess made a sound of disapproval at his boorishness.

Miss Hughes smiled again. "Indeed, Your Grace."

"Had you ever come to one of my parties here, dear, you would have known that," the duchess said archly.

Will took a deep breath, trying to pull himself together. His mother, loath as he was to admit it, was right. Had Will been present in her life more consistently, he would have known she retained a companion. A beautiful, worldly companion, but a companion Will suspected might not be at all appropriate for the position.

His mother needed security and consistency. Predictability and dignity. Not a snake-draped goddess, standing in the middle of a ruined hall, who had carried on a conversation with the dowager duchess that was better suited to a bawdy house than a dower house. Who didn't seem even a little concerned with any of it. How had he allowed this to happen?

Will suddenly needed a drink more than he ever had in his life. He rubbed his face with his hands. "Please explain. Why do you have a snake in your house, Mother?"

The duchess gave him a cheeky grin and lifted the snake from around Miss Hughes's shoulders. "This is Phillip, dear. And he is very misunderstood."

"And where did it come from?" Will asked, relieved his voice had not retreated into the realm of hysteria, which was where his instincts were currently dragging him as he watched his mother handle the reptile.

"Your cousin brought him back from India for me," the duchess told him, stroking the back of the snake now draped over her arm. "So I named it after him. I'm told it's called a python."

"And I assume my cousin told you this himself? Or did he leave a note before the damn snake swallowed him on the voyage back to England?"

"Mind your language, dear," the duchess admonished.

Will glanced in the direction of Miss Hughes, only to find her eyes dancing with ill-concealed humor. In fact, both women were regarding him as though he were a particularly amusing interloper.

Alarm bells were tolling loudly. When had this all become acceptable? When had this become *normal*?

"Your Grace?" A rough voice spoke up from somewhere behind Will.

"Yes, George?" The duchess looked past Will, and he turned to find an elderly man standing in the doorway with what looked like a dead rodent clutched in his hands.

"I found this outside." He held up the mass of gray, leaves and twigs sticking from it.

"What in heaven's name is that?" she asked, blinking.

"Pardon?" the man asked, leaning closer.

"What is that?" the duchess said loudly.

The man shook his head and cupped a hand to his ear. "I beg your pardon?"

Miss Hughes moved around and came to stand next to George. "What do you have?" she yelled into his ear.

Will started, though no one else seemed to find this odd.

"Ah." The man nodded. "I believe it is Lord Gainsey's wig, Your Grace." He shook it, and a few leaves fell to the floor. "Should I have it cleaned and returned?"

"Heavens, no," the duchess said. "Wigs are so unfashionable. Give it to the dogs to play with. He'll thank us for it later."

"Mother!" Will wheezed. "What is wrong with you?" He pressed his temples with his fingers.

The duchess looked at him reprovingly. "There is nothing wrong with me, dear." She hefted the snake in her arms. "At least nothing that a lemon tart won't remedy."

"A lemon tart," he repeated dumbly. *A lemon tart?*

This had to stop. It was one thing for his mother to be considered odd. It was another thing for her to be a laughingstock. He didn't want that kind of attention for her, and he certainly didn't want it for himself. In any event, it was quite apparent his mother had been left to her own devices for far too long.

Something had to be done.

"Would you care to stay for a bit, dear? Since you're already here?" his mother was asking.

Will forced himself to take deep, even breaths. "No," he said slowly.

"Oh, that's too bad." The duchess sighed.

"I'm not staying for a bit." Will straightened his shoulders, the solution to his dilemma suddenly very clear.

His mother and her mad household, the staff and the delectable Miss Hughes—all of it needed to be dealt with.

"I'm going to move in."

Chapter 2

Jenna Hughes forced her features into a mask of neutrality even as her heart dropped to her toes and the first stirrings of unease prickled unpleasantly against her skin.

"You can't be serious, darling," scoffed Eleanor, Dowager Duchess of Worth; her features were calm, but there was a brittleness to her voice beneath her dismissal.

"I've never been more serious in my life."

Jenna flinched. She believed him, if only based on the grim line of his mouth. She was well aware of the duke's reputation in polite society as a fun-loving, incorrigible rogue. The ton judged him charismatic, daring, and stylish. Good-hearted, but unserious. In short, a beautiful fribble of a man. But at this moment, if the duke's expression was any indication, he was feeling neither glib nor blithe. And even more worrisome was that Jenna had seen that very same hardened look on his face before.

At the Newmarket racecourses in Surrey. And again at Epsom Downs. When he was running his beloved thoroughbreds, he was always serious. And smart. And sober. And very, very successful.

Which was why he had to leave the dower house. Leave

as soon as possible and return to his bubble of friends, fun, and fast horses and not look back.

"There is no need for such extreme measures," the duchess told him, sounding convincingly blithe. "If you ever spent any time at Breckenridge in the summer, you would remember that the main house is hardly much of a ride from here. Stay there. Then you can simply visit, like I've been asking you to do for years."

"I visit you plenty when we're both in residence in London during the season, Mother," the duke sighed. "And you know very well I'm never at Breckenridge during the summer because I'm away at the racetracks." He glanced around pointedly. "Though it is quite apparent that my absence has become a problem. I'm not leaving."

Eleanor sniffed. "I'll send some of my staff over to the main house to help you get settled, then—"

The duke was shaking his head. "You misunderstand. The problem is not at the main house. The problem is here. I'm not leaving the dower house."

"You cannot move in." The duchess crossed her arms over her ample chest, her blue eyes flashing.

"This isn't a debate, Mother," the duke replied. "Please instruct your housekeeper to prepare my rooms. I believe I'll use the blue suite."

"No."

"No?" Worth's eyes narrowed. There was an edge of anger now. "I arrive here to find a half dozen lords and ladies fleeing, the hall in shambles, chickens in the drawing room, and my mother wearing a snake. And the worst of it is, you seem to find it funny."

Despite the dire circumstances, Jenna bit the inside of her cheek. Well, when he put it like that, really, who wouldn't?

The duke's dark eyes impaled Jenna's as if daring her to contradict him. Her breath caught. He was sinfully handsome, what with his height and his broad shoulders and his devil-may-care aura, but she'd never been on the receiving end of his determination. She'd witnessed his charm and consideration before, but he presented these so effortlessly and with such natural kindness that she had always judged him to be a malleable sort of man. His determination had transformed him into something more dangerous that she wasn't sure would be easy to manage. It sent an unwelcome shiver along her spine and raised the hair on the back of her neck. A determined Duke of Worth stole her breath.

"What I was going to say, dear, was that the blue suite hasn't been the blue suite in quite some time. The blue suite is rather the cream-and-gray suite now. With perhaps a touch of pink."

"They're my rooms," Jenna said, forcing herself to respond with an amiable dignity she hoped was appropriate for a companion. She cringed inwardly, wondering if the duke had overheard the wholly inappropriate conversation she'd had with the duchess earlier. Unfortunately, there was nothing she could do about that now. "I can't imagine they would ever suit. However, I would be more than happy to vacate them if that is your desire."

The duke was looking between the two women suspiciously.

"No one is moving anywhere. I can assure you, dear, there will not be a repeat of tonight," Eleanor said firmly. "And I am sorry if I have caused you undue distress this evening."

"It's not just this evening, Mother," Worth groaned.

"Tonight is simply the culmination of months of…" He threw up his hands in despair, groping for a word. "The whispers and gossip have taken a cruel slant."

"I don't really care," replied the duchess, and Jenna heard the truth in those words.

"But I do." The duke sighed heavily. "For your actions reflect on me as well."

Ah. And there was the crux of his dilemma, Jenna realized. She supposed, in all fairness, she couldn't blame him. His mother appeared to care not a whit for the opinion of the ton. But the truth of the matter was that the opinion of society mattered very much to the duchess. There were untold advantages to being dismissed as a scatterbrained ninny, and it was a facade that had taken Eleanor years to perfect. Not that Worth would ever understand.

"I'll get rid of the chickens, if that will appease you," the duchess offered.

The duke rolled his eyes. "I am your son, Mother. It is my duty to see to your well-being."

Eleanor raised a brow. "Your duty?"

Jenna watched as Worth colored slightly. "I admit, I may not have been overly attentive these last years, but that doesn't mean I don't care. Whatever shortcomings I may have had in the past will be rectified now. You need me, and I am happy to oblige." He put his hands on his hips, his face a grim mask of resolve. "I'm moving in, and that is that."

Jenna sent the duchess an alarmed look. Eleanor met her eyes helplessly.

"I would caution you that you may find residence here rather restrictive to your lifestyle," Jenna tried tactfully.

"She has a point, dear," his mother chimed in. "Don't

think I haven't heard stories about your fondness for pretty young widows. Or, for that matter, their fondness for you. And I will not abide by that sort of mischief in my house. I'll never get a good night's sleep if all I can hear is—"

"Mother." The duke visibly cringed. "Stop. Please."

The duchess sniffed. "You weren't dropped off by a stork, you know."

Worth closed his eyes briefly, his patrician features pained, before that damned determination reasserted itself across his face. "You will not lose a moment's sleep during my tenure, I assure you, Mother." He turned toward Jenna. "And for the record, Miss Hughes, I care little for your opinions on my personal life. You work for me, and if my lifestyle offends you in some manner, please feel free to find employment elsewhere."

"I work for the duchess, Your Grace," Jenna corrected him. "Not you."

The duke drew himself up to his full impressive height and straightened his shoulders. "I am the Duke of Worth, and I control the duchy and everything in it. That includes this household. So while my mother might have hired a companion with the manners of a princess and the mouth of a madam, it is I who have the final say on whether or not you stay. Or go. Don't test me, Miss Hughes."

Eleanor was staring at her son in shock. Truthfully, Worth himself looked a little dazed at his pronouncement.

Jenna cursed inwardly. This was the most inopportune time for the man to start behaving like a duke.

"Of course, Your Grace." Jenna met his gaze with feigned disinterest. She was rapidly running out of cards to play. She chose the only one that might prevail against his sudden onset of unwelcome gallantry. "Will you be forfeiting the Oaks then, to stay here?"

"The Oaks?" Worth froze.

Jenna waved her hand. "I understand that you race horses." *And damned well too*, she added silently.

"I do." He was frowning fiercely.

"I had been told you had entered the Oaks at Epsom Downs. But you'll miss the race if you move in now, won't you? Isn't it one of the biggest races of the year?"

The duke blinked.

"But I suppose there are some lovely bridle paths around here you could ride on," Jenna continued. "I'm sure—"

"How do you know about the Oaks?" Worth asked suspiciously.

"I don't live under a rock, Your Grace." Jenna was treading dangerous waters now. If he perceived she knew too much, he might get suspicious. But if she didn't emphasize the importance of the race enough, he might not fully comprehend the ramifications of his impulsive decision.

She opted for a half-truth. "You are a duke and a very single, very wealthy one at that. Your name comes up often in conversation in all sorts of circles. As do your hobbies. Everyone is talking about your success on the Newmarket track already this year. They say you might just have a champion in your stables."

With satisfaction Jenna could almost see the wheels turning in Worth's head. It would be a cold day in hell before the Duke of Worth sacrificed something so dear to him for some bizarre sense of duty he had discovered in the last ten minutes. And Jenna knew very well what he had in his stables. Worth had a black filly he had bred and trained himself that had thus far annihilated all challengers, colts included. Rumor among the racing set said Worth would sweep the stakes races this year and establish himself as one of the preeminent horsemen of the thoroughbred world with the filly he called Comtessa.

"Dammit." The duke was pacing, considering for the first time the problematic logistics of moving into the dower house.

Eleanor pounced. "Worth, darling, while I appreciate your sentiments and your good intentions, there is no need—"

"I'll skip the Oaks," he said to no one in particular.

Jenna's eyes widened. This wasn't sounding as if it were going anywhere good.

"I'll run her in the Gold Cup at Ascot instead."

Oh no. No, no, no. The blood drained from her face. The very reason everything they did worked so well was that the duke did not run his horses at Ascot. He favored the classics, keeping his horses and his acumen firmly on the turf at Newmarket in May, Epsom in June, and then finally at Doncaster in the fall. For whatever reason, he avoided competing at Ascot altogether, and until now his absence had left Jenna free to do what she did best over those four days of racing.

If he were to compete at Ascot, he would ruin everything. Panic began to bubble up. How could Jenna ever hope to outwit the duke in such close quarters and what would no doubt be closer scrutiny? Every crooked thing she did to further her cause would rest right under his nose, no matter how hard she might try to conceal it. She would fail, and those who counted on her would suffer.

"Makes a sight more sense anyway," Worth was muttering. "I have no idea why I didn't consider this earlier. She's better suited to the distance, and she'll be rested and ready." A gleam had crept into his eye, and a satisfied grin was stealing across his face.

"You can't." It was out before Jenna could call it back.

"I most certainly can." The full weight of his stare was on her now, and Jenna became aware of the keen intelligence burning behind those coffee-colored eyes. Intelligence that she should not underestimate. "One can change one's mind, Miss Hughes." He paused, considering her. "My mother goes every year to watch the races at Ascot, though I suppose you already know that. I would escort her this year. However, it would seem I must spend my time in the stables instead of the viewing platforms. Have you been to Ascot with my mother before, Miss Hughes?"

"No, Your Grace." It wasn't quite a lie. The duchess and she usually arrived separately and remained so. They were never seen anywhere remotely close to each other.

The duke turned to Eleanor. "Had you planned to go again this year, Mother?"

"I do like to wager on the races," Eleanor said weakly.

"Excellent. I'm sure Miss Hughes will be more than happy to accompany you in my place, since that is her *job*." He said the last pointedly. "And perhaps you could even place a wager on my filly. I assure you, you won't regret it. I believe you'll find it quite enjoyable."

A completely inappropriate snort of hysterical laughter threatened to erupt, and Jenna struggled to suppress it. Racing was not enjoyable. It was cutthroat and scheming and sometimes cruel. It was gritty and sweaty and dangerous and oh so rewarding when you could triumph over the odds. But there was no world that existed where the duke would expect or accept that Jenna Hughes, his mother's paid companion, knew that.

"Is there something you wished to say, Miss Hughes?" The duke was watching her.

Panic was beginning to rise again, and Jenna quashed it. It served no purpose, other than to provoke smart people into making very stupid decisions. "Of course not, Your Grace." She forced the reply. "I look forward to it."

"Very good." The duke sniffed, looking quite pleased with himself. He gave one last pointed look at the ruined hall. "I already feel better knowing that I'll be here to help and handle anything that might come up. Now, is the gold guest room available, Mother? Or should I be on the lookout for an errant camel?"

Saints above, this was really happening. The duke was not going away. At least not tonight. He was still proudly sporting that mantle of determination and duty as though it were a new set of fine clothes. But he couldn't possibly remain determined forever.

Could he?

Chapter 3

"Do you suppose the duke will have me hanged?"

The Duchess of Worth had been poring over a map of Quatre Bras, bold arrows clearly illustrating the advance and retreat of English and French troops. She set it down and leveled a stern look at Jenna. "No one is going to be hanged."

"So just transported then."

"No one is going to be transported anywhere," said Eleanor with an exasperated sigh.

"Have you forgotten what it is I do?" Jenna kicked the edge of the rug in frustration.

The duchess's nostrils flared. "Dramatics do not suit you, Miss Hughes."

"I am not being dramatic, I am being pragmatic. Every successful thief is pragmatic."

"You are not a thief. You use a unique set of skills to recover. Recoup. Retrieve."

"I steal."

The duchess made a derisive sound. "No more than anyone else."

"Except when the ton does it, it's not called stealing. When an earl or a viscount or a marquess steals the rightfully earned income of his tailor or cobbler, it's called *entitlement*."

"That may be so, Miss Hughes, but nothing has changed from yesterday. There has always been risk."

"Yes, but now there is a duke. And a damned principled one at that."

"He would be pleased to hear you say so."

"He would not be so pleased if he discovered what I do."

Eleanor's lips thinned but she remained silent.

"Tell me that your son would look the other way if he caught me swindling his friends and fellow peers out of their money. If he caught me fleecing his social contemporaries for what would appear to be my own gain. He wouldn't care who I was."

The duchess looked disturbed. "No, he wouldn't," she agreed quietly. "Strange, since it is the very opposite of how his father would approach a similar dilemma. Status and connection were the only things that mattered to my husband, and in his eyes, rank would excuse almost anything. And since you are connected to me, the old duke might have been tempted to overlook your transgressions. Particularly if he could personally benefit somehow. My son has a much better developed sense of right and wrong."

Jenna groaned. "I hear Botany Bay is nice. I've always fancied living near the ocean. And at least the winters would be warmer."

"Don't be ridiculous. I'd never allow that to happen."

"I don't know that you'd get much of a say, Your Grace," Jenna mumbled miserably.

The duchess returned her attention to her map, her brows furrowed. Jenna knew Eleanor did her best thinking when she retreated into her massive collection of military maps, and if there had ever been a time when the duchess's shrewd wisdom was needed, now was it. Because the man currently sleeping in the gold guest room upstairs was going to be a problem on an epic scale, and at the moment, Jenna had no idea what to do about it.

Jenna had spent a great deal of time studying the Duke of Worth. Specifically his horses, but by default the duke as well. It was her job to educate herself about the owners and the trainers and the jockeys and who out of the lot would offer up real competition each year. It was her responsibility to know who could be bought, and for how much. Who would be willing to drug a horse, lame a horse, or ride that same horse anyway. Who could be paid to steal a horse, replace a horse, or pull a horse. In her experience everyone had his price. Everyone, that was, except the Duke of Worth.

In fact, the Duke of Worth, for all his obvious disinterest in politics and the governance of the Empire, was an unexpected leader at the tracks. He was involved with the Jockey Club and was an advocate for the development of an accurate stud book, and, to the best of her knowledge, had never accepted a bribe for anything. All things Jenna would normally admire.

But these were also things that would make her job at Ascot much more difficult.

For all his sterling qualities as a horseman, Jenna knew William Somerhall would never understand what she did. And he would never forgive her absolute disregard for the rules of the track and the dignity of thoroughbred racing in fair Britannia.

"Do you think if we get rid of the chickens, he'll leave?" Jenna asked, trying to keep the desperation from her voice.

"I'm quite sure that will not be sufficient. Though I must admit the idea has appeal. Those damned birds are becoming tiresome. As is my supposed eccentricity," Eleanor muttered under her breath, rifling through a pile of notes and pulling out a page. "Why do you think the Prince of Orange didn't order square when the French cuirassiers attacked?" she asked abruptly.

"Because he was an idiot."

"I can't use that word in my thesis. It sounds inexpert."

"How about *uninformed*?"

"No, he certainly had the information he needed to issue the appropriate order."

"Perhaps he was distracted by the shiny tassels on his uniform?"

The duchess gave Jenna a long look.

Jenna sighed. "Perhaps *unwise*?"

"Better." Eleanor crossed out a word and replaced it.

"He'll want to see our stables." Jenna wasn't talking about the Prince of Orange anymore.

The duchess winced. "Yes, he will." She tapped the edge of her quill against the table. "There is no avoiding it, but I am hoping he will be too focused on his own mounts to pay much attention to ours. When the time comes, and it will, I am confident we can explain away my horses. Sadly, I do not think we will have the same success if we try to explain away your role with the horses. You'll need to appear to be simply my companion."

Jenna could do that. She'd posed as Eleanor's companion many times in the past and knew she did a damn convincing job of it. But that didn't mean she couldn't search for another solution to the problem that was the Duke of Worth. Every problem had a solution if one was willing to think creatively. And Jenna had always been good at creative thinking.

"What if we bought him a new horse?" Jenna demanded. "Something he could not resist racing. Something he would feel compelled to take to Epsom immediately. Lord Bering has suggested he might be selling that Eclipse colt he bought as a yearling a few years ago."

"And how would we explain that?"

"A birthday gift?"

"His birthday is in January."

"An early birthday gift?" Jenna was reaching.

"My son believes I can't tell the difference between a donkey and a draft horse. He would only become more suspicious."

Jenna cleared her throat. "Well, how about a woman to distract him then? Perhaps I could find him a mistress," she suggested, though somehow that thought rankled.

Eleanor shook her head. "He won't take a mistress, mostly because a mistress is an encumbrance. The last one he had was well over a year ago, and from what I understand, she could not accept that he spent more time at the track and in the barns than he did in her bed. She had a vilely destructive temper. He hasn't had one since."

Jenna groaned in frustration, well and truly backed into a corner with no discernible way out. "How about we get Margaret to tie him up and lock him in the dungeon until after the Cup? Please tell me the dower house has a dungeon."

The duchess sighed in sympathy. "I believe dungeons went out of style a few centuries ago, dear."

Jenna sank into a stuffed chair, defeated.

Eleanor watched her a moment, then approached, perching herself on the wide arm and putting a hand on Jenna's shoulder. "We'll find a way, Miss Hughes, and Worth will be none the wiser. We'll set him at the accounts first. If we're lucky, he'll give up after a day and leave on his own."

"And what if he doesn't? Leave, that is?"

"Then we'll still depart for Windsor and Ascot Heath as planned."

"You don't think the duke will find it suspicious that we depart so early?"

"And therein lies the beauty of my bizarre behavior. Who can explain what I do?" Eleanor's eyes twinkled.

Jenna rubbed at her eyes. "This has the makings of an utter disaster."

The duchess patted her on the shoulder, and her features became wistful. "I'd like to think my son would understand what it is we—you do. Maybe given enough time, maybe given enough evidence of why we do it, he would eventually even sympathize. He has a good heart— that I believe with all my soul." Her voice dropped even lower. "But time is something we do not have the luxury of right now. And I am not close to William the way a mother should be. That is my fault, and I will regret it until the day I die. For I fear now it is too late."

Jenna reached up and squeezed the duchess's hand.

Eleanor cleared her throat brusquely. "I want you to keep track of Worth while he's here. I don't think it is in our best interests to have him wandering around the property unsupervised. If and when he starts putting two and two together, it would be better if we had some warning."

"And what would make you think he will agree to my constant presence?"

The duchess smiled faintly. "My son has scores of

women vying for his attentions, either for his money, his title, or bragging rights. But you, Miss Hughes, are an enigma, if only for your clear disregard for all three. Like any man, he'll want to determine why."

"That's not true. I quite like the idea of his money."

"But not for yourself."

"That's not the point."

"That's exactly the point, dear." Eleanor's expression became grave. "Now listen carefully, Miss Hughes. The duke is going to have a great number of questions, especially when he gets a look at what lies beyond those oaks out back. Whenever possible, tell the truth. I've always found the truth is easier to remember. Establish yourself in the role he already assumes you fill. If he digs his heels in and decides to stick this out, there is only one thing that will enable you to do what will be required in just over a week."

"What is that?"

"As long as the duke believes you are simply my hired companion, no matter what happens at Ascot, you will be above suspicion."

Jenna forced herself to cast aside her discontentment, thinking of the people who were depending on her. She would succeed in outwitting the Duke of Worth because failure was simply not an option. Perhaps, if the fates were kind, the duke would reconsider his decision in the hours before dawn.

And leave before breakfast.

~

Sometime in the small hours of the morning, Will reconciled himself to his impulsive decision of the night before. He'd miss the stakes races at Epsom, that was true, and that still needled. But after witnessing the aftermath of his mother's ill-fated dinner party, he fully understood that the sacrifice was nonnegotiable.

He'd never liked Ascot. The turf itself was fine, as far as tracks went, though he found the longer distances of many of the races did not often suit his own mounts. It was everything else he rebelled against. To start with, Ascot hosted only four consecutive days of races out of the entire year—four days that seemed more dedicated to pomp and pageantry than to the pure sport of racing. Society descended en masse for the first races and then stayed for the entire four days, Ascot being just a little too far from London to allow for daily return. At least at Epsom on Derby Day, most people came, watched, and left by nightfall.

Ascot was of value to the ton only as a place to see and be seen. They used the damn turf as a promenade in between races, for God's sake, and required hired men to push them back behind the rails so that they didn't get trampled by the racehorses or—more importantly, as far as Will was concerned—cause injury to a horse or rider in their wanderings. It was one thing for them to conduct their social dramas at Almack's or Rotten Row or Vauxhall, but for them to make the racetrack just another backdrop for narcissistic theater maddened Will. The track was supposed to be where he could escape the political and matrimonial maneuverings of polite society. And it was for precisely that reason that he'd preferred to avoid Ascot entirely. Until now.

Though maybe this was meant to be, for this year was a year unlike any other. This year Will had a champion in his stable, a horse he had bred and trained himself. A horse that would, with success, prove to everyone beyond a doubt that the Duke of Worth was to be taken seriously.

Another peer might buy himself a winner. William Somerhall, on the other hand, had made one from scratch, and that was worth more than any amount of money.

He couldn't deny that the Ascot Gold Cup was a very prestigious race. The distance was punishing, the competition fierce, and it took a rare horse to overcome both. A win on the track at Ascot would establish him as one of the preeminent horsemen of England, and that could only lead to great things. Yes, Will thought, warming to the idea, perhaps Ascot was indeed a blessing in disguise.

And the extra time would allow him to deal with whatever was amiss in the dower house. He would devote himself to straightening out his mother's finances, reviewing her staff, and most importantly, reshaping her reputation. His first order of business would be a heart-to-heart with Miss Hughes. If she was to remain as his mother's companion, she would need to be more vigilant. Will planned to establish certain parameters for his mother's behavior, and it would be up to Miss Hughes to enforce them.

Though after last night's performance, he wasn't certain the captivating Miss Hughes could manage the burden. Will suspected she was too much of a renegade herself to keep the dowager firmly in check, but perhaps he was wrong. At the moment, both the woman and her motives were absolutely inscrutable.

Though if he was honest, Jenna Hughes was a mystery he was very much looking forward to solving. Especially if the delectable Miss Hughes should prove willing to reveal more than just her secrets.

Chapter 4

Her first mistake had been bathing before breakfast.

On her way up to the house from the barns, as the sun was just starting its ascent into the sky, Jenna had realized she was dusty and muddy and stank of horse. None of which was remarkable on an ordinary day, but all of which was unacceptable on this day. So she had chosen to remove the evidence instead of having to invent an excuse as to why she smelled like a stableboy. Jenna was quite sure paid companions did not work in the barns. Especially not before breakfast.

Except bathing took time, and when Jenna staggered into the breakfast room, she found it deserted. She wasn't sure whether she should be relieved or concerned. Perhaps dukes did not eat breakfast, she thought. Indeed, she was given to understand most aristocrats did not rise from their beds until midday. Just as well, she mused, as she piled a plate high with beef and eggs and toast. If the duke remained under the covers until noon or thereabouts, a huge number of her problems were solved. Almost all her daily duties would be completed by eleven of the clock, and a late-rising aristocrat would know nothing of them.

Wolfing down the contents of her plate, she considered her plan of attack. In the light of the new day, Jenna had made peace with the chaos that might be wrought by Eleanor's son. The two women would manage Worth as best they could, and they would do so without hiding the basic facts of their enterprise. It was a miracle really that they'd avoided detection by a horseman like Worth for as long as they had. Well, no longer. The duke would soon realize that his mother was keeping many important secrets from him—and that she had done so for a very, very long time.

Jenna reminded herself to take comfort in the idea that she and the duchess could still control this story. The only thing she had to do in order to perpetuate a convincing fiction was remove herself from the barns and the horses and anything that had to do with horse racing. She would have to be smart about it, of course. Worth was not likely to believe her completely ignorant of the duchess's horse breeding program. But betraying too much understanding of the enterprise would be a disaster. As of this moment, she was the genteel Miss Jenna Hughes, hired companion to the Dowager Duchess of Worth. Everything rode on the success of her deception.

She sat back, satisfied with her newfound composure and resolve.

The door to the breakfast room flew open, startling Jenna.

"Go," Margaret wheezed, her massive bosom heaving.

"Go?" Jenna echoed, perplexed.

Margaret pointed a sausage-like finger in the direction of the window. Jenna followed her gaze and nearly fell off her chair.

The duke was striding down the cobbled path that led from the house to the stables. He looked neither left nor right, intent only on the buildings barely visible beyond the trees and bushes that separated the house and the barns.

"Dammit," Jenna cursed as she sprang to her feet, bolting from the room.

The Duke of Worth could not be allowed near the stables without supervision.

And carefully rehearsed explanations.

The dower house was not a mansion exactly, certainly not anywhere near as big as the main Breckenridge house. But as his father had been fond of saying, it had been built and decorated to keep every unwanted female in the family out of sight and out of mind. Which, as far as Will had been able to determine, was every female his father had ever been related to.

But the house was indeed beautiful. It was two stories of rose-colored stone, topped by expansive attics housing the servants' quarters under a slate roof. It had a small ballroom, a generous dining room, and a collection of pretty and airy guest and drawing rooms. The bedrooms sat on the second floor, the windows open to the summer breeze this morning, and curtains fluttered behind the multi-paned windows.

When Will had walked through the hall on his way out this morning, he had been pleased that the mess of the prior evening had been set to rights. Aside from a faintly discolored square where the broken mirror had been removed from the wall, one would never have known anything had ever been amiss. At least the servants responsible for maintaining the house were competent, if the sparkling hall was any indication. Likewise, the gold guest room he had currently settled into had been kept clean and well dusted, the linens fresh, and he had wanted for nothing in the way of necessities. And the breakfast room earlier this morning had been a welcoming surprise, filled with sunlight and the scent of polished wood and mouthwatering aromas emanating from the sideboard, everything set out marvelously early. There hadn't been a soul around, but then he hadn't expected to see anyone. He very much doubted anyone save the servants was an early riser like himself.

The apparent normalcy of the morning routine encouraged Will. He couldn't discern any glaring problems with the servants who maintained the dower house, and so he figured further investigation on that end could wait. In the meantime he needed to turn his attention to the stables. He knew that somewhere in the back, behind the massive row of oaks, was a carriage house with space for at least six horses. With some embarrassment he realized that the last time he'd been back there, he'd probably been twelve years old. He wasn't entirely sure what to expect, but he was desperately hoping the buildings would be in suitable shape to be used for his own horses.

Will was mulling the quandary of housing and training his horses in substandard conditions when he came around the far side of the oaks. His mouth dropped open, and he tripped over his own boots as he stared at the vista before him.

The carriage house still stood, and the small stable alongside it. In fact, it featured a relatively new roof, gleaming white paint, and shiny hardware on the doors. But it was the entire other wing of stables that had been added behind the once-modest structure that had him gaping. Will was quite certain his own stables weren't as fine. There must have been room for at least an additional twenty horses here. Beyond the barns, fences had been constructed, rolling away in neat lines beyond the far ridge. And everywhere he looked were horses.

In the distance were a half dozen broodmares with foals at their sides, and a pasture containing frolicking yearlings. Small herds of leggy, athletic-looking horses grazed on the lush grass farther along the ridge, swishing their tails at flies. Nearest the barns, where enclosures with higher, heavier fences lay, Will's practiced eye easily picked out two stallions, holding court with all the equine arrogance they were entitled to.

What the bloody hell? Will thought, his brain finally starting to process what he was seeing. The duchess had never said anything about raising horses. For this was a dedicated horse farm if he had ever seen one. She had certainly never mentioned building another stable block or extending the pastures or hiring the staff it would take to manage this.

Perhaps she didn't know. That was almost easier to believe than the possibility that all of this had gone on beneath his nose, a bare mile from his Breckenridge mansion.

But then, that little voice that was quickly becoming unwanted reminded him, *you've never taken the time to visit the duchess in the summer.*

But to have done all of this and not told him? Not mentioned it, even once?

"Good morning, Your Grace." Miss Hughes suddenly appeared at his side, breathless, as if she had run all the way from the house.

Will jumped, startled from his engrossing train of thought. Had he not been so preoccupied, he might have made the effort to wonder why Miss Hughes would be so far from the house at such an unexpected hour. But then, Miss Hughes had yet to do anything expected.

A thrill of anticipation hummed through Will. There was no reason he could not take advantage of her sudden, though certainly not unwelcome, presence. He wanted some answers, and he wanted them now. Surely Miss Hughes could provide some intelligence about how the new stables had come to be. And if not, the manner in which this woman comported herself during private conversation would help him determine if she was a suitable companion for his mother.

Will assessed his quarry out of the corner of his eye, trying to remain objective, which was a great deal harder than he would have liked.

God, but she was stunning. Even dressed again in another horribly drab gown, this one the color of faded ash, more suited to a scullery than a drawing room, she was captivating. He wasn't entirely sure why she chose to dress like an antiquated crone, but Will could have told her that no amount of poor tailoring could conceal her elegant stature. Her hair was predictably pulled back, though wisps of jet black had escaped and framed her striking features. The corners of her eyes crinkled beneath a fan of sooty lashes as she smiled up at him, her cheeks glowing with that hint of the outdoors completely foreign to the pale complexions so common in society assembly rooms.

Will fought the urge to smile back. This was about duty, not pleasure.

"Miss Hughes. Good morning. I almost didn't recognize you without a snake wrapped around your neck." The words were light enough, but Will hoped his stony countenance would invite only the most solemn reply.

Miss Hughes dipped her head. "My apologies if I made you uncomfortable last night, Your Grace."

Will blinked. It was a passable start. He waited for more.

"I missed you at breakfast," she continued easily.

"Then you overslept."

Her lips quirked slightly, though she offered no argument or excuse. "I had hoped to give you a tour of the property myself."

"Well, as you can see, I am quite capable of finding my way around my own property." His voice sounded regrettably curt in his own ears. No matter. He was here as a dutiful son to resolve whatever sort of strange madness had taken over his mother's home, not flirt and play the part of a charming scoundrel.

Miss Hughes nodded agreeably.

"Did you know this existed?" he demanded, forcing himself to remember that this woman who claimed to be his mother's companion was to be suspected, not seduced. For all he knew, Miss Hughes could be stealing the family plate. Or the family fortune. Or—

She licked her lips, and Will's thoughts scattered.

Dammit, but he wasn't off to a very good start.

"I beg your pardon?" She was watching him with concern.

"This." He waved his hand at the scene before him impatiently.

"The barns?"

"Yes, the barns," he snapped.

"The barns have been here since I have, Your Grace. Did you wish to see them?"

"Hell, yes," Will grumbled, already stalking toward the carriage house.

Miss Hughes matched him stride for stride effortlessly, seemingly unfazed by his abruptness. In fact, Miss Hughes seemed unfazed by everything.

"Who is the stable master?" he demanded.

"That would be Paul."

"And where might I find Paul?"

"He is unavailable at the moment, Your Grace."

"Unavailable?"

"I believe he is in London at the moment, attending to business."

"What kind of business?"

"I couldn't say, Your Grace."

Of course she couldn't. Miss Hughes wouldn't be privy to the daily workings of the stables.

"Then whom can I speak to about"—he gestured to the barns with residual disbelief—"*this*?"

"I can fetch Joseph for you, if you like. He is Paul's brother and head coachman."

"That would be helpful, Miss Hughes." He tried to keep the derision from his tone.

"Very good, Your Grace." Miss Hughes led him into the cool interior of the old barn, the air sweet with the scent of freshly laid straw and the earthy aroma of horse.

With a swish of her ugly skirts, his escort moved off in the direction of the new barns, pausing only briefly to straighten a bridle that had slipped off a hook before she disappeared. He was left to examine his surroundings unobserved. The first glance left him satisfied. Further study left him reluctantly impressed. The stalls were in perfect repair. Not a nail or a loose board was visible anywhere. The stone alleyway had been swept immaculately, and Will was fairly certain he'd eaten off worse. Oats and grains were sealed in barrels stacked against the wall. Tack was hung neatly and properly along the wall—both harness and a selection of bridles and saddles. The leather gleamed dully in the dim light, evidence of a recent cleaning. The only item out of place was a worn cobalt-blue jacket left draped over a stall door, clearly forgotten by a groom or stableboy.

There were two horses in the barn—one was the mare he had ridden here last night, contentedly resting. The other was at the far end, and Will wandered down to examine it. The horse, seeing Will approach, stuck its head over the stable door in curiosity. Will peered at the imposing beast, noticing the mass of scars marring the glossy black hide. An old war-horse, perhaps? He put out a hand and scratched the horse's ears, catching a glimpse of the animal's right shoulder. Or what was left of it.

A twisted mass of scar tissue ran just in front of its wither, down along its shoulder and over the front of its chest. The muscles were grotesquely misshapen, damaged beyond repair.

And it was a ghastly shame, for the animal's breeding was evident in every line. Will took in the depth of the stallion's chest, the straight, strong legs that ended in a solid, well-formed hooves. A back end that promised speed and the ability to run forever. He shook his head in regret. The horse, though in otherwise perfect health, would never again walk soundly. For the life of him, Will couldn't imagine why it was still alive. It was, essentially, useless, and the kindest gift one could give this horse would be a swift, painless death.

"Now that is a damn shame," Will muttered under his breath.

"What is?" Miss Hughes asked, and Will spun, having failed to hear her approach. Again.

"Do you know if this horse raced before it was injured?"

Miss Hughes gave him an odd look. "I don't believe so. Why?"

"This, Miss Hughes, is what perfection looks like." He gestured at the stallion.

"Perfection?"

Will waved his hand in dismissal. She wouldn't have a clue. "Why is it here?" he asked instead.

Miss Hughes shrugged. "Your mother keeps it."

"My mother owns this horse?" *And why not?* Will thought impatiently. A lamed horse was hardly a stretch from a stiff python.

"Indeed she does," Miss Hughes said. "Vimeiro."

"Vimeiro?"

"That's what she calls it, Your Grace. Served in the cavalry corps for five years. Had four officers shot off its back before it ended up in the battle for Vimeiro in Acland's eighth under Wellesley. Brought its officer back to the safety of English lines, even after a French blade did that." She gestured at the scarred shoulder.

Will's brows shot into his hairline. "How do you know all this?"

"Your mother told me."

"How does she know all that?"

Miss Hughes shrugged.

"And she just keeps it here? For what reason?"

Miss Hughes shrugged again. "I haven't the smallest idea."

God, but he was beginning to despise that shrug.

Will abandoned the topic of the ruined horse and turned his attention to the boy Miss Hughes had returned with.

The lad couldn't have been more than sixteen and was thin and rangy, though Will knew his slope-shouldered frame held far more strength than might be assumed at first glance. His face was all sharp angles, dominated by a pair of large eyes, giving him a perpetual startled look. His hair stuck out from his head in all directions. This certainly wasn't the head coachman.

"Were you unable to locate Joseph?" Will inquired, making an attempt at patience.

The boy raised an angular brow. "I am Joseph, Your Grace. Joseph Lockhart," he said politely. The faintest hint of a Scots accent was evident in the boy's speech. "An honor to make your acquaintance."

Will stared.

"Miss Hughes said you had some questions about the stables. How can I be of assistance, Your Grace?" the boy asked in a manner more suited to a butler than to an adolescent coachman.

"When was this built?" Will demanded, feeling as though the rug had been yanked from beneath his feet and he had yet to regain his balance.

"The duchess had it built eight years ago, Your Grace."

Eight years ago. The year he had assumed his title. The

year he had done everything in his power to distance himself from everything and everyone still in the shadow left by his late father.

"I see," he said, pleased at how genial his voice sounded. "And what type of horses are you raising here on behalf of my mother, exactly?"

Joseph's eyes shifted briefly before they steadied. "Mostly fine hunters, Your Grace. Some carriage horses, if they suit."

"Why?"

"Why?" Joseph echoed, puzzled.

"Why does my mother raise horses?"

"I do not think I need to remind you how much your mother enjoys her animals, Your Grace." Miss Hughes helpfully reasserted herself back into the conversation. "She enjoys having the horses here, especially the young ones. And if you will forgive my vulgarity, the profit realized from the sale of the horses is handsome. Especially now that the war is over and there seems to be a scarcity of well-bred hunters suitable for a gentleman."

Will was still struggling to come to terms with the fact that all of this had been going on for years without his knowledge. He opened his mouth to say something, but failed to find words.

Joseph stepped into the silence smoothly. "We have set aside three stalls, Your Grace. Including the one your mare currently occupies. Will you require more during your stay?"

"No," Will managed to respond, at least able to address his own immediate needs.

"You only have two more horses?" Miss Hughes asked in apparent surprise.

"Two racing thoroughbreds, Miss Hughes. I saw no need to bring my carriage horses here. Especially now, since it seems my mother has a wealth of them." Sarcasm soured the last.

Jenna arched a slim brow, unperturbed by his outburst. "I would have thought you would own more. Racehorses, that is."

"It is about quality, not quantity," he intoned. "Otherwise you end up like Prinny, begging your father for more money to maintain an entire herd of middling racers."

"I see." She looked genuinely curious. "I heard you train your own horses. Is that true?"

"Yes." He was trying not to be flattered by her interest. "And your groom—"

"Has ridden for me for seven years. He knows me and he knows my horses and his loyalty is not for sale." He met her pale eyes and held them.

"Then you are a lucky man, Your Grace." A small smile played around her mouth. "Loyalty is a rare thing."

Will's lips thinned. Was she mocking him? What could Miss Hughes possibly know of horse racing?

Joseph cleared his throat discreetly. "I've cleared the south tack room for your use while you are our guest," the boy said with a quiet dignity characteristic of a man twice his age. "I hope you find it suitable. Please let me know if you require—"

"How old are you?" Will interrupted.

"I believe about seventeen, Your Grace. Give or take."

"Give or take?" Will's forehead wrinkled. "What kind of answer is that?"

"The best I can provide, Your Grace." Joseph trailed off uncertainly. "My brothers are fairly certain it was the winter of ninety-nine. On account they remember the heavy snow near Christmas."

"Ninety-nine?"

"The year Joseph was born, Your Grace." Miss Hughes sighed impatiently.

Will scowled. He had no idea what he hoped to gain by asking these questions, but it was becoming quite clear just how vastly oblivious about everything in his mother's life he was. He forged on.

"And aside from the absent Paul? You have other brothers?"

"Just one, Your Grace."

"Here?"

"Yes, Your Grace."

"Have I met him?"

"I couldn't say." Joseph was looking at him oddly.

Will collected himself. "What I meant to ask is, does he also work here in the barns or up at the house?"

"Luke is up at the house, though he has quite a few duties here as well."

"And have you always worked with horses then?"

Joseph suddenly grinned at him. "My brothers and I started with sheep and cattle, Your Grace, when we still lived near Glasgow," he said, the burr getting just a little stronger with the memory. "And then when we came to London, we specialized in horses."

Will frowned. "What part of London did you work in?"

"Mostly the western parts. The best horses are usually stabled there."

"The best horses?"

Joseph flashed him another grin. "I have a knack with fine horses. I believe that is why the duchess hired me."

Will sighed in frustration, at a loss as to how to extract something more useful. Clearly interrogation wasn't his strong suit. He felt like he was talking in circles.

"Is there anything else you need, Your Grace?" the coachman asked.

Yes. Will needed his old life back, where everything was easy and familiar and sane. "No. Thank you," he added.

Joseph grinned at him again. "Very good, Your Grace." The boy turned and loped away.

Will was left standing, bewildered and uncertain.

Miss Hughes, as if sensing his hesitation, moved to his side and casually tucked her arm through his as though they were out for an informal stroll in his mother's rose garden. Her fingers rested lightly on the sleeve of his coat, and her hip pressed against his. Will closed his eyes briefly, excruciatingly aware of every curve of her body.

He would have asked her to dance that night at his ball, had she not disappeared. Just to have her in his arms, if only for a few fleeting moments. Her memory had lodged in his mind, and since then, more times than he cared to admit, Will had imagined what this woman would have felt like next to him, her warmth merged with his. He had imagined repeatedly what it would have felt like to have stolen a kiss.

But he hadn't anticipated the raw desire that crackled over every nerve ending in his skin and lodged uncomfortably in his groin. Her slightest touch made him feel almost feverish with need. Without meaning to, he leaned forward slightly, inhaling her scent. Soap and sunshine.

The conundrum that was Joseph abruptly faded into the realm of the unimportant as Miss Hughes pulled Will forward slightly and he followed, unable to think of anything else to do. Unable to think, period, except to wonder at his intense and sudden urge to claim those curling lips. He shook his head, trying to regain some measure of control over his runaway libido.

"Joseph may be young," Miss Hughes was saying, "but I can assure you he is most capable."

Will tried to listen. But he'd noticed that an escaped tendril of hair had plastered itself to the side of her neck, and he imagined pressing his lips to the dampness. It would taste salty and—

"If you'd care for a closer look at the stock, Paul will be happy to accommodate you once he returns." Her voice was coming from a distance, but somehow he couldn't focus on her words, only her mouth. Why hadn't he noticed last night that he would barely have to dip his head to kiss her? There was a freckle near her upper lip that he needed to explore.

And why hadn't he noticed the way her breasts curved enticingly, begging to be worshipped? They weren't overly large, but they pushed up invitingly beneath her bodice, and Will had the irrational urge to rip that ugly gown away from a body it didn't deserve. She turned her head, gesturing to something in the distance, and her hair caressed his chin, a brush of soft silk.

He'd been hopelessly drawn to Miss Hughes that night of his ball, and now that he was in her presence, the affliction seemed to be getting worse. Perhaps because she was a complete departure from the overdone, over-scented, overindulged females he'd been dealing with since he inherited his bloody title. Normally, in his presence, women preened and primped. They giggled and fluttered and hung on his every word. Jenna Hughes did none of those things. She didn't tug or adjust the awful dress she was wearing, turning just so to give him the best view of her profile or her cleavage. She seemed oblivious to her appearance, and, even more fascinatingly, indifferent to what he thought of her appearance.

Perhaps it was that confidence that Will found so riveting. There was no pretense with this stunning woman. She would say what she meant and mean what she said. There would be no coyness, no games. When he took her it would be raw. And physical and—

"Are you all right, Your Grace?" They had come to a stop.

Will jerked to attention, realizing with horror that he was still staring at her breasts like a besotted schoolboy. Fantasizing about sex he would never have with a woman he should never touch.

"Yes?" Dear God, that sounded like a question. He was a duke, dammit. "Yes." There, that sounded more dignified.

"Have I spilled something?" She was examining her bodice, a worried crease in her forehead.

"No," Will stuttered. "I was thinking that dress is the singularly most ugly piece of clothing I have ever seen." He congratulated himself on his recovery.

"Good heavens. Your charm is overwhelming."

He smiled despite himself. "I don't need charm, Miss Hughes. I have a fortune and a title."

"True enough. And you're handsome."

He gasped like a little girl, a humiliating sound he quickly tried to hide behind a fit of coughing. Had she just called him handsome?

Miss Hughes shot him a wry look and said, "I'm sure you're quite aware of your assets, Your Grace. All of England is aware of your assets."

"I beg your pardon?" He couldn't have heard her right.

She began to count his attributes on her slender fingers. "You've a title. You're tall, dark, and handsome. And, yes, let's not forget exceedingly wealthy. In short, you're the ultimate prize for any debutante or eligible lady with even an ounce of feminine ambition."

Why did that not sound like a compliment? "That is rather cynical."

"I prefer *realistic*."

"Isn't that what *you* would want?" The question was out before he could consider the possibility that he might not like her answer.

"Ah." She resumed walking, and Will followed involuntarily. "Luckily for you, no."

No? Will waited for her to elaborate, but she remained mute. He frowned. If she didn't want wealth or titles, what did she want? The question reminded Will he still knew nothing about Miss Jenna Hughes. And this was the reason he was here, wasn't it? So regardless of whatever lustful urges he felt for her, he should be focusing more on his duty to uncover her past and her secrets and less on her physical attributes.

Will cleared his throat. "Tell me about yourself," he demanded, trying to remember why he should consider himself lucky she didn't want anything he had to offer.

She looked up at him, that half smile lingering around her mouth. "What do you want to know?"

Everything, he thought, shocked by the realization that it was the truth and that it had nothing to do with duty.

He decided to start at the beginning. "Where did you grow up?"

Miss Hughes tilted her head in thought. "I was born in Dorsetshire, but we moved around a lot."

"We?"

"My father and I." A crease appeared between her brows.

"Do you still see your father often?"

"He died."

Damn. He should have considered that likelihood; she was, after all, employed as a ladies' companion. "Pardon me for dredging up a painful memory. I am sorry for your loss."

Miss Hughes shrugged. "Thank you. It was a good while ago, but I still miss him sometimes."

Will let a respectful silence stretch for what he hoped was an appropriate amount of time.

"And your mother? Where is she?"

Miss Hughes shrugged. "If you find her, let me know. She disappeared the day after I was born." The last was said without malice or bitterness.

Will grimaced. He was making a proper mess of this.

"And what did your father do, Miss Hughes?"

"He was a surgeon." There was an imperceptible hesitation in her answer.

"Where?"

"He started his career with the cavalry corps. Then he built his own practice."

"And did you assist him?" Where had that question come from?

Miss Hughes looked at him sharply.

"I am only curious." Upon reflection, Will found he

was rather enamored of the idea that his mother's companion had some sort of medical knowledge. He was certain that would come in useful, if it hadn't already.

"Yes." Her answer was short. "I assisted him from the time I was very young."

Well, that would explain her forthright manner and confidence, at least. Miss Hughes would certainly not be given to fits of the vapors or fainting spells when presented with unpleasantness. Like the situation last night. It did not, however, explain the inappropriate conversation she had carried on with his mother. He was getting to that. Pleased with his progress so far, he pressed on.

"I must assume, given your address, you have never been married?"

Miss Hughes stilled slightly. "No."

"Engaged?"

Her eyes drifted to the horizon somewhere. "Once. When I was young and foolish."

"And now you're not?"

"Young?"

Will scowled. "I was going to say foolish."

"Of course." Her half smile resumed.

"Very well, then, Miss Hughes, how old are you?"

"Twenty-five, Your Grace," she said, and then with an impish grin she added, "give or take."

Will looked at her in surprise. "Twenty-five?"

"You sound surprised."

"No," he lied. Will was struggling to believe no one had tried to lay claim to such an exquisite creature. God, a woman like this should have hordes of men vying for her attentions and affections. She would have had her pick. "Marriage is not something you desire?"

"I am no longer foolish," she answered ruefully, her mouth curling and her dimple creasing. "So no, I do not desire marriage. The furtherance of my bloodline is not vital for the continuation of the world as we know it. You, sadly, are not so fortunate."

Will tore his gaze from her lips with effort, wondering again if she was mocking him. "I am a duke, Miss Hughes. It is my duty to the entire duchy that I marry and produce an heir." He made a face. "Probably three or four heirs."

"Sounds dreadful." Unfathomable eyes met his.

He had no idea if she was being serious or not. But Miss Hughes couldn't possibly understand. For a duke, marriage wasn't something to be enjoyed. It was something to be endured.

"Why did you decide not to marry him?" Will demanded, unnerved at the strange disquiet she was stirring within him. "The man you were engaged to?"

Miss Hughes dropped her gaze and continued walking in silence. "Why do you assume it was I who changed my mind?"

The question startled him. "No man with a shred of honor would withdraw from such a pledge, Miss Hughes. It simply isn't done. Only a woman may break a betrothal."

"Mmmm." Miss Hughes made a very noncommittal sound in her throat.

"Miss Hughes?" Will was still waiting for an answer. "You can tell me or I'll find out about your past another way."

"I'm sure you would," she muttered under her breath. "May I ask why this is important to you, Your Grace?"

Because, for the life of him, he couldn't truly believe any man would walk away from this compelling woman.

Will cleared his throat. "Because you are the single person who spends the most time with my mother. As her son and as a duke, I have the right to know exactly what kind of woman you are, Miss Hughes. I have the right to question your loyalty and your reliability. We are all a product of our pasts." He hated the words the moment he'd uttered them. As if he were one to cast stones.

"A product of our pasts." She echoed his words so quietly he barely heard her. She gave a small, humorless laugh. "Well, we certainly are that if nothing else."

Her hand dropped from his sleeve, and Will felt the loss keenly. He was already regretting his invasion of her privacy, but he didn't know how to call his demands back.

Miss Hughes had turned her attention to an invisible point on the horizon. "Very well, Your Grace, since it is so important to you. His name was Peter, and he was my father's apprentice. Our betrothal had been settled when I was seventeen, and he was only a few years older than I, so we both agreed to wait a year before we wed. Peter had no money of his own for us to begin a life together; he intended to use our betrothal year to save for our future. But those plans were ruined when my father fell ill and died a few short months after our engagement." She fell silent and continued walking in silence, the crunch of gravel beneath the soles of her sensible half boots muffled under her skirts.

"At first we were still full of hope. Peter picked up where my father had left off and he worked hard. We both did. Peter was skilled—he had been quite a good student. But he was young. He . . . we found it almost impossible to collect the wages owed to us for services rendered. Few of our customers felt obligated to pay for work performed by a green boy with no previous reputation. The worst offenders were those who, because of their pedigree, were beyond the reach of the law.

"We lost the house first. Not that it was much, but it had kept us dry in the rain and warm in the winter. After that it became hard to find enough food. We had to sell most of my father's instruments to keep from starving. It became a daily battle just to survive. Peter reached his limit right after winter set in, and disappeared. I found out later he joined the army. A job, a warm bed, and steady meals."

"He abandoned you for the goddamn army?" Will choked, aghast.

Miss Hughes had stopped walking, though she hadn't looked away from the horizon. "A surgeon with frost-damaged fingers is of no use to anyone, Your Grace. And we were both slowly starving to death. He couldn't support himself, much less me. He made the right decision."

"Like hell he did," Will snarled. "I would have hunted him down and torn him apart with my bare hands."

Her lips quirked at his declaration. "When I realized he wasn't coming back, the thought crossed my mind. Especially after I discovered he had taken what was left of my father's medical supplies."

"Why didn't you?"

The smile faded. "The day after he left, I . . . lost our baby. There was a lot of blood. I thought, throughout that night, that I might be dead by dawn." She said the last with the same amount of emotion she would apply to reading a shipping receipt. "But obviously," she continued, "I didn't die. I was in no shape to hunt anyone anywhere, mind you, but at least I was alive."

"He left you when you were with child?" Will said the

words with concentrated care, certain that if he unleashed the emotion coursing through him, he would say or do something he would regret.

"He didn't know I was pregnant. I only suspected." The wind loosened a lock of her hair, and it blew across her face, obscuring her expression. "It's not uncommon. Especially in the early stages of gestation." She might have been reciting a passage from a medical text.

"I'm so sorry," Will whispered. Sorry for her betrayal. Sorry for what she had endured. Sorry he had ever assumed the arrogance to pry into something he had no right to know. He squirmed, excruciatingly aware he had no idea what he could possibly say to excuse his conduct.

"Thank you for the sentiments, Your Grace," Miss Hughes said, pulling the hair away from her face. She met his gaze evenly. "But it is long in the past, and wallowing over something lost does not bring it back, no matter how precious it was. One must live in the present to... well, *live*."

Will found himself having a hard time reconciling the horror of her story with her calm and steady demeanor. "But what happened to you wasn't fair." Surely she thought so as well?

A strange smile touched her face, and her pale eyes assessed him. "Have you ever wondered why women become paid companions, Your Grace?"

Will stared at her in incomprehension.

"Forgotten at the side of every ballroom are women who once thought life would turn out far differently than it did. Individuals who have been hurt and betrayed and damaged in a manner far more grievous than I ever suffered." She paused. "Life is rarely fair, Your Grace."

"What you told me—does my mother know?" Will asked, adrift in a sea of disturbing uncertainty.

"Yes." She lifted her chin. "I hope what I've told you in no way makes you question my dedication to my duties or the duchess. Earlier you spoke of loyalty. Do not underestimate mine."

"No. Of course not." Will grasped the change of subject she offered him with alacrity, though somehow it made him feel like a coward. "Perhaps then, Miss Hughes, you might describe your duties here? What is it you do for my mother? Besides fetch her reptiles?"

That damned half smile he didn't understand reasserted itself firmly back on her face, and she resumed walking. "You don't approve."

"Of her snake? No. Of her chickens? No. Of her complete disregard for the good opinion of her set? No." Will knew he sounded callous, but this was the essence of why he was here. "I love my mother, Miss Hughes. But we can't go on like this."

"Like what?" Her voice had absolutely no inflection.

"You know very well what I am referring to," he said, irritation creeping in. "Everyone believes her to be a crazy old bat!"

"Yes, they do, don't they?" Miss Hughes murmured, and for the briefest of seconds, Will thought he caught a hint of pride in her words. "Do you think she's crazy?" she asked presently, not looking at him.

Will tried to swallow the annoying lump that had formed in his throat before responding. "I don't believe so, no," he began. "But as much as it shames me to say it, I haven't spent enough time in her company in recent years to know for certain. It is why I decided to move in—because I am concerned that the answer to your question may be yes. And in any event, I hope you will agree that we must manage her eccentricities for her own protection. Society can be cruel, and I do not wish to see her hurt."

"Society can indeed be cruel," Miss Hughes agreed.

"Is that a yes?"

"A yes?" She finally looked at him in question.

"That in the future I may count on you to do a better job supervising the way in which the duchess presents herself to the public?"

Miss Hughes regarded him for an impossibly long minute with eyes that seemed far older and far wiser than he'd realized. Twice it looked as though she would speak, but then she seemed to change her mind. Will felt as though he was missing something important.

"Very well, Your Grace," Miss Hughes said eventually. "I will endeavor to do my best."

"Excellent." Will nodded approvingly. He congratulated himself on this small victory, though something still felt off. No matter. At least they were moving in the right direction. "In that case, I must insist that you accompany her to all social events she attends. I do not want her loose in polite society unsupervised. If she hatches one of her eccentric schemes, it would be better if we had some warning."

"Of course, Your Grace." Miss Hughes had a peculiar expression on her face.

"Is there something amiss, Miss Hughes?"

"You are more like your mother than I believe you realize, Your Grace."

Will doubted that very much. He had nothing in

common with his mother. Or at least he didn't think he did. In truth, he barely knew her. And—

"And here we are," Miss Hughes announced, jerking Will from his musings.

Will looked up and blinked, startled to realize they were standing at the back of the dower house. How had that happened? They had just been at the barns.

"I've asked George to go over the accounts and ledgers with you today," she told him pleasantly. As if on cue, the door opened, and the elderly man who had rescued the wig the night prior appeared.

"The accounts?" Will asked, still flummoxed by how he had ended up back at the house.

"Yes. Since you have so graciously offered to assist the duchess and ensure everything is up to snuff, I figured that the household accounts would be the place you would wish to start." Miss Hughes looked up at him expectantly.

"Of course." Will couldn't think of anything he wanted to do less.

Miss Hughes gestured at George. "George will answer any questions you might have," she said. "He's been doing your mother's accounts for years."

"I beg your pardon?" George leaned closer to Miss Hughes, apparently catching his name and not much else.

"I said you'll help His Grace with anything he needs," she shouted at the secretary.

George's wizened face creased into a smile. "Anything, Your Grace," he said, all but saluting Will.

"Just great," Will muttered nastily.

"Beg your pardon?"

"I said, I can't wait!" Will yelled, feeling absurd. He

turned to Miss Hughes, keeping his voice low. "Why does my mother employ a deaf secretary?"

"George's hearing in no way affects his duties here." She put her hands on her hips.

"Duties? What, he has more than one?" Will couldn't imagine what other service this elderly man could possibly provide the duchess.

"George was Royal Artillery. Eighteen years. Cost him his hearing. But he was one of the best with a fuse and a barrel of black powder."

"And why does my mother need an artilleryman on staff?" Will heard his voice rise. Good God, but the idea of his mother with access to explosives made his knees a little weak.

Miss Hughes chuckled. "Artillerymen are usually quite good at math, Your Grace. Trajectories, angles, distances, that sort of thing. Now, off you go. Everything is set up in the study. I'll have luncheon sent up to you both, and then I'll see you later at dinner. I imagine it will take you a few days to get through everything."

Will scowled.

"Your mother is lucky to have you, Your Grace," Miss Hughes said, rueful sympathy lacing her words. "Now go easy on him, George," she was saying loudly. "And make sure you start at the beginning. His Grace has fully committed himself to making sure his mother is in good hands."

"Of course, Miss Hughes." The artilleryman-turned-secretary gave her a fond look before turning to Will. "Would you care to follow me, Your Grace?"

Will groaned. He did not want to follow George into the house for a day of accounting. But he couldn't possibly say no. This was what he had wanted. Or at least what he had declared he wanted in a compulsive spate of duty last night. To decline now would make him look like an indecisive idiot, especially to Miss Hughes.

He was already regretting the loss of her company. Will wanted more time with her. Time to make amends for his pretentious assault on her privacy. Time to understand how a woman who had suffered such adversity could find forgiveness. Time to simply bask in her beauty and confident nature.

In Will's world, beauty was common. Strength, grace, and loyalty were a sight more rare. He'd certainly admitted to himself that he was attracted to Miss Hughes. But now he feared that *attracted* might have slid into *smitten*, and for that reason, it was probably better he withdraw and create some space. Find some objectivity. Find some control. He didn't trust himself not to do something irreversibly foolish.

"I despise bookkeeping," Will grumbled under his breath as he stepped toward the house. "It's such a bore."

"I beg your pardon?" George cupped his hand to his ear.

"I said, I'd like nothing more!" he yelled.

George offered him an approving look. "Very good, Your Grace." He turned and disappeared back into the house.

Will shot Miss Hughes one last look. She was still standing in the sunshine, that easy smile on her face, watching him go. He sighed with real unhappiness and followed.

It occurred to Will only later that for all the information he had pried from his mother's companion about herself and her past, he'd completely forgotten about the barns.

Chapter 5

Jenna collapsed into a chair, feeling exhausted.

She'd been focused so thoroughly on the barns and the explanations she would need to provide that she hadn't anticipated or prepared herself for the duke's very personal interest in her. A reasonable, sensible interest to be sure, since a hired companion was always subject to the careful scrutiny of any employer. She closed her eyes.

Jenna despised speaking of her past, but not for the usual reasons a woman in her position might. She'd made peace with her youthful misfortune long ago; while thoughts of Peter and their unborn child still caused her some anguish, it was now more of a dull and muted pain. And to her surprise, a part of Jenna felt this pain had eased even further after she'd shared her story with the duke. It had been solace for her soul—a confidence given and received, and in that acceptance losing some of its ability to hurt. She wondered, with not a little shame, if she had been too quick to make unfair assumptions regarding his character. For his distress for her had been genuine, and it had certainly made her feel less alone.

However, the other, more practical part of Jenna feared she'd imperiled the duchess's entire operation by giving so much of herself away. The bulk of the duchess's activities were, of course, quite illegal, and too many of them could be traced back to events in Jenna's past. If Will continued to poke around the dower house like a bloody Bow Street Runner, he might make the obvious connections between what he found and Jenna's youth. And if that happened, she and Eleanor would be well and truly sunk.

For their entire scheme was a product of Jenna's own experience with unpaid debts. Jenna knew firsthand that a peer who chose not to pay the tradesmen and -women who toiled for him was, in most cases, exempt from prosecution. Members of the ton might think twice before skipping out on bills owed to established merchants, but newly minted professionals were entirely at risk. Many worthy businesses were shuttered simply because the proprietors were unable to collect what was due to them. And while it was considered dishonorable for a gentleman to ignore a debt to another gentleman, there was no recourse for those dwelling down on the lower rungs of society's ladder. Well, no recourse other than Jenna and the duchess.

Jenna had often marveled at the irony: the peerage had devised a robust system of laws to punish cheats and debtors while the peers themselves remained largely immune. So over the years she had come up with a rather ingenious method of rebalancing the scales, and to her delight she had found a willing partner in Eleanor. Together they swindled the worst reprobates of the ton—so-called nobles who lacked a single noble impulse—in order to save the destitute merchants these same lords and ladies cheated every day. And while they had worked other tracks in the past, Jenna's preferred theater had always been Ascot, where the majority of the popinjays placing bets knew more about their waistcoats than they did about horses. Jenna herself knew very little about fashion. She did, however, know a great deal about thoroughbreds and the people who raced them.

She'd taken Eleanor's advice to heart. Everything she had told the Duke of Worth had been the truth. Her father had indeed been a surgeon. He had indeed served in the cavalry corps before starting his own practice. And Jenna had assisted him from the time she was able to take basic instruction. What she had failed to mention was that her father's patients usually had four legs. In a pinch Papa would tend to critically injured soldiers, but though he was capable of treating human patients, it was the cavalrymen's mounts to which he gave priority. Her father hadn't just been a surgeon.

He'd been a veterinary surgeon.

Jenna's upbringing had been unorthodox at best, shocking at worst. Her father had done what little he could to raise a daughter on his own. But there had certainly never been governesses or lessons on the pianoforte—things that were of little use in the racetrack stables where her father had plied his trade. Instead Jenna was well versed in lancing abscesses and poulticing sand cracks, and had a deft hand with a needle and thread for mending fabric or skin. She possessed an impressive repertoire of raunchy tavern songs, and by the time she turned thirteen, a kindly coachman with daughters of his own had taken the time to teach her how to throw a decent right hook in case the need ever arose.

None of which skills would endear her to the duke or bolster her credentials as a proper lady's companion.

The good news was that Worth was unlikely to pry any

further into her past. The poor man's acute discomfort and horror had been stamped across his features when she answered his questions with brutal candor. Jenna only hoped her honesty would discourage him from interrogating the rest of the duchess's staff. Most of them had secrets far more dangerous than hers.

"Miss Hughes?"

Jenna jerked upright, realizing she was sprawled across the chair like a drunken hound.

"I beg your pardon. I did not mean to startle you. Are you unwell?" Luke's smooth voice held concern.

Jenna turned to gaze at the duchess's butler. "I'm fine, thank you." She paused. "Tell me, Luke, when the Duke of Worth demands to know how it is you became Her Grace's butler, what will you tell him?"

Luke looked at her thoughtfully. "Why, the truth, of course."

"Which is?"

"That I'm good at opening doors."

Jenna snorted. "Just doors?"

"And windows and latches and all manner of locks, but I see no need to boast. Humility better suits a butler, don't you think?" He gave her a languid smile.

"Indeed."

His smile faded. "I came to fetch you. You have visitors. Her Grace is already in the morning room."

"Thank you." Shoving all thoughts of the duke from her mind, she stood, shaking out her plain skirts. She allowed the butler to hold the door for her and waited until he fell into step beside her. "Who is it?"

Luke's blond eyebrows bunched. "Mrs. Monroe. And her daughter."

Jenna frowned. They had helped out the talented dress-makers once before, and while the women had accepted their assistance, they'd made it quite clear they despised relying on others to solve their problems. Things must be bad if the Monroes were seeking them out.

"How much are they owed this time?" Jenna asked.

Luke shrugged. "I don't know. Her Grace sent me to fetch you."

Jenna reached the morning room and slipped inside. The duchess was seated at a small writing desk, making notes on a scrap of paper, the elder dressmaker perched stiffly beside her on a straight-backed chair. Miss Monroe was standing awkwardly near the window, looking miser-able and uncomfortable.

Luke cleared his throat. "I found Miss Hughes, Your Grace," he said unnecessarily.

"Thank you, Luke," Eleanor said absently, returning her attention to the paper before her.

"Is there anything else you require?" Luke asked politely. His sharp eyes included Miss Monroe in his query, and the pretty girl blushed furiously.

Jenna felt a stab of sympathy for the young woman. Luke was an obscenely beautiful man.

"No, thank you, Luke," the duchess murmured, and the butler departed as silently as he had arrived.

"It's a pleasure to see you again," Jenna said to the two visitors. "Though I suspect the reason for your visit is less than joyous." She kept her voice gentle but direct.

"I made her come," blurted Miss Monroe. "We need help, and I didn't know what else to do or where else to go." She looked as though she might burst into tears.

Mrs. Monroe's mouth drew into a thin line. Jenna could

see substantial gray in her once-dark hair that hadn't been there before. "I don't like charity," she bit out.

"This is not charity," Eleanor told her, her voice hard. "Charity would mean that you accept something you didn't necessarily earn. You've earned every penny here and more." She gestured at the list in front of her.

"How much?" Jenna asked.

"Four hundred and eighteen pounds," Eleanor said.

"How much?"

"Four hundred—"

Jenna waved her off apologetically. She'd heard the first time. "From the same person or from multiple people?"

Miss Monroe moved to stand behind her mother, her knuckles white as she clenched her fists in her skirts.

"Lord Brockford ordered an entire wardrobe for his new wife. Two carriage dresses, three morning dresses, six walking gowns, a garden dress, four evening gowns, and a riding habit. We delivered everything four months ago. The last time we attended his address seeking payment, he had his footmen throw us out onto the street. Lady Caudel had ball gowns made for her daughters two months ago, but she claims Lady Louisa changed her mind about the color after wearing it and Lady Leticia was unhappy with the silk roses on the hem of hers. She's refused payment and refused to return the gowns."

Jenna felt a familiar anger build inside her chest. She took a deep breath, forcing herself to think. "How much do you need?"

Miss Monroe bit her lip. "We owe our landlord, but more pressing, we owe the drapers. They've refused to give us any further credit, and without fabric, we can't sew anything. We have four orders that are supposed to be filled by the end of the week for paying customers, and if we can't deliver, they will simply go somewhere else. And if we have no customers . . ." She trailed off in despair.

They'll end up on the street trying their best not to starve to death.

Eleanor tapped the desk with her quill, leaving tiny ink spots on the surface. "Leave Lady Louisa and Lady Leticia to me. Those two ninnies have barely a brain between them. Both of them chased my son endlessly last season. And while I would fall on my sword before I allowed either of them into my family, I can certainly shame them into reimbursing you." She scribbled a note on the paper.

Mrs. Monroe's face relaxed fractionally.

"I'll be able to collect Lord Brockford's debt at Ascot," Jenna said with conviction. "He's a perfect target. He's got loads of money, and he lives to impress. And most importantly, he has a grossly inflated opinion of his knowledge of racing."

"Ascot is not for over a sennight," Eleanor reminded her. "And his is the largest debt. I would imagine the Monroes need that money before then."

The dressmakers nodded, looking a trifle ill.

"I would forward you the money myself, except an amount such as that would require my son to sign off on it with the bankers." The duchess was frowning fiercely. "I need to avoid that, especially now that Worth has decided to take an interest in my affairs. Perhaps I can sell a diamond."

"No," Jenna replied immediately. "There are too many others who depend on the money those diamonds bring in. We've always kept it separate."

"The amount will be reimbursed," Eleanor said. "Gisele will understand."

Jenna had no doubt the former Marchioness of Valence would be more than understanding. In fact, if anyone understood desperate measures, it was Gisele. But those were her diamonds and they had come at a steep price.

Jenna wavered.

"How much do you think you can get out of Brockford this year?" Eleanor asked her.

"All of it," Jenna said.

"You're sure?"

"Yes."

"Well then, it's settled."

"Fine," Jenna capitulated.

The Monroes looked a little bewildered.

Eleanor reached behind her and gave the bellpull a yank. In less than a minute Luke reappeared. Miss Monroe blushed furiously.

"Please ask Joseph to prepare the carriage for me," the duchess told him brusquely. Of the Monroes, she asked, "And how did you arrive here?"

"We walked." Mrs. Monroe looked defiant.

"Good heavens. That must have taken hours."

"Only two," Miss Monroe mumbled.

"Well, I'm glad my ancestors saw fit to perch this pile on the edge of London and not the edge of Wales. And you shall certainly not walk home. I will drop you off on my way to visit the Caudel sisters. I know for a fact they are still in town."

"But they cannot know it was us who complained," Miss Monroe sputtered, looking horrified. "We'll never work again."

Eleanor waved her beringed hands airily. "Good heavens, I'm certainly not going to discuss anything quite so vulgar as merchants," she scoffed. "No, I am going to natter on about how my son, the duke—the *unmarried* duke—is currently holed up in my study, poring over my personal ledgers and accounts. It is quite tiresome, really, but the man has no tolerance for sloppy bookkeeping and even less patience for unsettled household debts. Why, any prospective duchess of his must be capable of keeping the estate records in perfect balance." She sneered. "You'll have the money by the end of the day, I can assure you. Will it at least be enough to get you started?"

The Monroe women nodded slowly.

"Excellent. Now, when was the last time you ate?"

An uncomfortable silence fell.

"Luke, please tell Margaret to prepare something for our guests. She can serve them here while the carriage is being readied. Miss Hughes, you will accompany me this afternoon. Please select a stone suitable to sell here in London. Something midsize but nondescript. Mr. Ross gave me an excellent price last time. I believe I will be patronizing his shop again after my little social call." She patted Mrs. Monroe on the arm. "I will see that you get the balance of what's owed you by morning. One of my servants will deliver it to your shop. You may settle your debts and continue doing what it is you do best."

"Thank you," Mrs. Monroe whispered, sagging in relief. Her daughter looked as though she was fighting tears again.

The duchess clapped her hands. "Now go." She made a shooing motion at Luke and Jenna. "I've people to see and things to do today."

"Very good, Your Grace." Luke gave Eleanor a brief bow, though his eyes lingered on Miss Monroe.

"Are you going to fight Joseph over the right to drive the lovely Miss Monroe home?" Jenna murmured as they moved toward the door.

"I'm sure my little brother is going to be very busy this afternoon," Luke whispered. "He's not the only one who can steer a team." The butler flashed her a grin and hurried out toward the stables.

"Oh, and Miss Hughes?" The duchess's voice followed her out into the hall, and Jenna stuck her head back into the morning room.

"Yes, Your Grace?"

"Please put a couple of chickens in the carriage for good measure."

Jenna hurried upstairs to the duchess's rooms. With no hesitation she strode across the sparsely furnished chamber to the carved wardrobe that loomed against the far wall. In her mind she was already cataloguing the diamonds that remained. A number of them were too big and too ostentatious to be pawned locally. When required, those stones were covertly sent to Lady Josephine, the duke's sister and Eleanor's daughter, who resided, as far as Jenna knew, somewhere in Italy. Jenna had never met her, but the vast sums she sent back to her mother had convinced Jenna the young woman was a very talented and clever negotiator. And that money had helped so many women escape horrifically impossible situations.

The wardrobe door creaked open, and Jenna dropped to her knees, pushing aside yards of silks and satins.

Stretching as far as she could, she reached to the very back, her fingers feeling for the hidden catch. With a pop a small panel at the rear of the wardrobe opened, and Jenna withdrew an enameled box. She flipped up the lid and a king's ransom of brilliant sparkle and glitter emanated from the velvet interior.

The diamonds were arranged by size and shape. Jenna bypassed those stones with a peculiar color or cut, and those that looked as though they should be mounted on a royal crown. Jenna rather suspected some of them had been, at one point in history, worn on the head of a monarch. Her fingers deftly sorted through the smaller diamonds, stones that would be suitable as a center piece in a brooch or mounted on a pendant. With a satisfied nod, she selected a diamond and put it aside.

Quickly she closed the box and replaced it deep in the wardrobe, shutting the panel and returning the cache to secrecy. Fluffing the duchess's gowns back into place, she shut the door, retrieved the diamond, and pushed herself to her feet to leave.

"Just what the hell do you think you're doing?"

Jenna jumped, nearly tripping backward.

The Duke of Worth strode into the room from the doorway. "I asked you what you're doing in my mother's rooms. Rifling through her things." His voice was hard, and his expression even harder. He looked furious and dangerous, and Jenna could feel her pulse pound.

"You startled me." She was relieved her voice came out evenly. She curled her fingers around the diamond and pushed her hand into the folds of her skirts.

His eyes narrowed. "I would imagine most thieves say the same thing when they are caught."

Jenna would have laughed if not for the fact that she was struggling to formulate a good excuse for what the duke thought he'd seen. "I am not a thief." *At least at the moment*, she added silently.

"Yes, I believe all thieves say that as well."

Jenna rolled her eyes. "There is no need for fuss, Your Grace," she said. "Your mother asked me to fetch her spencer for her. She is going out."

The duke didn't look convinced. "And she keeps her spencer in the bottom of her wardrobe?"

"No. It would seem she does not. Now, if you would be so kind as to move out of the way, I can continue my search."

Worth took a menacing step toward Jenna. "And why did she send you to find it? Surely she has a maid who looks after these things?"

"Of course she does," Jenna agreed. "But I was closer. All of your mother's staff have multiple duties. Speaking of which, how are the accounts coming?" She edged away from the duke.

"Don't think you can divert me," Worth growled. "I take a break from ledgers that seem to have been creatively tallied by a drunken jester, only to find you skulking about in my mother's rooms. I want to know what you were doing." His gaze flickered to the hands still clenched at her sides. "Show me your hands."

Jenna forced herself not to react. The diamond suddenly felt as if it were the size of an apple against her palm. "Are you accusing me of something, Your Grace?"

Worth let out a bark of what sounded like bitter, disappointed laughter. "I'm fairly certain I already did."

"Of course. You believe me to be a thief, based on the

fact that you discovered your mother's hired companion looking for an article of clothing in her rooms." She was stalling, and they both knew it.

The duke closed the distance between them again. "I don't believe, I know. Show. Me. Your. Hands."

Jenna swore inwardly. If she handed the diamond over to the duke, that would open a whole barrel of questions she had no interest in answering. Like why a supposedly dead marchioness had left a supposedly lost fortune in diamonds with a supposedly eccentric duchess to sell. And what that money was used for. And why Jenna was sneaking one out of the house. Goddammit, but the Duke of Worth was beginning to make life difficult.

"Very well." In a swift motion, Jenna brought her hands up in front of her chest, dropping the diamond down the front of her bodice even as she opened her fingers to him.

For a moment Worth looked stunned. "What the hell did you drop down the front of your dress?" he snarled.

"I have no idea what you're talking about," Jenna replied placidly. She had gotten herself out of stickier situations than this. Distract and deflect. She dropped her hands again.

"I demand to know what you took."

"Nothing, Your Grace."

"You have something in the front of your dress," he snapped.

"I have since I was twelve years old."

Worth started in shock before he swiped his hands through his hair angrily. "You think this is funny?"

"A little." She was forcing a sangfroid she didn't feel.

The duke let out a string of expletives better suited to the London docks. "You have five seconds to produce whatever you have in the front of your dress, or I swear by all that is holy, I will rip your bodice in half and retrieve it for you."

"Ah. Is this your area of expertise?"

That stopped him short. "What the hell is that supposed to mean?"

Jenna smirked at him and cocked a brow. "I thought bodice-ripping might be part of your overwhelming charm."

Worth's eyes darkened even further. "Very well, Miss Hughes, have it your way."

God's teeth, he was calling her bluff, and in truth, he had every right to do so. Though she'd be damned if she conceded. "Do your worst then," she dared.

She watched as the duke's hands went first to her shoulders, then to the edges of her bodice. She felt the backs of his fingers brush against her bare skin as he curled them under the seam at the tops of her breasts. Jenna remained perfectly still, her breath caught in her chest and her heart thundering against her ribs.

He had long fingers. Beautiful fingers, actually, covered in small nicks and scars and calluses that attested to the fact that this duke understood physical exertion. And they were tracing the neckline of her dress in slow, sure movements. Her stays were suddenly suffocating. The air around her had thickened. Every muscle in her body had clenched, and not in fear. In anticipation.

She closed her eyes, trying to block him out of her consciousness, but that only made it worse. Her skin was on fire, and with every minute movement of his fingers, the heat built. She wanted his hands on her. Wanted them everywhere. Now.

"Look at me," the duke said, and his voice sounded

strained. His fingers delved farther beneath the seam, and his palms brushed her nipples.

Jenna swallowed the moan that nearly escaped and forced herself to remain still. It had been a very long time since she had found herself in this position. She was hardly an innocent. But she didn't remember ever having this feeling of desperate...need. Every fiber of her being wanted to push her body into his hands and let him have his way. There was no doubt in her mind he would be magnificent. But this man was dangerous. This man had the power to destroy everything she had accomplished.

She tried to focus on something safe. Like the frayed edge of the counterpane draped over the bed. It really should be mended—

"Jenna."

The sound of her name on his tongue in that rich, husky tone nearly snapped her control. She wanted to hear it again. Preferably against the hollow of her throat. Or the sensitive spot below her ear. Or—

"What exactly are you doing to Miss Hughes, dear?"

The duke snatched his hands away from the edges of her bodice and took a smooth step back at the same time. Jenna forced herself to fill her lungs slowly and deliberately before raising her head and her eyes.

Eleanor was standing in the doorway, peering at the pair of them in absent confusion.

"Miss Hughes was going through your things, Mother," Worth said, managing a decent amount of indignation, though his voice cracked at the end.

"Well, of course she was," the duchess said. "I told her to."

That took a little wind out of his sails. "She has hidden

something down the front of her dress, and I mean to know what it was she took," Worth pressed on gamely. "That was what I was trying to determine a moment ago."

Jenna met Eleanor's eyes and winced. The duchess gave her an almost imperceptible nod.

"Oh, go ahead, Miss Hughes. My son may take a look if he wishes." The duchess sighed heavily as she shuffled into the room.

Worth appeared uncertain as he met Jenna's eyes. The duke at a distance was much easier to manage than the duke with his beautiful hands on her. She shrugged with a pleasing measure of indifference and reached into the front of her dress. Worth looked away.

She passed the diamond to the duchess, who rolled it around in her palm.

"Is that a diamond, Mother?" Worth asked, coming to stand next to the duchess.

"Yes, dear. One of the ones I no longer wish to keep. I had instructed Miss Hughes to fetch it for me."

"Tell me you're not going to sell this one as well," the duke said, disapproval coloring his words. "I had to hear about the last one you sold from the Countess of Baustenbury. She was worried you were dismantling the family jewels."

"The countess might just lose her nose one of these days if she keeps putting it places it doesn't belong," Eleanor huffed. "Of course I'm going to sell this diamond, Worth. And don't you even think about stopping me. Rest assured the Worth family jewels are still safe, gathering dust, waiting for you to pick a bride and present them to her. I've half a mind to give them to Miss Hughes out of sheer despair."

Worth's face tightened.

"These"—she gestured to the stone in her hand—"are baubles I've collected through the years. They mean nothing, and they do me no good moldering in a box. But I knew you wouldn't like the idea and I said as much to Miss Hughes. Which is why this piddling little diamond ended up in the bottom of her bodice, along with your fingers." She gave her son an arch look before turning to Jenna. "Thank you for your efforts at least, Miss Hughes."

The duke had the grace to look properly mortified.

"Miss Hughes," he said stiffly, "it would appear I was rather hasty in my judgment." A muscle worked along the edge of his strong jaw. "I am very sorry for wrongly accusing you. Please accept my apology."

She was impressed with his admission. "Apology accepted," Jenna replied.

Worth looked up at her, startled. "Accepted? That's it?"

"You were doing what you thought was right. Protecting your mother and her property. I can hardly fault you for that. In fact, I find it admirable." It was the truth.

The duke was staring at Jenna openly now, disbelief and something else suffusing his features. "But you can't just...accept. Not after what I...implied."

"Would you prefer I hold a grudge for a while?" Jenna asked, feeling a little devilish. "Would that make it easier for you?"

He continued to stare and made a funny noise in his throat.

"Is that a yes?" Jenna prompted. "What is an appropriate amount of time a woman should hold a grudge against a duke who has accused her of being a thief? A day? Maybe two?"

"I'd aim for a week," the duchess suggested slyly.

"That sounds exhausting." Jenna wrinkled her nose at Eleanor. "I think the best I could do would be a day. I'd probably forget during breakfast the next morning. Especially if there was bacon."

"I do like bacon," the duchess agreed. "It's hard to be angry when you're eating bacon."

"My sentiments exactly."

"Jesus." Worth pinched the bridge of his nose, something that looked like a smile threatening. "No, Miss Hughes, I would hate to burden you further by insisting you hold a grudge. It's just that in my experience, most women—"

"Your Grace," Jenna interrupted, "the matter has been settled. Though might I suggest you seek out a new circle of female acquaintances if your experience thus far has led you to believe that our gender is fixated on vengeance for such trivial issues."

The duke didn't look convinced.

"Well said, Miss Hughes." Eleanor nodded with approval. "Now, can we go? I fear Joseph will have fallen asleep with the carriage by now."

"I think Luke is driving today," Jenna said, slipping her arm through Eleanor's and steering her toward the door. "I believe he is rather taken with Miss Monroe."

"Where else are you going?" Worth demanded from the far side of the room behind them. "Besides the jeweler?"

Jenna clenched her teeth. They had almost made it. Beside her she heard Eleanor exhale in impatient annoyance.

"Nowhere that you'd want to go, darling."

"Let me be the judge of that, Mother."

"If the duke comes with us, he's not here, snooping around," Jenna hissed against the duchess's ear. "He'd probably agree to anything to escape George and the accounts. And if anyone could drive him back to his life and out of ours, it would be Lady Louisa and Lady Leticia."

Eleanor paused in consideration. "I suppose his presence would certainly help our cause. And who knows who else that family owes money to?" she whispered.

Jenna nodded. "A win-win."

"What are you whispering about, Mother?" Worth demanded from behind them.

With a feigned sigh, the duchess turned around. "I am going to call upon the Earl and Countess of Caudel. More specifically, their daughters, the Ladies Louisa and Leticia. They are back in town this week."

Worth's brows shot into his hair. "Why on earth would you want to visit those witless wonders? They've barely an entire brain between the two of them."

A bubble of laughter caught Jenna unaware, and she choked. Worth looked at her sharply.

Eleanor looked merely exasperated. "Watch your manners, young man. They are both pretty girls from a very good family, dear. You will eventually have to get married, you know. Someone in this family should be thinking ahead."

"Good Christ, Mother, you can't possibly think I would marry one of those nitwits. I'd fall on my sword before I'd commit myself to a lifetime of Caudel misery. I'd declare Phillip my heir. The cousin or the snake, either would be a damn sight better than one of their offspring."

Jenna was coughing into the sleeve of her dress.

"*Hmph*." Eleanor crossed her arms. "Well then, it is a

good thing your company is not required this afternoon. Miss Hughes will accompany me. We'll leave you to the ledgers."

"No, no, no, wait. I'll escort you," Worth said hastily. "In fact, I insist. I'm sure the books will still be here when we get back."

Jenna stared at the toes of her boots and tried not to laugh. "And endure an afternoon of Caudel misery?"

"Have you met the family, Miss Hughes?" the duke asked dryly.

"I have not had the pleasure."

"Then you're in for a rare treat." There was a wry amusement to his tone. "I can't think of any other women who, in my presence, better epitomize your rather cynical view of feminine ambition." Jenna glanced up at him and found him watching her with the humorous warmth of a shared private joke. That look made her breath catch and her toes curl. He held her eyes for a timeless moment.

"*Tsk*. That's enough, dear. If you can't be on good behavior, I'll leave you at home," Eleanor threatened.

The duke finally looked away from Jenna, leaving her feeling a little wobbly.

He strode toward the door. "I'll be on my best behavior, Mother. So long as you leave your damned chickens at home."

⁓

William paced at the bottom of the stairs as he waited for his mother and Miss Hughes to collect their belongings. He had no idea what had prompted him to volunteer himself to escort the duchess into town. London in the summer always seemed overly warm and more than a little malodorous. And worse, he had agreed even knowing they were headed to Lord and Lady Caudel's. Each of their daughters possessed a dearth of intelligence and a terrifying ambition to improve upon her title. Will shuddered.

If he was honest with himself, he might admit that his hasty offer had more to do with the woman he had accused of being a thief and less to do with the need to escape the stacks of ledgers that were making little sense. Will cringed, recalling his accusations. And then he cringed again, remembering Miss Hughes's graciousness. He'd labeled her a thief, had his hands on her bodice, and then called her Jenna as though he had the right. And if his mother hadn't interrupted him, who knows where his hands would have gone, because every time he was around Miss Jenna Hughes, he seemed unable to control his lust for her. He had no idea what she truly thought of him now, despite her declarations.

Admirable, my ass. He'd been a bloody cretin.

But despite his mortification, he hadn't failed to notice the undercurrents in the conversation that had passed between Miss Hughes and his mother. And their covert whisperings convinced Will he was missing something important. He would be paying very close attention to the behavior of both women this afternoon. Something odd was going on.

"Your Grace?" A strong baritone broke into his thoughts.

Will looked up to behold the most stunning man he had ever seen. He was short, with golden hair and blue eyes, and resembled a compact Grecian carving of perfect masculine proportions. Chiseled features, faultless posture, flawless comportment. Dimly Will became aware the otherworldly creature was wearing livery.

"Who are you?" Will demanded.

"My name is Luke, Your Grace." The man offered him a courteous bow, and Will imagined a heavenly fanfare echoing.

Luke. Why was that name familiar? In a second it came to him, along with the recognition of the slight burr in the man's speech.

"You are Joseph's brother." Pleased with his deductive reasoning, Will straightened his shoulders.

"Indeed, Your Grace."

Will suddenly frowned. "You two don't look like brothers."

"I would reckon that is because our fathers looked nothing like each other, Your Grace."

"Oh. Of course." Will cleared his throat awkwardly and then again with more conviction. It wasn't as though one got a choice in the matter of paternal selection. He of all people should understand that. "And what is it you do in my mother's household?"

"I am the butler."

Will snorted. "No, you're not." Butlers were older, formal, conservative men with a lifetime of training. They were masters of discretion and invisibility. The man standing before him was probably Will's age, and while Will could not evaluate discretion by sight, there was absolutely nothing invisible about this supposed butler.

The golden prince named Luke offered Will a small, almost indiscernible smile. "I simply came to inform you that your mare has been saddled and is ready out front with the carriage. I took the liberty of ordering it readied in the event you chose not to ride in the carriage with all four women."

"Four women?" Will asked in confusion, momentarily forgetting this man's bizarre claim that he was a butler.

"The Monroes, Your Grace, will be traveling back to London with you."

"Who are the Monroes?"

"The dressmakers, Your Grace."

"What dressmakers? Why are there dressmakers here? At this hour?"

Luke inclined his head. "I wouldn't presume to know, Your Grace, though I might suggest it would have something to do with making dresses."

Will nearly swore in frustration. Could no one in this damn house give a straight answer? And why was this man asserting himself to be something he obviously was not?

"Ah, Luke, there you are." His mother's breathless voice floated down the stairs behind Will.

"Your carriage is ready, Your Grace," the man said, inclining his head with respect. "Mrs. and Miss Monroe have already alighted and are waiting."

Will turned to watch the duchess and Miss Hughes descend the stairs. Miss Hughes had her arms full of his mother's belongings.

"This man says he is your butler, Mother," Will said bluntly.

The duchess reached the bottom of the stairs and blinked up at him. "Well, of course he is."

"Why?"

"Why?" His mother gave Will a queer perusal before she gazed fondly at the beautiful man.

"I am very good at opening doors, Your Grace," the butler offered.

Luke's explanation earned him a nod of approval from the duchess and a wide grin from Miss Hughes. The golden butler moved to relieve Miss Hughes of her burden, and even with Miss Hughes's superior height, the pair made a stunning couple, their contrary coloring only enhancing the physical beauty of each. Their body language around each other betrayed a long familiarity and made Will's fists and teeth clench.

"Come along, Worth dear," the duchess said over her shoulder, breezing out into the sunshine.

Will was left standing in front of the open door as Miss Hughes followed the duchess and the women were handed up into the carriage. He could make out two unfamiliar faces peering out at him uncertainly as Luke handed reticules and parasols up into the interior. The butler shut the door with a snap and climbed up onto the driver's seat.

"Are you still planning to join us, Your Grace?" the butler, who was now driving the carriage, asked politely.

Will frowned. "I thought you were the butler. Where's Joseph? Shouldn't the coachman be driving?"

Luke grinned, his even white teeth flashing. "Regrettably, my youngest brother is otherwise occupied, Your Grace."

He could see Miss Hughes watching him from the small window, that half smile lingering on her lips.

"Your Grace?" the butler prompted patiently.

"Yes," Will said, forcing his feet to move. "I'm coming."

Chapter 6

The Caudels' butler—a real butler with white hair and a stoic face—outdid himself. When the man opened the door to the Duke of Worth and his mother, he simply inclined his head and invited them inside, showed them up to the residence's best drawing room, and offered to take gloves and hats with a polite, expressionless voice. He offered regrets that Lord Caudel was not at home at the moment; however, Lady Caudel would be delighted to receive them, and would they require any refreshment while they waited? All said with pedantic deliberation, as though dukes and dowager duchesses showed up unannounced at regular intervals.

Lady Caudel, however, was not nearly as skilled.

The petite countess stumbled into the drawing room, her faint expression of skepticism fading first to horror and then to glee and finally to utter calculation.

"Your Graces," Lady Caudel said smoothly, recovered from the shock of seeing a duke standing in the center of her horribly patterned rug. She put a hand to her artfully arranged blond hair. "What a pleasant surprise. Please make yourselves comfortable."

Will eyed the excess of ornate furniture crammed into

the space and escorted his mother to a large overstuffed, red sofa. Miss Hughes followed them, taking a chair set slightly to the side of the sofa, her eyes downcast and her demeanor demure. Will glanced at her and then did a double take. Somehow, on the way into the town house, the woman Will knew to be Jenna Hughes had ceased to exist. The woman who was now settling herself awkwardly on the hard wooden chair behind his mother had slouching shoulders that diminished her height and gave her a faintly defeated air. And since when did she wear spectacles? And where had that horrid cap come from? Will was unnerved at how Miss Hughes had suddenly morphed from the unyielding woman who had challenged him in his mother's rooms to this sober, silent shadow. She was barely recognizable.

"What a lovely room," his mother was exclaiming, looking around with great interest. She peered up at Will. "Oh, do sit down, dear, you'll give me a crick in my neck if I must keep looking up at you."

Will tore his eyes away from Miss Hughes and gingerly lowered himself to the sofa beside the duchess.

"Why, thank you," gushed Lady Caudel. "I confess I decorated it myself."

Will followed his mother's gaze. Everything was covered in a rusty red, from the walls to the upholstery to the curtains to the rugs. He rather felt as though he were sitting in the center of an overripe tomato.

A commotion at the door distracted him from his perusal. Two young women swept into the room, and Will stood. Both curtsied deeply, expensive skirts billowing out around them though the tiny blond ringlets around their faces didn't so much as stir. Both brought their eyes up to meet Will's. If Lady Caudel's expression had been calculating, her offspring wore smiles that were positively predatory.

"You remember my daughters, Lady Leticia and Lady Louisa?" the countess asked.

"Indeed." The duchess acknowledged the young women with a watery smile that didn't reach her eyes. "I believe I saw you at the Countess of Baustenbury's ball. You were both wearing *breathtaking* ball gowns. Everyone said so."

The Caudel girls exchanged a smug, triumphant look.

She turned to Will. "Don't you remember, dear?"

Will remembered hiding in the cardroom drinking fine brandy and avoiding anything in a ball gown. "Of course," he lied. What else was he supposed to say? He sneaked a glance at Miss Hughes. She was still studying the floor in the center of the room, her face expressionless. He wondered if her presence had even been noted by their hostesses.

Lady Leticia and Lady Louisa both selected chairs directly opposite the sofa, and Will sank back down, feeling cornered.

"I've rung for tea and cakes," Lady Caudel said a little breathlessly. "Unless you would prefer something a little stronger, Your Grace?" The last was directed at Will.

"No, thank you." Will declined with real regret. He was quickly regretting a great deal, not the least of which was his current location. What the hell was his mother doing here? More to the point, what the hell had he been thinking in agreeing to escort her?

"We were sorry to miss your last ball, Your Grace," Leticia—or was it Louisa?—breathed. She leaned forward, giving Will an eyeful of pale cleavage.

Her sister, not to be outdone, strained even farther toward the sofa from her seat, putting Will in mind of a ship's figurehead, thin layers of muslin desperately working to prevent full exposure. "We were stuck in the country," she pouted, "and simply couldn't make it back in time. Though we heard about all the excitement."

That was one word for the disastrous events that had occurred at Breckenridge. Will did not wish to dwell on it.

"I heard the Marquess of Valence went mad," Leticia said. "Is it true?" She put a dainty hand to her throat and tipped forward a fraction more, threatening to spill her breasts into her lap.

"And the waltz that cavalryman danced? Was it as scandalous as everyone says it was?" Louisa interrupted with her own question, preventing him from replying.

Both women stared at him, waiting for him to say something.

"I believe accounts may have been somewhat exaggerated," he managed politely.

"Poor Lady Julia," Louisa breathed. "If I had been forced to suffer the humiliation of being engaged to a madman, I believe I would have sailed to the Americas. The gossip would be unbearable."

Will's eyes slitted. What had happened to the Earl of Boden's sister had happened through no fault of her own. "Lady Julia behaved with remarkable poise in circumstances she would never have sought and could not possibly have anticipated. No one could have anticipated them."

"Surely there were warning signs. Perhaps she didn't notice because she was untutored in the ways of polite society. Her family, after all, comes from mere—"

"I would, of course, expect there to be very little gossip," Will interrupted loudly, a hard edge to his voice.

"But I heard that—"

"Girls," Lady Caudel said sweetly, clapping her hands as if to round up a pair of unruly lapdogs. "Do not forget His Grace is on good terms with the Earl of Boden. Lady Julia's brother."

Louisa and Leticia sat back, paling slightly.

The arrival of the tea service saved them from an uncomfortable pause.

"How delightful," the duchess said, peering at the assortment of cakes the maid had laid out, seemingly oblivious to his stiff posture beside her. "Is there something with lemon?"

Lady Caudel eyed his mother. "I believe there is. Shall I pour?"

"No, no, Miss Hughes can do it. That's why she's here," the duchess said, her dismissive tone snapping Will's head around in astonishment. He had never heard his mother speak of Miss Hughes, or any other servant for that matter, with such indifference.

Miss Hughes rose without a word and expertly prepared and poured. Her expression remained serene, as if she found nothing amiss.

The duchess accepted her cup and waved her hand in the general direction of Jenna. "My hired companion, Miss Hughes," she said by way of shabby introduction.

"I don't believe I've had the pleasure," Lady Caudel replied by rote. Her eyes darted, then dismissed just as the duchess had. Her daughters took a moment longer to assess the other feminine threat in the room, and their hackles rose, the horrid gray dress not fooling them as completely as it had their mother. Miss Hughes carefully returned to her seat and lowered her eyes back to the rug, folding her hands in her lap silently. Placated, Leticia and Louisa sneered slightly before once again returning their full attention to Will.

Will felt his jaw clench as he proceeded to endure long minutes during which Lady Leticia and Lady Louisa prattled on about the weather, the last theater performance they had attended, and their favorite complexion cures. This was why Will hid in cardrooms. Or behind potted plants. Or, most successfully, in barns. Otherwise minutes of his life slipped by, wasted on heaps of . . . nothingness. He could barely stand it.

Sometime during a heated quarrel between the sisters over the aesthetics of a well-appointed barouche as opposed to a phaeton for a turn in the park, Will's attention wandered to Lady Caudel. He could almost see the wheels grinding in the countess's head as she examined every possible reason for their unexpected visit. He was quite certain, based on her giddy smile, that she fancied one of her insufferable daughters was under consideration for the position of duchess. He did not particularly like any of the Caudel women, but a small part of him felt a measure of guilt for encouraging the countess to hope. She might be a horrible, grasping harpy, but he supposed vicious mythological beasts had feelings too, somewhere underneath their scales.

"Peacocks are overrated," the duchess was opining beside him, and Will forced himself to resume interest in the conversation. "As are swans. But I do so love chickens. I travel with them everywhere."

Three expressions faltered slightly, and Will winced.

When they'd arrived he'd discovered his mother had smuggled two of her damn birds in the carriage. Thankfully, he'd had his way, and the chickens remained outside, locked safely in the equipage.

"I had swans once, in my pond," his mother was telling no one in particular. "But they kept drowning my ducks. Nasty birds, swans. Chickens are much gentler souls. They make wonderful companions."

"Quite," replied Lady Caudel, with a warning glance at both her daughters, who were looking at the duchess with ill-concealed distaste.

"Worth here does not appreciate my chickens," the duchess grouched. "Since he's moved in, he's made me keep them in the barn."

"Moved in?" Lady Caudel inquired.

"Just temporarily, of course." The duchess gave Will a fond pat on the shoulder. "He wants to make sure I'm taken care of."

"How wonderful," Leticia simpered.

"How munificent," Louisa sighed.

"Isn't he?" his mother agreed with pride. "Tell them what you've been doing all day, dear."

Will shot another glance at Miss Hughes, unable to help himself. She met his eyes, her half smile lingering as if she could see the string of thoughts that suddenly crowded into his brain.

I've imagined ravishing my mother's hired companion all day. Before and after I called her a thief. And especially when I had my hands down the front of her dress.

Miss Hughes's smile widened.

"Books," Will blurted, looking away.

"Like the kind you have to read?" Louisa blinked.

Will gaped. Dear God, but his mother couldn't truly be entertaining any idea of acquiring a daughter-in-law like this. He'd be in Bedlam before his first anniversary.

Miss Hughes found something fascinating on the ceiling that required her complete concentration, while Lady Caudel looked stricken.

His mother gave him a sharp elbow.

"Accounts," he said with an impressive amount of civility. He wondered what would happen if he simply walked out of the room.

"Oh." Leticia's face twisted in distaste. "How horrid. I don't like numbers."

"Ugh. Nor do I," Louisa chimed in.

"Pity," the duchess sighed heavily beside him.

"I beg your pardon?" Lady Caudel was sharper than her daughters.

His mother fluttered her hands. "It's just that a future duchess would need to oversee household accounts. Could you imagine what would happen if a duke's bills went unpaid and his debts were left unsettled?" She dropped her voice to a near whisper. "Now, I know some care little about such matters, but for a Worth, such behavior is anathema. Why, just this morning my son declared any future wife of his must have a deft touch with finances or risk the sterling reputation of the family! Isn't that what you said, dear?" She turned to Will and fixed him with a stare that dared him to disagree.

"Indeed," Will murmured out of a sense of self-preservation, more shocked at the intensity of his mother's challenge than at the fact that she was lying through her teeth. They had had no such conversation. This morning or ever. Had she lost her mind for good?

All three Caudel women were gawking at the duchess. Will adjusted his cravat, which suddenly seemed quite constricting, and gave Miss Hughes a pleading look. She had promised to handle situations like this. Surely she would do something.

"Your Grace," Miss Hughes murmured gently, "I'm quite sure Lady Louisa and Lady Leticia are not interested in bookkeeping. Or managing domestic accounts." She gave the women a faintly apologetic look.

The duchess set her lips in a mutinous line. "My apologies. I fear I speak sometimes without thinking in my old age. It's just that I so want my son married to the right woman—someone worthy of the title."

Will tore his gaze from Miss Hughes and transferred his attention to his mother. A nagging awareness began to hum quietly in the back of his brain. He suddenly suspected nothing the duchess had said in the last minute had been unthinking, even if her delivery had been exquisitely offhand.

Miss Hughes leaned forward. "I believe you wished to inquire about the ball gowns, Your Grace."

Will was aware she had seamlessly redirected the conversation.

"The gowns?" The duchess was tapping her chin.

"The gowns Lady Leticia and Lady Louisa wore at the Countess of Baustenbury's ball. You've mentioned your desire to have something similar made. Perhaps, if Lady Leticia and Lady Louisa would be so obliged, they might share with you the name of their modiste? We could make an appointment this afternoon, since we're in town shopping."

Will kept his face carefully blank. Not an hour

previously, they'd dropped off two dressmakers at their fashionable shop near Bond Street after they'd attended his mother at the dower house. Surely any necessary additions to his mother's wardrobe would have been addressed this morning? Why in God's name would they need to seek out yet another dressmaker this afternoon?

"Ah, yes, of course! Now I remember!" his mother exclaimed. "I was thinking of having something made just like them but in that new emerald green. I so adored the little silk roses on the hem. Do you suppose yellow roses would be too much with the green? Maybe they should be pink. I could even wear one in my hair." She patted her head as if a phantom rose were already there and cast an expectant look at the sisters. "You simply *must* tell me the name of your dressmaker. She'll be delighted, no doubt, to hear you've recommended her."

Lady Leticia and Lady Louisa were blinking rapidly. Lady Caudel looked as if she might be ill.

And in that moment, Will finally understood. The entire conversation, the entire visit, had been orchestrated to arrive at this destination. This excursion had never been about helping to select potential wives for Will. It had never been about discovering who had created the ball gowns in question. The duchess knew exactly who had made them. And they'd ridden back to London in his carriage.

"I don't remember," Louisa mumbled.

"You don't remember her name?" the duchess asked in surprise. "Good heavens. How can that be?" She let that hang. "Was it a shop on Bond Street then?"

"I don't remember." Leticia's eyes were darting between Lady Caudel and Will.

"Perhaps if they still have the bill for the gowns, Your Grace?" Miss Hughes suggested quietly and deliberately. "For the dressmaker's name and direction will be noted, I'm sure."

"Yes, yes. A bill of sale would be just the thing." The duchess beamed. "We can wait while you retrieve it."

Lady Caudel swallowed, no doubt thinking of the bill for the gowns that might or might not still exist. But a bill that had apparently never been paid.

Will wondered what the two dressmakers had done to earn such loyalty and kindness from his mother. His eyes narrowed. Or perhaps they had earned loyalty and kindness from Miss Hughes? It wasn't clear to him who was the puppet master here. The duchess had a generous heart, and Will could easily believe his mother would go far to help two women in need. But the more likely scenario was that Miss Hughes had devised this scheme and had plunged Eleanor into it the thick of it. Noble though the impulse was, Will wasn't sure he liked the idea of his mother's being dragged into such intrigues.

For the moment, however, the point was moot. In the matter of his mother, Miss Hughes, and their two dressmakers versus Lady Leticia, Lady Louisa, and their outstanding bills, picking sides was delightfully easy. He'd reserve judgment on the rest until after he had spoken with Miss Hughes.

"If they can't remember, Mother, I can make inquiries, if that would please you?" Will offered indulgently. "The gowns were indeed unique, and I'm sure someone will be able to recall who made them. Perhaps I might even inquire with the Countess of Baustenbury herself. She seems to remember everything."

"Oh, that is not necessary, Your Grace," Lady Caudel sputtered, looking horrified. "I'm sure I'll be able to find it. If you will but give me a little time, I will have the name and the address sent to you."

"That would be wonderful," Will replied, standing up. There was no need to remain a moment longer. "I do so like to pamper my mother. I'm sure your daughters are similarly minded." He forced his mouth into a broad smile. "Now I believe we've taken up too much of your time already. Thank you for such a charming visit, Lady Caudel. Lady Leticia, Lady Louisa, I look forward to seeing you again." He almost choked on the last.

He felt the weight of Miss Hughes's regard, though he kept his eyes on the duchess. He'd get to Miss Hughes in due time.

"Such a good son," the duchess chuckled, allowing Will to help her to her feet and past their gaping hostesses. "Now if only he'd give me my chickens back."

⁓

The Duke of Worth waited until his mother had decamped from the carriage and disappeared into the small jewelry shop across the lane.

Jenna was surprised it had taken him that long.

He tied his horse to the rear of the carriage and climbed in, drawing the door shut behind him. The equipage tilted slightly as he settled his weight onto the seat opposite her. He shoved the wire cage housing the two chickens to the side with the toe of his boot, and the birds squawked in protest. The duke leaned forward, considering her in measured silence.

Jenna shifted, the spacious carriage having suddenly

shrunk to minuscule proportions with the invasion of his long frame and his probing eyes.

"Do you wear spectacles often, Miss Hughes?"

Of all the questions he could have asked, she hadn't expected that one. "When I need to," she prevaricated.

Without warning the duke reached out and snatched the spectacles off her nose. He held them up to his own face and peered through them, the light reflecting off the shiny surface of the lenses and hiding his eyes from her completely. After a moment he removed them and handed them back to her.

His lip curled slightly. "You wear them when you wish to alter your appearance, you mean."

Jenna didn't have a rebuttal for that. He'd just seen for himself that they were constructed of nothing but clear glass. There was nothing useful about them, other than their ability to mask her eyes and do exactly as he said.

Jenna placed the spectacles on the seat beside her and shrugged. "Perhaps."

"Why?"

Jenna shrugged again. "Everything is less complicated when people are presented with what they expect."

The duke stared at her. "Less complicated?"

She returned his gaze mutely. She'd already said enough.

"Would you care to tell me exactly what transpired in the last hour at the Caudel residence?" he finally asked in the layered silence. To his credit the words were almost cordial.

"Shouldn't you be with your mother?" Jenna stalled, gesturing out the carriage window.

"She didn't want my help. She insisted on having Luke escort her."

Jenna snorted under her breath. Eleanor didn't want her son anywhere near a proprietor who had bought a fortune in stolen diamonds from her over the last five years. Explanations would have been awkward.

"You haven't answered me, Miss Hughes."

"I believe you know exactly what that was, Your Grace," she said carefully.

"An act."

Jenna shrugged. "Call it what you like."

"Who are they to you? The dressmakers?"

Jenna felt a flash of annoyance at his question, and he mistook her hesitation.

"Ah. They are related to you."

She shook her head. "No. They are simply two women living and working in London, who require payment for services rendered if they are to survive."

The duke sat back with a thump. "This is about you."

"I beg your pardon?"

"What happened to you—what you suffered. You're helping others who find themselves in the same situation."

Dammit, but this was what she'd been afraid of. Worth was too clever by half. Perhaps she should have lied this morning. But had he taken the initiative to question others on the staff without her knowledge, she would inevitably have been caught. Her story was hardly a secret among the duchess's employees.

Jenna forced herself to remain calm. So what if he had figured out what they had done this afternoon? It was harmless and even honorable. Let the duke believe the events of today had been a simple means of helping settle a score from a distant past.

It was a far cry from what she would do at Ascot.

"It is not about me, I assure you, Your Grace." Jenna forced a nonchalance into her words. "It's about people who don't deserve to be used."

The duke studied her intently, his elbows on his knees now, and Jenna resisted the urge to squirm. For once she couldn't tell what he was thinking. His dark eyes betrayed nothing, and in the relative dimness of the carriage, his sharp features were set and still. "Payment was never received by the dressmakers for the *breathtaking* ball gowns, I must assume."

"It was not." Jenna kept her answers short, simple, and precise.

"I would imagine the outstanding payment is on the way to the dressmakers right now."

Jenna allowed a small smile. "I would imagine you are correct. Before the Dowager Duchess of Worth, or worse, the duke himself, can discover the Caudel ladies have outstanding accounts. Before Lady Leticia and Lady Louisa might destroy any chance they might now have of becoming a duchess."

"And you speak of people being used," he growled. "You used *me*."

Jenna arched a brow. "If I recall, it was you who insisted on coming."

"You used my mother." There was more heat behind this accusation.

"She might disagree."

"I don't like to see her generosity and decency taken advantage of."

Jenna leaned forward into his space, tipping her chin up. "Tell me, Your Grace, who ensures your accounts are settled? Your tailor. The collier. The chandler. The bakers and butchers and booksellers. The saddler and haber-dasher and hatter."

The duke withdrew fractionally, and a crease formed between his dark brows.

"Is it you?" she asked.

"No."

"Then who?"

"I have a secretary. And stewards and housekeepers. They keep track of such details."

"And if they don't? If they miss a payment or forget a payment or simply can't be bothered to make a payment?"

The duke stared at her.

"Who is being taken advantage of then, Your Grace?"

He had no answer.

Jenna suddenly felt tired. "You sit in the House of Lords, Your Grace. Tell me, how many laws exist that force a peer to pay the milliner for the six hats his wife bought last month? Laws that are enforced?"

Worth spread his hands over his knees and rubbed at the fabric of his breeches. He shifted against the squabs. "I never thought about it," he said quietly.

"Most individuals of your station don't. But I have. And so has your mother," Jenna said gently. "The merchants who serve you and your kind have bills to pay as well, Your Grace."

"You've done this before." It was more a statement than a question. "Helped collect unsettled debts."

"Yes. When I can."

"And has my mother helped you? Before today?"

"Sometimes." It wasn't a lie, exactly.

"Is that what you were doing disguised as a princess at my ball? Helping someone?"

"Yes." That was the truth.

The duke reached forward and grasped her hands in his. Jenna froze, her gloved fingers trapped in the warmth of his.

"I'm sorry," he said.

"For what?" she asked in surprise.

"For any disrespectful treatment you suffered."

"From you?"

The duke dropped his head with a rueful sigh. "Among others." He looked back up at her, his dark hair falling over his forehead and partially concealing his eyes.

"*Hmph*. Well, Your Grace, it's true I am quite experienced at being mistreated by your social set. But I must admit, I've never had a duke with his hands down my dress before today," she teased.

The duke's fingers tightened on hers. "I'm sorry. I didn't—"

"Oh, for the love of God, stop," Jenna interrupted him, feeling a slight tug of guilt. "I was teasing you. There's nothing to forgive." *Forget* was another matter entirely, but Jenna shoved that aside ruthlessly for the time being. "You were doing the right thing."

Worth was rubbing his thumb over the backs of her knuckles and Jenna forced her hands to remain still. "Sometimes I have no idea what the right thing is," he said suddenly, staring down at their hands.

"Your Grace?" Jenna heard the uncertainty in his voice, and it surprised her.

The duke seemed to sneer at her address. "My father was considered a distinguished duke by the whole of society. He was respected for his ironfisted control of the duchy, but he was a hard and angry man despite his accomplishments. Most everyone despised him, including his own family. I don't want to be despised."

Jenna let the silence stretch until Worth brought his eyes back to hers. They were miserable.

"My father would have let the milliner starve in the street if it wasn't convenient for him to pay his bill." There were bitterness and bile in his words. "And he wouldn't have cared or given it a second thought. Because that is the prerogative of a peer. Of a duke. Dukes do not bother themselves with such trivialities." Worth looked stricken. "I've never concerned myself with such. I'm no better than he was."

Jenna was shaking her head. "That's not true."

"It is. Until this very moment, I've never really considered the consequences of my entitlement."

Something in her chest squeezed hard. "But you're thinking about it now."

"Yes."

"You're not your father."

"Not yet."

"Not ever." Jenna was vehement.

The duke glanced away helplessly. "You sound so sure of yourself. But you know nothing of my father."

Jenna studied his profile. She was well aware the conversation had now delved into territory studded with pitfalls and pain. She would need to navigate carefully, not only for herself but for the man across from her.

"I know people only held value to your father if they could provide him with something. They were no more than possessions to be used and discarded at his whim. I know it got worse as he got older, yet that same ruthlessness brought him recognition as a man his peers perceived to be ambitious and fearless."

The duke's face darkened ominously, but he remained silent.

Jenna took a deep breath. "I know why your mother sent you and your sister away when you were children," she said evenly, allowing no pity to taint her words.

Worth froze before slowly turning back toward her. He had retreated within himself, the honest emotion wiped clean from his expression, leaving only a brittle crust of warning resentment in his eyes.

"You have no idea what you speak of."

Jenna refused to look away, thinking of all the women the duchess had helped out of impossible situations. Situations exactly like the one Eleanor herself had been far too familiar with. "I know exactly what I speak of."

Worth pulled his hands from hers and balled them into fists on his knees. "I'm not discussing this with you."

"You should."

"Why would I do that?"

"Because you know my secrets," Jenna said. "And secrets like those lose their power when they are no longer secrets. Your mother has already learned this."

She could hear the harsh sound of the duke's breathing in the confines of the carriage, the noise of the outside world distant and muffled. "What did she tell you?" he asked finally.

"She told me that your father was an angry, abusive man. That he would take out his failures and frustrations on those closest to him, sometimes with words, but more often with his fists."

The duke flinched.

"Tell me this," Jenna asked quietly. "Do you hold yourself responsible for your father's actions? Are you the reason he was the man he was?"

Worth looked up at her, startled, before a flash of anger crossed his face. "No."

"Good."

The resentment in his eyes had faded, leaving a lingering unhappiness. "My mother thought that if she loved him enough she could change him. And when I was a child, I wanted to believe that too. Perhaps that was why I never told her that my own injuries did not really come from a tumble off my pony or a misstep along the top of a stone fence. I still clung to the same hope she had, that he could change."

"Men like that don't change."

"No. They don't," he agreed.

"Your mother's biggest regret is not recognizing that sooner," Jenna told him. "She did not know until it was too late that the violence visited upon her was visited upon her children. For that she carries a heavy burden of guilt."

The duke made a tortured noise in the back of his throat. "To what end? What could she have done differently? She could not have overpowered him. She did the only thing she could and sent me away to school. It was I who felt guilt every day that I was unable to stop what I knew was happening at home."

"You were a child."

"That didn't make it any less real. It took years before I was big enough and strong enough that my father could no longer threaten me. Yet that only seemed to anger him more, and I know my mother suffered for that. It was better for everyone if I stayed far away. My sister had figured that out for herself long before I did, even though I was the elder."

Jenna frowned in confusion. "I was under the impression your mother had sent her away for schooling as well."

A faint smile touched his lips. "Have you met my sister, Miss Hughes?"

Jenna shook her head.

"Joss is . . ." Worth searched for a word. "Different."

"Different?"

"Brilliant. Intellectually gifted. In another time, an unparalleled polymath."

"Ah." Jenna wasn't surprised, given the little she already knew.

The duke's face darkened. "My father called her unnatural, though I think he was a little afraid of her mind. When she was six, she made the mistake of correcting him on a political matter in front of a guest. He broke her nose for her efforts."

Jenna bit her lip. She hadn't known that.

"My mother sent Joss away the next week to live with distant cousins in Italy. My sister came home for the summer months to Breckenridge, as I did, because my father despised the country and rarely left the city. But she stopped coming home when she was fifteen. I haven't seen her since."

"I'm sorry."

Worth shrugged, though Jenna could see the discontent beneath the dismissive gesture. "We write. Often."

Jenna sat back and watched the duke, who was now staring out the window.

"Is this why my mother helps you?" he asked abruptly. "Does she have some sort of notion that she can help balance the scales after enduring so many injustices herself?"

"Perhaps," Jenna replied honestly. "Though I think that her compassion is part of who she is. I believe it was you who once told me we are all products of our pasts." Jenna was picking her words carefully. "Though it might not be immediately evident, I think the duchess has emerged stronger for the adversity." She paused. "As have you."

Worth frowned and turned back to her, uncertain. Without considering what she was doing, Jenna put a hand on the side of his face, pushing a heavy lock of black hair from his eyes.

"You didn't have to do what you did today," she told him. "But you did it simply because it was the right thing to do. You are your own person who makes his own choices."

Beneath her fingers she could feel a muscle jump. A strange expression stole over his face and Jenna caught her breath at the vulnerable pride she saw there. He gave an imperceptible nod and she let her hand drop, afraid that if she kept it there, she'd be forced to kiss him. Whatever had squeezed in her chest before was twisting painfully now.

She was terrified she was beginning to like this man far more than was safe. Jenna was no more immune to his devastating smile than the next woman, but it was the small things that were turning her insides to mush and threatening good sense. His imperfect humanity and his willingness to acknowledge it. His concern for his mother. His fair-minded honor.

Worth was shaking his head, his mouth twitching wryly, breaking the somber mood of the last minutes. "That's what my mother and you were whispering about before we left, isn't it?" he asked. "Whether or not I would ruin your carefully laid plans? Whether I would expose your cover?" He tugged on the graying cap she still had pinned over her hair.

"Umm. Yes," Jenna mumbled.

The Duke of Worth was a far better man than he gave himself credit for. And she should leave. Now. Get out of the carriage and run as fast as she could before she did something stupid.

He again picked up her hand, which had fallen against her skirts. Carefully he turned it over, his fingers tracing a worn patch on the palm of her glove. "And did you think I would do the right thing, Miss Hughes?"

Worth spoke so quietly that Jenna barely heard him. This was her opportunity to lie. To tell him she had doubted him every minute. Tell him he had surprised her with his actions. That would put some much-needed distance between them. Probably permanently.

"Yes." She whispered the truth instead.

The gentleness in those coffee-colored eyes shifted into something searing, and Jenna could see tiny flecks of black and gold in his irises. He threaded his fingers through hers and pulled her forward, her knees brushing his. She could smell the remnants of his shaving soap, something rich and exotic darkened by leather and the heat of his own body. He placed her hands on his thighs and trapped them there, bracing her palms against iron-hard muscle that flexed under her touch. His scent and the feel of him beneath her hands were dizzying.

"Tell me to stop," he ordered, his fingers beginning an ascent of her arms.

Jenna swallowed.

"Please tell me to stop," he repeated, his voice low and feral. "For if you don't, I'm going to kiss you senseless, and you're going to find my hands down the front of your dress again."

A wave of desire crashed through her, and she was drowning in it. Holy God, but she wanted him, and for now she didn't care to examine the wisdom of that. Jenna remained mute, not only unwilling, but unable, to do as he asked.

Worth groaned. "I'm trying to do the right thing here, Miss Hughes."

"Then do it." The words slipped out, inevitable and inciting.

Every inch of the duke's body shuddered, and his breath hitched at her reckless challenge.

Jenna's pulse pounded. Her gaze dropped to his mouth.

And the carriage was flooded with light.

"I was wondering where you'd got to, Worth dear," Eleanor said from the door, rummaging through her reticule. She frowned fiercely. "I can never find anything in here. It's like looking for something in the bottom of a stocking," she grumbled. The duchess stopped her mumbling long enough to peer up at Jenna and the duke. "Are you planning to return home with us in the carriage, dear?"

The duke had retreated as far back into his seat as physically possible. "I believe I'll ride my mare." He avoided Jenna's eyes. "I find the carriage somewhat constricting."

"It is rather warm in here," Eleanor sniffed. "Unfortunate. This day has worn me out. I'm sure I'll be asleep in no time, and Miss Hughes might have appreciated the company."

Jenna thought she was appreciating the company a little too much for her own good, if her hammering heart was any indication. Holy God, what had she been thinking? He was a *duke*.

She cleared her throat, allowing her pulse to slow before she spoke. "I'll be quite fine, Your Grace," she told Eleanor. "Were you successful?"

The duchess held up her despised reticule, and Jenna heard the unmistakable clink of coins. "Very."

Across from her, Worth was doing a spectacular job of appearing relaxed. "And just what are you going to do with that money, Mother?" he asked.

The duchess shrugged happily. "I haven't decided." She allowed Luke to hand her up into the carriage, and settled herself next to her son. "Thank you for not being a pest, darling."

"I beg your pardon?"

Eleanor motioned to her reticule. "You have to allow an old woman her indulgences."

The duke sighed, though his exasperation now sounded more like amusement. "I'm learning to pick my battles." He nudged the cage of forgotten chickens with the toe of his boot. "If you wish to sell a few baubles you no longer want, Mother, I promise not to interfere."

"Very good." Eleanor beamed broadly at her son. "Now, shall we be off? I'd like to return home. The heat is starting to bother me. You two look a little flushed yourselves."

Worth all but flung himself out the carriage door. "I'll ride," he repeated. His eyes touched on Jenna before they veered away, and he closed the door with a loud snap. Through the window she watched him retrieve his mare from where he'd tethered her to the back of the carriage.

"He seems angry," Eleanor commented curiously as the carriage lurched into motion. "I assume he deduced the true purpose of our little bit of theater earlier."

"Yes. No." Jenna stopped and collected her wits, which had been scattered like seeds on the wind. "He wasn't angry at what we did. He was angry that I had taken advantage of your good nature. He implied I used you and your position to achieve my own ends."

Eleanor's face softened. "And what did you tell him?"

"The truth. That we try to help those who need it when we can. That one might use one's position for good, even if it is contrary to society's expectations."

"*Hmph.* And what did he say to that?"

That he has no idea how to reconcile society's expectations of a duke with his own objectives as a man. That he dreads the idea that by embracing his title he will turn into every miserable thing his father was.

"He said it was very kind." Jenna couldn't bring herself to say the rest out loud. It seemed like a betrayal of trust.

The duchess studied her, and Jenna met her sharp eyes with a level stare of her own.

"*Hmph.* He didn't ask about anything else?"

"No." *He was too busy threatening to kiss me.*

Eleanor sat back with a satisfied grunt, though Jenna knew very well she hadn't fooled her entirely. "Well then, at least we've surmounted one hurdle. This afternoon had the potential to become a disaster."

Jenna turned her head and watched the Duke of Worth's mount trotting effortlessly beside their carriage. The duchess didn't know the half of it.

William needed to ride. Not a sedate trot or a pretty canter, but an uncontrolled, mind-numbing gallop that would
empty his brain of everything except the wind screaming
in his ears and the feel of unrestrained power beneath him.

And make him forget Miss Hughes.

The conversation he'd had in that carriage was the most
brutally honest conversation he'd ever had with anyone
about his family. Miss Hughes hadn't shied away from the
unpleasant and shocking nature of his revelations, nor had
she offered him placating pity. Instead she had given him
her faith and challenged him to use the hardship of his
past to do better. Will couldn't remember the last time he
had felt as exposed before another person.

Or, strangely, as safe.

And then he had almost kissed her. He wasn't sure if
it was her cleverness, her compassion, or her confidence
that had most intoxicated him, but together they were a
devastating cocktail made only more potent by her beauty
and grace and strength. All he knew was that he had never
wanted a woman as badly as he wanted her, and he'd had
no intention of stopping with a kiss. He would have had
her skirts up to her waist and his hands in far more intimate places than her bodice before she could have thrown
another bloody dare at him.

Then do it. Her words rang in his head over and over.

She had no idea what she had demanded. No, that
wasn't true. She wasn't an innocent untutored in such
matters, but she was his mother's hired companion and, as
such, off-limits. He clenched his hands around the reins,
and the edges of the stiff leather bit into his palms. He

was shaking, for Chrissakes. The Duke of Worth did not shake. Certainly not over a woman. Women were diversions, entertaining tangents of pleasure and, if he was lucky, pleasing company and conversation.

But Jenna Hughes was starting to consume him.

She was certainly making it difficult to ride with any degree of comfort. For the last hour he'd had an unceasing erection. It was making him irritable and frustrated and desperate. Everything he wasn't, even on his worst day.

In front of the dower house, the carriage had already rolled to a stop. Joseph held the horses, waiting for his brother to help the women disembark. Behind him William saw Isaac hurrying up from the direction of the stables. If his groom was here, that must mean his own horses had arrived as well. The sight of the familiar, capable face was a welcome relief. At least one thing was going right.

"Your Grace." His groom reached Will as he slid off his mare.

"I trust everything is well," Will barked, wincing at his tone. He forced himself to take a deep breath even as he adjusted the fall of his breeches.

"Indeed, Your Grace. I've barely arrived myself." Isaac glanced back in the direction of the row of oaks and dropped his voice. "I must confess, I was not expecting . . . this."

Will made a rude noise. "You and me both."

"The young coachman tells me your mother raises blooded hunters here. It is difficult to tell from a distance, but it appears she has some very fine animals."

Will made some sort of indecipherable reply. This thread of conversation was doing nothing to soothe him. "Are my horses settled?" he asked instead.

"They are, Your Grace. Your mother's staff is nothing if not accommodating."

A snort of ironic laughter escaped. "Accommodating, indeed."

The older man gave Will a curious look.

"Please have the horses ready by dawn tomorrow," Will instructed. "You and I will ride then."

"Very good." Isaac looked pleased. "I'll make sure Joseph and the rest of the barn staff are aware—"

"No." Will cut him off. "Tell no one we are riding."

"Your Grace?"

"I do not wish an audience," Will snapped. "Ever since I have arrived, I have had a minder every minute of the day. Artillerymen, lady's companions, Greek sculptures, and chickens. And one snake."

"Of course, Your Grace," Isaac replied, as if this made perfect sense.

Will was going to have to give the man a raise. "Thank you, Isaac. I'd like to ride the bay first tomorrow morning. And again, please do not share our plans with anyone."

"I wouldn't dream of it, Your Grace."

The day was already sliding into evening. He'd finish what he could of the damn books tonight and then he'd ride tomorrow. Away from George and the ledgers and the chickens.

And most important, away from Miss Hughes.

Chapter 7

The sun was still just a promise in the east when Will strode down to the stables. A faint mist hovered around the edges of the trees and grounds, making everything appear dreamlike. He took a deep breath, the cool morning air filling his lungs and settling his nerves. He'd barely slept, and it had nothing to do with the fact that he was no longer surrounded by the familiarity of his own bed and lodgings and everything to do with the woman who slept down the hall, on the other side of his mother's rooms.

Which only reinforced the notion that some distance from Miss Hughes was essential to his sanity. Perhaps Boden would fancy a lark into London this evening. Or even into the tiny village squatting a few miles south. Anything to put some real distance between himself and this house and Miss Hughes. Yes, that would be just the thing. He'd send a message round as soon as possible.

He already felt better.

"Good morning, Your Grace." Isaac met him at the crest of the hill on the other side of the oaks. He pulled his coat closer against the chill of the air and stifled a yawn.

"Late night, Isaac?" Will gave him an arch look.

"Might have had a few pints with the boys."

"The boys?"

"Joseph. Luke. Decent sorts, the lot of them."

"Mmmm." Will made a noncommittal sound, feeling a little envious. He could have used a pint or six last night. "Did they mention where the best place to exercise horses was here?" he asked, not wishing to discuss his mother's strange staff any further.

"Indeed, Your Grace," Isaac said slowly. "There is a wide track they use to train carriage horses. It runs a fair way towards the back of the property before turning back to the barns. Something of a circular nature."

Of course there is, Will grumbled to himself. Secretly tucked away behind the secret barns and secret horses.

"And? Is it suitable? I won't kill myself or my horses?"

"It is infinitely suitable." Isaac paused as if searching for words. "In fact, it appears to be in exceedingly good condition."

"Well, that's good news."

"Indeed, Your Grace. Whoever maintains it knows their business. I've seen racetracks with worse turf."

"It would appear my mother does nothing by half measures." A distant rumble intruded on their conversation. The thunder rolled, increasing in volume, and a familiar vibration began in the earth beneath his boots and then faded. Will strained to see the riders, but sunlight was still a half hour away and the curling mist that hugged the ground made the shapes hazy.

"Seems like someone else had the same idea," Will said, itching to be on his horse. Hack or hunter, it mattered not. The power and the freedom were intoxicating.

"Let's go," he said to Isaac, leading the way down to the old barn.

His bay was waiting, pacing its stall, as eager to get out as Will was. He'd bought the horse as a yearling, and it had proven a sound investment over the last four years, winning fifteen of its seventeen starts. Will was confident it would command a respectable stud fee once he retired it.

"Shall I saddle the filly?" Isaac asked.

"No." Will led the bay out into the alley. The horse snorted and tossed its head. "I want to ride Comtessa myself later."

Isaac nodded in agreement. "What would you like me to ride?"

"Did you get a good look at my mother's herd yesterday?" Will asked, realizing he had yet to do just that. There had been too many distractions, the one with ice-blue eyes and kissable lips the greatest of them all.

Isaac shook his head. "I'm afraid I didn't, Your Grace. It was dark by the time I was done with my chores in the old barn. But when I arrived, I thought I saw some hunters in the lower pastures that looked like they could run."

Will nodded, trying to recall his own impressions. "I agree. Pick the best of the lot that looks like it might have the most speed and stamina. It won't come close to beating the bay, but I'd like it to push him at the beginning."

"Very good, Your Grace. I will meet you at the bottom of the track." Isaac gestured to the murky pastures.

"Excellent." Will had already cleared the barn door and was swinging up into the saddle. "Let's teach them a little something about racing, shall we?" He was grinning, the feel of the horse beneath him familiar and glorious.

This was what he was good at. This was what he knew, and best of all, he didn't have to be a duke while he was doing it.

⁓

The bay was sweating lightly when Isaac appeared a short time later, riding a leggy black. The murk of the morning still hadn't relinquished its hold, but the mist was dissipating, revealing the packed ground. Will watched as his groom cantered his mount toward him.

Will frowned. "I said I'd prefer to ride Comtessa myself later," he said.

"It's not Comtessa, Your Grace," Isaac told him. "I pulled this filly out of the lower pasture." It was difficult to make out the groom's face in the dull light, but the man seemed troubled.

Will squinted at the horse. "Are you sure?" In the remnants of the gloom, Isaac's horse was the spitting image of his own black filly.

"I'm quite sure, Your Grace."

He must be more sleep-deprived than he realized, Will thought wryly. In the low light, he was mistaking fine hunters for racehorses. Will shook his head in dismissal, giving the bay's challenger one last perusal in the gloom. Whatever it was, the horse certainly seemed suitably capable and keen.

"Are you ready?" Will grinned at him, the anticipation of the race making him giddy.

"Yes." His groom slowed the black into a trot with some difficulty. "But Your Grace, I think—"

"Try not to fall too far behind," Will said, impatient with conversation and unwilling to wait a second longer.

The bay snorted and pawed the ground, and with a shout, Will turned it toward freedom. The stallion surged beneath him, racing into the wind, and Will laughed. God, but he needed this.

Each stride the stallion took increased its speed, the horse's head bobbing in time to the steady rumble of its hooves. *If a person could fly, this is what it would feel like*, Will thought fiercely, leaning low over the horse's neck. The trees and the pastures blurred beside him as Will guided the horse down the track.

A half mile slipped away, then another. The bay was running exceptionally well this morning, the last few days of rest clearly a benefit and not a hindrance. Turning his head slightly, Will could see Isaac galloping steadily behind them, the groom's face hidden by the black's mane. He was a little surprised Isaac's horse had hung on this far, though it wouldn't take him long to fall behind now.

The track curved to the right, threading a copse of trees, and just as Will reached it, the sun broke over the horizon. Golden light spilled everywhere, and for a moment everything was right with the world.

Until Will became aware of Isaac moving up on his left. Will frowned. He hadn't noticed the bay's pace decreasing. In fact, his stallion was digging in, and Will could feel the horse add more speed. He gave the stallion its head, and the animal responded, stretching to a strong finish. Up ahead the barns were coming back into view. Surely Isaac's mount should be flagging by now. The pace was punishing, yet the filly stuck next to him like an unwanted burr. Will sneaked another look, stunned to realize Isaac still had the horse in hand.

The two horses pounded down the stretch toward home, nose to nose. Isaac was cursing his horse roundly, fighting to check the animal's speed. The black pinned its ears and tore the bit from Isaac's fatigued arms, detonating into a blur of flying hooves, leaving Will gaping in its wake. It reached the end a full five lengths in front of Will's stallion, and was another quarter mile back up the track before Isaac managed to turn it, forcing the black into an unwilling canter.

The bay dropped into a trot, blowing loudly. Will barely noticed, fighting to understand what had just happened, too disoriented and dazed to make any sense out of anything. Isaac was wrestling his mount back toward Will, the groom's expression a peculiar mixture of horror and denial and awe.

"What the hell was that?" Will snarled at his groom, breathing hard. He swung from the saddle, keeping the bay walking.

"I don't know, Your Grace," Isaac said helplessly, also dismounting and walking his horse. "I couldn't hold her back." He rubbed a trembling hand over his head, distraught. Isaac had been riding thoroughbreds for more years than Will had been alive, and the confession was alarming.

In the harsh light of dawn, Will got a good look at the horse that had routed his stallion. And wondered how he ever could have missed it. Wondered if he'd lost his edge somewhere. For the filly Isaac was riding was as fine a thoroughbred as Will had ever seen. Its black hide glistened, slick with sweat, muscles bred for running bunching and flexing beneath its silky pelt. Its breeding was evident in every inch of the horse, and if this animal ever stepped into the auction ring at Tattersalls, mayhem would ensue. Disorientation was rapidly giving way to disbelief and something he identified as fury. He hadn't mistaken this filly for what it truly was.

His mother wasn't just breeding horses, she was breeding *racehorses*.

"Remind me where you got that horse from?" Will asked carefully, trying not to take his wrath out on Isaac.

"I just pulled it out of one of the pastures by the new barns, Your Grace. You said to pick the best of the lot. She looked fast in the dark. Looks fast in the light too. Bloody, bloody fast." His groom had been reduced to babbling.

"You pulled it out of one of the—" Will couldn't finish; he was too agitated. "You pulled it out of the pastures," he tried again. "Like a common cart horse."

Isaac nodded feebly.

"Please take my horse, Isaac. See that he's properly cooled along with the filly you just *pulled out of the pastures*."

"Er, where are you going, Your Grace?" Isaac asked.

Up close for the first time, Will stared out at the infamous pastures, taking a good long look and seeing exactly what type of horse made this farm profitable. Why had he not seen it when he had been down here yesterday?

Because you were too busy flirting, a snide inner voice mocked.

Will ignored the voice and focused on the more appalling, implausible matter. And that would be the fact that the duchess had kept this from him. Even knowing his passion for the sport, she had kept all of this from him. For years.

Will waited until the red haze had cleared somewhat from his vision. "I am going to speak with my mother."

"Is that wise, Your Grace? Perhaps you should wait. I mean, you've had a bit of a shock—" Isaac stopped abruptly as he caught sight of Will's face. "Very good then, Your Grace. I'll see you in a while."

Will turned in the direction of the house.

"Do try not to break anything," Isaac called after him.

⁓

Will crashed into the breakfast room not caring that he had mud on his boots. Not caring that he was sweating and disheveled and furious. Not caring when the door bounced hard off the plaster wall.

The duchess froze with her teacup halfway to her mouth, and Miss Hughes paused with a heaping forkful of eggs suspended over her plate.

"Good morning. You're just in time for breakfast, dear." The duchess beamed. "Please sit down. There are poached eggs and apricot—"

"No."

"No?" His mother raised a silver brow in his direction. "Are you not hungry? Miss Hughes said you'd gone riding. I would have thought you'd be famished by now."

His eyes swung to Miss Hughes, who had finished with her eggs and was devouring a generous helping of ham.

"Good morning, Your Grace," she said pleasantly, and then returned her attention to her food. For a woman he'd nearly mauled in a carriage yesterday she seemed remarkably composed. And how did she know he'd been riding?

The duchess *tsk*ed. "You're not feeling peaked, are you

dear? Lord Alfort said just last week his nephew caught a fever that—"

"I'm not sick," Will snarled, refusing to be distracted. By Miss Hughes or his mother's ramblings.

"Well, that's good to hear." The duchess blinked up at him. "You look a little worse for wear. Did your valet not arrive yesterday?"

"I was just at your barns, Mother." He waited for a reaction.

"That's nice, dear." She took another sip of tea.

"I rode one of your horses. Or rather, Isaac rode one of your horses. It thrashed one of my best thoroughbreds out on your track."

In the corner of his eye, Miss Hughes's fork paused before resuming its travels.

"Well, I'm sorry to hear you were beaten." His mother leaned forward with mild interest. "Which one was it? Isis? She's the black filly."

"All your damn horses are black, Mother. I can barely distinguish one from the other," he blurted, shocked that his mother wasn't even going to apologize.

The duchess sat back. "*Hmph*. That makes me feel better. I thought it was just I who couldn't tell them apart. Perhaps I should get some different colors next year." She looked up at him brightly. "Did it run well?"

"You're raising racehorses!" Will shouted, hating the wild accusation in his voice, but unable to do anything about it. "*Racehorses*."

The duchess smiled indulgently. "Well, not all of them become racehorses, darling. Only a handful of my thoroughbreds ever develop the speed required to race. The rest, of course, simply make splendid hunters. And a tidy profit."

"Why?" Will choked.

"Why what?"

"Why would you do that?"

"I dabble, dear."

"You dabble?"

She patted her hair. "You seemed to spend so much time in the stables and at the tracks, I decided to see for myself what it was all about."

Will flailed for an appropriate response. "So you purchased an entire stable full of thoroughbreds so you could dabble?"

The horses Will had seen run today were not the product of *dabbling*. He'd seen his share of dabblers. Those poor beasts were usually distanced in the first heat of a country race. No, the horses that flourished in his mother's pastures were the product of careful breeding, experienced training, and skilled handling.

The duchess laughed breezily. "What does your sister always say, dear? If you can't beat them, you might as well join them."

"Joss knows about this...hobby of yours?"

"I might have mentioned it in my letters." The duchess shrugged.

"And you never thought to mention it to me?"

Another shrug. "You are a busy man."

"Not that busy!"

"Worth, darling, there's no need to be upset. In fact, I thought you might be pleased."

Will began pacing. "And where do you race your horses, Mother?" He was hanging on to self-control by a thread.

"Ascot," the duchess replied, reaching for the teapot.

"I do so enjoy the viewing stands there. And they sell the most delicious lemon pies on race days. And sometimes there is cinnamon bread, dusted with sugared—"

"Mother." Will stopped and grasped the back of a chair in an effort to keep himself steady. Even if she only raced at Ascot, he still should have heard something. The racing world in England was not so big as that. Unless... "Where else do you race your horses?"

"Well, Paul usually takes them up to Scotland when they're two. He says the hills are good for them, and that it gives him a chance to see which ones will be worthwhile racing at Ascot when they are three or four. And of course he has family there he likes to visit. Now, I find the weather up north a little chilly for my tastes—"

"What happens to them after they race at Ascot?" Will interrupted, still stymied as to how he could have been unaware of this.

Eleanor added a dripping spoonful of honey to her tea and stirred. "Why, I sell them, dear. Otherwise I'd end up with dozens and dozens, and the stable lads tell me I simply wouldn't have room for them all. Not if I want to keep breeding my mares. And I do so love to see the little ones frolicking in the pastures. They bring such joy to my heart."

Will was frowning fiercely. If his mother were selling horses here, he would know about it. It was not as if they could simply disappear. Will would have— He stopped, the answer obvious.

"You don't sell them here."

The duchess made a face. "Good heavens, no. There is a lovely man who comes at the end of each summer to purchase my best. I've done business with Mr. O'Neill for years. So much more civilized than the disorder and hub-bub of the auction rings."

"You're selling them to Ireland." Will wasn't sure if he should be impressed or horrified, though it certainly explained why he, along with the rest of England, had remained oblivious.

"The Irish take their racing very seriously," his mother confirmed. "My horses are in good hands."

A thought struck him. "Who else knows you own racehorses?"

The duchess blinked at him. "Well, I can't imagine anyone, really. It's not as if I ride them myself. And I must confess, I find the barns a little dusty for my liking. I'm quite happy to let Paul and his brothers sort out the details when it comes to racing them."

"And are there details to work out this year, Mother?" Will demanded. "At Ascot?"

"Why, as a matter of fact, there are." The duchess beamed proudly. "I have entered two horses this year. One in the Yeoman's Plate and one in the Trafalgar Stakes."

Oh, dear God. Will took deep, controlled breaths and wondered, if he hadn't made the discovery this morning, if the duchess would have told him before they actually departed for Ascot. He brought his eyes back to Miss Hughes, who was now diligently working on a stack of toast smothered in preserves.

"Was there a reason you didn't think to mention any of this to me yesterday, Miss Hughes? When we were stand-ing in the barns?"

Miss Hughes looked up at him and delicately wiped at her mouth. "I thought I did."

"You most certainly did not." He said it with more

confidence than he felt, because there had been long stretches when he hadn't been paying too much attention at all to what she'd been saying.

"My apologies for the oversight then, Your Grace."

"The oversight. The *oversight*?" Will's eyes bulged. "Failing to inform me you borrowed a book from my library is an oversight. Not noticing the cobwebs on the dining room chandelier is an oversight. Not telling me my mother has a stable full of racehorses is not an oversight!"

Miss Hughes had a toast square in her fingers. "Then what is it?" she asked curiously.

"It's a . . . a . . . conspiracy!"

The toast tumbled to the plate.

His mother rapped her spoon on the surface of the table. "That is quite enough," she snapped. "Miss Hughes is not to blame for your ignorance. If you need to continue yelling, dear, please do so at me." His mother was genuinely annoyed. "Preferably from outside this room."

Will dragged in a lungful of air. He was acting like a barbarian. And a maniacal and paranoid one at that. "I'm sorry."

"As am I." His mother sniffed. "It was never my intention to cause you grief."

"It's just all a bit shocking." Will made a monumental effort at civility. "Is there anything else you're not telling me? Anything else I should know about you and your household? Now would be a good time to speak up."

The duchess replaced her spoon gently beside her cup. "Of course not, dear."

Will rubbed his face. "Thank God." He stared unseeingly at the floor. Then frowned. "Where are your shoes, Miss Hughes?"

Miss Hughes started and snatched her bare feet underneath her skirts. "I would imagine they are still in my room."

"Why are you eating breakfast without shoes on?"

She shrugged in that infuriating way of hers, but there was no clever retort.

Will stared at her suspiciously, noticing that her hair wasn't as tidy as it usually was. In fact, the knot at the back of her head was threatening to unravel, long tendrils of hair already having made good their escape. Her color was high, and she looked like a woman just returned from an invigorating walk.

Or invigorating bed sport.

Will cursed himself in disbelief. Despite the events and revelations of the morning, he was once again dwelling on Miss Hughes. And her bed. This had to stop.

He forced his feet to the door. "I am assuming I will find Paul in your barns."

"No, I believe he is still in London. I expect him back sometime tomorrow." The duchess gave him a warning look. "If you're going down to the barns now, do not terrorize my staff."

"Give me some credit, Mother. I am simply going to have a proper look at your stock. And an informative conversation with someone there who won't suffer from any further oversights." He avoided looking at Miss Hughes. "I will speak with this Paul in depth when he returns."

The duchess sat back, apparently satisfied with his recollection of common courtesy. "Very good, dear. Will you be back in time for lunch? Margaret is making the most delicious stewed pork with ginger—"

Will escaped before he lost what little composure he had left.

～

The outside door banged shut, the sound reverberating through the rooms and hallways. Jenna slumped in her chair, her forehead hitting the table. "I think I might be ill."

"I thought that went quite well."

"I had hoped we could avoid this," Jenna mumbled into the tablecloth. "It was my fault. We rode earlier than usual to stay well out of his way, but it seems not early enough. I'm sorry."

Eleanor shook her head. "Don't be so hard on yourself. It was inevitable. A stable full of racehorses is not something that can be easily concealed under a rug. He was bound to see them run at some point, and while we might have passed them off as high-spirited hunters in the pasture, there is no mistaking them for what they really are on the track."

Jenna groaned.

"The important thing is that he doesn't suspect you."

Jenna lifted her head and pulled back the hem of her skirts, revealing her bare toes. "We think."

She'd just finished her own ride with Joseph when she'd heard the horses on the track. She'd watched the duke and his bay stallion charging out of the mist down the stretch nearest the barns. And then, horrified, she'd seen his groom on Isis, closing the distance with a blistering gallop. She'd known then that their secret would be a secret for roughly five or six seconds longer. Just long enough for the black to catch the duke and blow by him.

Jenna had bolted then, running as fast as she could back to the house, startling the duchess, who was just leaving her rooms. One look and Eleanor had hustled Jenna down the hall and into her room, where Jenna had stripped out of her riding clothes and been unceremoniously stuffed into the closest dress at hand. She'd not had time to fix her hair, nor find her shoes. But it had worked.

The duke had no reason to suspect the stables were Jenna Hughes's principal domain.

"He probably believes you just rolled out of bed," Eleanor offered.

Jenna glanced down at her disorganized appearance and raised a brow at the duchess.

"I will assure him I have spoken to you about proper breakfast attire for a lady." Eleanor looked amused.

Jenna rubbed her temples with her fingers. What a bloody disaster.

Two days, she thought. Two days until they departed for Ascot. Two days in which she would need to slink around her home like a French spy, avoiding the duke and his meddling ways and his clever mind. Two days she couldn't afford to waste in preparing for the races.

The duchess, as if reading her mind, leaned forward. "Can Joseph or Luke manage until we depart? If you're not in the barns, there's no chance of being caught."

Jenna's mind instantly rebelled at the suggestion. "No." She needed intimate knowledge of exactly how her horses were running for a good portion of her scheme to work.

Eleanor grimaced. "I didn't expect you to agree." She sighed. "But if the duke is going to insist upon riding in the morning, you'll have to find a way around him. He'd have an apoplexy if he realized it was you riding. Worth is only human, after all, and let us not forget that he is also a man. He has his limits of what he can understand and accept, and I rather suspect we reached the end of those limits this morning."

That was putting it mildly, Jenna thought. The duke had been visibly furious that the duchess had concealed the truth from him for so long. She straightened her shoulders. While she understood and even sympathized, she could not afford the luxury of pity.

"I'll find a way," Jenna said. There simply wasn't another choice.

"Just don't let my son catch you in the barns. Certainly not in anything but a dress." Eleanor picked up her teacup again. "So long as he continues to believe you are simply my companion, he won't suspect anything out of the ordinary when we arrive at Ascot."

Jenna gritted her teeth. She was pretty sure it was already too late for that.

Chapter 8 _____

William spent the remainder of the morning perusing his mother's stock, his emotions swinging wildly from disbelief to disgruntlement to elation and back again. It wasn't a stretch to see how he might have missed it. There were less than a half dozen thoroughbreds destined for the turf, and they weren't kept indoors, blanketed and isolated in stalls. Instead they had been turned out in pastures and enclosures, hidden in plain sight among the rest of the herd.

And the bulk of the herd consisted of beautifully bred thoroughbred hunters, swift as the wind but not swift enough to compete on the turf. A handful of matched pairs intended for the finest phaetons and barouches and curricles of London were pastured together, mostly geldings, and Will could very well see why the profit from the sale of these animals was handsome. Will would happily have purchased any of them on the spot. Whoever this Paul was, he certainly knew his business, and despite himself, Will found himself looking forward to speaking with the man responsible for such distinction.

At the study in his townhome in London, there was an entire shelf devoted to racing calendars and reports. He was positively itching to go through them and see for himself what sort of success his mother's horses had had at Ascot over the last years. He'd ride there immediately, he decided. On a fast horse, it wouldn't take too long, and it would be a chance to clear his head. A chance to retreat from the turmoil of this morning's revelations and allow himself the opportunity to put his thoughts back in order.

It would also put distance between himself and the temptation that was Miss Hughes. Against his will his thoughts continued to delve toward the vision of her at the breakfast table, flushed, rumpled, and barefoot. He refused to consider the possibility that she had attended the duchess at breakfast having risen late and languidly from the arms of a lover after being well tumbled. Surely, even if she had a lover, she would not consort with the man while his mother slept not twenty feet away on the other side of the wall.

An image of Luke and Miss Hughes standing side by side, intimate in their familiarity, caught him. The idea that she might share her bed with the butler made his insides sour. Which was ridiculous. Will certainly didn't have a claim to her. Could never have a claim to her, other than by taking her as a mistress, and somehow that just seemed wrong. Will's rather limited experiences with mistresses had usually involved jaded women who were more interested in what material rewards could be earned from bed sport with a duke than in the man himself. Miss Hughes seemed utterly uninterested in material rewards. He'd never seen her wear any sort of jewelry. Her clothing was ghastly, and from her lack of concern, Will could only conclude Miss Hughes considered fashion irrelevant. Come to think of it, he'd yet to catch her sitting anywhere with a book or embroidery or a set of watercolors. He'd never met a woman so indifferent to feminine pursuits.

In the next breath, Will cursed himself. Miss Hughes's hobbies, assuming she had some, were no concern of his. Whatever this boyish infatuation was, it would pass. And if he wanted to maintain his sanity, he would do well to remember that. Abruptly he turned and made his way back toward the old barns. He would ride into London and avoid luncheon at the dower house. And continue to avoid Miss Hughes.

It was first thing he'd done all day that made sense.

～

"The Hambletonian mare is in season." Joseph was waiting for Jenna in the new barns, tapping his fingers on his leg expectantly.

Late-afternoon light filtered through the windows, illuminating the dust motes dancing through the rafters. The air was still stifling, though a bank of clouds had gathered on the horizon, promising rain by evening. Puzzled as to why she had been summoned to the barns for this pronouncement, Jenna raised a brow. Joseph was more than capable of managing the breeding barn without her.

"Then breed her." Jenna was trying to steer clear of the barns during the day at all costs, and the imposed inconvenience was making her grumpy.

Joseph's eyes darted beyond her shoulder in the direction of the house. "I wasn't sure where the duke was. I thought it prudent to ask before I got started."

"Ah." Jenna had managed to avoid Worth all day,

having no interest in getting cornered by the duke and the sharp questions he wielded. "The duchess told me he's gone back to London. Something about accounts and correspondence. She was under the impression he wouldn't be back until tonight."

Joseph snorted. "I would have thought the man would have had enough of accounts by now."

"George is making it as painful as possible," Jenna said with a sigh. "For all the good it's doing."

Joseph sniffed with disgust or admiration, though it was difficult to tell which. "Isaac just rode out to run the duke's black filly, so he's out of the way. And so long as His Grace isn't going to be spying, I reckon I'll get the mare covered now then. Hopefully again tomorrow."

"Very good," Jenna approved. "Would you like some assistance?" she asked on impulse. She was chafing at the inability to come and go in the barns as she pleased. And since the duke was safely ensconced in his own study over a mile away, Jenna didn't see the harm.

Joseph nodded. "I'd be obliged. I'll meet you in back."

Jenna strode quickly back in the direction of the old barn, snagging a halter from a hook on her way. She entered the cool interior and went to the stall door.

"Ready to go a-courting?" she murmured as she entered, slipping the halter over the stallion's head. She smoothed a hand over the glossy black hide and the patchwork of scars. The war-horse whickered softly.

The stallion should have been destroyed on the battlefield. But for some inexplicable reason, the horse had been allowed to live. Jenna rather suspected it had something to do with the exacting and eccentric persona of the lieutenant colonel whose life the horse had saved. The same lieutenant colonel who had served with an artilleryman named George and who had eventually given the damaged horse to the equally eccentric Dowager Duchess of Worth.

But every day for the last seven years, Jenna had looked out on the pastures full of black fillies and black colts and been grateful the horse had lived. Vimeiro, though it had never had the chance to compete at the tracks before being sent into battle, sired racehorses second to none. The stud was their best-kept secret. And no one had ever given the damaged war-horse a second look. No one, that is, except the Duke of Worth. Just another reason not to underestimate him.

Jenna led the horse out of its stall, the animal's gait making an uneven clopping beat on the stone floor. She cast another glance up toward the house and the top of the long drive visible beyond the oaks, but both path and drive remained deserted. Eleanor had said that the duke didn't expect to be back for dinner. That gave her all sorts of time, though she couldn't resist a final look. Jenna shook her head. She was beginning to become as paranoid as Joseph. Though if she had survived as a horse thief for as long as Joseph had, it would be second nature to her too.

Joseph had the mare hobbled and waiting in an enclosure behind the new barn. One of their other stallions was being led away by an undergroom, and Joseph held the mare's lead. Vimeiro, catching the scent of the mare, arched its neck and let out a piercing whinny.

"Bring him in," Joseph instructed.

Jenna gave the stallion a long lead as it approached the mare. Joseph handed his own rope to another waiting groom and moved to the side, ready to pull the mare's tail out of the way. This was one of their older, more experienced broodmares, and Vimeiro had covered it before. Jenna didn't expect any problems.

"All right, man, up and at 'em," Joseph said to the stallion. "And be quick about it today."

Jenna snorted. "Aren't they always?"

The stallion, as if taking Joseph's advice, mounted the mare with a grunt and little preamble.

"Depends," Joseph retorted, his voice from the far side of the horses somewhat muffled.

Jenna guffawed. "Oh really? On what?"

"On the lady's desire to prolong the moment."

"To prolong the moment?" Jenna snickered. "Are you speaking from experience, Joseph?"

"Perhaps," came his smug reply over the backs of the horses. Joseph popped out from behind the coupling horses, apparently satisfied with the progression of things, and put his hands on his bony hips.

Jenna eyed the young coachman with open amusement. "I think you're blushing."

"I am not." Joseph sniffed. "I've finally become immune to your attempts to make me blush."

"I'm sure I could come up with something," she teased.

"But you won't." Joseph rolled his eyes and gestured in the direction of the house. "Because if the damned duke were to—" The words died, and a look of horror suffused his face. "Oh, shit," he breathed.

Jenna followed his stricken look and nearly dropped her rope. Beyond the side of the barn, she could just see that the damned duke had emerged from the trees, mounted on his big mare, and was trotting down the path toward them.

"I thought you said he wouldn't be back until after dinner," Joseph choked.

"That's what the duchess said." But that didn't make her less of a fool for putting herself in this position. Jenna looked between the horses and the approaching disaster. There was no way the stallion would be done before the duke crashed in on them. There was no reasonable way to explain why they were breeding a crippled war-horse. There was no reasonable way to explain why Jenna would even be present, much less assisting.

"Please come and take Vimeiro," Jenna said to Joseph, as calmly as she could.

Joseph moved to take the stallion's lead, panic making his eyes seem even larger in his face. "What are we going to do?" the groom gasped.

"It's not what we are going to do; it's what I am going to do," Jenna muttered, easing her way from the enclosure so as not to disturb the horses.

"What?"

"I don't know. But I'm fairly certain it will require something that's going to make you blush," she hissed.

She left Joseph and broke into a run, heading for the old barn and the approaching duke. She came to a sliding stop in the center of the alley, breathing hard, looking frantically about her. The duke was close enough now that she could see his face through the windows. He looked a little windblown and weary, but more alarming was his fierce expression of determination. He was clearly a man on a mission.

"Dammit," Jenna swore softly, still at a loss as to how she was going to stall him.

The sounds of his mare's hooves crunched just outside. There was the jangle of a bit and then the unmistakable sound of boots hitting the ground as he dismounted. Jenna's eye fell on a bucket of freshly drawn water.

Without a second thought, Jenna heaved the bucket from the floor and dumped the contents over her head.

The icy shock made her gasp and drenched her hair and the top half of her dress. She let the bucket drop to the ground and wiped at her face, pushing the hair that had come undone out of her eyes. When she looked up, the Duke of Worth was standing in front of her, his mouth hanging open.

"What the bloody hell are you doing?"

Jenna squeezed some water from the ends of her hair, hearing the last valiant pin hit the floor with a pathetic ping. "I was hot."

"You were...hot?" The duke blinked. His gaze traveled the length of her, lingering on her bodice, then her neck, and then her mouth before returning to meet her eyes.

Jenna swallowed. She could only imagine what she looked like. Her hair streamed over her shoulders in a twisted snarl, and she could feel a cold rivulet of water snake down the side of her face to the corner of her lips. The threadbare fabric of her bodice was plastered to her breasts, leaving absolutely nothing to the imagination.

The duke didn't move. Or speak. He was simply watching her from under hooded lids, and if Jenna hadn't been hot before, she was now. In apparent deference to the humidity outside, the duke had abandoned his coat and waistcoat and shoved his shirtsleeves up to his elbows, revealing well-muscled forearms darkened by the sun. Equally dark was the skin at his throat, dipping down toward his chest. Black riding breeches hugged his narrow hips and powerful thighs, tucked into well-worn, dusty boots. His hair was slightly disheveled, falling in thick waves over his forehead. He'd never looked less like a duke. He'd never looked more perfect.

"And is this a regular occurrence?" the duke asked, his voice low and soft and dangerous. His gaze flickered to the puddle at her feet.

Just when I'm near you, Jenna thought, fighting desperately to remain composed.

His eyes darkened, and he took a step closer to her. "Is it?"

Yesterday Jenna had recklessly dared the duke to kiss her for reasons that had nothing to do with deception. Now, in a perilous situation that teetered toward real risk and needing to say something witty and distracting, Jenna discovered the power of speech had deserted her.

"Why are you down here in the stables?" the duke asked, his eyes narrowing.

Jenna bit her lip. What could she possibly say that he would believe? Why couldn't she think?

"Um." Dear God, but she'd been reduced to a halfwit.

Something shifted in his face, and Worth reached out and brushed a drop of water from the corner of her mouth with his thumb. Jenna shuddered and closed her eyes, the feel of his skin against hers electric. *This is getting away from you*, some practical part of her brain was warning her. She'd done what she'd set out to do. He was sufficiently distracted. Now was the time to stop. Now, before it was too late. A taste of this man would leave her starving indefinitely. And likely ruined for any other.

She remained motionless, adrift and disoriented.

Worth's hand moved from her mouth to her neck, pushing a strand of sodden hair over her shoulder. Her eyes opened. Very deliberately he twisted his fingers into the hair at the nape of her neck and pulled her head back ever so gently, tipping her face up toward his. Jenna could barely breathe. There were a hundred recriminations and warnings clamoring about in the back of her head, though she was damned if she could remember one.

He took another step closer, now close enough that she could feel the heat from his body through the wet fabric of her dress. Close enough that she could see the glint of gold in his dark eyes. Close enough to feel the brush of his hair as it fell forward and smell the dizzying scent of spice and man.

The duke brought his lips close to hers, and Jenna nearly whimpered with anticipation. With an agonizing deliberation, he pressed his mouth to the corner of hers, his tongue flicking out to catch another drop of water. Lust spiraled through her with a violence she hadn't been prepared for. She sucked in a breath, her legs suddenly unsteady, her skin on fire and her insides molten liquid.

Worth brought his other hand to her head, cupping the side of her face. His lips continued their tortuous path along the side of her jaw to just below her ear and down to the hollow of her throat. His fingers slid from her hair downward, over her collarbone, and then, with exquisite purpose, to the side of her breast. His palm settled against the underside of her bodice while his thumb drifted over the peak of her nipple.

Want pulsed at the apex of her thighs and she squeezed her legs together, aware of the dampness that had gathered. She heard his breath catch, and then his mouth was on hers, hot and demanding, and she opened herself to him, feeling her own need answered in kind. Her hands went to the bottom of his shirt and shoved it up and out of his waistband so that her palms met his heated flesh beneath. Her fingers explored the ridges of muscle along his abdomen, the scattering of hair across his chest, and the hard pebbles of his nipples.

Hazily she thought she might drag his shirt over his head so that she might fully appreciate the splendor that the linen concealed, but she was loath to leave the heat of his embrace for even a second. The hard planes of steel across his back flexed and tightened beneath her hands as she moved them toward the hollow at the base of his spine. The duke groaned into her mouth and pushed his hips into her and she could feel the hard bulge at the fall of his breeches, heavy against her lower abdomen. Her inner muscles clenched and spasmed, and with some shock Jenna wondered if the Duke of Worth had the power to undo her right then and there. Simply by kissing her.

What had started as an exquisite tasting had turned into an uncontrollable tempest of raw need. Jenna nipped at his lower lip, and Worth hissed in response, pressing even harder into her, forcing himself between her legs. His hands dropped to her bottom, and he hauled her up against him, her skirts riding up above her knees, her legs wrapped around his waist.

Jenna's head dropped to his shoulder, her breathing ragged and her vision blurred. In two steps the duke had backed them up against the stall door, the wood at her back as hard as the man who held her. She wrapped her arms around his shoulders and found his mouth again, suddenly needing to be closer. She wanted to fold herself into this man, have his heat and his power and his strength consume her.

The duke surged up against her, his arousal straining

against her very core and sending uncontrolled tremors racing across every nerve ending. Uncompromising in their intent, his fingers delved between them, finding her throbbing, aching entrance. With one smooth motion he thrust his finger into her, and Jenna bore down on that pressure, need obliterating any rational thought.

She tried to form a word, an indication of her pleasure, but she lacked the breath to do so. Her attempt came out as a sound in the back of her throat that she barely recognized, though Worth seemed to distinguish it just fine. With an answering groan, he withdrew, then thrust again, and without warning, Jenna simply shattered. Her hands curled into the fabric of his shirt to keep her from spinning into oblivion, and she pressed her mouth to his shoulder, muffling the moan that escaped. Worth jerked, burying the sounds of his own release in the hollow of her neck.

It was a long moment before Jenna slid silently back to her feet. It was an even longer one before she could look up and meet Worth's eyes.

"Holy God," the duke rasped.

Jenna was relieved it wasn't just she who was shaken to the core. "That was unexpected," she croaked.

"Christ." Worth ran an unsteady hand through his hair. "I don't ever . . . do that."

"Nor do I," Jenna assured him. She should feel regret or guilt at her utterly shameless behavior, yet all Jenna could muster was a feeling of intense exhilaration. And a fierce sense of rightness.

"I feel like an untried boy who's just taken his first tumble in the hayloft."

Jenna chuckled. "We didn't make it to the hayloft."

The duke stared at her for a moment before he let out a surprised laugh. "Next time."

Jenna found herself grinning back. "You're a cocky bastard."

"That sounds like a challenge."

Jenna bit her lip. "I don't know if that's wise, Your Grace."

"Consider it a promise then. And it's Will."

"I'm sorry?"

"William. That's my name. Not my title. I want you to call me Will."

Jenna balked. "I'm not sure that is wise either."

"Please."

Will suggested intimacy. *Will* suggested friendship. Two things that could not be supported by deceit. The guilt Jenna had expected earlier arose now, and with some unease, she realized she very much liked the idea of friendship and intimacy with this man.

What had just happened between them had been real. Their physical attraction to each other was undeniable and not a little frightening in its power. If Jenna were to tell herself she'd done it out of necessity, she'd be lying. She'd wanted the duke to kiss her. Hell, she'd wanted him to do everything he'd done and more. But physical attraction was not intimacy. Or friendship.

The duke, apparently tired of waiting for her answer, dipped his head and kissed her, a soft, teasing brush of lips. Jenna's insides melted, and her reservations blurred.

She was making more out of this than was necessary. Whatever existed between them would be physical and fleeting, and both of them knew it. A year from now—hell, *days* from now—they would certainly not be friends.

Each would simply be a memory to the other, sporadically recalled with a smile of pleasure and maybe a small measure of fondness. He was a duke and she was, well, a servant. Neither had unrealistic expectations as to how this would end. But that knowledge did not make her want him less.

Despite her better judgment, Jenna smiled against his mouth. "William it is, then."

He stilled slightly before he moved his mouth to her ear. "I don't like to share."

"I can't imagine you do." Jenna shivered.

His hands had caged her hips, and now they slid around to the small of her back. "Perhaps you should change into something dry."

"A good idea."

"I could help." Will nuzzled her neck.

Heat curled. "If I weren't afraid you'd threaten to rip my bodice again, I might let you."

Will plucked at the worn seams along her shoulders with distaste. "Someone should put this dress out of its misery."

"What's wrong with my dress?"

"What you are wearing is not a dress. It is an abomination. You should have better."

"I am a servant, Will. I don't need better. As a hired companion, who am I going to impress with my fashionable attire?"

"Me?"

Jenna scoffed. "You are not a person who measures another's merit based on a few yards of pretty silk."

The duke stilled suddenly, as if her words had startled him.

Jenna rolled her eyes. "If that were the case, you'd have

married one of the Caudel sisters a long time ago. Their dresses, after all, are *breathtaking*."

Will's lips twitched. "I—"

A bucket clattered to the floor behind them, the sound followed by a string of muffled curses and a great deal of shuffling.

Against her, Will froze before slowly turning around, and Jenna peered over his shoulder.

Joseph stood at the entrance to the barn, trying to right the forgotten bucket he'd tripped over, a task made all the more difficult by his desperate attempts to keep his eyes anywhere but on Jenna and Will. The lamed stallion was standing patiently on his lead, looking relaxed and quite satisfied.

"I'm so sorry, Your Grace," Joseph was sputtering. "I didn't see you there. So sorry."

Jenna glanced down at the front of her saturated dress and then at the sodden spots that had plastered Will's shirt to his chest. She suspected her lips were swollen and red.

It didn't take much imagination.

"I was just bringing him back," Joseph was mumbling. "I'll come back later. Much later. Tomorrow, perhaps."

Will sighed and stepped away from Jenna. "Joseph. I trust your discretion extends beyond the stables?"

Joseph bobbed his head frantically. "Yes, Your Grace. Of course, Your Grace."

The duke turned back and shoved his shirttails into his breeches before offering his arm to Jenna. "I was just escorting Miss Hughes up to the house. It would seem she had a bit of an accident with a water bucket."

"Of course, Your Grace." Joseph was staring pointedly at the ground. "Tricky things, water buckets. Could happen to anyone." His face was scarlet.

Jenna was biting her lip in an effort not to laugh. "Thank you, Your Grace. Good day, Joseph." She accepted Will's arm and they moved past the mortified groom.

"Will he be a problem?" the duke asked as they cleared the doorway. "I don't want you put in a difficult spot."

"Joseph?" Joseph and his brothers knew enough secrets about all manner of lords and ladies that Jenna could operate an extortion business had she the mind. It was an occupational hazard that came with sneaking through aristocrats' property at very unexpected times. She schooled her features. "No. Joseph may be young, but he most certainly isn't stupid."

"*Hmph.*" Will didn't look convinced.

"Your mother can't dismiss me," Jenna said lightly. "Don't forget that you are the duke and therefore control the duchy and everything in it. Including my employment. Your words, if you remember correctly."

Will winced. "I sounded like a pompous ass."

Jenna tipped her head in consideration. "I disagree. You sounded like a man determined to see something through. It was commendable."

He slanted her a strange look.

"You are a duke, whether you like it or not, Your Grace—er, Will. Your opinions and your words carry weight. You have the uncommon opportunity to use that to your advantage." She looked up at him. "The Monroes got their money from Lady Louisa and Lady Leticia. Every penny they were owed. Delivered to the shop not an hour after we left."

"How do you know that?"

"They sent a note of thanks that arrived this afternoon. They also asked me to pass along their gratitude for your presence and support. And that if you need anything at all, you have only to ask."

Worth was silent, and they walked on, gravel crunching beneath their feet.

"Is this why you kissed me? Because I'm a duke and you think by seducing me I can further this crusade you and my mother have undertaken?" he asked suddenly.

The complete and utter irony of his question was too much. Jenna started laughing.

"Why is that funny?" He sounded annoyed.

"Let me make myself clear." Jenna stopped, forcing the duke to stop with her. "First of all, you kissed me. Second, I kissed you back *despite* the fact that you are a duke. This *crusade*, as you like to call it, is the direct result of dukes. Thoughtless ones. And uncaring earls. Selfish marquesses and inconsiderate viscounts." Her eyes grew serious. "So no, Will, I don't want you to further anything. I don't want you to interfere. I want you to stay out of my way."

Will was staring at her.

"Generally I have no use for dukes. Or any other titled men. I try to avoid them."

"But you've made an exception in my case? Why?"

Christ, but that was a good question. One Jenna wasn't sure how to answer. Once again she opted for a version of the truth and chose her words carefully.

"Because you are a good man, William Somerhall." She deliberately used his name and not his title. "I didn't plan on...this. And while I don't precisely know what *this* is, we both know what this can never be."

Will shifted uncomfortably. "Jenna, please don't think you are a mere convenience—"

"Let's be realistic," Jenna interrupted gently. "As much

as I might like to disregard your title, it will always exist, and as such, I do not suffer from any illusions about you." Jenna shrugged, an unexpected twinge of regret pulling within. She ignored it. "But it would appear I am not impervious to your overwhelming charm," she teased, trying to lighten a conversation that had gotten much too serious for her liking. "Rest assured that will suffice."

Will was silent, and Jenna pulled back, puzzled.

"Everyone wants something from me," Will said, sounding surprised. "Even the women whom I have, ah—I've had a, er, arrangements with. They are quick to demand things. Or favors. For friends, family, or themselves."

Jenna made a face. "Good God. Are we really going to have a conversation about the other women you've tupped right now?"

"No! It's just that—"

"I'm going to say this once more, Will, and then never again. I want nothing from you. No favors, no baubles, no wealth or privileges. No pledges of love, no offers of holy matrimony. What happened this afternoon should probably never happen again. But it happened because I simply wanted . . . you."

The duke seemed to have stopped breathing. "Honest to a fault, aren't you?"

Jenna recoiled inwardly. *No*, she mumbled silently, *not really.*

"I haven't stopped thinking about you," he said suddenly. "Since the night I first saw you at my ball."

Jenna bit her lip. She didn't want to hear this. She didn't want his words to distort reality.

"No one knew who you were." Will reached out and fingered a wet clump of hair. "I thought you were an enchanted princess in that glittering gown." He smiled faintly. "I wanted you then. I want you more now. Here. Like this."

"I'm not a princess," she said. "Believe me, I'm the furthest thing from."

His eyes crinkled in the first genuine smile she'd seen from him in a while. "You are nothing like any woman I've ever met, Jenna Hughes."

Jenna couldn't help but return the smile, her heart skipping at the way he was looking at her. God, but she could get used to that. It made her feel treasured and needed and wanted. All of that being dangerous in itself. She began walking back toward the house.

"When can I see you again?" the duke asked, meaning something else entirely.

Now, she yearned to say. And tonight. And tomorrow. And for every minute of every day after that.

"I would imagine at dinner," she replied, fighting the irrational part of herself wanting to throw herself into his arms like an infatuated dairymaid.

"Will you be wearing shoes?"

Jenna took a steadying breath before she answered. She needed to remain focused, even if her better judgment had spiraled away in a tide of longing and desire. "Of course."

"Pity to go to the effort." Will covered her hand on his arm with his own. "You won't need them later."

Chapter 9 ————————————————

Will spent the little time before dinner holed up in his rooms. On the delicate writing desk in the corner sat his ancient scuffed satchel, a holdover from his days at Eton. When he had arrived at his town house at midday, he'd rifled through the racing reports twice before remembering that he'd loaned the Ascot reports out. Annoyed with himself, Will had written a hasty note to one of his Jockey Club colleagues asking for course results for the last seven years to be delivered to the dower house. He'd stuffed what reports he did have, as well as the stack of correspondence his secretary had left neatly stacked on his desk, into his satchel. Will had fully intended to review everything in his own home before returning to the dower house, yet the moment he had sat down behind the stately desk, he'd felt he couldn't leave fast enough. Solitude had suddenly presented itself as loneliness, and he knew now exactly why he'd been in such a hurry to return.

He was thoroughly smitten with Jenna Hughes. Hadn't even tried to pretend otherwise, even before this afternoon. He'd always scorned the idea of love at first sight or, more accurately, lust at first sight, but since that night at his ball, Jenna had been a constant presence weaving through his memory and consciousness. She'd humbled him with her blunt sincerity, and for the first time, Will truly believed he'd had an honest conversation with a woman who was more interested in him than in the trappings pinned to his name.

The unguarded passion Jenna concealed took his breath away. The feel of her in his arms, beneath his mouth, and under his hands had been electrifying. And when she had come apart against him, he had lost control like a bloody adolescent. He should have been mortified, but Jenna had only grinned up at him with an expression of utter satisfaction and made him feel as though he'd just handed her the keys to Whitehall.

And now the need to have Jenna at his mercy was enough to leave him reeling, drunk with anticipation. Will fully intended to make up for his earlier deficiencies, and in style. In a manner she wouldn't soon forget. Tonight he would eat, probably play a game of cards with his mother, enjoy a glass of brandy, and bid everyone a good night. And then he would find Jenna Hughes and finish what they had started. It would take a long time. A very, very long time, and there would be no interruptions. In fact, Will didn't much care if the house burned down around his ears. He would have Jenna and he would have her tonight.

A knock on his door broke the silence. "Your Grace," came a servant's disembodied voice, "dinner will be served shortly. And your guests have arrived."

Guests? Will frowned. His mother had said nothing about guests. Visions of lords and ladies pulling up in front of the dower house to be greeted by pythons and chickens had him suddenly scrambling for the door and clattering down the stairs. But the hall was mercifully empty, with the exception of three people being relieved of their gloves and hats by a very proper-looking Luke.

"Good God. Boden?" Will asked incredulously, a broad smile stretching across his face immediately. "What on earth are you doing here?"

Heath Hextall, Earl of Boden, turned to greet Will. But before he could utter a word, there was a delighted squeal and Will suddenly found himself with an armful of lavender lace.

"Lady Viola," Will said affectionately, disentangling himself from Boden's youngest sister. "You look more beautiful each time I see you." She was pretty in a conventional way, with dark hair and the same round, mischievous face she'd had since she was three years old. She was also a consummate flirt, and while it pained her brother, her harmless posturing amused Will to no end.

Viola giggled. "Your mother invited us for dinner. I couldn't believe it when I heard you'd moved in. Now you have no excuse not to come and visit us all the time." She fluttered her lashes.

"Duly noted," Will replied. "Though I will be busy reviewing my mother's accounts and making sure her household is shipshape."

Viola pursed her lips. "You sound like my brother. Heath has been such a bore since Father died," she complained, oblivious to the tightening of Boden's expression. "Perhaps you can shake him out of his rut. He has no time for parties or anything fun, and without him to chaperone us, we're stuck. He's always busy doing paperwork and . . . stuff."

"Your brother is working to make sure you are taken care of," Will chided gently. "You should be thanking him."

Viola looked as though she would argue, but her sister moved forward, preventing her.

"Lady Julia," Will greeted her. "You look wonderful." Will meant it. After the end of her engagement the year before, Julia had seemed to withdraw, which had concerned Will and worried her brother. But today there was some color back in her pale cheeks and some life in her pretty blue eyes. She was the opposite of her sister— petite, fair, and reserved.

"Thank you," she said. "It was very kind of your mother to extend the invitation."

Will nodded his head, disappointed with himself that he hadn't thought of it sooner.

"Tell us, Will, how long are you planning to stay at the dower house?" Julia stepped into the silence smoothly.

"I'm not sure," he replied.

"What about the rest of the racing season?"

"I have decided to take this opportunity to race my horses at Ascot."

"Ascot?" Boden raised a brow. "I thought you didn't like the track there."

"I like the track just fine. It's the people who insist on attending who wear my patience."

"Well then, Heath will have to let us go now if you're going to be there," Viola pouted. "Since the races are the only Ascot events we will actually go to."

"I'd have thought you'd have a slew of invitations picked out," Will said, surprised. London society seemed to take full advantage of any excuse to hold a collection of balls and parties in and around Windsor during the week of racing. Another reason he avoided Ascot.

An awkward silence fell.

Julia cleared her throat. "It would seem that our invitations have been lost in the post."

"Oh, come off it, Jules," Viola stamped her foot, anger and hurt making her voice rise unpleasantly. "We have not been invited to anything because our very recent title was inherited through an obscure branch of the family tree, our fortune was assembled through trade, and my sister was engaged to a barking madman before he disappeared. Or died. Depends on whom you talk to."

"That's enough," Heath said, his voice low. His frustration was unmistakable.

Anger rose like a sullen mist, and Will's jaw clenched. God, but the ton was malicious. "Let me rephrase the question," Will said slowly to the two women who had been childhood friends long before their father ever inherited his unexpected title. "Which events would you like to attend?"

Viola sniffed loudly. "Lady Kewitt's Gold Cup ball was the one I wanted to go to. There is an orchestra and dancing and—"

"Done," Will said coldly. "Julia? Did you wish to attend anything in particular?"

Julia blushed slightly. "I had hoped to go to the Countess of Newsham's country garden party. I have heard she has the most spectacular damask and China roses, and I would love to see them for myself."

"Very good." Will was struggling to remain calm.

Heath was running his hands through his hair unhappily. "Worth, I don't expect you to—"

"Shut up and let me make the sisters of my best friend happy," he snarled at the earl. "I have discovered rather recently that as a duke, and an unmarried, filthy-rich one at that, my opinions and desires have more weight than I ever credited. Lady Kewitt and Lady Newsham will be delighted to welcome your sisters, believe me."

Heath threw up his hands in defeat. "I have more money than you, you know," he said. "And—"

"Your Grace," came a throaty voice from the far end of the hall, "the duchess sent me to tell you that dinner will be served in five minutes."

Just the sound of Jenna's voice set his heart pounding and his temperature rising. Dear God, how was he going to make it all the way through dinner without his intentions written across his face like a banner for all to see? He turned to watch her approach, taking in the smooth knot at the nape of her neck, the pleasant expression on her face, and another gown that wouldn't fetch a penny in Petticoat Lane. He clasped his hands behind his back so he wouldn't be tempted to touch her or simply tear the offending garment from her beautiful body. At least this dress was dry.

"Thank you, Miss Hughes," Will replied neutrally, using every ounce of propriety that had ever been beaten into him. He waited until she had reached them before making the expected introductions. "Miss Hughes, may I present my oldest and dearest friend, Heath Hextall, Earl of Boden, and his sisters, Lady Viola and Lady Julia. Miss Hughes is my mother's hired companion."

"A pleasure, Miss Hughes," the earl said with marked appreciation, taking Jenna's hand.

"And mine." Jenna gave Heath one of her best smiles,

and Will watched as the earl responded with a smile of his own.

Something that felt a little like jealousy rose up in Will's throat.

"I was very sorry to hear of your father's passing," she continued gently, including the women in her words.

"Thank you." The smile slid from Boden's face, and Will felt like a cad for his petty resentment. His friend had smiled far too infrequently in recent months.

"I do hope I didn't interrupt anything important."

"Not at all," Heath assured her. "In fact, the conversation had become rather uncouth. Your timing was impeccable," he said lightly.

Jenna cast a questioning look toward Will.

"We were discussing money," Will explained, giving his friend an arch look. "And the fact Boden would trade all of his for my dashing good looks."

Beside him, Jenna rolled her eyes, startling a laugh from Heath.

"It appears your legendary charm has suffered out here, my friend," the earl said, grinning broadly at Jenna. "Most women don't roll their eyes at the Duke of Worth. At least when they're not pretending to swoon into his arms."

Will kept his eyes trained on the earl. "Indeed, Boden, I can assure you Miss Hughes is not most women, which is a most desirable, nay, necessary quality for her role as my mother's companion."

"I don't understand," Viola said loudly, drawing attention back to herself.

"I'm quite proficient at the safe handling of pythons," Jenna explained gravely. "And poultry."

Viola stared suspiciously at Jenna even as her brother dissolved into laughter again.

"Then my sincere compliments, Miss Hughes," the earl managed, and Will realized he'd not heard Heath laugh in a very long time.

Jenna glanced over at him, and he met her gaze, knowing she understood. He smiled at her, holding their shared confidence close to his chest.

"Will you be coming with us then?" Viola's question brought him back to reality. She had her hand on his sleeve and was looking up at him with wide, adoring eyes.

"With you?" he asked, confused.

"To the Gold Cup ball?" Her earlier snit seemed to have dissolved at the prospect of a party.

His gut reaction was to refuse. Will avoided such things whenever possible. But given the circumstances, it would seem his presence could do a world of good to reassert Lady Julia and Lady Viola in society.

Perhaps the ball would be enough. He could do without garden parties and roses. Maybe he could send his mother to that one instead.

"I would like nothing more," he said to Viola.

She squealed in delight, and Julia smiled faintly. Jenna had an odd expression of dismay on her face.

Heath's forehead creased. "You're serious."

"Yes. Why not?"

"You hate balls."

William shrugged in the manner Jenna seemed to have perfected.

Heath was staring at him. "I'm sorry, good sir, but I can't seem to find my friend. Perhaps you've seen him? Tall, dark hair, can usually be found at this time of year somewhere near Epsom hiding in barns? Hates dancing, loves cards, avoids anything smacking of bookkeeping or balls?"

"Very funny, Boden."

"I wasn't trying to be funny." The earl was still staring at him, clearly perplexed.

Will frowned at the intimation that he would duck such duties when it was clear that he could very easily help. He wasn't that man, was he? That man sounded horribly self-absorbed.

"I believe we should go in to dinner, Your Grace," Jenna said beside him. Her peculiar expression was gone and had been replaced with one of bland politeness. "I was assured Margaret has once again outdone herself."

"Excellent idea," said Boden cheerfully. "I'm quite famished."

"Of course," Will murmured. Viola tightened her grip on his arm as Julia took her brother's.

"Miss Hughes?" Heath asked, holding out his other arm. Jenna smiled at the earl and accepted the invitation.

Will wasn't aware he was staring until Heath winked at him. "In the event of a sudden onset of pythons or poultry, I'd like to be prepared," he said.

"Of course," Will murmured again, distressed by the flood of envy and possessiveness that had suddenly risen at the sight of the earl escorting Jenna in to dinner. He watched as Jenna said something to both Heath and Julia, and Heath dipped his head toward her to better hear. Will's stomach turned.

"What will you wear to Lady Kewitt's ball?" Viola was asking as she led Will toward the dining room. "I was thinking of wearing blue. It would be nice if our attire was complimentary, don't you agree?"

Viola chattered on but Will barely heard her, a far more critical question bouncing around in his brain and making him cold.

When had the sight of Jenna Hughes on another man's arm become excruciatingly, piercingly intolerable?

~

Dinner was a pleasant affair, due mostly to good company, good food, and the absence of anything resembling reptiles or birds. His mother was gracious and inclusive, drawing both Julia and Viola into conversation about fashion and flowers, two topics all three women seemed to be well versed in. Jenna, seated next to the dowager, seemed content to listen and enjoy her meal. Will shifted again in his seat. Jenna was too close and too far away all at the same time. So available yet utterly inaccessible, and it was driving him mad.

It was almost a relief when the duchess signaled that the post-meal rituals should commence—the ladies retiring to a drawing room with gossip and sherry, leaving Will and Heath free to escape to somewhere else. In the absence of a study, Will wasted little time in making for the deserted breakfast room at the back of the house, needing space and a good quantity of the brandy he knew was stored in the depths of the sideboard.

The door clicked shut behind them, and Heath wandered to the far side of the room to peer out at the long line of oaks. "Are you sleeping with her?"

Will nearly dropped the bottle he had just hauled out of the musty depths. "Am I— Jesus Christ." Will tried to muster more indignation. "I beg your pardon?"

"Miss Hughes. Are you sleeping with her?"

Will put the bottle down on top of the sideboard with a little more force than he'd intended. "Whatever would give you that idea?"

Heath clasped his hands behind his back and walked toward Will. "You stared at her all night like a moon-eyed puppy. I was going to suggest she accompany us to Lady Kewitt's ball, but I was afraid I might lose my head. You looked like you wanted to run me through when I took her in to dinner."

"I did not!"

Heath reached for the bottle and poured two healthy measures of brandy into waiting tumblers. He pressed one into Will's hand. "We've been friends almost our entire lives, Worth, but this is the first time I've ever seen you besotted."

"I am not besotted. Dukes do not become besotted."

Heath took a long swallow and leveled a challenging stare at Will.

His pathetic righteousness was pointless. The earl knew him far too well. "It's her," Will muttered.

"Her?" A blond brow rose.

"From my ball."

"From your— Holy hell. Miss Hughes is your mysterious woman?" Both brows shot into his hairline. "The woman you've spent a year inquiring after in London?" A disbelieving smile spread across Heath's face. "Your enchanted princess is your *mother's companion*?"

"Yes." Will didn't see what was so damn funny about it.

"Your perfect woman is no longer invisible." The earl looked delighted.

"No, she's not. She's very real and clever and compassionate and beautiful and funny."

Heath guffawed. "God, Worth, you're not just besotted, you're in love."

"I will not deny that I am attracted to her, but I am certainly not in love." Will said the last word with disdain.

"Of course. Such adoration is reserved solely for those females in your life with four hooves and a winning turf record." Heath was openly mocking him now. "Does Miss Hughes know what she's up against?"

"I'm not exactly courting her, Boden." He frowned.

"Yes, I suppose that would be a little redundant since you're going to marry her."

"Since I'm going to *what*?" Brandy sloshed out of Will's glass and ran over his fingers.

"I distinctly remember you saying she was the one you would marry." Heath was grinning wickedly.

Will didn't even deign to answer that, only shook the drops of liquor off his fingers, trying not to spatter his coat.

"Ah, but that bold declaration was made when she didn't exist, of course." Heath was having far too much fun with this. The earl drained his brandy and watched Will over the rim of his glass.

"Miss Hughes has no interest in the institution of marriage."

Heath choked. "You've actually thought about it? You've asked her?"

"Good God, Boden, don't be ridiculous. I simply asked if she had ever been betrothed," Will snapped. "In an effort to learn more about my mother's staff." He sniffed. "And when I am sufficiently drunk or more adequately armed, I will find the courage to ask my mother's cook the same thing."

"Hm-mmm." Heath filled his glass again and pulled out a chair, straddling it and resting his arms on the seat back. All the better to study Will. "So Miss Hughes just shares your bed then?"

"No."

"No? Or not yet?"

Will took a long swallow of his drink, letting the fiery liquor burn down his throat.

Heath correctly interpreted his non-answer. "And when, exactly, do you plan on taking advantage of Miss Hughes?" There was reproach in the casual question.

"I'm fairly certain she's taking advantage of me."

The earl made a funny noise in the back of his throat. "Right."

"Miss Hughes suffers no illusions."

"How do you know?"

"She and I have had some very...enlightening conversations."

The earl stabbed a finger at him. "Don't do anything stupid, Worth. You're not that man."

"Thank you for the unsolicited advice." Will crossed his arms. "Are you done now?"

"I suppose." Heath toyed with the rim of his tumbler. "Speaking of thanks, I must thank you for what you did— are doing for my sisters," he muttered, abandoning the topic of Miss Hughes.

"Of course." The mere mention of their exclusion had Will's blood heating again.

"It's a competition, you know."

"What is?"

"Which matriarch can get the elusive, debonair, and

elegant Duke of Worth to attend her Ascot event. Word is out you'll be in Windsor."

"I'm not elusive. I like the sound of the rest of that, though."

Heath snorted.

"How do you know this?"

"Viola keeps me informed of all the gossip. The scandal sheets and gossip rags are as necessary to her as the air she breathes. Even when they are horribly cruel."

Will's lip curled. "I take it back. I am elusive. And that is why."

"It's not my sister's fault. The title, our fortune, or Julia's debacle of an engagement. None of it."

"No, it isn't," Will agreed. "But there are a great number of people who must make others feel small so that they may feel more substantial." He paused. "Julia looks better, though."

Heath propped his elbows on the chair back. "Julia has a suitor."

"She does? Who?"

"His name is Lance Morgan. He is the son of a vicar. He is honest and gentle and not even the slightest bit insane. And Julia adores him."

Will smiled. "Then that is a good thing."

"It is. They have known each other a long time. My father would not consider his suit because Morgan does not possess a title. I've encouraged his suit because he makes her happy. I've suggested that, in light of the events of the past year, it might be prudent that they wait a few more months before they marry. They've both agreed. I'm sure my father is turning in his grave as we speak."

The late earl had indeed aimed higher on the social

ladder when it had come to his eldest daughter. For all the good that had done anyone. "What does your mother think?"

"My mother is in Bath with her sister taking the waters for her fragile nerves. She has declared herself too beleaguered to deal with anything."

"I'm sorry to hear that." The countess was a frail, nervous woman at the best of times.

Heath shrugged. "It's probably easier if she's out of the way. Her constant fits of the vapors and wailings were starting to wear. On us and the staff."

"I would imagine." Will was beginning to gain a new respect for his own mother.

"Can you do me a favor?"

"Anything."

"Will you help me keep an eye on Viola?" the earl asked. "She has embraced her newfound status and is determined to improve upon it. But she is impulsive and reckless and a little immature. I'm afraid, if she is given enough rope, she just might hang herself. And I just can't deal with another scandal right now."

"Ah. So no vicars' sons for Viola."

"No." Heath sounded unhappy. "She swears nothing less than a marquess. A duke would be acceptable, and a prince would be even better." Heath sighed wearily. "You ought to watch yourself, Worth," he said, and Will realized he wasn't laughing. "She'll set her sights on you if you're not careful."

"We wouldn't suit at all," Will balked. "I'd make her miserable. She needs far more attention than I would ever be able to give her." Will had, up to this point, given no thought to the happiness of his future wife, but Viola was different. She was the sister of his best friend, and Will would like to see her find some measure of joy in marriage.

"I know that. You know that. Viola only knows that you've always been kind and tolerant to her, and that you come with a duchy." He rubbed at his forehead. "She doesn't always think before she acts."

"I'll keep an eye on her," Will promised.

"Thank you." Heath heaved a weary sigh.

"You look tired," Will commented.

Heath gestured helplessly. "I've managed and expanded my father's business for the last years, which had always been the plan. During that time I assumed the earl was managing the earldom. But it appears the task of managing an earldom steeped in debt completely overwhelmed my father, who was too damn stubborn to admit it and ask for help. He had no idea how to rectify the mess the earldom was left in without drawing even more attention to our family and causing more scandal. So now I've got a crumbling house, fallen fences, and fallow fields. There are bills and banknotes and statements of revenue for all manner of things. I'm not at all confident the estate ledgers have been balanced in the last year. I'm not even sure if the sweeps actually got paid when I had them clean the chimneys after my moldy library almost caught fire a fortnight ago."

"Well, that's no good. The sweeps have bills to pay too."

Heath gave him a startled look. "Indeed they do."

Will leaned against the wall. "I could help."

"Help?"

"Sort out some of that mess. I'd be happy to take a crack at the estate's books."

"Did you hit your head?" Heath asked, sounding baffled.

"No."

"Fall off your horse?"

"No."

"You might not remember hitting your head if you fell off your horse."

"I did not fall off my horse. At least not recently." Will scowled.

"And you're not drunk?"

"Jesus, Boden, do you want my help or not?"

Heath held up his hands. "Yes. God, yes. But you don't even do your own books, Worth."

"Not...recently."

"Not ever."

"I'm remedying the oversight. Just ask my mother."

Heath blinked. "I just..."

"You just what?"

"I was just wondering what happened to suddenly make you so...conscientious."

Jenna Hughes walked into my life with a snake wrapped around her neck, Will thought. And his priorities had tilted along with his world.

Will cleared his throat. "I've been staring at my mother's ledgers for much too long. I feel the need to be able to get to the bottom of a page and have a number that I can understand."

Heath held up his hands in defeat. "Then I'd be happy to have the assistance when you have time."

"Good." Will tapped his finger on the side of his crystal glass. "I'll have time soon. Once next week is over, everything will go back to normal."

The earl gave a bark of humorless laughter. "Dear God, Worth, I've been saying that for the last year and a half."

"And?"

Heath tossed back the rest of his brandy with a grimace. "And it hasn't worked. Let me know how you make out."

⁓

The women were still in the drawing room when Will and Heath emerged. All the women, that is, with the exception of Jenna.

"Where is Miss Hughes, Mother?" Will asked casually as the party moved into the hall and their guests prepared to take their leave.

The duchess brushed an invisible thread from her skirts. "Miss Hughes is out, dear."

"Out? Now? Where?"

"She was called to a . . . neighbor's."

"A neighbor's? For what?"

The duchess blinked at him. "Well, to help with a . . . ah, feminine issue."

"A feminine issue?"

"Stop repeating everything I say, dear. It's stilting the conversation."

"What kind of— Oh." Will stopped abruptly. "I can't imagine I wish to know exactly what that might entail. Well, I suppose that makes sense."

His mother froze. "I beg your pardon?"

"Her father was a surgeon," Will reminded her unnecessarily. "And she told me she assisted him from the time she was young. I'm sure she's exceedingly well qualified to help with a feminine issue."

The duchess's eyes cleared. "Indeed. Very well quali-fied. She is a remarkable woman."

"When will she be back?"

"Miss Hughes seemed to think she might be needed most of the night."

Will quashed the disappointment that washed through him, feeling a prick of guilt at his selfishness. Jenna would never turn her back on someone who needed help. And Will certainly wasn't going anywhere. He'd be here when she got back.

"Did someone go with her?" he asked suddenly, not liking the idea of her out somewhere by herself.

"Luke is with her."

That didn't make him feel much better. In fact, if he'd been envious of Heath for escorting her into the dining room, the thought of the golden butler's spending the night with Jenna made him nearly woozy with an envious resentment. His jaw clenched.

"She'll be fine," his mother said, patting him on the arm as if he were a troubled child. "She's done this many times before."

Of course she has, Will thought. In fact, she had told him not to interfere. She had told him to stay out of her way. And if he was a man of his word, he would respect her wishes and do just that.

"Thank you, Your Grace, for such a wonderful eve-ning." Lady Julia had moved toward them.

"You're always welcome here, dear." The duchess beamed at her.

Heath had joined Will on his other side. "Did your enchanted princess retire early?" Heath asked in low tones as he accepted his gloves from a footman.

"Miss Hughes had to leave unexpectedly," Will muttered.

The earl's lips compressed, and Will was sure Heath was fighting a grin. "It would seem this happens to you a great deal, Worth. The lady disappearing without explanation. Do you suppose it's just you, or was it something you said?"

"Oh, do shut up, Boden."

The earl smirked. "You know, Worth, if you married her, she might feel compelled to leave you a note next time."

Chapter 10 _____

Simon Wright's wife had been three months pregnant when he had lost his shop and his tailoring business. He'd specialized in exquisitely crafted waistcoats and evening coats and had been wildly popular with the young bucks of the ton who couldn't resist the latest in cut and color. Unfortunately for the tailor, most payments for such luxuries had been elusive.

For the last six months, Wright and his wife had lived in the back half of a wretched room in a wretched building in the most wretched part of St. Giles. The couple stayed one step ahead of starvation by mending and sewing for pennies, and with a little monetary help from the Duchess of Worth. It was only through sheer fortune that today, when Paul had arrived to deliver that help, he'd found Mrs. Wright in the early stages of labor and the tailor in the early stages of panic. The duchess's stable master had immediately sent one of the footmen flying back to the dower house on the fastest horse to fetch Jenna. There were very few doctors who would attend a birth in St. Giles, and among those who would, one could never count on sobriety. Or competence.

The footman had arrived just as dinner had concluded.

Jenna politely excused herself, and within ten minutes she'd changed, collected her surgeon's kit, and met Luke at the foot of the driveway. The footman had remounted on a fresh horse, and Luke held two other mounts ready and waiting. In a heartbeat the three riders had been galloping toward London.

Jenna had been in St. Giles many times before, and still each time she was shaken by the hopelessness that rose like a miasma from every corner and crevice. That she was flanked by two men familiar with the twisting warren of streets and alleys and armed with pistols had made her feel safer but no less saddened. Climbing the rotten stairs to the suffocating space that the talented and once-successful tailor now occupied had only stoked her determination that, by this time next week, Simon Wright and his family would have back what had been stolen from them.

The birth itself had gone smoothly, and Jenna had needed only to provide guidance and reassurance as a new little life was brought into the world. As she held the tiny baby in her hands and watched as she took her first breaths, a familiar heartbreak fused with joy pressed ruthlessly against her diaphragm, making it hard to breathe. A reminder of what Jenna had lost and a reminder that life was still full of new possibilities and hope. But humans seemed so fragile compared to horses. Especially here, surrounded by a morass of misery, where life was worth very little and death was always hovering, eager and remorseless.

Jenna had no idea what time it was when she finally made her way back down the stairs, but it was still dark, meaning it could be minutes after midnight or minutes before dawn. She found Paul leaning against the wall just inside the crooked doorframe, peering out at the sheets of rain pouring down on the streets. The acid stench, always pervasive, seemed to have abated somewhat.

"When did the rain start?" Jenna asked, hefting her bag in her hand.

"'Bout the same time the screaming stopped," Paul said dryly, looking down at Jenna in the gloom. Luke and Joseph's oldest brother was a giant of a man, barrel-chested and loud with dark-red hair and a heavy brow that sat low over his eyes. Jenna doubted he really needed the pistol he held casually to intimidate anyone, though she was glad for it.

She peered around him. "Where is Luke?"

"Right here." A shadow blew in from outside and shook itself off like a dog, water droplets scattering over the floors and walls. "Here." Luke pulled the hood of his cloak down and held out a small leather purse that clinked dully with the unmistakable sound of coins.

"Jesus, Luke, tell me you weren't out doing what I think you were doing."

Luke shrugged, unapologetic. "A man's got to keep his skills sharp."

"Luke!"

"Bloody hell, Jenna, but I couldn't stay here and listen to that." He made a weak gesture in the direction of the stairs. "I always imagined that was what the inside of Newgate would sound like." He caught sight of Jenna's face and sighed. "For the record, I didn't break into anything. I found an incoherently drunk gentleman lying on the side of the road before I could get that far," he muttered. "Gin and bad judgment do not make good bedfellows. I escorted him to a much safer and drier location until he might be in a condition to see himself home, and he was kind enough to ... offer me recompense."

"I'm sure he did."

Luke pressed the purse into her hand. "He could well afford it based on the cut of his clothes. He'll never miss it. The Wrights will need it far more, especially now."

Jenna shook her head in defeat.

Paul plucked the purse from Jenna's hand. "I'll see that they get it," he said. "But you two should head out," he advised, pulling up the hood of his heavy cloak and handing Luke the pistol. "Won't be much good in the rain, but I imagine the weather will keep the worst of the riffraff inside. Don't want to be running into any fool thieves tonight, present company not included." Paul cuffed his brother on the shoulder and let out a piercing whistle. In a minute their horses appeared, led by three bulky footmen. "Tell Her Grace I'll be back by tomorrow night latest," he told her. "Hadn't planned on this small delay."

"Thank you for waiting," Jenna said.

Paul grinned at her, his cheeks bunching below his eyes. "Someone had to keep Luke in line," he chuckled before stepping out into the pouring rain.

Jenna shrugged into her coat, stuffing her hair under her worn cap. By the time they got back to the dower house, they'd be soaked, but there was no help for it. A warm wash, a change of clothes, and a dry, comfortable bed beckoned. An empty bed, she thought with a mixture of relief and regret.

It was just as well she had been called out tonight. Where the Duke of Worth was concerned, she felt a little as though she were clinging to a runaway carriage heading for a cliff, unable or unwilling to throw herself clear. She wanted him; there was no denying that. The two of them together were like bonfire sparks drifting over a pan of black powder, igniting in an explosive conflagration at the slightest touch. What was more alarming was how much she found herself enjoying every moment of his company, and the loss she felt when she wasn't with him. Because of that, Jenna desperately needed some time. Time to step back and figure out how she was going to reconcile her selfish desire for William Somerhall and her obligations to those who needed her most. Because after the emotionally exhausting reminder tonight of what was at stake, Jenna couldn't for the life of her see how she could possibly satisfy both.

She buried her chin in her coat and swung herself up into the saddle, water already seeping down the back of her neck. As her horse moved off, she glanced back at the second-floor window covered with shreds of tattered cloth, the faint glow of candlelight winking feebly through the rain. The new parents were huddled up there, and the tiny newborn they held in their arms faced astronomical odds among the filth and the vermin and the disease that riddled her home. Jenna's face hardened.

Simon Wright's pride might be keeping them here for the moment, but his daughter would not grow up like this. Not if Jenna could help it.

Will must have fallen asleep. He awoke with a jerk, his neck protesting at the movement, to find himself slouched in the desk chair. The candle had gone out, leaving him sitting in the dark, and he blinked, trying to get his bearings. A gust of wind rattled the windowpanes, and the room was suddenly pierced with a beam of moonlight as the clouds parted. The earlier downpour had ended, though somewhere water dripped even as the wind continued to whine. Will remained motionless, trying to determine what had woken him.

Uncertain, he stood, a forgotten racing calendar sliding from his lap onto the soft rug beneath his feet, and padded to the window, peering out toward the road. The moon was suspended high, and the light filtering through the wildly shifting clouds sent strange and eerie shadows dancing across the ground. Puddles glittering like icy mirrors dotted the drive, and trees swayed, their darkened branches twisting up through silvered leaves. Had he been a superstitious type, Will would have expected ghostly faery folk to materialize under the pale light.

A movement out on the road caught his eye. *Jenna*, he thought instantly, straining through the shadows and distance to see telltale skirts underneath the riders' cloaks. A breath he hadn't realized he was holding hissed through his teeth as he realized it wasn't Jenna and Luke returning, but two horsemen, mounted on dark horses, riding hard and fast. They turned down the drive, hunkered over the backs of their mounts, their horses' heads slung low against the gusts. A spurt of trepidation sent Will's pulse jumping. Who the hell was riding for the dower house at this ungodly hour? His eyes strained to make out the identities of the horsemen, but it was impossible to see faces.

A cloak-wrapped figure was running up to greet the riders, and Will recognized Joseph's loping gait. The riders slowed their horses, and the young coachman raised his hand in a welcoming greeting that was returned.

Friends then, Will supposed with a cautious relief. It was clear Joseph had been watching for them, so they must have been expected. At the very least, Will felt reasonably certain they weren't highway brigands come to ransack the dower house. The horses and riders passed beneath his window and out of sight, heading toward the back of the house and the stables. But where was Jenna?

Probably already in her bed, Will suddenly realized. Judging from the position of the moon, it had to be close to dawn, and Jenna had very likely returned while he'd been sleeping. He shook his head, feeling foolish. What did he think he was doing, waiting up for a woman who hadn't needed his concern for the first twenty-five years of her life? A woman who hadn't felt the need to share the details of her departure and would undoubtedly be even less interested in notifying him of her return? Jenna certainly owed him no explanations, and yet here he was, bleary-eyed and pacing like an anxious nursemaid. God's teeth, but Will didn't even recognize himself anymore.

The sound of a downstairs door opening froze him in his tracks. But the house relapsed into silence, and Will wondered if it had been the wind pushing and pulling on a sash or shutter. He inched closer to his bedroom door, pushing it open just enough that he could see out. There was definitely someone moving in the house, though it could very well be a maid, up to check on the windows or the flues in the wind.

Will drew back into the darkness, still able to see the hallway and Jenna's bedroom door. Someone was moving up the stairs now, quietly and unhurriedly. A flickering glow from a candle grew in brightness against the patterned wallpaper. A figure appeared, but it wasn't Jenna. It was a man dressed in a sodden coat, its bulky silhouette and the cap, pulled low, offering no clues as to the intruder's identity. The figure crept down the hall, unerringly

stopping just outside Jenna's door. With a quick movement, he glanced up and down the hall, then eased his
way into the room, shutting the door behind him with a
soft click. It was very apparent this was not the first time
he had done it.

Something vile rose up inside Will. Something bitter
and uncomfortable. Something that felt horribly like a
sense of betrayal.

There was a man in Jenna's bedchamber. A bedchamber she had left unlocked, clearly expecting nocturnal
company. Will spun from his door, frozen in the darkness
with indecision. Perhaps even now Jenna was smiling at
the man, welcoming him into her bedroom. Welcoming
him into her bed. An image of her wrapped in the arms of
her unidentified lover stirred all sorts of things Will did
not care to examine. She was his, dammit.

But she wasn't his. A few moments of fumbling passion in a stable did not make Jenna Hughes exclusively
devoted to him. She'd never made him any promises.
She'd never pledged her fealty to him like some harem
mistress. She'd never promised him loyalty like a blushing bride. In fact, if he thought back to her words, she'd
specifically told him not to interfere. To stay out of her
way. So why the hell would he ever have assumed she was
his and his alone? Will was astounded at the magnitude
of his arrogance. And what had probably been an equal
measure of stupidity.

He thought back to breakfast and her bare feet tucked
under her skirts. The truth had been there all along, and
realizing it was like a slap in the face. Goddammit, how
could he ever have been so naïve? Will had always fancied himself reasonably clever, but when it came to Jenna,

he seemed to have lost every modicum of intelligence and instinct. He had no one to blame for any of this but himself.

Still. He couldn't pretend to lie here in bed while some other man had his way with her. Not under his mother's roof. He ignored the fact that he had intended to do exactly that himself, and pulled open his door with a little more force than necessary. He stalked down the hall, his steps muffled by the heavy carpeting. He pressed an ear to her door, but could hear nothing except the occasional creak of the floorboards as someone moved about. At least she wasn't making noises like the ones he'd elicited from her against the stall door. Yet.

With a vicious curse, he turned and rapped on her door.

Behind the wood he heard a muffled exclamation and then silence.

"Miss Hughes?" he said as loudly as he dared.

"Will?" came her incredulous reply.

He had been right. She had already returned. "Open the door."

"What?"

"Open the door."

"Have you lost your mind?" Her voice was closer to the door now.

"If you do not open this door in five seconds, I will open it for you."

She might have laughed. "Remember what happened the last time you threatened to count backward from five?"

Will swore silently at the reminder. Still, this was a far cry from a diamond down the front of her dress. This was a man in her bed. He knew what he'd seen.

"Five. Four."

A string of what sounded like muttered curses filtered through the wood. Scuffling followed by a thump.

Will shoved the door open.

Miss Hughes was standing alone in the center of the room, wrapped in a sheet and, as far as he could tell, nothing else. The single candle burning in the corner of the room guttered and flickered at the intrusion, sending shimmers of gold across her skin. Her hair was loose, tumbling over her shoulders in rumpled waves of inky black, and she was simply staring at him, her beautiful features shadowed and unreadable. No surprise, no alarm, nothing except a faint furrow between her brows. As if a duke's barging in on her at an outlandish hour were a regular occurrence.

Jenna shifted, and the sheet dropped perilously low across her chest, exposing smooth shoulders and a swath of skin interrupted only by the shadow of her breasts.

Will's insides turned molten, and his mouth went dry. "Explain yourself," he rasped.

A dark brow rose slowly and deliberately as she gestured at her state of dishabille. "I would have managed a robe had you not missed the three-two-one part."

Will forced his eyes away from the vision that was gutting him and sending whatever shreds of intellect he still clung to further from his brain and closer to his groin. "Where is he?" he demanded, his voice sounding strained in his own ears.

"Who?" Jenna's sheet slipped a little farther as she shifted, the entire slope of her breast kissed now by candlelight.

Will nearly broke.

"You know very well who," he snarled instead, prowling around the room, peering behind the curtains, which were still drawn, and poking his head into her tiny dressing room. "I saw him come in here."

"I don't know what you think you saw, but it's quite obvious there is no *him* in here. With the exception of you roving about like a lunatic, of course."

Worth yanked the single window in the room open and leaned out. It was a daunting drop to the ground. There was no balcony, no ledges, no convenient lattices or vines or trees. Anyone who'd attempted an escape by this route would most likely be in a broken pile on the stone below. He slammed the window shut with a bang.

"You'll wake the entire household doing that."

Will didn't care. He had never cared less about anything except the all-consuming need to discover the identity of the man she had chosen over him. "There's no one here except you." He was pacing now, ridiculous given that the width of the room gave him only four strides before he had to turn around.

"That's correct. Now stop moving. You're making me dizzy."

He dropped to his knees, peering into the darkness beneath her bed.

"What the hell are you doing, Your Grace?"

Dimly Will registered the stony use of formal address and not his name. But not before he found what he'd been looking for. He reached under the bed and retrieved a crumpled ball of clothes. Men's clothes. Never had he felt so miserable in triumph.

"Explain these," he growled, tossing the clothing to the bed one item at a time. An oiled coat, still dripping rainwater. Men's riding boots, scuffed, well worn, and damp but wiped clean of mud. A pair of breeches, similar to what a jockey might wear, reinforced with leather on the insides of the thighs and knees and spattered with what almost looked like blood in the dim light. A thin shirt, functional and unfussy. A cobalt-blue jacket, worn at the seams and sleeves and soft as satin from hard wear. And a simple cap, also sodden from rain.

Jenna was staring at the clothing, refusing to meet his eye.

It was the jacket that tugged at Will's memory. He'd seen it before. Seen it, in fact, hanging in the barns that very first morning. He snatched it from the bed, bringing it to his nose. The unmistakable smell of the stables drifted from the fabric.

"Who is he?" Will said, the anger he'd been relying on fading uncomfortly to despondency with proof in his hands. Obviously a groom. Or someone who worked in the stables from time to time. Like the man she'd been out with all night. "Is it Luke?"

Jenna jerked. "You're such a bloody idiot."

"Is it?" Will pressed.

"No." Jenna sneered. "You think I have him stuffed under my mattress? Under the rug? There's a book by my bed. Check between the pages. I'll wait if you'd like to look."

"Don't push me, Miss Hughes."

"What irks you the most, Your Grace? Your assumption I'm entertaining a man in my bed or the knowledge it isn't you?"

Will felt a maddening resentment rise. "Both," he growled. Why bother lying?

Jenna laughed, a disdainful, humorless sound. "There's no one here, Your Grace. No one in this room except for me and you."

"I know what I saw," Will repeated stubbornly.

"No, you don't. You have no idea what you saw." Jenna raised her eyes to him. There was fire there now, burning in those icy depths. A breathtaking defiance was set into her features, color rising in her cheeks, her posture straight and unyielding. At that moment she could have led an army to battle and men would have fought for the privilege of dying on her behalf.

Will swallowed, unable to answer. An excruciating awareness was starting to infiltrate, his muddled mind awakening and assimilating the evidence that lay before his eyes.

"These are yours." He thought back to the riders flying through the mud and the moonlight. Neither had ridden sidesaddle. Neither had worn skirts.

Jenna's eyes flashed. "Yes."

In two steps Will closed the distance between them, threading his fingers through the hair spilling over her shoulder. It had been hard to tell in the candlelight, but up close he realized it was wet. One of those riders had been Jenna. Another more pressing notion was dancing on the edge of his consciousness, but it refused to crystallize.

"And why were you out dressed like a common stable-boy?" Her hair slid through his fingers, and he dropped his hand.

Jenna seemed to be considering her answer. "Because it was expedient," she finally decided to say.

Will didn't like her hesitation. "Expedient? Dammit, Jenna, stop talking in riddles!"

"It's not a riddle. It's an explanation."

"Where the hell were you?" he demanded. Where could she possibly have been that abandoning skirts would ever be considered a good idea?

"Nowhere that is any of your concern." Jenna tipped her chin up in challenge, her eyes blazing.

Will wondered how he ever could have mistaken her for a princess. Jenna Hughes wasn't a princess, but a warrior through and through. He almost gave in to the wild impulse to kiss her. Kiss her without stopping because kissing Jenna was the only thing he'd done that had made sense since he'd arrived. But kissing Jenna made him forget everything around him, and for that reason he simply couldn't.

Will took a step back. He snatched the stool near the small washstand in the corner and swung it in front of him, placing it deliberately in front of the bedroom door. Very slowly he lowered his weight onto the seat, crossing his arms and leaning back against the doorframe, the blue jacket still in his hand. "Since I have arrived here, others have dictated what is and isn't my concern, Miss Hughes, including yourself. And I am damned tired of it." Will considered the jacket in his hands. "I've got nowhere to be, so let's try this again. Where were you tonight?"

"Why don't you tell me, Your Grace, since you've been spying on me?"

"I wasn't spying on you."

"No? What would you like to call this then? A coincidental ambush?"

"Answer my question."

Her eyes shifted angrily in the candlelight, and she pulled the sheet closer around her shoulders like a shield. "Fine. I was assisting with a birth tonight. Your mother should have told you that. Perhaps it would have saved me the displeasure of returning to a duke charging into my room like a bull on a Smithfield Sunday and accusing me of bedding the butler."

Will refused to back down. "Where?"

She narrowed her eyes but answered. "St. Giles."

"St. Giles?" Will couldn't possibly have heard her right. "But that's in London."

Jenna snorted. "Yes. Not even six miles from here as the crow flies. I'm surprised you know where it is, Your Grace." There was a mocking edge to her words that he didn't like. "I was under the impression your set stayed safely west of Haymarket."

"Jesus Christ, Jenna, are you out of your mind?" Will forced himself to lower his voice. "St. Giles in the middle of the damn night? You could have been hurt. Or killed. Or worse."

Jenna shrugged in that infuriating manner of hers. "Babies don't get to choose when and where they're born, Your Grace."

"Don't be obtuse."

"Says the man keeping me prisoner in my room and interrogating me while I'm in an objectionable state of undress."

"You've been in an objectionable state of undress all night," he retorted, ignoring her barb.

Jenna sneered. "Skirts betray one's identity as the fairer gender. Compared to a man, a woman is perceived as weak, vulnerable, easy to prey upon. Why would I tempt the odds when I could change them?"

"The odds are never in anyone's favor in places like that," Will snapped.

"And that is exactly why I was there." Her response cracked through the room like a whip.

Will thumped back against the door in frustration. "If my mother knew where you'd been—"

"Your mother knew exactly where I was. And it is vastly apparent why she didn't choose to share my where-abouts with you."

Will raked a hand through his hair, a familiar wrath rekindling. "My mother said you were at a neighbor's."

"*Neighbor* is so subjective, don't you think?"

Will surged to his feet, his patience at an end, tossing the blue jacket to the side. "Why were you called to attend a birth in St. Giles, Jenna?"

"Because no one else would have come," she said evenly. "Because the tailor who lost his trade and his home when the members of the ton couldn't be bothered to pay him had no one else to call." Her jaw was set. "You may consider it part of my little crusade if it makes it easier for you to understand why I did what I did. I might have lost my child, but I'll be damned if another woman loses hers for lack of help. Help that is in my power to give."

Will stared at Jenna for a long moment, every modi-cum of anger and irritation draining entirely, leaving him feeling weak and unsteady. "I'm sorry."

"As am I. Circumstance is not often kind." Her words were tight.

A well of emotion was bubbling up in Will and he tried desperately to sort through the tangle. Mostly guilt, for his pitiable, self-centered assumptions. He had some-how twisted everything to be about him and his damn ego. And while he was sulking, Jenna had been out all night, disregarding her own safety and painful losses to help another soul simply because she could. An unnamed yearning clawed, something so intense and sharp it was making the back of his throat burn. "My God, but I'm an idiot," he groaned.

"Then we're agreed." Jenna sighed, sounding tired. "And if we're done here, I'd like to go to bed. Without the butler."

In two steps Will had closed the distance between them and caught her face in his hands. He searched her eyes, wanting to understand how one person could hold so much selflessness and kindness and integrity within. Wanting to absorb true beauty that had nothing to do with what the eye could see. Jenna Hughes made him want to be better.

"Don't ever do such a reckless thing again," he said, his voice harsh.

Jenna's lips thinned, defiance instantly igniting.

"Without me," he added.

Surprise flared.

"If you are going to risk life and limb, please let me help."

"You already helped the dressmakers," she hedged. "At the Caudels'."

Will tucked a strand of tangled hair behind her ear. "That wasn't me. That was all you. The only thing I did was facilitate a faster escape."

Her mouth quirked, and her face softened. "And I appreciated it."

"Please, Jenna. I want you to show me what you do and how you do it. I want to help. Please." Will was well aware he was nearly begging, but he didn't care. "I don't want to be a man remembered for his fine clothes or practiced charm. I want to do something that matters."

Jenna was watching him, clearly conflicted. She bit her lip, her eyes grave.

"Tell me what you're thinking," Will whispered.

"I'm thinking that I'm a damn fool," Jenna said. "And you're a duke."

"You're not a fool," he said. "You're the most incredible woman I've ever met." He traced a finger along the side of her cheek. "But I am indeed a duke. Use what I can offer."

Jenna closed her eyes as if in pain. "I can't do what you ask."

"You can."

"God, Will, I want to. You have no idea how much. But—"

"I'm a duke." Never had he hated his title as much as he did then.

"Yes. It's better if you don't know."

"Know what, Jenna?" Will asked desperately. "Let me in." His subconscious was still nagging, but the truth it held remained concealed, clarity compromised by the emotions battering him. He was still missing something important, he knew. And her words only confirmed it.

Jenna shook her head, her eyes pools of anguish. "I'm not who you think I am."

"You are exactly who I think you are." Will searched for the right words, knowing they would fall short. "Strong. Brave. Real. I don't care about anything else."

Jenna laughed, a horrible, forlorn sound. "You should care." She looked away. "A week from now you'll be back in your old life, and I won't be—"

He kissed her then, unwilling to let her finish that sentence. He didn't want to think about next week. He didn't want to think about losing this woman he had just found.

She stilled beneath him for a moment, and then he

heard her groan, and whatever fears or worries she had shielded herself with fell away.

"Just tonight," she whispered, and he thought he might argue but it was becoming very difficult to think. All he could do was feel. Feel her skin, hot under his hands, feel her mouth against his, feel the way his body was responding with uncontrollable need. He took a step back and moved to extinguish the candle.

"Don't."

Will froze.

She looked up at him, her eyes heavy with desire, her lips swollen and red. "I want to see you."

Will turned back to her, his pulse roaring in his ears, and, grasping the top of the sheet she still had clutched in her hands, he pulled it free. It caressed her body as it fell, pooling at her feet, and Will sucked in a hard breath as Jenna stood before him, candlelight dancing over her skin. She met his eyes, unflinching and unashamed.

She was different from any woman he had ever been with, all long lines and fluid muscle. Her body was sleek and strong, a powerful grace contained below a surface of smooth skin. He ran a hand along the side of her breast, over the subtle ridges of her ribs, and against the slight flare of her hip. Jenna shivered under his touch, not for a second looking away. He was shaking, he realized, and it was becoming increasingly difficult to remember why he needed to take this slowly.

"You're beautiful," he rasped. "So goddamn perfect."

She might have smiled then, though she was already reaching for the bottom of his shirt and pulling it over his head, letting the garment fall to the floor with the forgotten sheet. She ran her hands over his chest, tracing the ridges and planes of his abdomen. Her fingers drifted to his waist, and he could feel his erection surge hot and hard against the fabric. With no hesitation her fingers started working on the buttons at the fall of his breeches. It was torture.

"This is what you do to me," he groaned, unable to stop himself from pushing into her hands. "I have wanted you like this since the moment I first saw you."

His breeches fell open, and Will shoved them down his legs, needing to feel Jenna against him. He took her mouth savagely again, his hands pulling her toward him. They moved to cup her high breasts, his thumbs stroking their smooth slopes and caressing her nipples. They were hard already beneath his touch, and she made a noise of pleasure in her throat, and it was everything he could do not to shove her back on the bed and bury himself within her.

He bent his mouth to taste her skin, his teeth grazing her shoulder. Her hands coursed down his back, her fingers kneading the muscle at the base of his spine and then playing with the ridge of muscle over his hip. Between them his cock pulsed heavy and hot against her stomach, and she closed her hand over his length, stroking and exploring. He shuddered violently.

Jesus, but this was going to be over before it even started.

"Jenna." It was desperate, and Will didn't care. "I don't think I can wait."

"Then don't," she whispered.

He caught her at her waist and spun her, pulling her to the bed and lowering her down before him, trying to gain some control. He knelt over her, bending to explore her glorious body with his mouth while his hands traveled over her hips and thighs, coming to rest at the juncture of her legs. She was wet, and as his fingers delved, she came off the bed with a hiss.

"I love how you feel," he whispered, pushing harder against her folds.

"Will," she groaned, and he heard his own desperation echoed.

He withdrew his hand, wanting to be inside her when she came this time. Wanting to feel her tighten and convulse around him when she lost control. He grasped her waist and turned her over so that she was on her stomach. He moved between her legs, kneeing her thighs apart and grasping her hips to pull her up to him. The tip of his erection teased the entrance to her core, and she gasped, her head dropping to the mattress, her pelvis jerking against him.

Will thrust into her heat.

His vision dimmed for a moment, so excruciating was the pleasure that ignited and licked through his body.

Mine, he thought incoherently, *always*.

She was hot and tight and perfect, and Will wanted to say something to make her understand just how exquisite she was, except he couldn't seem to catch his breath, much less form words. Beneath him Jenna moaned softly, adjusting the angle of her hips to draw him deeper. Will withdrew slightly and then surged forward again, feeling her stretch around him. He was sweating now, restraint slipping with every pull of her body. His hands reached to stroke her breasts as he rocked, circling the hardness of her nipples.

Jenna was breathing hard, her fingers clutching the

coverlet. She was making those small sounds of pleasure he so loved, muffled by her thick hair, which had fallen on either side of her face. In the soft light he could see her muscles straining and flexing across her back and shoulders beneath the smooth expanse of her skin. He thrust into her hard, his teeth clenched against the rising need he was powerless to stop.

When she came her inner muscles gripped him with an intensity he hadn't been prepared for. He slammed into her with a hoarse moan, his own release so powerful he was left panting helplessly as he pulsed and throbbed deep within her. He shook as the aftershocks swirled through him before his muscles gave out and he collapsed beside her on the bed.

Eventually Jenna stirred and turned over so she was facing him. Gently Will kissed her, unwilling to ruin the perfection of the moment with words he wasn't sure he could find and promises he wasn't sure he could keep. He gathered her into his arms, pulling the coverlet over them against the chill of the night air, sharper now against damp flesh.

Jenna rested her head against his shoulder, and Will smoothed her tangled hair back from her face. Eventually her breathing became even, her body languid and boneless against his.

Just tonight, she'd said, though he wasn't sure if she'd been trying to convince him or herself. Either way it was irrelevant.

One night was never going to be enough.

Chapter 11 _____

Jenna wasn't sure how long she dozed, but when she opened her eyes, Will was no longer wrapped around her and dawn was making itself known along the edges of the curtains. An acute sense of loss warred with relief. Not that a fleet of servants would descend into Jenna's rooms without a specific request, but the Duke of Worth could not be found in her bed when the household awoke. She stretched, feeling muscles in her body protest in a delicious, satisfied manner. Dear God, but he had been magnificent. She'd been right to be afraid that day in the barn. A taste of this man had indeed left her starving for more. And definitely ruined for any other.

He'd claimed her for his own last night, as surely as if he had branded her. He'd taken her control and her caution and he'd obliterated them with his body and his mouth and his words. And when he had driven into her, the pleasure he had given her had robbed her of her senses, her wits, and left her reeling. He was an addiction, she knew, something she would find difficult to indulge in only once.

But they'd be leaving for Ascot at first light on the morrow and she didn't fool herself into thinking that whatever this was between herself and the Duke of Worth would transcend that time or distance. What they'd shared last night was all she would have. Once they arrived in Windsor, Jenna Hughes would cease to exist. She would set her stage and deliver the performance of a lifetime, and William Somerhall would not be part of that. Could never be part of that. No matter his professions of good intentions, he had no idea what he asked. And it needed to remain that way. It was safer for everyone involved.

With no little regret and sadness, Jenna pushed herself up, intending to dress against the morning chill. She froze, suddenly realizing Will hadn't left at all. He was sitting motionless and silent on the end of the bed, facing away from her, his broad back a beautiful canvas of defined muscle and smooth skin. He'd donned only his breeches, as though something had distracted him from completing his task of dressing. And it was his stillness that had Jenna's heart banging hard against her ribs. Something was wrong.

"Will?" Jenna slid closer to him.

He didn't answer. Didn't even turn his head to look at her.

Tentatively she reached out, brushing his hair from the side of his face. She glanced down, and her arm froze. Her forgotten blue jacket was draped over his knee, and her mud- and blood-splattered breeches were in his hands. He was turning the garment over with his capable fingers, tracing the edges of the leather sewn over the insides of the knees and thighs. After a moment he placed the breeches on the edge of the bed and steepled his fingers under his chin. "Isaac has a pair of these," he said into the silence. "With the leather sewn into the inside."

Jenna could barely breathe. Panic was rising.

"Type of breeches you need for only one thing." Without looking up at her, he reached up and grasped her hand, still suspended near his shoulder, and pulled it toward him. His hands were warm and unyielding, and Jenna tried to snatch her hand back, but she was too late. He trapped her hand between his, turning it so that her palm lay exposed before him. Jenna was left leaning awkwardly, her chest pressed to his back through the covers, her cheek resting on the top of his shoulder. She closed her eyes, knowing exactly what he was doing and knowing she had only herself to blame for this.

"I never realized what a good rider you were, Jenna Hughes," Will said conversationally, "until I saw you return last night."

Her mind was racing, her thoughts darting wildly, seeking a rational escape, but she was coming up with nothing.

"Somehow I automatically assumed you'd borrowed those clothes," Will said quietly. "But you know what they say about assumptions." His finger traced her palm, rising and falling as it caressed every one of her thick calluses.

Jenna opened her eyes but remained silent.

"I saw this blue jacket the first morning you came down to the barns with me. It had been left over a stable door, and I remember thinking it was the only thing out of place. Well, that and the bridle that had slipped off its hook. But you straightened the bridle before you went to fetch Joseph for me. Looped and tucked the reins neatly and efficiently so that it wouldn't fall off again. You even made sure the bit hung straight."

Jenna let out a miserable, shaky breath. She didn't even remember doing that.

"Tell me these aren't your clothes." His voice was even and unhurried.

"Those aren't my clothes," she parroted unhappily.

"You're a terrible liar."

"It's an affliction I seem only to suffer with you. And I don't know why." Jenna tried to pull her hand away again, but Will only tightened his grip. The pads of his fingers stroked the outside edge of her hand, the flesh scarred and toughened from the bite of leather. Jenna knew her carefully crafted facade was crumbling further with every touch of those skilled fingers.

"Tell me why my mother hired you, Jenna Hughes," he said. He examined her corded forearm, her thickened wrists, and then her scarred knuckles. Silently he traced the blunt end of each of her fingers with his thumb before enfolding all the evidence he needed within the warmth of his own hands once again. Jenna dropped her forehead to rest against the solidity of his back, admiration somehow mingling with her distress.

Damn the duke and his clever, clever mind. Damn the duke and his exquisite attention to detail. And damn her inability to lie to this man.

"I'm her companion," she said tonelessly.

Will shifted suddenly, turning so that he faced her on the edge of the bed. "I'm quite certain you are from time to time. But that's not why my mother hired you." It wasn't a question. His eyes bored into hers, black and bottomless in the dim light. Will's face was a mask of granite, and Jenna couldn't tell if he was furious or merely indifferent.

She dropped her gaze. "No." Was there a point to

trying to lie at this juncture? Will held all the evidence to refute her protestations. A woman did not have hands like hers from years of embroidery and painting.

Will reached out and tipped Jenna's chin up, forcing her eyes back to his. "Was your father really a surgeon, Jenna?"

"Yes," she answered on a sigh. "Though I might have left out the veterinary part. He was a track surgeon. At the time it didn't seem relevant."

"What about the rest of it? Peter? Your—"

"The truth. All of it."

He was silent for a moment. "This is what you meant, isn't it? When you said you weren't who I thought you were."

Jenna's eyes slid away.

"Tell me how you came to work for my mother. The truth."

The truth. A funny word, that. Especially when omissions kept leaving gaping, treacherous holes.

"Jenna."

"I met her at Tattersalls. She was debating the wisdom of buying a chestnut colt that had just been brought out. I was standing beside her, debating the wisdom of stealing two meat pies instead of one."

"Why?"

"Because I hadn't eaten in three days."

"No, I meant why were you standing with my mother?"

"Because she was standing next to the vendor's cart."

Will's lips might have twitched. "She bought you a pie, didn't she?"

"She bought me two. But only after I told her the colt she was about to bid on was so low in the heel and upright in the hind pastern that it wouldn't last a half dozen races before it broke down."

Something shifted in Will's eyes. Something dark and hungry, and it took Jenna's breath away. "And then?" His voice sounded off.

"The duchess told me she wished to purchase good breeding stock. Perhaps something that might win a race or two. She asked if I could do that for her," Jenna murmured, watching Will carefully.

The duke had tightened his hold on Jenna's hand. "What did you say?"

Jenna couldn't entirely suppress the smile that threatened. "My answer trounced your bay yesterday morning."

"Those are your racehorses in my mother's barns."

"Well, technically your mother owns them, even though most of the time we list Paul as the owner on race days. But yes. They're mine. I've overseen their breeding and training, and ultimately I'm the one responsible for their successes and failures." God, but it felt good to say that to this man. To take ownership of everything she had put into the past eight years and know that effort was understood, and maybe even appreciated, was exhilarating.

Will was blinking rapidly, and his hand was crushing hers now. Yet he said nothing, only the sound of his harsh breathing puncturing the silence.

Jenna shifted, uncertain at the duke's curious reaction. Alarm was sounding, though the expected regret was suspiciously absent. Jenna knew it was her own actions that had landed her here and betrayed her secrets. Had she kept her distance from the Duke of Worth, she wouldn't be in this position. But what had happened last night had been incredible. With one kiss William Somerhall had filled her world with everything she had thought lost to her forever. Passion and compassion. Closeness and companionship. He had obliterated her defenses with his tender words and persuasive lips, and damned if she could bring herself to say she wouldn't do it all over again given half the chance.

But now that the truth had been exposed, it didn't matter that she believed William Somerhall to be a man of quiet dignity and unsurpassed honor. A man with a kind heart and a noble soul. It didn't matter that she was wildly attracted to him. What mattered was what he would do now that he knew she wasn't at all what she had pretended to be.

Jenna raised her head and met his gaze squarely. Better to get this over with. This was certainly a blow—something she had tried to avoid—but there was nothing to be done about it now. Even if the worst happened, she would still find a way to succeed. She always did.

"Are you going to dismiss me?" Jenna asked, her voice steady and challenging.

Will started, his grip on her hand lessening. "Dismiss you?" He seemed to be having a hard time with the words.

"Yes. Now that you know what I do, that I am more often than not more fully and exclusively dedicated to your mother's horses than to the position of her hired companion, will you dismiss me?"

"Holy God." He started laughing.

Jenna stared at him, uncomfortably aware she seemed to have missed something vital. For there was absolutely nothing funny about any of this. "Is that a yes?"

He was still laughing, a low, rolling sound with an edge

of lunacy that came from deep within him. Jenna yanked her hand out of his, furious and confused.

Will lunged forward, pushing Jenna back against the pillows, the covers sliding away. He rested on his elbows above her, his hands smoothing her disheveled hair away from her face. He bent his head and kissed her hard before pulling back slightly. "I'm not going to dismiss you, Jenna Hughes," he said roughly. "I think I'm going to marry you."

A snort of laughter born of shock escaped. "Marry me?"

"I think I'm in love." He grinned down at her.

Jenna rolled her eyes, relief making her giddy. "Luckily I'm not the marrying kind, so I won't hold you to that," she said. "And you'll come to your senses soon. The novelty won't last long, I promise."

The duke was shaking his head, incredulity glowing from within. "I have the most beautiful woman in my bed, who shares the same passion I do. I'm struggling to believe I haven't died and arrived at the gates of heaven."

"Mmmm. To be honest, I was half afraid you'd have my head for such a breach of accepted racing conduct."

He grinned again before his eyes grew serious. "A title means nothing to a horse. Racing has been the single forum where my measure may be taken not from the circumstance of my birth but from the product of my work and ability, for better or for worse. The reason I take the laws of racing so seriously and strive to improve upon them is that it has been the only honest thing in my life. Before I met you, that is."

Guilt pricked, and she bit her lip.

"But you have a rare gift, a gift many men spend a lifetime trying to achieve. And the beauty of such a gift is that it is independent of gender or class or wealth." Will brushed her hair back from her forehead. "Why didn't you tell me before?"

"Would you have believed me?" Jenna deflected, unwilling to build another set of lies at this moment.

"Yes. No. Perhaps." Will shifted, his weight pressing Jenna into the mattress. He bent and kissed her again, reverently, as though she were a newly discovered and breakable treasure.

"For what it's worth, I'm sorry," Jenna said against his lips, apologizing for more than he would ever realize. "It wasn't personal. No one knows about what it is I do here. And it must remain that way."

Will was grinning idiotically again. "Why?"

Jenna leveled a long look at him. "I thought the entire reason you moved in here in the first place was to curb the scandal and gossip that dog your mother. I might suggest that your esteemed Jockey Club colleagues, sitting smugly in their club rooms on High Street, might have some very strong opinions regarding both my, and by default your mother's, very direct involvement in their world. I'm certain there would be nothing kind in those opinions."

"Women race their horses from time to time," Will protested.

"Ah, yes, those delightful country races, described as lovely, but indecent, entertainment." Jenna knew she was being testy, but there was a more immediate underlying reason to make sure her secret remained just that. "I don't want notoriety. I want the focus to remain on my horses and not on the gossip and scandal that would be me. And your mother. I think we have enough already."

Will blew out his breath. "You're right," he conceded. "Your secret is safe with me."

"Promise?" Jenna needed to hear it.

"You have my word."

She believed him. The tension bled from her limbs.

Will rolled to the side, propping his head up with his elbow and studying her, a bizarre array of intense emotions playing across his handsome features. Wonder. Possessiveness. Confusion. Joy. Jenna watched them all, trying to make sense out of any of them.

"You are incomparable," he said softly.

Jenna abandoned her deliberation and simply allowed herself to bask in his happiness. Never had she felt as cherished and exceptional as she did at that moment. It was something that she would hold and keep safely tucked away to be examined later when the duke had long departed and solitude became too suffocating. When she would once again be watching William Somerhall from a distance.

He had caught her hand again and was caressing her palm with his thumb. "I always wondered why you wore gloves," he said. "Especially given your disregard for fashion. You were hiding your hands from me."

Jenna brought his fingers to her lips. "This is rather ironic, but did you know it was your hands that I noticed first?"

Will gave her a quizzical look.

"You can tell a great deal about a man from his hands," she said, considering his. "And yours are exquisite. They are your best feature."

Will wrapped his fingers around hers, a small smile playing around his mouth. "I'm not sure if I should be flattered or insulted. Though I must confess, no one else has ever commented on my hands. What do they tell you?"

"Your hands speak of a man who isn't afraid to do for himself, even though he has others who could." She traced the nicks and scars over the tanned skin. "They're strong but not cruel. Gentle when they need to be. Capable. Sure."

Will was watching her intently, his eyes dark, all humor gone.

Jenna brushed the sparse hair over the backs of his knuckles and touched the blunt, callused ends of his fingers. "I've heard it said that the eyes are the window to the soul, but I disagree. Beauty is as beauty does, not as it appears." She threaded her fingers through his.

Will kissed her then, rolling over her and pressing their entwined hands into the pillow above her head. His kiss was almost desperate, as if he was seeking something he was afraid he could not find.

With her free hand, Jenna stroked the steel of his arms and the hard ridges of his back, letting her lips communicate what could never be put into words. She sucked on his mouth, her tongue twining with his, meeting his every challenge. With a sudden urgency, Will reached for the buttons at the fall of his breeches, yanking them open. Jenna hooked a foot in the waistband and shoved his breeches down below his knees, and in the next instant, she felt him heavy and hard as he touched her core with the tip of his erection.

He stilled then, slightly, and Jenna could see him gather his control. She arched against him, impatient and dissatisfied, trying to find release. Will was moving his hips now, small, inestimable movements that penetrated her ever so slightly before he withdrew again, infuriating in their torment.

"God, Will, what are you doing?" she ground out in frustrated pleasure as the friction built and then vanished, and then built again.

"I want to do this slowly," he gasped, "so that I know it's real and not a dream. I want to watch you come, want to see you fly apart under me."

"I don't want slow." Her fingers dug into the muscles of his back. "I want all of you. I don't think I will ever be able to get enough of you," she whispered raggedly, unable to stop the truth that tumbled out.

He groaned and bent his head, worshipping the sensitive skin at her throat with his mouth. Then his tongue found the slopes of her breasts and the sensitive peaks and swirled over each one with an exacting deliberation.

She wrapped her legs around his waist, opening herself farther, and heard his breath hitch. He pushed into her then, every inch sliding with exquisite sensation against her until he was buried deep.

"Yes," she mumbled on a near sob of relief. The way this man filled her, the way his body slid over hers, left her writhing with a need that would not be denied or delayed.

He throbbed deep inside her and shifted, a subtle withdrawing before he pushed back into her, impossibly deeper. He held her eyes the entire time, his arms braced on either side of her shoulders. Jenna wrapped her hands around his forearms, anchoring herself and feeling his muscles flexing and trembling beneath her touch. He rocked against her again, both of them settling into a rhythm ancient in its compulsion and increasingly desperate in its pace. He was still watching when she felt herself come apart, her body reaching within itself only to hurtle away into tiny pieces she would never be able to recover. He followed a second later, whispering her name.

Jenna pressed her lips to the skin below his ear, tasting the salt and musk of his skin.

It was going to be so hard to let this man go. She had one day. One day before they departed for Ascot and their lives diverged forever.

A single day before she said goodbye. A single day to pretend that she wasn't falling for the Duke of Worth.

Chapter 12 ⸻⸻⸻

It hadn't taken long for Will to come to terms with the knowledge that there had been a change in him—one indefinite but irreversible. And he couldn't decide if he was thrilled or terrified. Ever since he'd slipped from Jenna's bed that morning, he hadn't seemed able to go longer than two minutes without thinking of her. Every two minutes his breath became short, his pulse pounded abnormally, and his breeches seemed to have become perpetually snug. His insides were twisted and his composure scattered, and he'd never, in all his life, suffered the like before.

Everything reminded him of his inability to be with Jenna at every possible moment. Though being close to her was worse. Breakfast with his mother and Jenna had been like some form of medieval torture in which he was expected to smile pleasantly and converse civilly, all the while dwelling on how desperately he wanted to simply drag Jenna into the first empty room he could find and remind her exactly how completely she belonged to him. Or he to her.

The Earl of Boden had been right. Will was besotted. And he didn't care.

For the first time in his life, Will was seriously considering his future. Normally when he tried to imagine what his life might be like two or five or ten years from the present, he didn't think past his racehorses, his clubs, and his friendships. The idea of marriage instilled dread, and for the most part, he'd avoided thinking about it at all. But he was a decade past twenty and it was long past time to consider exactly what he wished for himself, for his wife, and, when the time came, for his children.

His parents' marriage had been carefully arranged, a perfect example of the correct melding of titles and fortunes. And for all that proper planning, only heartbreak and misery had ever been generated. There had been no joy or happiness within that union, and Will had watched his family splinter as his mother tried to love a man incapable of emotion while he and his sister distanced themselves from the desolation as best they knew how.

He would not allow that to happen to him. Not when he had control over his future and his fate. He wanted a genuine partnership. Something better than what his mother had suffered through. At the very least contentment. Compatibility. Company. A union with a person who might care for him as a man and not just a duke. And with a surreal sense of comprehension, he wondered if Jenna Hughes was that person. The single person who had looked beyond the trappings and seen him for who he truly was.

I think I'm going to marry you, he'd blurted, the words born of shock and wonder, and Jenna, being Jenna, had simply laughed. It was absurd, he knew, and he should follow Jenna's lead and dismiss the notion out of hand. Yet the idea lingered like elusive wisps of a beautiful dream after waking, the fragments swirling just beyond reach.

Idly Will wondered how much scandal would be generated if he married his mother's companion. In the next breath, he wondered if he would actually care. The irony of that wasn't lost on him. As Jenna had so recently pointed out, he had moved into his mother's house to suppress the gossip and scandal his family generated, and now here he was, contemplating creating more. But he was not prepared to lose Jenna Hughes. Not when he had just found her.

A firm tap on his door jerked him out of his musings. "A message for you, Your Grace," came Luke's disembodied voice through the door. "Would you care to receive it or shall I leave it in the hall for you?"

Will strode to the door and yanked it open. The butler stood at attention, a thick envelope held casually in his hand.

"I'll take it." Will glanced down and saw it was the Ascot racing reports he'd asked for.

"Very good, Your Grace." Luke handed the envelope to him and made to leave.

"Tell me, Luke, why is it that you accompanied Miss Hughes into St. Giles last night?"

The butler froze before slowly turning around. "I did not know you were aware of our destination," he said carefully.

"I was not informed until after the fact." He willed his expression to remain neutral. "But I do know how dangerous such a place can be. Why you?"

The butler blinked. "I am well familiar with St. Giles," he said. "I used to live there."

"You used to live in St. Giles." Will wasn't sure if that

was a question or a disbelieving statement. Who the hell had a butler who used to live in St. Giles?

"It was during a leaner time in my life," Luke said. "Though no less important in its experience."

"And this...experience makes you capable of protecting Miss Hughes?" Even he could hear the condescension in his question, and he wasn't sure if it stemmed from irrational jealousy over the fact that Luke had somehow been appointed Jenna's protector.

Luke moved so swiftly, Will had barely time to register the motion. "You tell me, Your Grace."

Will became aware of cool metal being pressed to the side of his throat. "Jesus Christ." His heart skipped a beat, he was sure. Possibly two.

Luke pulled back and straightened, flipping the wicked blade he had seemingly pulled from the air over in his fingers to hand the weapon to Will hilt-first for inspection. "In such an environment, one learns a more distasteful skill set." The statement was utterly incongruous coming from such an angelic-looking man. "So in answer to your question, yes, for what it's worth, I feel I am quite capable of protecting Miss Hughes. And your mother, should the need ever arise."

Will wasn't sure if he should be incensed or impressed. Unwilling to show either reaction to this man, he examined the knife methodically. It had a long, narrow blade with a slight curve to the point, set deep into a polished bone hilt. This was not a gentleman's frippery. It was a weapon, unadorned and pure in its lethal purpose. Slightly unnerved, Will handed the knife back to the butler. Luke gave him a brief nod of thanks, and then the blade impossibly disappeared again.

"I know I may not be as...conventional as you might like, Your Grace, but please do not doubt my loyalty and devotion to the duchess. I have a great deal of admiration for your mother." Luke had retreated back into his butler persona, and the words were delivered with a steady, firm cadence.

"Then I am glad to hear it." Strangely, Will thought he believed him. They were almost the exact words Jenna had used in declaring her own loyalty. In fact, for the many peculiarities of his mother's staff, each of them seemed completely dedicated to the dowager.

"Very good, Your Grace." Luke beamed at him. "I will be downstairs if you need anything further." He turned to leave for the second time.

"Wait," Will blurted.

Luke's blond brows rose fractionally in question as he paused.

"I want you to take me to St. Giles."

Luke paled. "I beg your pardon?"

"You heard me. I wish to visit the tailor and his wife you were with last night."

Luke was blinking rapidly. "May I ask why?"

That part of this entire impulsive decision was still a little muddy to Will as well. All he knew was that he needed to understand. Understand what Jenna did and why she did it. And for some reason she was holding back. There was something he was still missing, and he was damned if he wouldn't do all he could to discover what that was.

"No, you may not ask. You may have two horses saddled and meet me in front in ten minutes."

"Your Grace, I must caution you that—"

"You may take me or I will find my own way there. And if I get my fool throat slit because you refused my request, you may have the pleasure of explaining that to my mother."

Luke looked like a rabbit backed into a corner by a pack of hounds.

"Ten minutes, Luke. That is not a suggestion."

The butler took a deep breath, as if trying to shore up his wits. "Of course, Your Grace. As you wish." He paused, his eyes touching Will's attire. "Might I advise a change of clothing?"

Will glanced down at the casual garb in question.

"Something a little less ducal would be...helpful. Your boots alone, should they be skillfully fenced, would feed an entire family for months."

He gave Luke a curt nod. "Understood." The butler began to hurry off. "Oh, and Luke?"

The man stopped, misgiving stamped across his face. "Yes, Your Grace?"

"What sort of things does a baby need?"

⁓

There were three horses saddled by the time Will met the butler out front, and he eyed the fast, swift, sleek hunters, knowing all three were beyond the abilities of an average horseman. Will frowned in momentary confusion before he realized who was effortlessly swinging up onto the back of the third horse, mainly because she was dressed again in her breeches and coat, her cap pulled low over her face. Under the brim her eyes were intense and considering.

"You're not coming," he said stiffly, with an epic effort

averting his gaze from the smooth lines of her thighs and hips straddling her horse. If he lived to be a hundred, the sight of Jenna Hughes in riding breeches would haunt him for the rest of his life.

Jenna smiled a slow, pitying smile and adjusted a leather pouch she had slung across her shoulder. "I might say the same thing to you." She made no move to dismount.

Will accepted the reins of his horse from Luke, giving the man an accusing look. Luke shrugged. "She'd already planned to go see the wee bairn this morning," he told Will with no apology.

"It's dangerous," Will tried again with more effort, even knowing it was futile.

Jenna snorted. "Perhaps you should stay here then, Your Grace, if you fear for your safety."

Will growled something indecipherable under his breath.

"Is there a particular reason you fancied a ride into London this morning, Your Grace?" Jenna asked. "St. Giles is not much of a destination even in the daylight. While I have a newborn to check on, I am uncertain as to your motivations."

"I want to help. I want to understand. I believe I made myself clear earlier, Miss Hughes, though it would seem you might have misunderstood. Perhaps you were distracted." He kept his answer clipped and precise.

Will was gratified to see a faint stain color her cheeks. Luke was looking at the pair of them with a slightly raised brow.

"Very well, Your Grace," she conceded abruptly. "Then if you insist on accompanying us, please try and keep up." Jenna turned her horse down the drive, urging her mount into a trot and then a swift canter.

Will stared after her, watching her handle her powerful hunter with effortless skill.

"You'd best do as the lady suggests, Your Grace," Luke advised, even as he mounted his own gelding. The leggy animal danced and pulled at the bit, eager to run.

Will frowned slightly. "I beg your pardon?"

"Try and keep up," the butler advised, pulling his own cap down more firmly over his ears as though he were preparing for the start of the Epsom Derby. "Miss Hughes rides like a damned Valkyrie."

Will had been to St. Giles once, as an adolescent, on a dare. The details were a little blurry, though he remembered the clandestine excursion's being exciting and adventurous and foolishly dangerous. Now that he saw clearly, it just seemed sad and demoralizing and foolishly dangerous. He'd heard many long diatribes in the House of Lords on the evil combination of alcohol and poverty and crime so rampant in the parish. But he'd never paid a great deal of attention, certainly not enough to prompt him to investigate the situation on his own. Just like so many other things, he'd simply not taken the time to think about it.

He was certainly thinking about it now. They'd flown into London, slowing only when they'd reached the roads and streets with increasing traffic, the daily commerce of London well under way. Traveling deeper into the city of London, they'd left their horses stabled in a livery near St. Martin's Lane, as Luke had rather caustically commented that he'd not be able to watch three horses and a duke at the same time. On foot they'd worked their way north through Seven Dials and into a maze of alleys Will quickly lost track of. Buildings loomed over their heads, most of them threatening to topple, blocking the light and keeping the streets in perpetual gloom.

And everywhere were people. Walking, staggering, sitting, brawling, and lying in the streets. Some met their eyes with emotions ranging from suspicion to hatred to despair, while others stared sightlessly at the ground. Some were moving with a purpose, others seemed to be adrift. In doorways children crouched, their sunken eyes following each and every move the group made.

Luke kept them moving quickly and confidently through the maze, hopping cesspits and kicking fly-ridden offal and grasping hands from their path with brutal efficiency. Eventually he veered into the darkened doorway of a two-story structure, the smell of rotting wood, sewage, and the despair of humanity almost choking in its potency.

"We're here," Luke said shortly, gesturing at a staircase missing a number of steps and listing hard to port.

Will nodded, at a loss for words. The wretchedness of his surroundings had left him mute.

Jenna had already started up the staircase, nudging the carcass of what might have been a cat from a stair onto the floor below and motioning Will to follow. Luke brought up the rear. She stopped at a small landing, stepping around an insensible woman propped up against the wall. A tattered blanket had been nailed to the doorway beyond, the door and its hinges long gone.

"Wait here," she instructed Will.

Jenna ducked around the blanket, and Will could hear low voices from beyond. He glanced down at the woman in the corner of the landing. She might have been eighteen or eighty, her face haggard and lined, open sores running on her cheeks. Her dress gaped open at the neck, bones jutting from her chest, her breasts exposed for anyone to see. Will crouched down, feeling the need to cover her.

"For God's sake, don't touch her," snapped Luke from behind him.

Will straightened. "But—"

"She'll be crawling with vermin. And she's probably sick. Cholera. Consumption. Syphilis. One or all of them. Don't touch anything. Or anyone, unless I tell you. Understand?"

Will nodded uncomfortably.

"You can come in now," Jenna said, suddenly reappearing.

She led Will into the tiny room as though she were showing him into one of the finest St. James drawing rooms, her body warm against his in the close confines. Luke followed, taking up a position just inside the door. The room had a window, allowing a decent amount of light to flood the space, and Will blinked after the dimness of the stairway. It was about a third of the size of his dressing room at Breckenridge, a tiny pallet shoved up against the wall under the window and a table constructed of a board balanced on two stacks of broken bricks to one side. A second board had been nailed to the wall above the table, and here sat a ragged collection of possessions that included a battered mug, a wooden bowl, and three dented tins.

"Good morning, Your Grace." The polite greeting came from the far side of the room, where two people stood uncertainly, wedged between the pallet and the table.

"Good morning," he replied, transferring his attention

to the man who had spoken. "I— Dear God. Mr. Wright?" Will felt recognition punch through him with horror.

The young tailor inclined his head. "At your service, Your Grace. A pleasure to see you again, though I'm afraid I can no longer offer you coffee or tea. Or a chair." His voice held a faint note of bitter mocking.

Will knew he was staring but he couldn't help it. He'd had cause to meet Simon Wright on multiple occasions, always in the tidy confines of his shop, surrounded by luxurious fabrics and only the best furnishings. Last year Will had been mystified when the tailor had simply disappeared, his shop closed up and reopened as a haberdashery a week later. But he hadn't thought to ever determine why.

His answer lay in brutal starkness before him.

"This is where you live?"

The tailor shrugged, looking weary. "For the moment."

Behind him a muffled squawk had him turning, a woman Will could only assume to be his wife shifting a squirming bundle in her arms. The new mother looked pale and exhausted, and Will jumped forward. "Good Lord, you should be resting." He gestured toward the tiny pallet. "Please don't stand on my account."

Mrs. Wright looked up at him with wide-eyed indecision, and Will understood that the etiquette of their former business had followed her here to this room.

"Please. I must insist." Will gestured again to the miserable little bed.

"Thank you, Your Grace," Mrs. Wright breathed and sank down gratefully.

Jenna gave him an approving look and immediately moved to join the woman and child. With practiced ease she took the tiny infant from its mother's arms, smiling down at the downy head. Will couldn't tear his eyes from the sight, an ache like nothing he'd ever experienced building within his chest.

"Congratulations," Will managed awkwardly. "I understand you have a daughter."

The tailor smiled in pride, though there was an underlying worry. "Yes."

Jenna had laid the baby on the pallet and was unwrapping the blanket. With gentle, sure hands she examined the child, all the while murmuring encouraging whispers. She reached into her pouch for a jar of something and handed it to Mrs. Wright to open. The rich scent of herbs cut through the air, and Jenna scooped out a daub of salve. Carefully she applied it to the infant's abdomen around the crusted stump.

Will edged toward Mrs. Wright. "I brought you some things," he said, depositing a wrapped parcel next to the tailor's wife. "Some food. Soap. A couple of blankets." He was twisting his hands in front of him like a nervous boy, and he forced them to still.

Mrs. Wright colored slightly but smiled up at him, and Will saw a pretty woman below the exhaustion and hardship. "Thank you, Your Grace." Her eyes were suspiciously bright.

Beside her, apparently satisfied, Jenna was rewrapping the little girl in a manner that looked more complicated than a cravat knot.

"Would you like to hold her?" Mrs. Wright asked Will.

Will started, completely at a loss. He'd never held a baby. Babies were the responsibility of nurses and nannies, brought out briefly before dinner to be dutifully admired and then whisked away abovestairs until they were old enough to be sent off to school. Slowly he nodded.

Jenna picked up the squirming infant, running a finger over the little girl's cheek. Will could see the tender wistfulness stamped across her face, and he knew she was thinking of the child she had lost. The ache in his chest grew unbearably sharp. God, but Jenna deserved to have her own. Boisterous and burly sons, strong and beautiful daughters. All with her raven-dark hair and her courage and heart. Never in his life had Will ever wanted to give someone something so badly.

Jenna looked up at him and faltered slightly, and Will wasn't certain what she had seen in his eyes. She pressed the wrapped bundle into Will's arms, and he looked down to find a little pink face, tiny fingers curling against the blanket. She was hopelessly small and innocent and vulnerable.

"She's perfect," he said.

"We named her Eleanor," Mrs. Wright told him shyly.

Will stared.

"Without your mother's help, we would never have survived as long as we have."

Will looked sideways at Jenna, and she gave a slight nod. He could only assume the duchess had provided them with some sort of financial support, though she had never mentioned it. Then again, she had failed to mention a lot of things, so the revelation wasn't as surprising as it should have been.

Out of the corner of his eye, the tailor stomped on something that had appeared from a hole in the wall near the plank table. With a smooth motion, he scooped it up and threw it out the window. Wright caught sight of Will watching and averted his eyes.

"Damn rats," he muttered.

In Will's arms the baby fussed, and Mrs. Wright reached for the child. With something that felt like regret, he relinquished her back into the care of her mother.

"I'm so sorry," Will said suddenly, overcome by the unfairness of the entire situation.

"I beg your pardon?" Wright looked back at him in surprise.

"I didn't know you had lost your shop. I didn't know you were...here. Living like this."

Wright sighed unhappily. "Thank you for the sentiments, Your Grace, but it wasn't your fault, to be sure. You always paid your bills on time."

"My secretary paid my bills on time," Will murmured.

The tailor might have smiled. "Then my thanks to your secretary. I only wish more of your ilk had employed similarly prompt assistants."

Will's heart sank. "You don't deserve this."

Simon Wright's face hardened. "No. I don't. And I don't intend to raise my family here. But—" The tailor didn't finish before a deafening crash came from the landing, followed by the sounds of men yelling and pounding boots on the stairs. The blanket over the doorway was torn from its tacks, and a filthy body crashed in through the opening. The man staggered to his feet, a rusty mallet clutched in his hands, his eyes wild and glazed. Behind him another man had the unconscious woman in a headlock and was dragging her down the stairs.

"Saw 'er first," the man dragging the woman down the stairs bellowed. "Find yerself another."

Mrs. Wright whimpered in distress, pulling her daughter closer to her chest. The sound caught the attention of the trespasser and he spun, a rotten sneer spreading. Jenna threw herself in front of the tailor's wife and her daughter, Wright was rushing forward, and Luke had drawn his knife, but Will was closer. Without thinking, Will snatched a broken floorboard from his feet and swung it at the wild-eyed man with all his might. The wood connected with a sickening thud, and the mallet clattered from his hand as the man went down in a heap.

Will glanced up at Luke, who was staring at him with no little shock, and then over at Simon Wright, who was trying to comfort his wife and crying daughter. He met Jenna's troubled eyes over the chaos.

"Get your things," Will said into the ensuing silence.

The tailor looked up at Will, his expression now mirroring Luke's. "I beg your pardon?"

"You're not staying here."

Wright shook his head and glanced at the body on the floor. "This happens from time to time, Your Grace. Though I thank you for your quick action, please, do not concern yourself."

"I'm not concerned," Will snapped. He threw the board to the floor with a loud clatter and gestured around the room. "Is there anything here that you wish to take?"

Wright looked at him in bewilderment.

"Luke was on his way to hire a hackney, weren't you, Luke? Pay the driver whatever it takes to get him here. Mrs. Wright should not be walking far."

"But we have nowhere else to go," Mrs. Wright said.

"I have a house that has twenty-eight rooms, none of which are currently in use. You will stay at Breckenridge."

"No," blurted the tailor. "I couldn't possibly."

The man on the floor suddenly groaned and vomited

across the warped planks. A new layer of vileness was added to the existing stench.

Will shuddered and edged back. Holy God, but this was untenable. They could argue all they wanted later. Much later. From far, far away.

"We're leaving," Will snapped. "All of us. Now."

Wright hesitated. "But—"

"But what?"

"You're a *duke*. And I am—"

"A father. With a wife and a newborn daughter who cannot live like this and survive. Again, is there anything you wish to take?"

The tailor's mouth had fallen open, and he made a visible effort to close it. "No," he managed. "But why are you doing this?"

"Because I can." Will said it with a vicious satisfaction.

"We can't go without Christian," Mrs. Wright suddenly said.

"Who's Christian?" Will demanded. He would take anyone along so long as they could leave their contemptible confines as soon as possible.

"Sam won't like us interfering," Simon hissed. "There's no way he'll let us take his boy anywhere."

"He might not have a choice," his wife snapped back.

"Who is Christian?" Will demanded again, louder this time.

"He's the son of the furniture maker downstairs. Samuel Frost. It was Sam who helped us find this place when we came here. Helped us survive at the beginning. He lost his business the same way I did two years ago. Couldn't collect what was owed."

Samuel Frost. Will had never met the man, but he was

quite certain the ornate rosewood library table and book-
case in his London town house had *S. Frost* stamped into
their undersides.

"What's happened to Christian?" It was Jenna who
asked, trepidation quieting her words.

"He got into a fight. I think he might have been cut."

Jenna made a noise of distress, followed by a curse. She
hurriedly began placing everything back into her leather
surgeon's pouch. "Badly?" she asked.

Mrs. Wright looked worried. "I don't know. Sam
wouldn't tell us much. Too proud to admit he might need
help. That he can't handle things on his own."

Will had a cynically clear picture of a mercurial young
man, out on the streets, spoiling for a fight and getting the
short end of a confrontation. This Christian didn't sound
like someone he had any interest in putting up at Breckenridge next to the Wright family. "Does this Christian
usually choose his opponents unwisely?"

Jenna stopped just long enough to give Will a bleak
look. "Christian Frost is only five years old, Your Grace."

Will felt the air leave his lungs. "I beg your pardon?"

"He tried to stop the men who were set on stealing
the bread he'd been bringing back. But they caught him
and beat him and took the bread anyway." Mrs. Wright
hugged her daughter closer and no one else spoke. "Sam
thinks he'll be fine but I don't know."

"They beat a child for bread?" Will blurted.

Four sets of eyes leveled with his own as if the answer
should be obvious. Jenna was already pushing past him,
heading for the stairs.

Will turned, helpless anger making it necessary to
speak carefully. "Get your things, Mr. Wright. Luke, find

a hackney. Or a cart or a wagon, or whatever it takes." He spun and hurried after Jenna.

In front of Will, Jenna headed deeper into the noxious confines of the building, their feet squelching across pools of water that had run in from last night's rain. At a doorway similarly covered with a rotting blanket, Jenna knocked loudly on the doorframe.

"His wife died last year," she whispered to Will. "The boy is all Samuel has left."

An instant later a man peered out, his face haggard and lined with worry.

"Hello, Sam," Jenna said quietly.

"Miss Jenna." Samuel Frost's eyes darted to her face and then to her bag.

"How's Christian?"

Christian's father shook his head, defiance rising. "He'll be fine. My boy is strong."

"He is very strong," Jenna agreed. "Mrs. Wright thought maybe I could take a quick look at him. I might have something that could make him heal a little faster." She gestured to her bag.

"Mrs. Wright should worry about her own."

"Mrs. Wright is worried about Christian too," Jenna said gently. "He is very much loved. Everyone just wants to see him well again."

Samuel's face softened slightly. "Well, perhaps you could take a quick look. Since you're here and all." His gaze landed on Will, and Jenna turned.

"This is His—"

"William," Will interrupted.

"William," Jenna repeated deliberately, "and he's helping me."

The man looked up at Will. "You a surgeon too?" he demanded.

"No," said Will, having never in his life regretted the shortcoming more than he did at that moment. His heart was slowly crumbling into little tiny pieces at the unjustifiable circumstances he had descended into.

Samuel hesitated for just a moment, then stepped aside and gestured them in.

The child was lying on a pallet above the damp and the filth, though the lower edges of the soiled sheet on which he lay were wet. He was tiny and thin, his cheeks sunken with hunger. Bruised circles under his eyes and a profusion of dark curls across his forehead accentuated his paleness.

The boy opened his soft brown eyes and looked up at Jenna. "Miss Jenna," he said, smiling faintly. "Did you come to see the new baby?"

Jenna smiled. "I did. And I thought I'd come see you too."

Christian's eyes drifted to Will. "Who are you?" he asked.

Will crouched down beside him. "I'm helping Miss Jenna. My name is William but all my friends call me Will. Do you think you can do that?"

The boy nodded, looking to his father for reassurance.

Samuel was hovering behind them, and for just a brief second, Will saw the wrenching despair and terror in his eyes as he gazed upon his fragile son. The furniture maker gave the boy a brief nod.

Christian returned his attention to Will. Jenna had placed her bag up on a corner of a pallet and crouched down beside Will.

"Where are you hurt, Christian?" she asked gently.

Alarm flared. "My side." He gestured with a bony hand to his right side. "It hurts."

"I know." Jenna nodded, her voice low and soothing. "I'm going to look." She leaned over. "Keep him talking," she whispered against Will's ear.

"I heard you were very brave," Will said to Christian.

A shadow passed over the boy's face. "They took the bread," he said. "I couldn't stop them. I'm so sorry."

Will's throat constricted. "It doesn't matter."

Jenna reached for the edge of the filthy sheet and pulled it back from the tiny torso. Someone—Will assumed it was Samuel—had pressed squares of cleaner linen over the wound, and she pulled these aside as well.

The wound looked innocent enough, a puncture just below the boy's protruding ribs. But the surrounding skin was an ugly purple and red, dried blood mingling with tiny amounts of new blood seeping from the gash. Will had seen similar wounds in horses many times. He cursed roundly in his head.

"Tell me, Christian, do you prefer butter or honey on your bread?" Will asked, forcing a grin.

Jenna was feeling very carefully around the wound, and Will knew the skin under her fingers would be hot.

The boy flinched and bit his lip. "Both," he gasped, a tear leaking from the corner of his eye.

"Ah, a man after my own heart."

It earned him a tremulous smile.

Jenna had replaced the bandages, and as she stood, Will could hear her talking to Samuel in low, urgent tones.

Will leaned forward. "I'm going to take you somewhere where there is bread whenever you want it. You may have as much as you like," he whispered. There was no other option. At Breckenridge the boy might have a chance. Here he would not. And if Will had to tie up the child's stubborn, proud father to do it, he would.

Christian looked at Will suspiciously. "Really?"

"Absolutely. But that means that we have to take a trip. An adventure."

"I like adventures."

With as much care as he could manage, he bent and scooped up the weightless boy, steeling himself against the whimper of pain the movement provoked.

He stood and faced Jenna and Samuel, uncaring what decisions had been made. Hell would freeze over before Will left this boy behind.

"We're leaving. Now."

"No." Samuel was shaking his head violently. "My boy is—"

"Hurt badly. You know it and I know it, and if you want to help him, you'll allow me to help you."

The man's face crumpled, stubborn pride giving in to grief.

Will softened his tone. "You have done all you can. Now let me do what I can. Please."

Miserably the man nodded.

"Thank you."

At Breckenridge the Wrights and Samuel Frost were provided with scrounged clothing and large quantities of soap and hot water. The local doctor was fetched, something Jenna was violently opposed to, snarling at Will that Christian couldn't afford to lose more blood by lancet or leech. Will assured her he was an army surgeon, and a veteran of Waterloo at that, someone more qualified than most to treat stab wounds. That seemed to mollify her somewhat, though she insisted on being present as he examined Christian. Will hovered, for some inexplicable reason feeling responsible for all the misery that had been pressed upon the souls now under his roof. As though he represented everything and everyone who, through negligence and arrogance, had created such a nightmare for these two families.

The doctor left Breckenridge looking grim, leaving an array of bottles and instructions behind and a promise to return on the morrow. Will sent Samuel to the kitchens with the Wrights and crept into the room where Christian rested. Jenna was still there, sitting on the end of the bed, talking quietly with the boy.

She looked up as he entered, her eyes meeting his, her expression unfathomable. She stood, and her eyes slid from his. "I'll go and check on your father," she told Christian. "Make sure he's not getting into too much trouble downstairs."

Christian smiled, as if the idea of his stern, serious father causing mischief was implausible. Washed and re-bandaged and dressed, the boy looked marginally better.

Jenna glanced back up at Will as though she might say something, then seemed to change her mind. She simply touched his arm ever so briefly and then silently withdrew.

"I like your house," Christian told Will solemnly as Jenna disappeared. "It's very grand. Are you a prince?"

Will pulled up a chair. "No," he said. "I'm just a very lucky man."

"A nice lady came and brought me some bread. With butter and honey."

Will glanced over at the small table near the bed and saw the plate his cook had left was untouched.

"I'm not very hungry right now," the boy said, a worried expression on his face. "My side still hurts."

"You can eat whenever you want," Will assured him, apprehension settling into his bones, though he forced it back. "I brought a story." He held up a worn book, the cover ragged with wear. He'd unearthed it from the depths of a dusty trunk in the nursery, where he and his sister had once played. "It was my favorite when I was your age. Would you like me to read it to you?"

Christian nodded his head. "What is it about?"

"This is a story about a prince and a dragon. A real prince."

"And a real dragon?"

Will laughed. "Of course. Is there any other kind?"

"Does the prince have a horse?"

"He does. A noble white charger."

"I like horses," Christian told him. "We had a horse once. I remember him. His name was Leo and he was brown and he used to pull my father's cart."

"And did you ride Leo?" Will asked.

Christian frowned. "No. Leo didn't like people sitting on his back. Do you have a horse?"

Will smiled. "I have five horses."

"Five?" Christian asked, his dark eyes wide. "How can you ride five horses?"

"Two are for my own...cart. One I ride wherever I need to go, and two are racing horses."

"Racing horses?" Interest sparked in the boy's eyes. "Can I ride them?"

"Perhaps one day. When you are a little older."

Christian's face fell.

Will studied him. "Perhaps when you are better, I can find you a pony to ride." An image of a little dark-haired boy trotting through the pastures of Breckenridge slid before his eyes, and Will smiled. The idea of teaching a child to ride appealed immensely. And when Will had sons and daughters of his own, he would teach them to ride too. Provided their mother didn't beat him to it.

The last thought startled Will in its certainty and longing. Shaken, he cleared his throat, unsure when that had become his truth.

"Will it be a fast pony?" Christian's voice pulled him out of his thoughts.

"The fastest," he assured the boy.

Christian nodded, apparently satisfied. "Is there a princess?"

"I beg your pardon?"

"In the story?"

Will lifted the book. "Ah. Yes, there is."

The child blinked at him, considering. "Does she need to be rescued?"

Will bit his lip. "I rather think it is the prince who needs to be rescued."

Christian made a face. "Princes don't need to be rescued. They're strong. Like you."

"Princesses can be strong too. Stronger than everyone realizes. Sometimes it is the prince who needs a little help," Will said quietly.

Christian yawned even as he made a face, clearly not convinced.

Will smiled faintly. "Shall I start?" At the child's nod, he opened the book and started to read.

Christian fell asleep almost immediately. Will sat for

a long time after he'd stopped reading, the book forgotten in his hands, watching the rise and fall of the little boy's chest.

It could have been he, this tiny dark-haired child who now slept in a duke's bed. Hunted down in the slums of London for a loaf of stale bread. But because of an accident of birth, it was not. And the worst part of the matter was that, even given the differences of birth, none of it had had to happen. The child's father was a skilled tradesman, capable of providing a secure life for his family. Until that life had been stolen away by people just like Will. Rich. Titled. Selfish.

Quietly he stood, leaving the book by the bed. He tucked the covers up under the chin of the sleeping child, brushing a stray lock of dark hair off his pale forehead and feeling shaken and powerless and not a little angry.

Three feelings that, until now, had never troubled the Duke of Worth.

～

Jenna hadn't gone to check on Samuel Frost. She hadn't gone anywhere, only leaned against the wall just outside the door of the bedroom where a duke read a children's story to a furniture maker's son. She swallowed hard, trying to dislodge the weakness that had become stuck in her throat and was burning the backs of her eyes.

She hadn't quite known what to make of Will's determination to accompany her to St. Giles. She certainly hadn't been prepared for what had unfolded. It was ironic, in a way. She had on multiple occasions begged the Wrights to leave and come stay at the dower house, at least until their baby was born, but they had always refused, their pride one of the few things they had left. Yet in the space of mere minutes, the Duke of Worth had swept that pride aside like so much dust, while managing to leave their dignity intact.

Very few men would have done what he had done. And he'd done it with no consideration for anything beyond the very real desire to give something that was in his power to give. A very large part of her wanted to confess everything. Wanted to believe that Will's actions today provided irrefutable proof that, if she were to tell the Duke of Worth everything, he would support her. Understand. At the very least not have her arrested. She wanted to believe that so badly it hurt.

She closed her eyes, hopelessly torn.

"You're eavesdropping." He had come out of the room, his boots silent on the thick carpets.

"It was a good story," she said weakly. She was afraid to look at him.

She felt his fingers brush the side of her face, and she opened her eyes. His face was grave, his eyes soft as they probed hers. "I'm so sorry," he whispered. "I'm sorry for what happened to you in the past. What you lost. I don't think I understood it—understood anything until now."

Jenna reached up and grasped his fingers in his. "Thank you."

"You will make an incredible mother. I want you to have that. I want you to be happy."

Jenna nearly gave in to the urge to cry.

She twined her fingers through his instead. "You did a good thing today."

"I didn't do it for you."

"I know." She thought her heart might have exploded, so painfully sweet was the emotion coursing through her. He hadn't done what he had done today with any sort of ulterior motive or hidden agenda. He had simply done what was right.

He was staring down at her as if memorizing her features. And then, in a single movement, he caught her face in his hands and kissed her with an urgent tenderness that left her weak and gasping.

"You've ruined me," Will said suddenly.

Jenna drew back, searching his eyes. "I beg your pardon?"

Will caught her hand in his and pressed his mouth to her knuckles. "Every woman I will ever meet from this moment will be compared to you and found wanting."

She couldn't go here. Not with this man, and ever hope to remain in one piece.

"It's my attire," she jested weakly, gesturing at her worn, dusty riding clothes.

"That's just it. It's not the clothes. It's not jewels or money or pretty baubles. It's you. There is no one else like you, Jenna."

"I'm far from perfect, Will," Jenna said, guilt building with each word.

"Perhaps, but you're perfect to me." With his free hand, he slipped a finger along the inside edge of the neck of her shirt and traced the ridge of her collarbone. "God, Jenna, but I want you."

Jenna closed her eyes, not wanting to hear any more. William's words threatened to blur the unpalatable strictures of reality, and there was only heartbreak down that road.

The duke bent his head and kissed the hollow of her

throat. "I think you might even be a better rider than I," he murmured against her skin.

"I doubt that," she whispered, trying to regain control of a situation that was rapidly spinning away from her. "I think I just ride better horses."

Will choked out some sort of sound between pain and laughter and buried his face in the side of her neck. "Marry me," he breathed.

Jenna shook her head and stepped away from him.

"You already asked me that once, and I gave you my answer." She forced a wry humor she didn't feel into her words.

"I'm serious."

"No, you're not. And you don't have to marry me to ride my horses."

In two steps Will was back at her side, her hands clasped in his. "I want you."

Jenna gently extricated herself from his grasp. "I'm flattered, Will, really I am. And there is no denying that what we have"—she waved her hand as though it could encompass everything they were—"is extraordinary."

Will stood silently.

"But you are a duke," she said, hating the resistance in his eyes at the reminder. Jenna put a hand to his cheek. "I am not a duchess," she said, "nor will I ever be."

"Why not?" It came out harshly.

Jenna sighed. "Because it is not the way of things," she said.

"And when has that ever stopped you, Jenna?" Will demanded. "Everything you do goes against the way of things!"

"Yet for it all to succeed, everything I do has to be

done in secret, Will," she said gently. "There is far more at stake than just my own interests and wants and needs. People depend on me. Do you understand?"

Will looked away.

"One day you will marry a suitable girl who will be able to give you everything you need. And if she can't, you will acquire a mistress—"

"Never," Will snarled.

Jenna stopped, frozen.

"My father," Will spit, "had a string of mistresses a mile long, each one more disposable than the last. He didn't bother with discretion, and he didn't care if it embarrassed or hurt my mother. In fact, he flaunted them in front of her. In front of society. As if to illustrate what my mother lacked. When I am married, I will never have a mistress. I will never do that to my wife." He stopped abruptly.

Jenna placed her other hand on his face and kissed him softly on the lips. "You are not your father, Will. The decisions you make on how you live your life are yours and yours alone." She kissed him again. "You will make a wonderful husband. Somewhere there is a woman who will make you insanely happy."

"I know that. I've already found her. She's kissing me right now."

Jenna dropped her head to the solid warmth of his chest, unwilling to let him see how much his words were torturing her. Will thought he knew her. But he didn't, really. And he never could.

"I don't want you to think that is what you are to me, Jenna. Disposable."

"I've never thought that."

Jenna felt his breath on the back of her neck even as his arms went around her. "I won't let you go."

"You don't have to. I'm not going anywhere." *At least for now*, she added silently. She would deal with tomorrow when tomorrow came.

Will pulled her against him, and Jenna's hands came up to rest against the solidity of his chest. She ran a finger down the lapel of his uncharacteristically worn coat and slipped her hand inside its warmth, feeling the steady beat of his heart.

Foolishly Jenna had thought herself happy these past years, doing what she was good at, surrounded by people she liked. And she had been . . . content. But now she knew something had always been missing. A hole that had been torn in the fabric of her life years ago had been, for a time, mended. Damn this man and his beautiful heart. Damn the circumstances that were forcing her to let go of something she hadn't known she wanted until it was too late.

"If you won't agree to marry me, at least promise you'll think about it," he demanded.

"Will—"

"I'm yours," he said quietly. "Whether you want me or not. So promise you'll think about it."

Jenna laid her head against his chest, letting his warmth enfold her. "I promise."

She was afraid to hope. Afraid that if she allowed that crack to widen, it might split open and leave a wasteland of disappointment and desolation and disillusionment on both sides. Years of trying to save lives endangered by those of Will's social set had left deep chasms of mistrust and cynicism. And Jenna knew she had projected undeserved assumptions on the duke simply because of his title. But just beyond her sight, a small child lay sleeping, and if Will's actions today did not bear witness to his true character, what did?

She cared about Will. More than was safe and more than was wise. And at the very least he deserved better than half-truths and deceit.

Carefully she extracted herself from his embrace. "We need to go back to the dower house."

"Of course." He was looking at her with concern.

She pulled on his hand. "I need to show you something."

"Of course." He paused. "Jenna, are you all right?"

"Yes," she lied. She was not all right.

She was in love with a duke.

Chapter 13 _____

Low clouds had gathered, threatening more rain, and a chilly wind pulled at the seams of his coat. Twilight had descended, offering only a weak light through the veil of gray as it fought off complete darkness. Jenna had been strangely silent and pensive on the short ride back from Breckenridge. Every so often she would look at him, her ice-blue eyes troubled and offering him no clue as to what was churning through her head. Their horses, eager to get home, ate up the ground with long strides and left little opportunity for conversation.

It wasn't until they had deposited their mounts in the barns and were almost back to the house that Jenna abruptly turned to him.

"I need you to promise me something now," she said.

Will nodded, frowning. It sounded ominous.

"You have to promise me not to say anything until you've had a moment to think about it. Until I can explain so you can understand." Her eyes searched his. "Can you do that?"

Will nodded again slowly, apprehension touching him with cold fingers. The first drops of rain splattered down around them.

"Promise me."

"I promise. Jenna, what—"

Jenna caught his hand and pulled him into the house.

It was silent, the occupants having already retired early in anticipation of a long day tomorrow. Steadily Jenna drew him into the small drawing room the duchess used as her study. Very deliberately she circled the room, lighting the candelabras and filling the room with a soft glow. Will watched her, sensing her need for space. When she had finished, she stood in the center of the room and gazed at Will for a long moment. She blew out a steadying breath and opened the drawer of a small side table, pulling out an old-fashioned key. Very slowly she approached Will and pressed the key into his palm.

"It opens that armoire," she said quietly.

"What is this?" Will asked. His pulse was pounding, and for the life of him, he couldn't begin to understand what was happening.

"It's the truth, Will. And you deserve to have it." She kissed him.

"The truth about what?" he demanded. "God, Jenna, you're scaring me."

"Just open it. And remember your promise."

Will walked over to the armoire, the key heavy in his hand. Carefully he fit it into the lock and turned it, the sound of the bolt loud in the suffocating silence. He had no idea what he expected. Weapons. Chickens. Witchcraft. More snakes. He steeled himself and yanked the double doors open. And stared.

The maps were of military quality, labeled with painstaking detail. Quatre Bras, Waterloo, the ridge near Hougoumont, even a map of roadways in and out of Brussels.

Troop movement was shown in colored ink, the times of the assaults noted, and the result of each skirmish. Stacks of bound leather journals stood at attention across the shelves, and Will pulled one out, flipping through the pages. These went back to earlier peninsular campaigns, effusive notes on cavalry and foot regiments, lists of artillery and naval support. At the top of each page was a date, and in some cases a name of an officer and what appeared to be his remarks or opinions. Will replaced the journal and snatched at a handful of loose papers detailing the Prince of Orange's disastrous movements against French artillery and cavalry. It was a thesis on commanding officers, arguing the need for leadership based on merit and experience and not title, presented with shining logic and insight. All of it written in his mother's neat, loopy hand.

Will stumbled back, shock and denial squeezing the air from his lungs. All of what was displayed before him was evidence of a brilliant mind capable of understanding the nuance of strategy, and complexities most military officers couldn't grasp. Yet in public, she feigned ignorance of the difference between an admiral and a captain, professed disinterest in anything more complicated than a lemonade recipe. She bumbled along, buffeted by a storm of gossip and criticism and pity and never, not once, stood up to that tempest. Eleanor Somerhall had everyone fooled. Including her own son.

His breath was coming in harsh gasps, and his composure was being threatened by overwhelming hurt and betrayal. Why? Why would she pretend to be something she wasn't? It had been bad enough to realize she had kept the details of her everyday life from him. It was worse knowing she had kept her true self from him. When had this happened, this irreversible rupture of bonds built by blood? Will realized he had no answer. When his father had died, he'd fled so far and so fast, he'd never looked back. Not once.

His eye fell on a thick envelope sitting benignly on the bottom shelf, simply labeled *Ascot*. He was terrified to open it. He was more terrified not to. Will reached for it, pulling out the thick sheaf of worn paper, folded in thirds. He opened the papers, pleased to see his hands weren't shaking as badly as he thought they should be at this point. The top page contained a comprehensive list of racehorses and owners, many of them names Will recognized immediately. Along the left-hand margin of each entry was the kind of basic information one might find in a racing calendar, but what wasn't similar was the notations beside each entry. He read the first three, frowning fiercely.

> *Mr. Bell. Whistler, 3 yo b f. Slow early, consistent late rally.*
> *Ld. Edgrehill. Bishop, 4 yo ch. h. Brief speed. Not a contender over 1½ miles.*
> *E of Gafton. Summertime, 3 yo br f. Likes outside. Kept out of traffic, will settle.*

So the three-year-old bay filly that Mr. Bell owned might catch competitors from behind at the winning post, while Bishop, Lord Edgrehill's four-year-old chestnut, would start fast and fade over distance. Will thumbed through pages of similar entries, all written with concise detail. It was a guide, he realized with shock, to the tendencies and recent past performances of racehorses. Most of which would be competing at Ascot. Will had never seen anything like it. Its value was incalculable, given there was often very little information on horses that had raced previously on lesser-known tracks.

I do like to wager on the races, his mother had said a lifetime ago. Will might laugh at the ironic truth of that statement now were he not so numbed. The duchess wasn't intending merely to wager, she was planning a careful assault on the turf at Ascot with the same attention to detail and accurate information she so valued in her military champions.

Forcing a calmness he didn't feel, Will carefully flipped through the entire sheaf, stopping abruptly as the entries changed toward the back. Here was a list of jockeys, grooms, and owners, and the notations beside each of their names chilled his blood.

> *S. Lowell. Jockey. Will pull. Min £10 paid in coin before post time.*
> *J. Framwell. Groom. Grain opium avail. Will supply.*
> *E of Grassmere. Owner Whisker, 5 yo bl h, by Colonel. switched for Bluebear, 4 yo bl h by Damascus. Cheltenham Stakes, 50 guinea purse. May 18.*

Will wasn't stupid. Cheating went on all the time at the track, though the Jockey Club had managed to curb the worst of it. But this, if it was true—Good God, this was intolerable. *S. Lowell.* Will knew exactly who Stuart Lowell was. He'd ridden for a lot of men, including the Duke of York. But Will hadn't known he could be bought. Will hadn't been aware that for ten pounds the jockey would physically prevent his mount from winning a race. He'd had no idea that J. Framwell, whoever he was, would happily supply opium to be added to a horse's feed before a race to render that horse either dead or useless. And if the last entry was to be believed, the Earl of Grassmere had secretly switched horses to win the Cheltenham Stakes.

What Will held in his hands hadn't been put together in a day. The information spoke of eyes and ears everywhere—at every track, in the barns, in the coffeehouses, and on the turf. There would be a web of spies in all these places who were somehow trusted to collect accurate information. All of which was compiled before the races at Ascot were to start, to best plan a successful campaign. The Duchess of Worth was not a duchess at all.

She was a goddamn general.

And had never once considered trusting her only son enough to give him the smallest clue about who she truly was.

❧

Jenna watched Will's face, the expression of fury and hurt bewilderment. Of everything that the duke might have discovered, his mother's deception could only be the most painful. Jenna knew Eleanor had not wished it to be this way. But distance and dissociation had thrust a wedge of uncertainty and guardedness between them that required careful mending. Something that could only be accomplished with time and truth. And a great deal of trust.

"You've known all along." It was an accusation, flung out of anger and a sense of betrayal.

"Yes."

"Why?" He sounded lost, and Jenna's heart ached for him.

She gestured to one of the chairs. "Sit."

"No."

"Please."

"I'm her son," he snarled. "Her own blood."

"Yes." She could see the wildness in his eyes, a man standing on the edge, ready to pinwheel into space.

"I've done all this for nothing," he hissed. "Because all along it's been an act." He slammed the doors of the cabinet closed. "An act, worthy of the very best theaters. She's made herself the laughingstock of society, and you've helped her do it. And I've played the fool this whole time, dancing right along to your tune."

"It hasn't been for nothing. And you're not a fool. But you need to ask yourself why."

"Another riddle." Worth's face was set, his jaw hard. "I've tired of riddles."

Jenna pushed herself away from the door. "Tell me what you see when you look at your mother." She moved to block Will's path, forcing him to pull up. "Before you saw that." She gestured at the cabinet.

Will was seething, a promise of violence quivering beneath the surface, barely leashed. "This is ridiculous. I'll not stand here and play your damn games anymore—"

"Tell me." It was a command.

Will's nostrils flared, his eyes bright with resentment.

"Tell me what you see." This time it was gentle.

Will looked up at the ceiling as if searching for control and patience. "I see a doddering old woman, absent and scattered. Oblivious to the opinions and judgments of all those around her."

"What else?"

"I see eccentricities that are tolerated by society only because she is a duchess. She does things no one in their right mind would even consider."

"Odd behavior that isn't questioned because of her rank."

"Yes." His eyes slitted, his breathing stilling.

"There is a great deal that can be hidden behind odd behavior, isn't there?"

Will was silent for a few moments. "Are you saying my mother is some kind of criminal?"

"I'm saying the rules of the ton rarely pertain to its own members. And that sometimes the law fails those it is supposed to protect."

"You're speaking of the dressmakers. And the tailor and his family."

Jenna inclined her head. "Yes. But there are others for whom the line between right and wrong is more... complicated."

"Others?"

"The last Marchioness of Valence, for example."

"What does that poor woman have to do with any of this? She's long dead."

"She'll be happy to hear that."

Will stared. "What the hell does that mean?"

She ignored his question. "It is said the marquess treated her with unspeakable cruelty before her death, though I suppose it was within his rights as her husband."

Will dropped the papers still in his hands onto a side table and pulled at his cravat irritably, tugging the linen free and balling it in his hands. "He certainly incriminated himself. But if you are suggesting that I condone—"

"Had the marquess not shown himself to be an unsuitable spouse, the Earl of Boden's sister, Lady Julia, would be married to him now, would she not?"

Will was looking at her with blank incomprehension. "The marquess was her father's choice for her. The old earl wanted Valence's title, and Valence wanted his fortune. Valence lost his own when his wife died."

"Ah, yes. A fortune in diamonds, if I am not mistaken." Jenna's fingers lingered along her collarbone.

"But . . . ," he croaked, his dark eyes darting as his mind examined each possibility from each impossible angle. "I saw her die."

"No. You saw an explosion."

He blanched as he was left with the obvious. "My mother . . ."

"Helped her escape unendurable abuse. Helped make sure Lady Julia would never suffer the same. The law may not be able to help those in impossible situations, but your mother and the marchioness can. And those diamonds have provided a means of allowing them to do that."

Will's legs folded beneath him, and he sat in a graceless heap on the wing chair behind him. "Why are you telling me this? Trusting me with this now?"

"Because I see the man who is William Somerhall. I see his honor, his heart, and his strength. And if you give the duchess a chance to get to know you, she will see what I see." Jenna dropped to her knees in front of him, reaching for his hand. "Your mother loves you, Will. But you both needed distance to escape your father. Time has healed, but that distance has made you strangers. She can't trust you, not because she doesn't want to but because she doesn't know you."

Will was blinking furiously, and he turned his head away, the muscles in his neck and jaw flexing. Beneath her touch his fingers were kneading and twisting the balled-up linen still clutched in his hand. Jenna remained still, allowing him time to absorb everything that had been hurled at him in the last minutes.

"Who else?" Will asked, still looking into the distance. "Who else knows? About my mother? About...all of it?"

"Besides those she's helped? Just us," replied Jenna. "Her staff. Everyone here has been a beneficiary of your mother's kindness and selflessness in some regard. Including me, as you well know."

The duke was silent for a long minute. "Are there others?" Will asked, turning back to look at her. "Others like the marchioness and the dressmakers and the tailor, whom my mother is helping now?"

"Yes. There are always others."

"This is why she didn't want me at Ascot. She didn't want me to interfere."

Jenna winced. "Yes. Though that was before she knew she might have your support. Some things would be harder to explain than others."

"Like this?" He picked up the papers at his elbow and opened them again. "I am assuming my mother ordered this compiled."

Jenna nodded slowly. "Her contacts simply send the information by post to her barrister's office. Before Ascot week Paul collects it and prepares a report for her. For us. That is why he was in London." Jenna couldn't tell if Will was appalled or impressed.

"These contacts she has—who are they?"

Jenna shrugged. "Beneficiaries of her generosity and

aid, or family or friends of those she's helped. Mostly grooms. Stableboys. People no one notices."

Will raised a dark brow fractionally and gestured at the many pages. "That is a lot of people."

"That is a lot of help," Jenna countered and confirmed all at once.

"And she uses this information for what? To wager?"

Jenna hesitated. "Sometimes. Sometimes to make sure our own horses win or simply to avoid a race entirely that will be unwinnable. Forewarned is forearmed."

"And what is your role in all of this?" His eyes were black and unreadable.

Oh, God. Jenna wanted to look away from him but she couldn't. She'd reached a crossroads, one at which she was going to have to make a choice. She had told the Duke of Worth she trusted him and it was time to prove it. Time to take a leap of faith. She needed to come clean and tell him exactly how she would manipulate the Ascot races and those individuals who had so unfairly profited off the backs of others.

Jenna pushed herself to her feet and wandered to the perimeter of the room. She stopped in front of a painting of a farm scene, hens and roosters scattered across the canvas with populous regularity. She took a deep breath, trying to find an angle that wouldn't make her sound like a complete felon.

"I determine if a race has been bought. For how much and by whom." God, but that hadn't exactly come out right. There were certainly benefits to knowing the outcome of a race before it was ever run, especially if it involved anyone from whom she wished to collect an outstanding debt. But the information Will held in his hand was more valuable in its potential to provide leverage for further information. More than one titled charlatan or crooked groom had been…persuaded into providing assistance when discreetly presented with allegations of his sins.

"Why have you not brought this to the attention of the Jockey Club?" the duke demanded, looking incensed.

Jenna sighed. "Some of it has been. For all the good that it does. Knowledge and hard proof are two totally different entities, as you well know. There are always rumors. But Will, it's more than just—"

"These individuals are despicable," Will erupted, venom coloring his words. "I cannot tolerate the idea that an individual would scheme to interfere with the purity of sport and competition. I've half a mind to call each of these idiots out for his iniquitous arrogance."

"Please don't," Jenna mumbled, her heart slowly sinking to her toes.

"I would certainly make sure they would never race again." The duke was grim in his declaration. "I don't care who they are. I don't care what their reasons are, for there is no reason that exists that could justify it. They are nothing but contemptible criminals. And they deserve to be treated accordingly."

There was a fortress at her crossroads, Jenna suddenly realized hopelessly. With a deep moat and a drawbridge that had just slammed shut. For William Somerhall, racing was a last bastion of honor and chivalry, where competitors could test each other stripped of titles and wealth and prejudice. Manipulating and breaking its code was akin to waiting until your foe turned his back before burying your blade deep in his flesh. No matter that flesh was already rotting from the inside out.

This was it then, Jenna realized suddenly. This was goodbye. She had known it was coming, known even beyond titles and impossibilities that this was what would separate them forever and always. Yet when she was presented with the immediate reality of it, her heart broke. While Will might be sympathetic and supportive of her cause, he would never understand or accept what she was about to do at Ascot. He could never know. She couldn't bear for him to see her as one of the despicable, criminal individuals who used racing for their own gains. For some selfish, nonsensical reason, she wanted him to remember her as something better.

"Jenna?" Will asked, concern in his face. He put the papers aside and stood. "What's wrong? You're white as a ghost."

She waved her hand weakly. "I'm fine."

He strode over to where she stood. "You're not fine."

"Isn't that supposed to be your line? You've just discovered your mother has kept an entire facet of her life from you, and I've helped her do it. *You* should be not fine." She wanted him to move away because, God help her, she couldn't. This would be easier if he were furious and bitter.

Will stared at her. "Tell me something," he said abruptly.

"What?"

"Does my mother really like chickens that much?"

Jenna hiccupped, a sound somewhere between a laugh and a sob. "Braised in cream sauce. Served with fennel and carrots."

"Jesus Christ." A smile might have lurked somewhere behind his curse. "She's like Robin Hood and Walsingham and Wellington all rolled into one."

"You need to talk to her."

"Yes."

"Are you very angry?"

"Probably."

"You are a good man, William," Jenna said, touching his face with her fingers, trying to fix in her memory the feel of his skin beneath hers.

"Jenna?" Will's breath brushed her ear. "Are you cry—"

Jenna kissed him them, trying to say what she would never be able to tell him.

"Jenna—"

"Please, Will." Once more. Once more before she walked away forever.

Will's eyes darkened instantly with desire. "Yes," he breathed. In a fluid motion, he backed her across the room, pushing her down on the long chaise lounge near the fireplace. Kneeling before her, he pulled at her boots, tossing them to the side. He ran his hands over her legs and spanned her pelvis. With quick fingers he worked at the buttons of her breeches, leaning up to kiss her.

Jenna lifted her hips, and Will slid her breeches over her bottom and down her legs. They joined her forgotten boots, and Will wrapped his hands around her calves, smoothing his palms up and over her knees and along the outsides of her thighs. He bent and pressed a trail of fiery kisses along her inner thighs, up to where she throbbed and ached. She could already feel the slickness between her legs.

Will pressed his mouth there, his tongue teasing and torturing, but it wasn't enough. She wanted to feel his weight against her, wanted his heat around her, wanted his strength deep inside.

Wrapping her fingers in his hair, she urged him up, pulling him against her. "Hurry."

He made a feral noise, shoving her back against the cushions, all gentleness gone. She could feel her urgency mirrored now as he ravaged her mouth, his tongue thrusting with a promise of what was to come. Reaching down between them, she yanked at the fall of his breeches, pulling aside the fabric so that his erection sprang free.

His hands gripped the backs of her knees, pushing her legs wide, tilting her hips so that she was open to him, exposed completely. Jenna let her head fall back with a whimper of anticipation, feeling the steel of his fingers curl into the muscles of her inner thighs, and without any further warning, he surged into her.

It was visceral and rough, Will withdrawing and thrusting with a punishing force, grinding against her with blind desperation. Instantly she felt her body start to coil, tiny stars gathering on the edges of her vision. Will must have felt it too, for he dropped her legs and covered her body with his, his chest slick with sweat, his mouth hot. He pistoned violently into her, and those tiny stars on the edges of her vision exploded into a white light as her body convulsed and she soared into a wrenching oblivion. Will buried his face against her hair and shouted, a muffled, tortured sound, as he spent himself within her, shuddering for long moments after.

Eventually he raised himself, levering his weight off of her. Jenna felt the loss keenly, though she knew it was something she would need to get used to. He dipped his head and kissed her, and the reverence with which he did broke her heart all over again.

"I'm not sure what I did to deserve you," he said, and

Jenna turned her head away so he couldn't see her stricken expression.

Taking a deep breath, she gathered her courage and faced him, forcing a brave smile. "Besides not demanding I abandon my breeches?" She was pleased with how light it sounded.

Will pushed himself to his feet and straightened his clothing, bending to fetch Jenna's from the floor. He watched as she righted her own clothes with an amused grin on his face. "Dear God, please do not abandon them on my account." His eyes roved over her legs and backside with a wolfish delight.

Jenna pulled on her boots, stalling for just a few more precious seconds with this man. Slowly she stood, looking up at him. She was out of time.

"You need to go find your mother, Will," she said evenly, forcing another smile. "For I believe you will like her very much. You two are quite alike, you know."

Will heaved a sigh, reality crashing back in. "It's late. She'll be sleeping."

Jenna smiled sadly. "Your mother never goes to sleep before midnight. She reads until then. Usually something that involves tactical artillery offenses. Or theories on equine breeding."

Will shook his head in rueful amusement. "Of course she does. Very well; I will seek her out."

Jenna went up on her toes and pressed her lips gently to his. The kiss was soft and sweet and tasted of goodbye.

Chapter 14 _____

She'd left Will a note this time.

Before she'd vanished from his life again, Jenna had at least left a scrap of paper behind. Her neat, slanted words apologized for her sudden disappearance but assured him it was for the best. She cared for him very much, she went on to say, and because of this, she could not stay. Nothing about any of that was sitting well at all with the Duke of Worth.

He should have known. Should have sensed it in the last, impulsive kiss she had pressed to his mouth. But he'd been distracted by the revelations of last night and he'd missed the signs. Instead he'd done as she'd suggested and spent the rest of the evening with his mother, a strange experience, though a surprisingly pleasant one. Jenna had been right. He and Eleanor were more alike than either of them could ever have imagined. There was still a great deal left to be said, as a handful of hours could never surmount years of lost time. But it had been a start.

At least until he'd found Jenna's note this morning.

"Where is she?" Will demanded, stalking into the breakfast room. The sun had barely crested the horizon, though the house was already buzzing with activity for their impending departure.

The duchess looked up from her plate. "Ah." She didn't pretend not to understand. "She left earlier with the grooms and horses. Isaac and your filly are traveling with them in the interest of expediency. We will follow with the carriages and trunks."

Will clenched his fists. "Why didn't she tell me this?"

His mother gazed at him in speculation, and Will was abruptly reminded of the shrewd intelligence behind those sharp blue eyes.

"Will she be with you at Windsor then?" Will demanded, not caring how his question might be interpreted.

"Sometimes," his mother replied slowly. "But like you, she will have duties outside my household. I will certainly not be able to account for her whereabouts for a great portion of the time. It is like this every year."

Will's lips thinned. No matter. He'd find her, of that he had no doubt. He'd find her and make it very clear her declarations of what was best for him were not acceptable. He would be the judge of what was best for him, and Jenna Hughes was very much included in that list. If she thought he would simply walk away from her, she didn't know William Somerhall as well as she thought she did.

"Here." The duchess was holding a folded paper out to him. "Your housekeeper sent it over early this morning."

Will snatched the note from her hand. He'd instructed his housekeeper to keep him apprised of the situation at Breckenridge.

"Any change in Christian?" asked his mother.

"No," Will said, reading the brief note. "He's the same." He wasn't sure if that was good or bad. For now he'd take it as a good sign.

"You did a wonderful thing, William," she said softly.

He shrugged. "It doesn't seem like it's enough."

Eleanor watched him, indecision creasing her face. "Perhaps..." She trailed off.

"Perhaps what?"

The duchess gave a small shake of her head, regret marring the tight smile she gave him. "Perhaps this is a matter you can address in the House of Lords," she suggested, though Will was certain that wasn't what she had initially been going to say.

"I intend to." Will was surprised he meant it. Up until now he'd been a mere spectator in every session, half the time listening with one ear while his mind wandered to more pleasurable pursuits like women and horses and cards. No more.

"Very good." The duchess pushed herself away from the table and stood. "Now if you will excuse me, I have a few last things to attend to. We leave at midday."

Will groaned. What he wanted to do was to saddle his mare and gallop after Jenna. With the racehorses in tow, she'd be traveling at an easy pace, not wishing to tire the animals. Yet if Will remained with his mother and the carriage, they'd not achieve a much better speed.

He took a deep breath, trying to find a modicum of patience. It mattered not what time he arrived at Ascot. He knew where the barns were, and if he knew Jenna, she would not stray far from her beloved thoroughbreds. It was only a matter of time before he found her.

⁓

Six days and Will had yet to find Jenna.

Six days of loitering around the barns, the turf, the town, the coffeehouses, and of course their own lodgings, hoping for a glimpse of her. But it was as though she had disappeared from the face of the earth. His mother was no help, providing only sympathetic apology. Joseph and Luke were worse, assuring Will that Jenna was around but offering conflicting memories of where they had seen her last. If she wasn't sleeping in the barns, she was supposedly at the hunting lodge. Yet returning to the lodge earned only a shrug and the vague suggestion she had departed for the barns. Even Isaac could offer him no real information, though he did give Will a slanted look clearly meant to convey he believed his employer's attentions would be better focused elsewhere. Like on the fast-approaching races.

Normally Will was quite fond of Berkshire. The forests in and around Windsor were spectacular and the road that led from Windsor to Ascot and the wide heath where the racecourse sprawled was beautiful this time of year. Elder bushes in full bloom lined the roads, while roses climbed every fence and facade in riots of color. The surrounding countryside beckoned with a lush, inviting greenery not seen in or around London. The county was, at any other time of the year, quite idyllic and peaceful.

The idyll, however, was quickly giving way to insanity as the first day of Ascot week drew near. The course itself was roughly circular, with two long extensions that stuck out from it, the old mile start that extended a short distance from the northernmost turn and the newer, longer stretch that lay straight to the east. Roads ran around and across the infield of the track, but very quickly they became difficult to navigate. Carriages arrived in droves and became stuck and blocked thoroughfares. Crowds thronged the course. Will couldn't move without running into someone he knew who wanted to talk politics or gossip or dig for inside information on the horses and riders assembling in the barns, preparing to compete. Tents and booths started popping up in the infield and all around the course at an alarming rate, selling everything from beer to bread to buttons. Gaming hells that were little more than a few stout poles covered with thick canvas proliferated, beckoning to the unwary and the unwise with great promises of fortune. Entertainers arrived in hordes—jugglers, dancing troupes, and singers. And there were three entire tents where, for a penny, a person could enter to view a collection of misshapen souls who, for a glimpse of their physical peculiarities, appeared quite happy to take a man's money.

On the track the turf had been stripped of its grass by thousands of trampling feet, and Will cringed when he looked at it. Picnickers took full advantage of any open space, and lavish meals were spread out while servants scurried and hurried. By Monday afternoon, the day before the first races were to be run, Will had been reminded at every turn why he avoided Ascot. And the Gold Cup wasn't to be run until Thursday. Will had three more days of this madness to endure.

Three more days to find Jenna and convince her he was never going to let her say goodbye again.

Jenna Hughes had never made it to Ascot. While the grooms had taken the horses directly out to the track and the barns, she had remained behind in Windsor, making her way to the Briarwood Rose Inn. Garbed in her most forgettable dress, her spectacles, and a gray bonnet pulled low over her forehead, she claimed a set of reserved rooms, tipping the young lad who hauled her heavy trunk up the stairs. Her mistress, Jenna explained to the proprietor, would arrive on the night before the races but had sent her maid ahead to prepare the rooms as she liked them.

Jenna almost never went near the barns during Ascot week. Joseph and Paul and Luke were more than competent to see to the horses, and there was little she could contribute from that end at this point. Staying away also allowed her to keep a believable distance from the Dowager Duchess of Worth and her household. And this year, the duchess's son.

She'd kept herself hidden from Will since she had arrived, though it had almost killed her to do so. She missed him with an intensity that was a constant physical pain. What had started as an attraction had turned into something far deeper, but wishing for things that could never happen was pointless. *Marry me*, he'd said twice, though she knew the words had been more of an endearment than a genuine request. At the time he'd been captivated by the notion that he might possess a partner who shared similar interests and skills. But if Will knew what she really did with those skills, he would walk away from her and never look back.

Now, late on Monday afternoon, Jenna wandered over to the window and pulled aside the curtains. She couldn't see the track from here—even viewed from the second floor of the inn, the heath was too far away. What she could see was a steady stream of horses and carriages and wagons and men converging on Windsor and Ascot like a massive army mustering its troops. And it was exactly that, she thought. A battlefield. One on which she would carefully choose her targets and exact her price.

This year she had the added benefit of possessing two thoroughbreds that had extraordinary ability and speed—enough that Jenna could confidently say they would win the races she had selected for them. It wasn't like this every year. Some years she had only one horse of adequate ability, other years none. The two horses now stabled in the barns out at the track gave her better opportunities and options.

Jenna turned from the window, nerves and something nameless sending her pulse speeding. She hoped beyond hope that William was not searching for her. The races would prove a distraction, she believed. This was his world, after all, and the filly that had made the journey with Jenna's own horses had the potential to take the Gold Cup and bear out before thousands of witnesses that the Duke of Worth had achieved success not by his title or his wealth but by his own merit.

Jenna sighed and ran her fingers along the edges of her trunk, knowing the excruciating ache in her chest would linger for a long time to come. Pressing her lips into a determined line and straightening her shoulders, she pushed the lid of the trunk open, crimson silk catching fire in the afternoon light. Jenna Hughes and all her self-pity and regret would disappear as of this moment. Because three days from now, on Gold Cup day, the most popular day of the entire meet, when fortunes were won and lost, Jenna would need to be ready. And she would do what she needed to do.

With no regrets.

Chapter 15 _____

Will watched the first two days of racing with a strange detachment. He should have been completely engrossed in the contests that unfolded before him, keenly observing, evaluating, discussing and debating the merits of each horse and its performance with others of like mind. Yet everything just seemed off somehow. Jenna had failed to reappear, and he had stopped asking about her whereabouts because it had become clear no one knew where she had gone. He was filled with a restless energy, unable to concentrate on anything for long, and found himself relentlessly scanning the crowd every time he ventured out of the barns. Because of that he used the barns as his bastion, where the sanity of routine chores ruled and the worst of the crowds were kept at a distance. It was here that the Earl of Boden found him, in the depths of a stall, stripped down to his shirtsleeves.

"They told me I'd find you in here, though I didn't quite believe them. I thought you employed people for this kind of work," Heath drawled as he stood watching Will fill a wheelbarrow with horse manure. He eyed the shovel Will had appropriated from a horrified stable lad. "Where's Isaac?"

"He took my filly out for a gallop, far away from this

debacle. She was getting edgy." Will had half a mind to follow his groom on the first fast horse he could get his hands on, only he wasn't entirely sure he'd come back. He stabbed the shovel into a pile of straw. "I can't be out there anymore."

"I can understand why." Heath glanced back at the churning masses beyond the barn door.

Will wiped the sweat from his brow, the sight of his friend somehow easing the agitation he'd been wrestling with ever since he arrived. "I wasn't even sure you had come, but I'm glad you did. You're a sight for sore eyes," he said with sincerity.

Heath made a face. "I would have sought you out sooner, but my sisters have kept me running, Viola especially. Did you know that people come to a horse race not to watch horse racing but to watch other people? Two days of racing, Worth, and I've been able to watch three races." He sounded disgusted. "Thanks to your meddling, we've been inundated with a blizzard of invitations. I've attended two picnics, one garden party, and the theater. Twice."

Will leaned on his shovel. "So don't go. You can say no."

"And leave Viola to her own devices?" The earl shuddered. "She'd crawl out her window if I locked her in her room and refused to let her attend any social engagements. She's much easier to manage if I simply accompany her to whatever entertainment she insists upon. And it's hardly fair to ask Julia to miss everything because she has an impetuous sister." He cleared his throat uncomfortably. "Speaking of whom, Viola wished me to ascertain exactly what color of waistcoat you intend to wear to the Kewitt ball this evening."

Will blinked at the earl blankly before cursing. "I forgot all about that." A ball was the last place he wanted to be.

"And are you planning to continue your memory loss into the evening?" Heath asked with amused curiosity.

"No," Will groaned. "I made a promise to your sisters." He leaned the shovel against the stall door in irritation.

"I'm sure the delectable Miss Hughes will agree to a dance?" Heath ventured. "Perhaps then you wouldn't find it so odious—"

"No," Will snapped. "Miss Hughes will not be there."

"Your mother will not attend?"

"Oh, the duchess will be there, I'm sure." Will did not want to discuss this. Not even with Heath.

Comprehension filled the earl's eyes. "Ah. Miss Hughes has disappeared again. Did she leave you a note this time?"

"Yes," Will snarled, the restlessness and feeling of loss surging back with a vengeance.

Heath stared at Will in wonder. "My apologies," was all he said.

Will waved his hand, feeling like an idiot. "Sorry. I've just been a little tense. Tomorrow is a big day."

"Mmm." Heath made some sort of sound that didn't convince either of them.

The men stood in silence for a long moment, each with his own thoughts.

Finally the earl spoke. "What color shall I tell Viola?"

Will looked at Heath blankly until he remembered the earlier question and rolled his eyes. "Gray," he grumbled. "Surely there are lots of things that match gray?" He wondered idly at his lassitude. Clothes used to interest him far more.

Heath shrugged. "Beyond my scope of expertise. But sounds good to me."

"Come, let me buy you dinner before we charge into the breach."

"You're referring to the pandemonium out there?" Heath gestured at the teeming grounds just visible beyond the barn doors.

"No," muttered Will darkly. "I was talking about the damn ball."

⁓

There was a life-size statue of a horse standing in front of Lord and Lady Kewitt's country mansion, something that hadn't been there last year.

It was quite well done, Jenna thought, carved out of white marble, and in the dying light it looked downright ghostly. That is, if you ignored the ridiculous wreaths of roses that decorated it. Jenna watched the guests who had alighted from their carriages and had stopped to gush effusively over the sculpture and sniff the fragrant blooms.

Though there was no shortage of roses. The gray stone-work of the mansion was covered with them, the plants twining their way upward on ornate trellises. The gardens that fell away on either side were equally impressive, landscaped and cultivated to perfection. From experience Jenna knew the ballroom would be no different, with massive arrangements of greenery spilling out of vases and pots. The refreshment table would be elaborate, delicacies and drinks laid out with a lavish splendor rarely seen at such events, if for the cost alone. The orchestra would be talented and seamless. And overhead, a thousand candles mounted on shimmering crystal chandeliers would provide a magical, flattering light to the entire scene. There was a reason invitations to the Kewitt Gold Cup ball were coveted. It was an event known for its daring extravagance, and everyone who was anyone attended.

Jenna paused on the wide stone steps leading up to the imposing mansion. He was here somewhere, she knew. She'd been there when William had made his promise to Boden's sisters, and if she knew anything about the Duke of Worth, it was that he was a man of his word. He'd be easy to avoid because he would stand out in the crowd as he always did with his height and dark looks. Women would flock to him, all hoping to catch the eye and the interest of one of the most eligible bachelors in England. And if Jenna allowed herself the weakness, she could easily be consumed by jealousy, because the thought of another woman on his arm made her stomach churn. But she couldn't afford such a petty indulgence because she couldn't lose sight of who she was or why she was here.

She took a deep breath, wincing as she did so. Her stays were nearly suffocating, and every time she glanced down, the amount of padded cleavage on display startled her. Her head itched under the blond wig, and the jewelry at her throat and ears felt heavy and foreign. If all of that wasn't a stark reminder of the reality of the situation, she didn't know what was. Nevertheless, Jenna knew her disguise was flawless. It had been an entire year since Margot Maxon had set foot in fair England, and the wealthy widow had just returned in style.

The whispers started the moment Jenna entered the already-crowded ballroom, just as she'd expected. Holding her head high, she sauntered through the crowd, a suggestive, mocking smile touching her lips. Her dress was scarlet, bordering on bordello, and stretching the very limits of French fashion. It was constructed of the finest glacé silk, trimmed with satin and edged with obscenely expensive blonde lace. Rubies dripped from her ears and throat, and more were wound through her golden ringlets. Long white gloves reached past her elbows, the leather impossibly soft, and dainty slippers of the same material peeked out from under her hem. Jenna Hughes had ceased to exist, and in her place was the elusive French widow, Margot Maxon, a woman of inestimable wealth and an obsession with horses and gambling.

And tonight she would be seeking out a very specific list of men.

"Madame Maxon." A gravelly voice cut through the hum that followed her. "We've missed your delectable presence all year."

Ah, her first mark. How convenient he should come to her.

Jenna stopped and turned, carefully arranging her face into a mask of enigmatic invitation. "Lord Brockford," she purred. "We meet again. A true delight, *n'est-ce pas*?" Her accent was as manufactured as her coiffure, yet no one had ever questioned it. The men on whom she bestowed her fleeting company were generally easily distracted. It was Ascot week, a week of dalliances, debauchery, and daring, where the rigidity of London society slipped.

The old earl let his eyes slide down her body, though he made an effort at subtlety. "It is indeed," he replied.

"I have heard the year has been kind to you since we last met. You are a bridegroom again, *oui*?" Jenna asked. She leaned forward slightly, and the earl's gaze followed. "And a young, beautiful bride, I hear."

The earl frowned slightly, as if annoyed by the

reminder of his spouse. "An expensive, impulsive bride," he grumbled.

Jenna laughed, a gay, tinkling sound. She knew more merchants than just the dressmakers of London were well acquainted with how expensive his new wife really was. "But I'm sure your generosity is well rewarded, *non*? What else is a fortune for if not to be spent on things that can give us pleasure?" She breathed out the last word.

Brockford gave Jenna a sly look, his eyes darting to the side to ensure they would not be overheard. "Rumor has it you have done quite well for yourself these last two days. And I know you made a fortune here last year, betting on the races."

Jenna shrugged with a coquettish smirk. "Perhaps."

"How?"

"How?" Jenna put a hand to her throat, playing with the diamonds around her neck. "Why, luck, of course."

"No one has that much luck," he growled. "I lost a great deal of money last year, and I want it back."

Jenna smiled at him. "Are you insinuating something, my lord?"

"Tell me how you do it."

Jenna let her gaze linger, as if she were considering his demands. "I might know...things," she said slowly and then smirked. "Men do so like to talk."

"What sort of things have you heard?"

Jenna smoothed the soft leather of her long white gloves with insolence. "Information is very valuable, my lord."

The earl narrowed his eyes. "What do you want?"

"What is it worth to you?"

Brockford frowned and reached for his cravat. Yanking a diamond pin from the linen, he held it out to Jenna for inspection. "Have it made into a necklace," he said carelessly.

Jenna plucked it from his fingers and examined the stone. It was comparable in size and quality to the one the duchess had sold to help the Monroes. How very fortuitous.

"Very well." Jenna tucked the pin into the top of her glove, secure against her skin. "I have heard the Duchess of Worth has two horses running tomorrow. A colt, in one of the earlier races, and a filly in the Trafalgar Stakes. It is the three-year-old filly that is of interest."

The earl made a rude noise. "The Duchess of Worth? That crazy old harridan? What the hell does she know about horses?"

Jenna tipped her head patiently. "*Mais oui*, my lord, you are correct. The old woman knows nothing, other than a desire to indulge her fancies. But her son is different."

Brockford had frozen. "The duke?"

"The duke knows a great deal about racehorses— everyone is aware of that. I have heard it said that her son has spent a great deal of time with his mother as of late. And her filly."

The earl was frowning. "He would have chosen and bought it for her. Had it trained for her."

Jenna shrugged and said nothing, letting the earl draw whatever conclusions he wanted.

"But how does this help me?" Brockford demanded. "Even if this horse is as good as you seem to think, this is nothing everyone else won't already know."

"Ah, but the duke does not choose all." Jenna dropped her voice to a whisper.

"What does that mean?"

"The duchess, she insists on choosing the jockey for her horse."

"Who is the jockey?"

"A very . . . how do you say? A very *enterprising* young man. A shame should the Worth filly become stuck behind the field at the winning post, *non*?"

The earl's eyes narrowed. "Indeed? Do tell."

Jenna smiled.

Will was hovering behind a marble column, trying to make himself invisible. Three times he had been pressed to dance, and twice he had failed to make good an immediate escape afterward. He'd done better the last time and was not about to ruin that meager success. He checked the timepiece in his pocket and groaned. He'd been here a bare forty minutes, when he had been certain it had been hours.

"You're going to have to come out eventually," Heath said, sidling up beside him. The earl had a decidedly hunted look on his face.

"Why didn't you tell me there was no cardroom when I agreed to this?" Will growled.

"An oversight on my part. My apologies." Heath paused. "I don't suppose you've seen Viola recently?"

Will shook his head. "No. Whom is she with?"

"The last I saw of her, she was with one of her friends, Lady Sara Pennington."

"Who?"

"The youngest daughter of Lord Mayberry."

Will shrugged. He knew nothing of the Penningtons. "Is that a bad thing?" he asked, catching sight of Heath's worried frown.

"I don't know. Lady Sara is sweet, but I don't know that she would object should my sister suggest they both jump off a cliff."

"Ah." Will edged around the column, surveying the crush across the ballroom. "Surely she's here somewhere?" A flash of red caught his eye. "Good God." The crowd shifted, and a woman in a crimson ball gown was revealed briefly before the crowd swallowed her again. "Who is that?"

Heath had followed his gaze. "Ah, yes, you wouldn't be acquainted with the notorious Madame Maxon, since you never attend any Ascot festivities." The earl sounded a little envious of Will's absences.

"Madame who?" Will could see her again, turned slightly away from him. He had an impression of a statuesque blonde, her ringlets glittering with threaded rubies and a bosom threatening to spill over the top of a truly scandalous dress. Her attire was not only shocking in its cut but in its color, and in a sea of pale pastels, the Frenchwoman stood out like a tropical bird in a flock of sparrows. The very type of woman he tried to avoid.

"She is a regular at Ascot every year, though apparently she lives somewhere in France. A widow, I've been told, and richer than God. And smarter than Him too, if her gambling success is any measure. I hear she is unearthly lucky at picking winners. Rumor has it she's been on a tear the last two days."

Will looked at Heath dubiously. "Rumor has it? Since when do you listen to rumor?"

Heath shrugged. "Since the Earl of Melthorpe told me he won over a thousand guineas wagering on Lord Darlington's colt Belville in Tuesday's Oatlands Stakes at her

urging. Which is of particular note, especially since Melthorpe confided he had fully intended to wager on Lord
Lowther's colt Garus again. Garus, if you might recall,
won the same race last year at twelve-to-one odds and
Melthorpe won almost two thousand guineas then, thanks
to the guidance of Madame Maxon."

"Melthorpe?" How was it that Heath seemed more
familiar with London society than he was?

"I do some business with him. He also helps fund the
foundling hospital up by the spa fields." The earl looked at
him expectantly, as though the last should jog Will's memory.

Will shook his head in defeat. He wasn't familiar with
the man, though he certainly sounded like a good sort.
Out of the corner of his eye, he watched as the woman in
red threw back her head and laughed, the crowd of gentlemen she was entertaining utterly captivated. That crowd
included the young Lord Braxton, heir to the dukedom
of Havockburn. There was something familiar about her,
Will thought, before dismissing the notion almost immediately. She was familiar because he'd met women just
like her a hundred times.

He had no interest in making it a hundred and one.

⁓

Viscount Carthart slurped noisily on his punch, darting
his eyes from side to side and twitching as if Jenna were
imparting Crown secrets.

"I don't understand," he grunted.

Jenna scoffed. "The betting post? So provincial, *non*?"
She leaned forward, glancing surreptitiously over her
shoulder. "The betting post is for...how do you say it?
Amateurs."

The viscount, when he tore his eyes from her décolletage, blinked at her.

"Numbers and odds, my lord, are what drive your profit, and Mr. MacGregor at the Four Kings can offer far better opportunity than the bookkeepers. You will find him and his establishment just behind the betting stand. Tell him I sent you, and he will take good care of you."

"It sounds risky."

Jenna smiled, her gaze smoky and full of promise. "Ah, but with risk comes great reward, *non*? A man such as yourself cannot be a stranger to that."

Carthart's chest inflated with vanity. "You are right, of course." His eyes narrowed. "And the other? You are confident he can be trusted to go through with what he promises?"

Jenna shrugged. "As confident as one might be in a man who offers himself for sale. For one might never know when there is a higher bidder."

"Perhaps I ought to offer further... encouragement."

Jenna offered the cadaverous viscount a wide smile of approval. It was unfortunate the viscount hadn't offered the same monetary encouragement to the masons who had spent five months repairing his decaying country manor. It was unfortunate he hadn't yet offered them any money at all.

Nearby someone was hailing the viscount. He rubbed his hands together, naked avarice gleaming. "I'll bid you a good evening for now, Madame Maxon. Thank you for such an... enlightening conversation. It's been a pleasure." He offered her a deep bow, his eyes lingering well below her chin, before he lumbered off.

Jenna watched him go, careful to keep her expression serene and her voice low. "No, Lord Carthart," she whispered to his retreating back, "the pleasure is all mine."

⌐

"I don't see Viola," Will said, scanning the crowd.

Heath was visibly nervous. "I'm going to go take another look. I don't like the idea of her unsupervised. There are a lot of titled gentlemen here tonight. Who knows what sort of plan she might concoct?"

"I'll help. Perhaps she's out on the terrace? Or in the gardens?"

"Oh, God." The color drained from Heath's face.

"Alone," Will added hastily. "Or with Lady Sara."

Heath gave Will a strained smile.

"I'll go take a look outside," Will reassured him. There was no way in hell he was going to venture back into that crowd, not even for Viola.

"Thank you," Heath said, before hurrying off, his blond head visible above the crowd as he threaded his way through a morass of bodies.

Will took the safer route through the potted palms, escaping into the cool night air.

⌐

Jenna had retreated to a chair deep in a corner of the ladies' retiring room, hidden by a massive Chinese vase from which a profusion of hothouse flowers sprouted. A maid had approached her carrying a decorated chamber pot, but Jenna had waved her off. She simply needed a moment to rest her brain and her wits, feeling exhausted but fiercely satisfied with her efforts tonight. Starting with Lord Brockford, she had spun her stories and woven her web, pulling in a dozen lords and gentlemen who had stolen the very lives of those who served them. She was almost done. Everything else would unfold starting with the first race tomorrow.

She had just stood when the sound of Will's name snapped her head around.

"He's divine," giggled a voice from the other side of the room, which Jenna identified instantly as Viola's.

"And rich," breathed an unseen friend.

"I don't care about th' money," Viola said with care, and Jenna realized Boden's sister was quite drunk. "My brother has loads and loads already." There was a long pause punctuated by a hiccup. "D' you think he's good... you know..."

"Good?"

"In bed?"

Scandalized gasps and more giggles all around. Jenna sank back onto her chair feeling hot and cold all at once. *A resounding yes*, she thought. He was better than good.

"I want him."

Jenna froze. Viola sober was impulsive and self-involved in the innocuous way young girls sometimes are. Viola drunk was impulsive and selfish and a nightmare waiting to happen.

"I'm goin' to have him," she continued. "I'm goin' to *marry* him."

"You can't just make a duke marry you," a voice of reason piped up.

"Yes, I can," Viola giggled, but it had an edge now. "What if we were caught?"

"Caught? What do you mean?"

The voice of reason wasn't very clever, Jenna thought rudely.

"If I was comprised."

"Comprised?"

Hic. "No. Compris—com-pro-mised." Viola finally got the syllables right.

"Oh. Goodness. Is that a wise idea?"

Of course it isn't, seethed Jenna. Did Lady Viola not understand how much grief such an idiotic plan would bring down on herself? And her brother? And Will?

"We're fam'ly friends. He likes me. He'll 'ave to marry me. So will y' help me?" Viola demanded.

"I suppose."

"Good. Listen caref'ly. He's on the terrace. I'll go out there an—"

"How do you know he's on the terrace?"

"I saw 'im go out there. He hates dancing. An' there's no cardroom tonight. That's where he hides."

"Oh."

"Wait one minute then follow me. An' bring a bat." *Hic.*

"A bat? Like a wooden one?"

"Like an old one. Lady Gainsey or Lady Baustenbury will do. Unnerstand?"

"Oh. That kind of bat. Yes, I suppose. Are you sure?"

"Of course I'm sure. He's a duke. I'll be a duchess. I need t' be a duchess. No one looks down on a duchess." There was no giggling with this vehement statement.

A swish of skirts swept by, and Jenna shrank back behind the vase. Dammit. She peered around the giant flower arrangement only to watch Viola and her friend exit the retiring room. Viola's color was high, her eyes were bright, her mouth was set, and she looked like a woman on a mission. Albeit one who wasn't walking very steadily.

Jenna cursed inwardly and hurried after them, impeded by a steady stream of women coming up the stairs. She almost reached Viola at the bottom landing, only to find herself helplessly swallowed up by the crushing crowd. Lady Viola and her imbecile friend dispersed like smoke in a storm. Even with her height, Jenna quickly lost Viola in the press and was left frozen in indecision.

Jenna had heard far more outlandish vows born of alcohol in her lifetime. Given enough wine, any eligible lady with a pulse would be giddily declaring her desire to possess a very wealthy and sinfully handsome duke. But to actually attempt what Viola had sworn to do was another thing altogether.

Jenna would like to believe Will could handle the situation even if Viola did the unthinkable. But he wouldn't be expecting a childhood friend to manipulate him in so cruel a manner. He wouldn't suspect anything until it was too late. Jenna swore under her breath, frantically looking about for Eleanor, but the duchess was lost in the crowd. The Earl of Boden was nowhere in sight either. There was no one she could prompt to warn Will of what Viola intended. No one to protect the reputation of a lady and the future of a duke except the notionally licentious Madame Maxon.

Her eyes fell on the tall terrace doors on the far side of the ballroom, and she took a steadying breath. She'd take a quick look. Make sure Viola wasn't doing anything stupid. It was possible Will wasn't even out there any longer and there was nothing to worry about.

One quick look. Will would never even see her or be any the wiser.

*Chapter 16*_____

William leaned over the stone balustrade and then glanced up at the moon, trying to estimate how much longer he would have to endure this excruciating ball. He'd been pleasantly surprised to find the terrace empty, and he'd been in no hurry to abandon his newfound privacy. He was content to be out here alone with his thoughts, the raucous sounds muted beyond the tall doors.

He desperately wished Jenna were here. He missed her laughter, her banter, her company, her warmth—he missed everything about her. A small part of him was desperately afraid that she was lost to him forever. What seemed like forever ago, she'd said goodbye, and somehow he'd foolishly dismissed it, confident he would find her and convince her...convince her of what? That he needed her? Wanted her? Loved her?

The last idea left him short of breath. Yet what other explanation could there be, when a single night with her was not enough? A lifetime with her might not be enough.

"Your Grace?" A feminine voice cut through his musings, and he started.

He turned around to find Lady Viola standing hesitantly

at the frosted glass doors leading from the ballroom. He felt a measure of relief at the distraction as well as a vague needling of guilt at the knowledge that he hadn't done much to seek her out and ensure her well-being. Well, no matter now.

"Lady Viola," he said, pushing himself away from the railing, "whatever are you doing out here by yourself? I would have thought your dance card would have been full." He smiled at her.

Viola didn't say anything, only staggered toward him, a strange expression on her face. She stumbled, and he caught her, realizing she was utterly foxed. Good God, but her brother would be furious.

"Don't let Heath catch you like this," he warned her. "He'll have an apoplexy. How much wine did you drink?"

"Don't 'member." She was gazing up at him with something that looked suspiciously like adoration.

"Coffee," he said, "always does the trick. But don't tell Heath I told you that."

Viola stared at him, swaying and silent in the moonlight. She must be more intoxicated than he'd thought. Usually he couldn't get her to stop talking. Dammit, but he should have been keeping a better eye on her. He'd promised Heath he would, and now—

Viola raised her hands to the top of her bodice. Oh God, was she going to be ill?

"Lady Viola, are you quite all right? I don't— *Jesus*!"

Viola had yanked down the front of her dress, and her rather generous breasts popped free, pale and heaving.

"What the hell are you doing?" William hissed, trying his best to pull her dress back up over her chest.

"Marry me," she said, then giggled.

"Are you insane?" The fabric of her dress ripped as he struggled.

"No." *Hic.* "You're jus' so handsome." Lady Viola lurched on her feet and gave him a victorious if somewhat blurry grin. "An' you're a duke. An' I'll be a duchess. I wanna be a duchess, Will."

The sound of approaching conversation intruded, and in that moment, Will knew he'd been played. Tricked like a green boy and well and truly caught. Through the frosted pane, he could make out a blurry gaggle of colorful skirts, bearing down on the terrace doors like a company of executioners to seal his downfall. The Duke of Worth was about to be caught in a blatantly compromising position with Lady Viola Hextall. He'd do the right thing and marry her, of course, because this was his best friend's sister. A woman he'd known almost all his life. And a woman he'd severely underestimated.

Goddammit all to hell. And back again.

"*Mon Dieu*," a voice murmured. "This is awkward."

Will's head snapped up, and he watched in horror as the woman in the outrageous red dress sauntered out from the shadows. "This isn't what it looks like," he rasped.

"I see a very desperate woman trying to trap a duke. This is not correct?"

"No! Yes!" Will heaved on Viola's bodice frantically.

"Go 'way," slurred Viola, narrowing her eyes at the intruder. "I'm gettin' married."

She tilted sideways and the Frenchwoman jumped forward to steady her with a surprising strength. "Perhaps not tonight, *chérie*," the woman murmured as she propped Viola up and peered over the edge of the terrace.

The gems in the widow's pale hair glittered, and the feeling of familiarity assailed Will once again.

Shrill, indignant voices intruded. Whoever was approaching had almost reached the terrace doors—the only remaining barrier between Will and a prison of matrimonial disaster. This wasn't happening.

"Do you want to marry this girl?" the Frenchwoman asked calmly.

Viola was hiccupping and snorting, her bared breasts jiggling in the moonlight. "Yes!" she garbled. "He wants t' marry me!"

"No!" Will wheezed. "Hell, no!"

"Just making sure," the Frenchwoman said as the handles to the terrace doors rattled.

In a casual movement, she gave Viola a gentle push, and Heath's sister tipped sideways over the low balustrade just as the doors swung open.

"Jesus!" Will yelped, staring at the spot where Viola had just been standing.

A posse of women tumbled out onto the terrace, led by the Countess of Baustenbury, their eyes sweeping the expanse and finding nothing except a duke in conversation with the very wealthy, if somewhat risqué, French widow. Nothing that might not be expected of the roguish Duke of Worth.

Will forced himself to steady. He drew himself up and gazed with icy annoyance at the countess. "Lady Baustenbury," he said with exaggerated politeness, "is there something amiss I can assist you with?"

The countess turned on a quailing young woman beside her and scowled. "I heard a rumor that a young lady was in danger of being compromised out here." She snapped her fan open and shut.

"By me." He didn't mean it as a question but as a statement, laced with the promise of terrifying retribution should her response be something he didn't like.

The countess sputtered slightly. "Of course not. I gave the rumor no credence, Your Grace," she sniffed.

Beside him the Frenchwoman uttered a low, throaty chuckle, and Will jerked at the sound, a strange, surreal sensation beginning to curl through him.

"Your concern for my virtue is noble," his companion said, clearly amused. "But this duke, he is ten years too late to ruin my virtue, *non*?"

The smoky innuendo was unmistakable. It had haunted Will's dreams and his days, and he would have recognized it anywhere.

A buzzing started in his ears, and it grew even as he watched the countess suck in a scandalized breath and saw her face pinch. Without another word Lady Baustenbury turned and waddled back in the direction from which she had come, the others slinking after her. The terrace doors snapped shut, and Will whirled.

"*Jenna?* What the hell?" he wheezed. Then in the next breath, "Holy God. Viola. She's—"

"She's fine," his rescuer said. "See for yourself."

Will peered over the railing and realized it was a very small drop, given the massive hedges growing directly beneath them. Viola was sprawled in the center of one, her pale gown glowing in the moonlight, alternatively giggling and hiccupping.

He turned back, only to find the widow was almost at the terrace doors, intent on escape. In a heartbeat Will was in front of her, blocking her path and staring at the top of her lowered head.

"Look at me," he hissed.

She was shaking her head. "Don't do this."

"Look at me, goddammit." Will put his hands under her jaw and forced her head up.

In the light filtering through the glass of the doors, he got his first good look at her face. Ice-blue eyes expertly outlined with the barest hint of kohl met his, troubled and pleading.

"What are you doing, Jenna?" he asked hoarsely. "What is this?" His fingers touched a blond ringlet, the red silk, the cosmetics on her face. Bloody hell, but he might have passed her on the street and never recognized her.

Jenna closed her eyes. "It's nothing."

"Bullshit," Will snapped. "You disappear from my life without so much as a farewell and then you show up here, dressed like a Parisian whore, flirting your way through the cream of London society."

"It's not what you think," Jenna mumbled.

Anger rose, choking and virulent. "You have no idea what I'm thinking right now," he hissed. "But I'm still not good enough for you, am I?" he asked, hurt cutting deep through the fury. "After everything, I'm still not to be trusted. I'm still just a duke."

"No. Don't say that. This was never supposed to happen. You were never supposed to happen." Her eyes glittered suspiciously in the pale light. "You're more than just a duke. God, you're so much more."

Will wasn't moved. "Then prove it. Or I swear I'll march into that ballroom and expose you for who you really are." It was reckless and callous, and Will no longer cared.

Jenna's complexion had gone ashen, and she swallowed

with difficulty. Very slowly she reached into her beaded reticule and pulled out a pretty dance card.

Will snatched it from her hand. Turning so that the muted light from the ballroom spilled across the surface, he read a list of names—viscounts and earls, barons and a marquess. Beside each of their names was a number.

"It's what they owe," Jenna said into the silence, her voice wooden. "It's what they've stolen from people who have no recourse to claim what is rightfully theirs." She stopped. "It's what I will get back for them."

Will read down the list. Many of the names he knew—men he often dined with at one of his clubs. Men who sat in the House of Lords with him, who had invited Will and his family into their homes in the past for meals and music and other entertainments. He glanced back at Jenna, who was standing ramrod stiff, staring somewhere over his shoulder, her face expressionless.

Madame Maxon, he heard Heath's voice say in his ear. *A regular at Ascot every year. Unearthly lucky at picking winners.* Will remembered the list of horses and their performances he'd found at the dower house. The list of men who could be bought and bribed.

"You're fixing the races." He said it with disbelief and horror.

"I'm making sure these men believe them to be fixed." Jenna met his eyes, her features rigid.

"You're swindling them." He was still having a hard time wrapping his mind around it. "You're a goddamn confidence artist. A thief."

She smiled, a terrible, brittle gesture, sad acceptance in her eyes. "I suppose you would see it like that, Your Grace. But yes, I am."

The formal address and her admission hung in the air, insurmountable in their pairing.

"Jesus Christ," Will cursed and spun away from her. "You do it every year, don't you?"

"Yes." There was no apology in her answer. "I don't expect you to understand. You've made your views quite clear on the worth of those individuals who trespass on the sanctity of the sport. Unfortunately, it is not about me, nor is it about your opinion of me."

Will seethed, a maelstrom of emotion swirling and surging, making it hard to think. Disappointment. Anger. Disbelief. Betrayal. Heartache. His next thought iced his blood. "My mother is in on this, isn't she?"

"Yes." Again it was without remorse. "Will you have me arrested?" Her question was cold.

"Arrested?" Will was brought up short. "No!" He couldn't do that without implicating his mother. And ultimately calling his own integrity into question.

"Thank you." She paused. "Will you expose me then, as a fraud? A thief?" She gestured to the ballroom. "Your audience awaits."

"I—" Will opened his mouth to speak but found he had nothing to say. He should expose her. He was the Duke of Worth. A member of the Jockey Club. A thoroughbred owner and competitor in good standing. A vocal opponent of those who would sully the sport with corruption.

But he couldn't do it. No matter what happened, no matter what Jenna Hughes did, he couldn't do what society or the rules of racing demanded.

And he didn't want to examine why.

"No." He felt defeated, breathless, and empty.

"Thank you then, Your Grace, for your compassion

and leniency. There are many families such as the Wrights and the Frosts who will have cause to thank you for it."

"There has to be a better way!" Will realized he was almost shouting and checked himself.

Jenna looked at him, a tired, jaded slant to her features. "You think I like doing this? You think this makes me happy?"

Will stared at her.

"Please let me know when you find an alternative manner in which to collect not just money but entire lives that are owed, Your Grace. Until then, I bid you a good evening." She turned to leave.

"Wait," Will blurted. She couldn't walk out of his life again. Not like this. "What about the Gold Cup?" he demanded. The race his filly would run in. The race he had pinned his reputation on.

Jenna smiled faintly. "Fandango will likely go in the favorite, but you should tell Isaac to keep an eye on Blake's colt, Sir Richard. That colt will be carrying less weight, and he likes the distance. Mr. Blake will instruct his rider to keep his horse steady with the field, and he'll make his move in the last furlong when the others are fading. Your filly will beat him, but you'll need to ask for speed at the end."

Will remained silent.

She stopped, then closed her eyes briefly. "But that's not what you're asking, is it?"

"No."

"I have no agenda for the Gold Cup, Your Grace. If the race is tampered with, it will not be by me."

Will wanted to scream. To punch something or kick something—anything to release the emotion that was threatening to suffocate him. Never before in his life had he been so torn. Never in his life had right and wrong been reduced to such a morass of muddy confusion.

"You need to fetch Lord Boden," Jenna said tonelessly. "His sister is starting to get loud. Someone is bound to hear."

Startled, Will realized he had forgotten all about Viola, and suddenly became aware of a horrible caterwauling coming from the hedge beneath them. From somewhere on the grounds, a dog began howling in answer.

"It would be better for everyone if her brother found her first and took her directly home. The Countess of Baustenbury might not be so understanding." Jenna took a step backward.

Will moved faster, capturing her face with his hands, searching her eyes.

"Please let me go."

"I can't."

"Don't make this harder than it needs to be, Your Grace." Jenna refused to look at him.

"It's too late for that," he whispered, anguished.

The terrace doors behind them suddenly rattled, and light spilled across the terrace.

"Worth?" The Earl of Boden stood in the doorway, peering into the darkness. "Are you out here?"

Jenna slipped from his hands.

"Yes," replied Will, watching helplessly as Jenna drifted past Heath and back into the ballroom.

"Have you seen Viola?" Despite his distraction, the earl gave Madame Maxon an odd glance and raised an eyebrow as he finally located Will in the darkness.

"Good Lord, Worth, but what were you doing out here

with—" he stopped abruptly. "What is that god-awful noise?"

Will raked his hands through his hair, the feeling of loss so intense it was blurring his vision.

"Worth?" Heath strode forward, frowning fiercely. "Are you all right?"

"No," rasped Will. "I'm not. I'm not sure when I will be."

Heath stared at Will, perplexed.

With heavy arms, Will began shrugging out of his coat. "Get your carriage, Boden. I found Viola."

Chapter 17 ——————

Numb and heartsick, Will had returned to the ballroom after he'd helped Heath smuggle Viola out of the garden and into the earl's waiting carriage. He'd agreed to remain just long enough to offer explanations and regrets on behalf of Heath, who, for any who inquired, had kindly taken his youngest sister home when she had complained of a headache. He'd also promised Heath he'd fetch Julia and see her home safely, but as he searched the ballroom with increasing frustration, she remained elusive, swallowed by the crowd.

But not Jenna.

Now that he knew who the woman in red was, he couldn't seem to avoid her. She was everywhere he looked, this woman he knew intimately but somehow had never known at all. It was like an arrow punching through his chest every time he caught a glimpse of her. And no matter how hard he tried, William hadn't been able to reconcile what he knew to be right with everything he knew to be wrong.

Jenna was a thief. And not just the simple sort that was everywhere, picking coins and watches from pockets, but the kind that swindled men out of entire fortunes. The kind that set up elaborate schemes and ruses that sucked men in and saw them stripped of their wealth. And she had, from what he understood, been doing it for years. And she didn't apologize for it.

But then, a little voice whispered in his ear, *the men she targets did the very same. Except their victims didn't have titles.*

But that did not make what Jenna did right. That did not give her the liberty to steal and cheat. And to do it here, at the racetrack, was an unspeakable betrayal of the very thing Will believed in. No matter his feelings toward Jenna, he did not think he could ever forgive her for that. It was deplorable.

Like the conditions you found the Wrights and the Frosts living in. The little voice was back, but Will pushed it to the side.

These men William knew. Surely, if given the chance, they would do the right thing and settle their debts. Surely, if presented with the consequences of their actions, they would rectify their failings.

His eye was once again drawn to the flash of crimson silk. This time it was along the edge of the ballroom, where Will could see the young and decadently dressed Lord Braxton loitering. Nineteen, handsome in a pretty way, and all too aware of it, he had his eyes fixed eagerly on the form of Jenna as she approached. Will watched as Jenna drew a small square of paper from her reticule and passed it to Braxton with discreet smoothness. The young lord clutched it to his chest while Jenna only inclined her head and moved off casually. The entire exchange had taken mere seconds, and by everyone else it went unnoticed. Braxton glanced about him before unfolding the paper, peering at it with a cunning delight.

Without thinking of what he was doing, Will strode forward, closing the distance quickly, and crashed into the back of the duke's son, knocking the man forward and sending the paper fluttering to the floor.

"Good heavens, Braxton, my humble apologies," Will spluttered, putting out a hand to steady the slight man. "I wasn't looking where I was going. Here, let me get that for you." He bent, leaning over the message. He had mere seconds to read it.

It was a track surgeon's receipt dated two days ago. Instructions to a M. Billeck for the proper care and poulticing of a severe quarter crack in a left hind hoof. A recommendation that the horse should not be run until the crack grew out, and a warning that the horse would show poorly or be permanently damaged should it be raced. Along the bottom, in Jenna's distinctive handwriting, *Dalliance* had been scrawled and underlined twice.

What the hell was Jenna up to?

He scooped up the paper and handed it carelessly back to Braxton. "Enjoying the races, Braxton?" he asked with forced joviality.

"Indeed," the young man said, and slid the paper back into his pocket furtively. "I understand you're running a horse in the Gold Cup tomorrow?"

"I am," Will responded automatically.

"Is it a filly?" Braxton asked.

"I beg your pardon?" Will's eyes wandered in search of red silk despite his best efforts.

"Your horse. I believe someone told me it was a filly. Normally I do not like to wager on the weaker sex. I simply do not like to be seen supporting a losing cause, you understand."

Will turned to stare at the youth in distaste, wishing now only to get away from this fluff of a man. "Couldn't have that, now could we?" he said, though Braxton didn't appear to have heard him but was instead studying Will's waistcoat intently.

"I say, Your Grace, is that new?"

Will looked down. It was indeed new, crafted out of the finest dove-gray silk woven into an exquisite brocade pattern. The cut and high collar were the very height of fashion, and it was stitched with the precision that was Simon Wright's signature. It had been delivered to the lodge yesterday morning from Breckenridge, wrapped with a single note that simply said, "Thank you."

"It is," Will admitted reluctantly.

The young lord was peering at the stitching. "That looks almost like a Wright piece," he mused. "The buttons and the brocade are classic."

"It is." Will frowned. He should have known a fop like Braxton would recognize the tailoring on sight.

The man clapped his hands together in delight. "Then he is back in London?"

"Not exactly," Will hedged.

"You lucky dog," Braxton sniffed. "I almost died when I discovered he had simply up and left London. Though I suppose his rather abrupt departure was a blessing."

"And how is that?"

The young man looked at Will as though it should be obvious. "I owed Mr. Wright a small fortune," he said, laughing. "It was not my fault—he was too talented. I simply had to have such finery. Just as well I never got around to settling my account. My father would have had my hide."

"You never paid the man?" Will asked carefully, and something in his face must have alerted Braxton to the possibility that the Duke of Worth did not find that amusing.

"You know how it is, Your Grace. We're busy men." He looked at Will in confusion. "He's only a tailor, Your Grace. A nobody."

A dull fury swelled within Will, and for a moment he couldn't speak. "I see," he managed finally. "And what of his family?"

"Whose family?" The man looked baffled.

"Simon Wright's family."

Braxton scoffed. "What about them? I have far more weighty matters to concern myself over than a few low-born brats."

Will felt his hands curl into fists. "Well then, Braxton, let me offer you some small advice. Admitting you do not possess the wherewithal for such basic courtesies as settling your domestic debts leaves me doubting not only your intellectual ability, but your honor as well."

Braxton gaped at Will, slashes of color high on his cheeks.

Will turned away, afraid he would say or do something further he might regret. He pushed his way through the crowd out of the ballroom and into the soaring hall, finding himself taking deep, calming breaths, trying to put his thoughts in order. Lord Braxton had been on the list he'd forced Jenna to show him. And given the man's uncaring admission, it was quite apparent why.

"There you are, dear." The duchess's voice broke into his thoughts. "I had given up hope I'd ever find you in that crowd. I understand Boden took Viola home early ..." She trailed off. "Is something wrong?"

Will turned to find his mother standing not three feet away, Lady Julia hovering behind her.

Will gazed at Eleanor, unable to reconcile everything that had been revealed in the last hour, including his mother's own complicity. If he spoke now, he would say something he would regret later, of that he was certain. He needed time. Time to sort out the tumultuous thoughts that were careening wildly inside his head.

"No, Mother," he said with perfect politeness. "But I should like to return home now."

"Of course," the duchess murmured. "I shall call for our carriage." She turned to Julia. "We will see you home first. I do hope your sister is feeling better tomorrow."

"I am quite certain she'll be fine," Will growled before he could stop himself, and his mother looked at him sharply.

He wasn't so certain about himself.

⁓

Will remained silent for the entire ride back to the lodge. Conversation swirled around him, but neither woman made any attempt to force his participation. Even when Julia was deposited back into the care of her brother and Will found himself alone with the duchess, she only sat back as the carriage rumbled on, assessing him openly. It wasn't until they found themselves in the lodge's hall, abandoned and empty at the late hour, that she addressed him.

"Are you going to tell me what's going on or are you going to stew for the remainder of our sojourn?" They had come to a stop near the heavy hall table, where a small pile of the day's correspondence lay. "Does this have something to do with Lady Viola?"

Will stopped short and tried to rein in the spurt of anger that escaped at the question. It had everything to do with Viola. And Jenna. And Eleanor. And the impossible position they had all put him in. He snatched at the envelopes and shuffled through them to stall before he answered.

"I must assume the reason Lady Viola left the ball was not because she had a headache?" the duchess ventured.

Will made a noise that might have been mistaken for a laugh. If Viola didn't have a headache yet, she would by morning.

"I take that as a yes?"

Something inside Will snapped. He could no longer flit about the edges of this entire mess, waiting for bits of information to be thrown out to him that might help him understand. He could no longer tiptoe around courtesy and civility when he was still struggling to make sense of it all. He faced his mother.

"Viola left the ball because she was drunk enough to believe taking off her dress in an effort to become the next Duchess of Worth was a good idea. It was only the clever actions of Miss Hughes, or should I say Madame Maxon, that saved you the pleasure of having Viola Hextall as your daughter-in-law."

Eleanor's face lost color, though her expression didn't change. "You don't say."

"Just what do you think you're doing, Mother?" Will hissed through clenched teeth.

"I'm doing what needs to be done," she replied evenly. "We're doing what needs to be done."

"You can't do it like this! And neither can Jenna."

Two white brows shot up into her hairline, and color flooded her cheeks. "Then tell me how we should be doing it," she snapped back, echoing Jenna's words. "For I don't get to have a voice in parliament. Women can't possibly understand the law or the changes that desperately need to be made to it. Why, the delicate constitution of a female would positively crumble should she be presented with the distasteful unpleasantries of real life beyond her bubble of glittering, insulated dependency." She sneered. "I lived as a prisoner in that damn bubble for far too long, William, put there by your father, who sought to control everything and everyone around him for his own ends. I was punished for daring to have a voice. Punished for fighting back. And I will not live like that again. Not even for you."

Will stared at the duchess, his fingers crushing a piece of stationery, afraid that he would be driven mad by the wickedly thorny conundrum that had no answers.

His mother collected herself first and reasserted her dignity. "How is Christian?" she asked stiffly.

"I beg your pardon?"

The duchess gestured at the envelope, and Will recognized the stationery from his own desk. "I don't know," he said, breaking the blob of wax. He unfolded the paper and stared at the words, and he had to read them twice before they penetrated.

I regret to inform you . . . Christian . . . fever . . . died.

There was a brief footnote scrawled by the physician, assuring Will he'd done everything he could to save the child, but the internal damage from the stab wound had festered and been too much for the boy to overcome.

Will slumped against the wall, feeling nauseated and

winded. Eleanor pulled the paper from his unfeeling fingers and scanned the note, her face creasing into lines of distress and sadness. She let her arm drop.

"I'm so sorry, William," she said. "I know you liked the boy."

"I barely knew him," Will mumbled. He'd spent but half a day with Christian, yet somehow it had seemed longer. In Christian, Will had seen a brave resilience most men could not ever hope to achieve. "I thought he was getting better," he whispered harshly.

Eleanor put a hand on his shoulder. "You gave him his best chance."

"I put him in that situation."

"No, you didn't," the duchess said firmly. "It was others who—"

"I am still a part of that, Mother," he snapped, anger starting to fill the void left by grief and shock. "I am a duke, and since birth I have been a part of the grand mechanisms of a society that allows the selfishness and arrogance of a few to inflict suffering on many. If not directly, then by my ignorance and passiveness. Yet somehow, this is acceptable."

"Is it?" Eleanor challenged.

"What?"

"Acceptable?"

He imagined Christian, lying small and fragile in his bed, cheated out of life. "Of course not!"

The duchess crossed her arms over her ample chest and stared hard at her son. "Well then."

In that instant Will understood. Understood that, if he looked hard enough into the quagmire of uncertain gray, there were black-and-white battle lines that could not be erased or blurred. When he stopped trying to reconcile right and wrong with the expectations of society and instead started reconciling right and wrong with his own conscience, those lines became quite vivid.

Jenna Hughes had drawn her line a long time ago, choosing her side with conviction and courage, but Will hadn't recognized that. His mother had also taken a stand long ago, deploying her artillery and her spies and her troops out of simple human compassion. With sudden clarity, Will realized he was not beholden to the strictures of an aristocratic society that had failed so many, simply because he had been born one of them. He could make a choice. He could make a difference.

Will crumpled the note in his hand, his wrath crystallizing into an icy determination. "Tell me where she is."

Eleanor tipped her head. "Why?"

"Because I want to do the right thing."

Eleanor smiled, a gritty, resolute gesture. "Well, why didn't you just say so at the beginning, dear?"

⁓

There had only been one other night in Jenna's life when she had felt as hopeless and as miserable as she did now. As on that terrible night long ago, she knew she had possessed something of infinite value, and it had slipped through her fingers, a victim of fate and circumstance she was powerless to control. Had she the energy, she might have cried, except crying would bring nothing back. Certainly not the past. And certainly not the man she loved. She would never forget the hurt and betrayal that had etched themselves so deeply in William's face when he finally understood what she truly was.

She sat in the dark, clad only in her chemise, and the cool air raised gooseflesh on her skin, yet she made no effort to find a robe. Instead she stared out sightlessly at the blackness beyond. For the first time since she had undertaken her crusade, she wondered if the price of success might finally have become too high. Jenna leaned her forehead against the cool glass and tried to predict what the dawn would bring. She had no idea if the duke would keep her identity and her scheme a secret, and the uncertainty, along with the suffocating feeling of loss, was making it hard to breathe.

When it came, the tap at the door was like a gunshot, though in reality it was barely audible. Jenna lurched to her feet, upsetting the chair she was sitting on, and she cursed at the resulting clatter. They had come for her, she realized, though she supposed she should have expected it. If she was lucky, it would just be a local constable and not a horde of angry aristocrats. Her mind raced. She could answer the door as a simple lady's maid and pretend ignorance, or it might be better to escape now, unseen. *Escape*, she decided almost instantly, for the risk of a clever interrogator was too great. Her heart in her throat and doing her best to keep panic at bay, Jenna scanned the room. The window was her only option, she realized, though how she was going to get from where she was standing to the ground in one piece was unclear.

"Jenna?" The word was a muffled hiss.

She froze, not daring to trust her ears. Silently she crept to the door on her bare feet. On the other side she could hear faint, impatient movements.

"Open the door," the unseen voice demanded in a harsh whisper.

Jenna squeezed her eyes shut. "Are you alone?"

"Am I— Oh, for God's sake. No, I'm standing in the dark whispering through a door while the King's Guard awaits my pleasure." He paused. "Of course I'm alone. And if you do not open this door in five seconds, I will open it for you."

Jenna choked.

"Five."

Jenna fumbled at the latch and swung the door open.

"You're getting better at that," Will said and stepped into the room, closing the door silently behind him.

Jenna retreated deep into the room, needing to maintain a space between herself and the man she had thought never to see again. His presence here, now, offered a tormenting glimmer of hope, though she forced herself to remain distant and guarded. She didn't know if she could survive having to make the same impossible choice all over again.

Will followed her into the room and stopped before her. In the deep shadows, his expression remained obscured. She stood motionless, waiting for him to speak.

"You're a hard woman to find," he said presently.

"That's the idea." She offered no apologies. The time for deception and excuses was long over.

Will reached for her in the dark, finding the side of her head with his hand. He wound his fingers through her hair, which hung loose down her back. "I didn't like the wig."

"I don't like it either. It makes my head itch terribly."

"The dress was an improvement." His fingers touched her shoulder and then traced the edge of her arm. "Though I'm not sure I approve of the cut."

"It has its uses." Jenna might have smiled faintly, but the duke couldn't see it. In that, the darkness was for the best, stripping away everything between them but the truth.

"Who is M. Billeck?" Will asked into the silence.

She hadn't expected that. Briefly Jenna wondered how Will might have known to ask, though she supposed it no longer mattered. "Martin Billeck," she replied. "He owns Escapade. The current favorite in the Windsor Plate."

"Ah, of course," Will muttered, sounding annoyed with himself that he hadn't made the connection earlier. "And based on the surgeon's receipt, I must assume his colt suffers a quarter crack and is not sound."

"One would assume that, yes."

"Lord Braxton is meant to assume that, you mean."

"Yes. Among others."

"But it isn't true, is it? The surgeon's receipt was forged." The duke's voice was strangely expressionless, as though he were idly examining a mundane puzzle.

Jenna shook her head. "The receipt is real enough. If you ask the track surgeon, he will attest he treated Mr. Billeck's gray thoroughbred colt for a quarter crack on the left hind hoof. He will tell you he prepared the initial poultice himself and warned the man that the horse should be put on pasture or risk permanent damage. And he would not be lying."

"Then I don't understand."

"Mr. Billeck owns two gray thoroughbred colts. Escapade is one of them. I might have gotten the horses... confused. It happens sometimes."

There was a long silence. "I see."

"Do you?"

"Braxton will not wager on a losing cause." There was a mocking edge to his words.

"A lame horse will not win," Jenna concurred.

"He'll wager heavily on Escapade's challenger, Dalliance, now that he possesses inside information no one else has."

"One can only hope."

"Dalliance will never beat Escapade."

"No," Jenna agreed.

"Braxton will lose a fortune."

"Yes."

"Good." It was said viciously.

Jenna stilled at the duke's response and his tone. "Why are you here, Will?" she asked.

Will shifted. "I was wrong."

Jenna took a cautious breath. "You were wrong," she repeated. "About what?"

"About what was real and what was right. It took me an unforgivable amount of time to understand that what you do is right. Justified. Necessary."

"And how exactly did you come to that conclusion?"

"Christian died."

Jenna recoiled. "Oh, God." The tears that wouldn't fall earlier suddenly found release and spilled unchecked.

"I'm sorry. I'm sorry for not understanding. For not believing. For not doing what was right the first time I had the chance."

Jenna was pressing her fingers to her eyes as if she could dam her grief.

"I want another chance to do the right thing, Jenna. For Christian. For those who depend on what you do. Please let me help." He caught her hands in one of his and pulled them against him while the other caressed her cheek, smoothing away the dampness.

An anguished desperation was burning in her chest. "It's too late."

"We couldn't save Christian. But there are still so many others for whom we can make a difference." Without warning he kissed her. "I love you, Jenna Hughes," he said against her mouth.

She made a strange sound in her throat, and he kissed her again, not allowing her a response. He gathered her against him, tucking her head against his shoulder and holding her tightly.

Jenna held on to him, hearing the sound of his heart against her ear and feeling the heat of his body through their clothes. She wasn't sure how long they stood there in the dark before he pulled back slightly and scooped her into his arms. He carried her to the bed and placed her in the center, leaving her only long enough to divest himself of the evening clothes he still wore. Jenna lay on her side, watching the shifting shadows as he finished and crawled in next to her, drawing the coverlet over the both of them.

Jenna nestled into his warmth, suddenly exhausted beyond measure. Will placed soft kisses on her forehead, her cheeks, and her mouth before his arms went around her as if he could protect her from a world that was not always kind.

"Sleep," he whispered. "I won't let you go again."

Surprisingly, Jenna slept, waking sometime in the early dawn to find herself still firmly encircled in Will's arms, his breath steady and even as he slumbered beside her.

She studied his beautiful face in the gray light, thinking that if ever she could choose a manner in which to wake every morning, this would be it.

I love you, the Duke of Worth had said, and it had not been muttered in the throes of passion or spoken as a casual endearment. It had been said in a tempest of honesty and truth, a gift given freely with no expectations in return. And she believed him. Just as she believed she owed him the same honesty, no matter that it would change nothing.

She shifted, tipping her head to brush her lips to his, feeling them curve slightly as he woke with her touch. She ran a finger down the side of his jaw, dark with a day's worth of stubble, and he opened his eyes. For a moment she was content to watch him, the love he had declared last night visible now in the depths of his own gaze.

"I wasn't sure I would ever see you again after last night's ball," she said quietly.

Will's eyes darkened, and he opened his mouth to speak, but Jenna placed a finger over his lips.

"I would still be in love with you."

He had stilled, a fierce joy shining from his face.

"Do you feel the same way you did last night?"

"About you?" Will asked hoarsely. "Know this, Jenna. Nothing will ever change how I feel about you. You've become my stars and my sun and everything I need to find my way in this world."

Jenna's heart constricted in her chest, and she nearly gave in to the wild urge to abandon reality. "And what about the rest?"

"Everything I said last night I meant. I am on your side, Jenna Hughes. Now and forever." He paused, searching her eyes. "Marry—"

Jenna kissed him before he could again ask the impossible, unwilling to deny this man anything at this moment. She could feel a brief hesitation, a second when she thought he might insist on an answer, but then he groaned and his mouth became hot and demanding. In one motion he rolled over her, claiming her as only he could.

They made love slowly and tenderly, unhurried in the pale light of dawn. When they lay spent and damp beneath the sheets, still cocooned against the inevitability of the day, Jenna simply gazed at the man who had crashed into her life and stolen her heart. She wished everyone could see the man she saw.

"What are you thinking?" he asked, caressing the skin on the insides of her wrists.

"I want you to be happy," Jenna told him.

"I am happy. Happier than I've ever been in my life. There is only one thing that could make me more so."

Jenna closed her eyes briefly. Alongside the Duchess of Worth, as her paid companion, Jenna had experienced firsthand the malice society inflicted on those it judged as anomalies. But Eleanor had chosen that, sought it out, cultivated it even, for a purpose that had been shaped and forged from her own adversity.

A far different set of circumstances would prevail if she were to stand alongside the Duke of Worth as his wife. Jenna could not be the woman who would set him apart, creating dissension and derision at his every turn. Not when he had so recently found peace and purpose within himself. The opinions and regard of Will's peers and contemporaries still mattered to him. She could not risk the chance that one day she might become the woman who held him back and the very real possibility he would come to resent her for it.

"Winning the Gold Cup," she said, hating herself for her cowardice but unwilling to sacrifice this tiny taste of heaven to discord.

Will's fingers paused before resuming their pattern. "Yes," he lied.

"You will tell Isaac what I told you last night?"

"Of course."

Jenna shifted, kissing Will softly on the lips, the only apology she could offer, though she knew it wouldn't be enough.

Will watched her as she drew back. "Tell me how you collect the money," he said suddenly, granting Jenna her reprieve.

"The money?"

"The money that the men on your list will wager. I must assume they do not place their bets at the communal betting post."

"No, though there are two bookmakers who work with us from time to time. They, however, have a fairly limited role."

Will frowned. "Then how?"

Jenna studied him for a moment before pushing herself up with a curious mixture of regret and anticipation. It would seem the day, and everything that would come with it, was already intruding.

"Perhaps," Jenna said slowly, "it would be better if I showed you."

Chapter 18

The Four Kings was located a stone's throw from the edge of the track, dwarfing the smaller, more ragged tents and booths that clustered around it. It was barely more than a raised wooden floor with large timber beams and a crisscross of stout ropes rising up to support the canvas that protected its patrons from the elements. It appeared each year at Ascot, then vanished again, another temporary oasis of entertainment. Yet for all the simplicity of the structure, the interior was decadently sumptuous. The inside was covered by wide swaths of crimson and gold-colored cloth that shimmered over every wall. Large gaming tables had been set up at regular intervals across the floor space, offering people the chance to try their hand at faro, hazard, vingt-et-un, and even the novel and popular rouge et noir. At the front of the tent, a list of the day's races had been posted on a large board, showing each horse, owner, and rider.

Will stood near the entrance, allowing his eyes to adjust after the bright sun, getting his bearings. Even at this early hour, the place was surprisingly crowded, well-dressed men and the occasional woman crouched over the many tables of chance. Will wondered if they had arrived early or simply never made it home the night before. He suspected the latter in most cases.

From somewhere along the side, a man the size of a rhinoceros appeared, moving far more stealthily than should have been possible. He looked like a champion pugilist, with the exception of the well-made, if simple, black clothes he wore.

"Good morning. Can I help you?" the man asked blandly, all the while blocking Will's path into the tent.

Will frowned slightly. "Er, indeed. I would like to gain admittance."

"Do you have an invitation?"

"An invitation? No."

"Then I'm sorry, sir, but I cannot help you." The giant motioned to indicate that Will should return the way he had come.

"I am the Duke of Worth," Will said in a low voice.

"I see. Then I'm sorry, Your Grace, but I cannot help you."

"I beg your pardon?" Will wasn't sure if he should be amused or scandalized.

The man crossed his arms over his chest. "You must have an invitation or a personal recommendation to be granted privileges within this establishment, Your Grace."

Suddenly Will understood. "Would a recommendation from Madame Maxon be suitable?"

The guard inclined his head. "It would. Of our exclusive clientele she is a valued patroness."

"Indeed I am," murmured Jenna as she slid from behind Will.

The guard's eyes widened fractionally before narrowing in confusion.

"It's all right, Jacob," she said, keeping her head low and shifting the crate she held in her arms. "He's with me. Is everyone in the back?"

"Yes," Jacob said reluctantly, eyeing Will with suspicion.

"Very good. Thank you, Jacob. Please, Your Grace, follow me."

She was dressed in her most shapeless dress and a bonnet, the garments neat but worn. Her hair, like her face, was almost invisible under the deep brim. She looked, for anyone who cared to see, like a servant or a merchant's maid making a delivery.

"Since when does a duke need an invitation to anything?" he whispered wryly as Jenna moved by him.

Jenna might have smiled under the shadow of her bonnet. "There is just something about an inner circle and a need to belong to it that men just can't resist. A little like an Almack's voucher, don't you think?"

Will shook his head and trailed after her. None of the patrons even looked up, so intent were they on their games, though pretty serving girls stepped aside as they passed, trays of fine liquors balanced on their bare arms and shoulders.

A redhead saw them coming and abruptly changed her direction as she caught Will's stare.

"Isn't that one of my mother's upstairs maids?" he hissed at Jenna.

"Indeed it is," she murmured.

Will looked around and realized with some shock that he saw more than one familiar face. A scullery maid, two footmen, and a kitchen maid. He would have asked something further, except Jenna was disappearing behind a heavy length of canvas guarded by two more battle-scarred leviathans. The guards turned their assessing eyes toward Will, as if they were considering the best method to achieve his demise should it be required.

Without hesitating, Will ducked through after Jenna.

The room's sole occupant froze, his pencil hovering over a massive ledger that lay open before him. Piles of currency lay stacked neatly across the wide surface of the table behind which he sat. "Good morning, Your Grace," he said, recovering admirably. "We must stop meeting over ledgers." He shot a questioning look at Jenna that was just short of being alarmed.

"He's here to help," Jenna said quietly.

"Indeed?" The old man's features were unreadable.

It was a good five seconds before Will realized the man was, in fact, his mother's secretary, and another five before Will realized Jenna hadn't yelled when addressing him. "George?" he blurted. "But you're not deaf."

The secretary blinked. "Only when necessary," he replied slowly, a gleam in his eye. "People say the damnedest things when they believe you can't hear them. Useful, that."

Will winced.

"My father was an artilleryman before me," George said, taking pity on him. "And he always extolled the value of fine wool packed well." He gestured to his ears.

Will gazed around, noting a massive safe behind the secretary, and the substantial fortune spread out on the table. "And did your father also teach you about running a gaming establishment? For I must assume I am speaking with the infamous Mr. MacGregor." Will took in the fine cut of George's clothes and the neatly groomed silver moustache that hadn't been there the last time Will had seen him. Shiny spectacles sat on the bridge of his nose, giving him a rather scholarly appearance. There was no stoop to his shoulders, and the illusion of frailty was absent. Without Jenna's presence, Will doubted he would have recognized George had the man shaken his hand.

"No, you can thank His Majesty's fine army for that. War, Your Grace, consists of a great deal of waiting around trying to find ways not to think about dying. I was happy to provide such distraction and quite quickly discovered that any man who understands numbers can be successful when it comes to gambling. At least on this side of the table. The odds are always in favor of the house."

Will nodded. "Like the odds you provide to those who wish to wager on the races?"

"Ah. Yes, well, one must have received an invitation to be eligible to wager through the Four Kings. And only on Gold Cup day, when the stakes are highest and the horses fastest, and the crowds largest."

"And the wagers most aggressive. And ill-advised." Will cast a sideways look at Jenna.

"Madame Maxon's advice has won a number of philanthropic gentlemen a great deal of money over the years," Jenna protested mildly. "It is hardly her fault there are others who do not fare as well."

"I prefer to think of it as a method of precise debt collection, Your Grace." George smiled a smile that didn't reach his eyes. "And yes, one must beware of pitfalls when it comes to wagering. Sometimes things are not as they seem."

"No, they are not," Will agreed quietly. "Which is why I want to help."

"And what, exactly, is it you believe you can do, Your Grace?" George asked skeptically but not unkindly.

Will was aware of two pairs of eyes on him, though it was the ice-blue ones he sought out. Everything he aspired to be as a man and a duke was in those crystal depths. "Whatever it takes."

Chapter 19 _____

Jenna slipped through rows of carriages lining the inside rail. Everywhere people crowded, standing on the tops of their equipages and filling the spaces in between. She was less concerned about being able to see the winning post than about having a clear view of the horses as they were brought out from the barns to be saddled and mounted. Around her, bodies pressed and chattered and shouted and pointed, either at people they saw in the crowd or at the horses and riders. She craned her neck in anticipation, not sure if she was looking forward more to watching her colt race or to watching Eleanor Somerhall do what she did best.

Men with long whips were starting their slow travels down the rail, pushing people back behind the barrier and chasing the urchins and beggars away. They were alternately cheered and booed, and a great roar of laughter arose when a youth in tatters and bare feet slipped around one of the prickers and stole his horsewhip, instigating a chase across the turf the man would never win. The laughter changed to an interested buzz as the first horses were led out and the urchin forgotten.

All the horses were covered in thick rugs, like destriers of old, caparisoned in heavy quilted fabric from the tips of their ears down to their hocks. All except Jenna's colt, and there was a definite pause in the hum of the crowd as it got its first look at the horse owned by the eccentric Duchess of Worth. Jenna nearly giggled through her nerves as Paul led the colt out onto the turf, Joseph trailing behind with the saddle and Luke sauntering in the rear, dressed in his racing silks. All three brothers were utterly expressionless, which was a credit to their self-control. Because, based on the titters and outright laughter that were building around Jenna, they had certainly outdone themselves.

The horse had been decorated like nothing short of a May Day pole. A narrow pink ribbon had been woven through the colt's forelock and another had been braided into the top of its tail. A dainty red rose had been tucked behind its ears. The animal, to the casual observer, looked like a ridiculous child's plaything, a rocking horse toy in a herd of sleek, spirited thoroughbreds. The duchess herself sailed out to greet her grooms and her horse from where she had been waiting, flushed and clapping her hands in girlish delight. Her gown, the same pink as the ribbons adorning her horse, billowed behind her in the breeze, and a pretty red rose was pinned into her white hair just above her ear. And escorting the duchess was the Duke of Worth.

He was dressed casually in simple buckskin breeches and a black riding coat. He was easily a head taller than anyone around him and moved with absolute authority and confidence as he guided his mother closer to her horse. More than a few smirks were hastily snuffed as the duke passed, replaced with polite nods and sideways glances.

Eleanor had almost reached her colt, and she was beaming broadly. "Look, Worth dear, doesn't he have just the cutest ears?" she trilled loudly for all to hear, glancing back at the duke. "I just *love* a horse with pointy ears. It was his ears that made me sure I *had* to have him."

"The horse does indeed have lovely ears, Mother," Will said easily, an indulgent smile affixed firmly to his face. He was greeting those he knew with good humor and an occasional chuckle. He came to a stop beside Paul and appeared to be in casual conversation with the stable master while the brothers saddled the colt and Joseph gave Luke a leg up. He was still smiling and laughing, even as he disentangled a ribbon that had wrapped itself around his coat sleeve, blown loose in the wind.

The duchess was doing her part, thrilling the gawking spectators with expansive hand gestures and loud, gleeful laughter, and once Luke was up and mounted, she pressed an effusive kiss to the colt's nose. The horse pinned its ears, and Luke turned it away even as the audience sniggered in unison. Jenna watched as her colt went by, passing the collection of stands and lines of carriages as it headed in the direction of the new mile start. As they passed the betting stand, Luke slowed the horse from a canter into a rough trot. The silk of Luke's racing colors fluttered in the breeze, a brilliant rose hue with the silhouette of what looked suspiciously like a rooster embroidered in royal blue across the back. Laughter rippled along the crowd, following the horse's progress. Luke made no effort to pace the colt with the other horses as they made their way along the track, doing everything in his power to make the animal a laughingstock.

Jenna grinned. The odds on her colt were lengthening by the second.

～

He'd not thought he'd find Jenna in the throng surrounding the track—dressed as she was as a servant, he knew she would be invisible. But he couldn't stop himself from looking. There was so much more he needed to say to her. For now, knowing she was out there somewhere watching, he would do everything he could to make sure his actions spoke for him.

Will escorted his mother to a good position in the small stand near the winning post. She fanned herself against the warmth, a pretty flush coloring her cheeks.

"You were splendid, dear," she murmured as they both turned to view the turf that had by now nearly been cleared of bodies. Across the track in the infield, chaos still ruled, a sea of spectators, tents, carriages, and horses.

"Thank you," Will acknowledged.

"You should have pinned a red rose to your coat." Eleanor smirked.

"For enough money, I might be persuaded next time." His lips twitched.

"Speaking of money, I heard a rumor Lord Braxton lost a small fortune earlier this afternoon. Children these days. So irresponsible. His father will have his head." The duchess *tsk*ed.

Will kept his face serene. "It would seem a number of gentlemen made the same mistake. One must wonder why they would not have favored Escapade, for the colt ran a brilliant race. Never looked better." He watched as the horses disappeared from sight.

Eleanor gave Will's arm a tight squeeze. "I'm so very proud of you, William," she said quietly, looking up at him. "I never told you that enough over the years."

Will covered his mother's hand with his own. "Thank you. I think."

Eleanor raised a brow.

"I would imagine most men would seek admiration from their families for more noble endeavors than fixing a horse race," Will murmured in her ear.

"Most men seek admiration for selfish endeavors where praise can be given easily and lavishly. Genuine nobility is a sight more difficult to achieve, and rarely is it visible enough to earn accolades. I regret I did not confide in you earlier."

Will considered his mother. "I'm not sure I would have been ready. I'm not sure I would have truly understood earlier."

"I see." Eleanor was watching him with her sharp, shrewd eyes. "And now?"

"Now I understand because I've witnessed true bravery and honor."

"You're speaking of Miss Hughes."

Will held her gaze. "Yes. And you."

Eleanor sniffed and squeezed his arm again. Her eyes looked a little misty, and she cleared her throat. They both stared out at the track, waiting for the start of the race.

"Will you marry her then?" the duchess asked.

After everything, Will had thought himself immune to further shock. But now he found himself staring at his mother, slack-jawed.

"Oh, don't look at me like that, dear," Eleanor chided. "I'm not blind."

"Um." Will was having a hard time constructing a sentence.

"Do you love her?"

"Yes." He could manage to answer that at least.

"Then that is all that matters. Do not make the same mistake I did," she told him. "Follow your heart and give yourselves a chance at happiness. Forever is a long time."

Will fumbled for a response, but the duchess was drawn into conversation by a well-dressed matron on her other side.

"Your Grace." The greeting intruded as a man squeezed in next to Will. He suppressed his irritation and turned to find Viscount Carthart hovering at his elbow, his bushy gray brows drawn low over his gray eyes. In fact, Will thought, everything about the viscount seemed rather gray, from his hair to his complexion to his coat.

"Lord Carthart," Will said, forcing a smile even as he fought back his distaste. The outstanding debts the viscount had accumulated were worse than Braxton's. And it wasn't because of lack of funds. Will knew Carthart's name showed up habitually in the betting books at almost all the gentlemen's clubs. The viscount could never refuse a wager, no matter how asinine, and Will suddenly sensed an opportunity.

The man cleared his throat. "I was surprised to see your mother's name on the racing sheets," he said. "I must confess, I did not realize Her Grace had an interest in horse racing."

"Neither did I until quite recently," Will replied.

"Did you purchase the horse for her?" Carthart asked carefully.

"Good heavens, no. I had nothing to do with...that,"

Will told him with perfect honesty as he gestured out in the direction of the turf.

The viscount opted for tact. "The ribbons were a trifle irregular."

Will dropped his voice. "I think you and I know a great number of things my mother does are irregular," he said, allowing a little distress to creep in. "But she is still my mother. And I should endeavor to show her support somehow." Will sighed.

Lord Carthart looked thoughtfully at Will. "Perhaps you might place a wager on her horse?"

Will pretended to consider this. "That is an excellent idea. But I fear it is too late. The race will start in minutes, I'm sure, and I imagine you've already placed your bets for this race."

"I have. But I would honor a wager with you, Your Grace, made right here, should you wish to show your support for your mother's horse." The viscount looked almost giddy, and he was pulling out a small black book and a pencil stub.

Will wrinkled his nose. "That is very kind of you, but I don't think—"

"No, no, I insist," Carthart maintained.

"Indeed. Very well then, I would be obliged. I shall pick my mother's black colt as the winner of this race against the rest of the field as the terms of our wager?"

The viscount nodded eagerly, writing down the details.

"You may name the sum," Will suggested, allowing the viscount control over his own fate.

The viscount settled on an amount that startled Will, but only for a moment, and his surprise was quickly replaced by a delicious satisfaction. His mother's beribboned colt had, in light of the earlier spectacle, been wholly dismissed as a serious threat. A long shot that would be lucky to finish the race, much less win it. Which, Will knew, was precisely what the proprietor of the Four Kings was counting on when it came to his patrons.

Will accepted the scribbled note the viscount handed him and slid it into his pocket. He certainly hadn't planned this little side wager, but he would take this man's money with no remorse. He craned his neck, but the horses were long out of sight now. They'd be nearing the far end of the track and the new mile start. From there it would be a straight sprint in front of the stands to the winning post.

"Heard you had some work done at your country manor last summer," Will said conversationally as they waited.

The viscount preened. "Indeed. Had every stone re-pointed. Took forever. I'm having the gardens land-scaped now. My wife saw those blasted marbles Elgin had carted over from some Greek ruin and has taken the notion she wants similar sculpture amid her plants."

"And will you pay the gardeners once they are done?" Will asked blandly.

"I beg your pardon?"

"Everyone knows you've yet to pay the masons that did your stonework last summer. One must wonder if it is because you've run out of funds or you've run out of memory."

The viscount's mouth had dropped open in slack shock.

"If you've run out of money, I would be happy to provide you with a loan," Will continued, as though this were an everyday conversation. "I do warn you, however, that I am not nearly as patient as your stonemasons. If it's your memory, I'm afraid I can't help you with that, other than to recommend a good physician versed in such matters."

Carthart's mouth opened and closed a few times. "I can assure you, Your Grace, that is not necessary," he finally managed.

Will shrugged carelessly. "As you wish." In the distance, still beyond their view, a rumble was slowly growing as a dozen horses began their sprint down the turf. "Ah, here they come."

The viscount stared at him before snapping his head around as the horses came into view. Or, more accurately, as the beribboned colt came into view. Luke was crouched low over the horse's back, riding effortlessly. Some distance behind thundered the rest of the field, and the only race that was left was the one for second place. A disbelieving hum went up, followed by shouts and laughing cheers as the Duchess of Worth's colt swept across the winning post ten lengths ahead of its nearest challenger.

"Well, will you look at that," Will commented idly. "It would appear my mother knows more about horses than I gave her credit for."

Carthart was nearly white. "But it had ribbons," the viscount wheezed. "Pink ribbons."

"My mother does like pink," Will agreed with a humorless chuckle. "Though in all fairness, I've never seen a little scrap of ribbon slow a horse down."

Carthart was gasping like a landed trout.

"Well, you know my direction," Will said coldly as the crowd around him started to shift and move. "I'd prefer you settle your debt with me before the end of the day, Lord Carthart. You may settle your betting stand wagers first if you need to."

"Didn't use the betting stand," the viscount mumbled in misery. "Wagered at the Four Kings."

"Ah. You took a chance on the better odds."

Another miserable nod.

"That is unfortunate. For I understand Mr. MacGregor, like me, does insist on prompt payment."

The viscount wiped at his brow. "Dear God."

"Perhaps you will have better luck next time." Will left the viscount staring sightlessly out at the turf, a vicious satisfaction taking the edge off his revulsion.

He joined the duchess and gave her a brief nod as her eyes slid past him to rest on Lord Carthart.

"I understand you earned some money," his mother murmured, as she linked her arm through his.

"You heard our conversation."

"Of course I did." She paused. "How does it feel?"

"It feels like justice."

Eleanor squeezed his arm with a crooked grin. "I do so love pink."

Chapter 20

Luke scuffed at a pebble in the dirt with the toe of his boot, sending a small cloud of dust puffing up into the air. He shifted his weight, the rough lumber of the booth he was leaning against rubbing unevenly against his back. Over his head, bright-blue pennants mounted on the long pole snapped in the wind. *Crawley's Spruce Beer*, said the lettering painted on the pennants, and from the enthusiastic crowd that never seemed to diminish, it was clearly very good beer. Or very cheap beer. Or quite possibly both.

Luke found himself suddenly thirsty and dug his hands deep into his pockets, searching for a coin, but as usual finding none. He sighed, disappointed, and instead drew out the apple he'd stuffed into his pocket earlier. Producing a small knife, he slowly started slicing.

The sound of a deliberately cleared throat made him look up.

A heavyset gentleman was standing before him, wearing a tattered coat in an effort to blend in with the lower classes; however, he'd left his hideously expensive silk top hat perched on his head and his Wellington boots were nearly blinding in their sheen. He was clutching a folded newspaper of some sort under his arm and was doing his best to affect a casual stance.

"Luke?" the gentleman asked.

Luke shoved himself off the wall of the booth. "It would depend who'd be asking." He let the Scottish burr run strong.

"We have a mutual friend, I believe." The stranger avoided his question, his eyes darting around him.

Luke put a piece of apple into his mouth and chewed slowly. "I have lots of friends."

The gentleman double-checked his timepiece and then gestured at the blue pennants flying overhead and the apple in Luke's hand. "Our mutual friend was very specific."

"I'm sure." Luke smiled, though it didn't reach his eyes.

The man inched forward and laid the newspaper down on a crate. "I trust you will find everything in order."

Luke glanced at the newspaper and then out at the crowd. "I'm verra sure I will."

"How good is the old bat's filly?"

Luke appraised the sweating man before him. "Didna you see her colt race?"

"Yes. Are you saying the filly is as good?"

Luke snorted rudely. "I'm saying the filly is better."

"You're sure?"

"I ride the wee beasties, don't I?"

The man stared at him, wiping his brow nervously. "I must have your word that you will honor your end of our agreement. That black filly she calls Isis cannot win the Trafalgar Stakes, do you understand?" The last was almost desperate.

"As long as I am riding that wee filly, she willna come close to winning," Luke said with a slight sneer. "You'd not be the first to solicit my services, milord. The money I earn in a year as a riding groom isna enough to buy the left front hoof of the horses I ride," Luke growled bitterly. "I suffer no conscience, only appreciate the extra business."

The gentleman nodded in satisfaction. "Then I look forward to a mutually beneficial arrangement."

In a smooth motion, Luke swept up the paper and walked away.

~

The races, as always, had fallen behind schedule. There had been dozens of false starts, people had had to be repeatedly cleared off the track, and just after two, a phaeton had crashed at the homeward turn of the old mile loop when two young bucks had taken it in their heads to race their equipages on the track between races. It had taken nearly a half hour to cut the struggling horses from their traces, help the injured driver from the wreckage, and collect all the broken pieces strewn across the packed ground. Jenna was perched in her usual spot near the outside edge of the track, a residual satisfaction over her colt's performance warring with a brooding impatience over this delay. She was trying not to fidget, or worse, give in to the urge to find Will and kiss him senseless. He had been brilliant at his mother's side.

Jenna had just turned back to the turf when a rough hand grabbed her elbow. Instinctively she jabbed her arm hard and high, pulling away even as her elbow made contact with hard flesh.

"Jesus," Paul snapped, flinching from the blow.

Jenna stared in horrified disbelief. "What the hell are you doing here?" she hissed, shrinking away. Even in disguise, she was never seen with anyone who might be traced back to the Duchess of Worth.

"Looking for you."

For the first time, Jenna got a good look at Paul's face. His usual grinning bonhomie was absent, and instead the big man looked pale and on the verge of outright panic.

"Dammit, Paul, what's wrong?" Jenna hissed, icy unease slithering through her.

"I'm so sorry, Jenna," he mumbled. "We weren't gone long, but—"

"Paul." Jenna grabbed his arm. "What are you saying?"

"You need to come to the barns," he said. "Now."

～

Will was on his way down to the barns to meet Isaac when Luke found him. There were only two races before the Gold Cup, and Will had intended to wait with his filly and Isaac until then.

"Your Grace," Luke gasped, coming to a shuddering stop in front of him. His face was flushed from the exertion, and his eyes were wide with worry and what looked like desperation.

Will's heart missed a beat. "What's wrong?" he demanded.

Luke shook his head, still winded from his frantic search. "She needs your help," he finally breathed.

"Where is she?" A hundred scenarios flooded his mind, each more horrific than the last. Jenna had been exposed or caught or hurt or—

"The barn."

Will froze. What the hell was she doing in the barns?

"Go," he urged Luke and bolted after the butler.

~~~

Will found them in the end stall where her filly was stabled. Paul was standing guard outside the door, visibly the worse for wear and glowering at anyone who might consider coming too close, though the only people left in the barns were the stableboys unlucky enough to have drawn the short end of the straw and be stuck with the chores while everyone else watched the races. Will forced himself to walk casually, as if nothing were amiss, and followed Luke into the cramped stall.

Jenna had her back to him, braced against the shoulder of her filly, while Joseph had wedged himself against the filly's flank. The horse was covered in rugs, but Will could see the rapid rise and fall of the filly's ribs. The horse shifted and threw its head before being soothed and restrained by Jenna. With a sinking feeling, Will moved silently to the head of the horse, noting the dilated pupils. Quickly he ran a hand under the heavy rugs along the filly's chest, feeling the twitching, shivering skin and the way the filly's normally sleek black coat was standing straight up, the hair stiff against his palm.

Opium. And a lot of it. Probably slipped into a bucket of oats or mash. It wasn't the first time he'd seen this.

"You shouldn't be here," Jenna whispered, her expression haggard.

Will ignored her. "Who drugged the filly?" he demanded, turning to Luke and Joseph. "Did anyone see anything?"

"No," said Luke miserably. "Whoever he was, he waited

until we had all left with the colt for its race. Paul came back and found her already sweating and weaving. The Earl of Brockford would be my guess. He appeared the most desperate of the lot, though in truth it could have been anyone who didn't want this horse to win."

Will doubted the filly could gallop in a straight line at the moment, much less win a race. It would recover, but not in time. "How much is at stake here?" he asked.

"Too much," Jenna whispered in furious frustration. "I should have anticipated this."

"You couldn't have."

She was shaking her head. "Isis is going into the Trafalgar Stakes as the overwhelming favorite. Everything hinges on those men believing Luke will ride this filly in that race and keep her from winning." She blew out an angry breath. "But I won't run her in this condition. I'll have to withdraw her from the race, and every penny of every bet made on her will count for nothing. There is no money to be made off a horse that doesn't run." She rubbed at her eyes. "We've failed so many who were counting on us."

"No, you haven't," Will said suddenly.

Jenna stared at him with despair. "What other choice is there? I'll not ruin—"

"You'll run a horse in the Trafalgar Stakes," Will said, the solution laughably clear, a fierce determination roaring through his body. "You'll run a three-year-old black filly, and she will destroy the rest of the field because she is one of the finest thoroughbreds of her class."

Jenna's mouth had dropped open, and she was gaping at Will as she understood what he was suggesting. "No," she said. "No, you can't. All your hard work, everything you wanted—"

He kissed her then, in the middle of the stall, uncaring who saw.

"Everything I want is standing next to me," Will told her, his tone unyielding. "Everything that matters, everything that is right here." He took a calming breath. "I'll undoubtedly be enraged when I discover my horse has been drugged right before her race, and I'll be sure to throw my best ducal temper tantrum. But Jenna, I don't need a Gold Cup to prove anything to anyone. Not anymore."

Her eyes were as wide as saucers.

"The fillies are as physically identical as you will ever get. They are the same age and the same color, with no distinguishing marks. I have confused them myself on more than one occasion. Whoever had the horse drugged will simply assume you're running Isis despite her condition, and by the time they realize the horse running in the stakes is not the horse they drugged, it will be too late. Or perhaps they will believe the wrong horse was poisoned. Either way, they can't do a damn thing about it. No one is going to admit they drugged the Duke of Worth's horse." He stopped. "Comtessa will run the race she's meant to run."

"But how..." Jenna trailed off, her voice uneven.

Will turned to Joseph with urgency. "My mother has informed me quite recently, among other things, that you used to be the best damn horse thief in all of England. Can you get Isis out?" Will asked. "And bring my filly in without anyone noticing?"

The wiry horse thief gave him a wicked grin. "Of course I can."

"How?" There were eyes everywhere, and they didn't

have much time. Very soon the horses for the Trafalgar Stakes would be fetched to be prepared and saddled.

Joseph winked at Will. "Leave that to me, Your Grace."

Just after three o'clock there was a fire in the barn. Not a large one, as it turned out, but a brief flare-up contained in a steel bucket. Nevertheless, the copious smoke pouring from an initially unseen source had horrified stableboys dragging every horse out of the west barn. Animals milled in alarm, men were yelling for water, and everywhere were pandemonium and confusion. Luckily, the source of the fire was quickly located, the flames extinguished, and more than a few choice words hurled at the unknown idiot who had obviously emptied his pipe or discarded the ashes of his cheroot in a bucket of straw and old hay as he passed by.

Eventually the horses were brought back in, and the grooms and stableboys began the task of resettling the animals after the excitement. The filly belonging to the Dowager Duchess of Worth seemed to settle easily, and its groom even stripped it of the rugs it had been wearing all morning. Rid of the heavy fabric, the horse looked alert and keen and ready to run. In no time it was being led out toward the track for the Trafalgar Stakes.

Chapter 21

Jenna had stayed hidden in the crowd just long enough to see Comtessa led out onto the turf and saddled. She'd stayed just long enough to watch the Dowager Duchess of Worth, once again escorted by her long-suffering son, sail out onto the track to inspect her filly. And she'd stayed just long enough to witness Eleanor's riveting performance as the duchess demanded quite publicly that her compact blond jockey dismount and be replaced right then and there with her dark-haired groom because the lad's complexion better matched the color of her filly.

Jenna didn't need to see the faces of the men who had bribed a jockey who had, in truth, never intended to ride. She did not even need to know which one of those men had poisoned her horse or how much he had lost to the coffers of the Four Kings when he'd been beaten at his own game. Jenna had accomplished what she had set out to do at Ascot, and as much as she wanted to stay and watch the final act of their performance, she needed to make sure Madame Maxon disappeared without a trace before anyone could come looking. At least for another year.

She found a ride back to Windsor in the bed of a farm

wagon, wedged among a dozen others, another unremarkable woman of no particular station or interest returning to town. As the wagon pulled away, she covered her face with the sleeve of her dress against the rising clouds of dust, hearing the roar of the crowd as it swept across the stands like a tidal wave. Jenna knew what they were cheering for. Out on the turf, a lone horse would be coming into view, guided by a dark-haired boy who rode like the wind. The filly's black coat would be rippling in the sunshine like polished obsidian, and its head would be stretched forward as it effortlessly devoured the ground with the unflagging stride its owner knew so well.

A filly that would have won the Gold Cup had it not been running at this moment for the good of many as opposed to the pride of one. A filly that would have brought recognition and regard to an owner who deserved it more than any other. Before he'd done the unthinkable without a second of hesitation.

I was wrong, the Duke of Worth had told her when he had come to her last night. *About what was real and what was right.*

Jenna dropped her head, afraid she might cry for the second time in two days, whether from joy or regret or fear it was difficult to tell. For she knew now that she had been wrong too. About what was real and what was right.

And she wasn't sure if she would get or even if she deserved a second chance to rectify that failing.

⁓

Through the windowpane the setting sun cast a strange golden hue into her room at the Briarwood Rose Inn.

The silence she had returned to would soon give way to commotion as racegoers returned from Ascot Heath, full of gossip and stories and excitement. Already a handful of attendees had trickled in, their voices rising from the common rooms downstairs. The stories on everyone's lips were the success of the eccentric Dowager Duchess of Worth with her beribboned horses, and the scandalous sabotage of the duke's filly.

There was still another day of racing to come tomorrow, though Jenna wouldn't be there to see it. All of Madame Maxon's belongings were gone now, carefully packed away by the same forgettable maid who had unpacked them. The wardrobe stood empty, a hollowed shell that was a perfect representation of her own feelings since she'd left the barns and the track. Jenna picked up the last garment to lay in the trunk, smoothing the crimson silk and watching the fabric dance and glow like embers as it caught the slanted rays of light. It was time to go.

"You left the door open."

Jenna stilled, her heart crashing into her throat. She was afraid to turn around. Afraid to see what would be written across his face. "I grew tired of dukes threatening to open it for me," she said with effort.

"Understandable." Will stepped inside, taking care to close the door in question behind him. He advanced into the room, coming to a stop before he reached her. "I can't say I favor the color."

Jenna glanced down at the red silk still in her hands. Her pulse hadn't slowed.

"I prefer you in blue." Will moved closer. "No, that's not entirely true. I prefer you in breeches."

Jenna turned then, meeting his eyes. They were dark and intense and unreadable.

"Thank you," she blurted, hating the inadequacy of the words. "For what you did today. For everything. I am in your debt."

Will cocked his head. "Indeed? Well, that's good, I suppose. For I have wicked plans for repayment."

Jenna's fingers were curled into the red silk so hard that she thought they might tear the fabric.

"Did you think you might simply return to the dower house without saying goodbye?" He gestured at the open trunk.

Jenna stared at him mutely. She had been terrified she would have to do exactly that. That she had squandered everything she had ever wanted because of her own flawed preconceptions. Dear God, why couldn't she answer?

"For such an intelligent woman, you seem to have a selective memory, Jenna Hughes," Will said, closing the distance between them and reaching for the crimson dress. Slowly he pulled it from her hands and tossed it carelessly on the bed. "When I told you I wasn't ever letting you go again, I meant it."

A rush of joy and longing swept through her, leaving her breathless and weak.

"You can't begin to know what you've given me," Will said, and his voice shook. "You've given me my family back. You've given me the courage to believe in myself and to believe I can make a difference. I love you. And even if you won't—"

Jenna reached up, pressing a finger to his lips before dropping her hand to press her palm over his heart. "Ask me again," she whispered. Her breath was coming in painful gasps. "Please."

Will squeezed his eyes shut before opening them. Grasping her hand in his, he slowly dropped to one knee. "Marry me."

"Yes," she said, the word catching in her throat. "A thousand times yes. It would be my greatest privilege and honor to be your wife."

Will surged to his feet and kissed her, and Jenna surrendered herself fully to the feeling of complete rightness.

"You should have said yes the first time," he grumbled warmly against her ear. "I was assured when I was younger that a duke would never need to beg a lady for her hand. Especially one he was madly in love with from the moment he first saw her."

"Had the lady in question found the courage to trust her heart earlier, she would not have been so difficult. She would have understood that the man who told her she was strong and brave and real was all of those things too. She would have realized that her soul would always be a part of his long before this moment. I promise you it will not happen again."

"See that it doesn't," he murmured.

"The scandal will be incredible," she whispered.

Will pressed his mouth to the hollow beneath her throat. "Indeed it will. And I believe I am looking forward to it. I've had some experience with scandal, you know. I have a very peculiar mother."

"Oh, God. The duchess." Jenna sucked in a breath.

Will looked down at her, a gleam in his eye. "Yes, I almost forgot. My mother told me to tell you you're dismissed. Though she still expects you to continue riding her thoroughbreds."

Jenna's eyes widened before she grinned. "Then I am forced to ask, Your Grace," she said with devilish indignation, "do you think by marrying me I can further this crusade you and your mother have undertaken?"

Will laughed. "Dear God, but I hope so."

And then he kissed her again, a slow, sweet promise of forever.

The Earl of Boden wants to settle down with an irreproachable lady. But when a mysterious puzzle falls into his lap, so does his best friend's sister, Joss, who's anything but demure—and impossible to ignore...

Please see the next page for a preview of

You're the Earl That I Want.

Chapter 1 _____

I need a wife."

Beside him the Duke of Worth choked on his drink.

"And I need you to help find me one. As soon as possible," Heath continued, ignoring his best friend's reaction.

"I must be drunker than I thought," the duke said, dabbing his chin. "For I could have sworn the Earl of Boden just asked me to find him a wife. And if that weren't strange enough, the aforementioned earl is supposed to be in Liverpool turning everything he touches into gold. He couldn't possibly be in a London ballroom, certainly not without having let me know he was back in town prior." He sounded affronted, though he was grinning as he said the last.

"Don't be an ass, Will." Heath felt his own mouth twitch in response in spite of him.

"Well, I've missed you too." The duke thumped Heath on the back and signaled to a footman to bring another drink. "Did you just get back?"

"This afternoon," Heath sighed.

"How were the roads?"

"Cold. Miserable." Heath leaned on the balcony railing, the din of a ball in full swing filtering up to where they stood. "But passable."

"And after days of being confined in a coach, you chose to come *here*? To the Baustenburys' ball?" Will said the last with some disbelief, eyeing the crush of people below them.

"You're here."

"I have an excuse. My mother wanted to come."

Heath kept his face carefully neutral. "Yes, I saw her earlier. You know she's carrying, ah, a live chicken around under her arm again?"

"Is she? I thought she was going to leave the poultry in the carriage tonight." Will shrugged, and then his eyes lit up. "Did you know Josephine is back in town? She's here somewhere tonight too."

Heath frowned, both at the duke's dismissal of the dowager's bizarre behavior and the sudden and unexpected reference to his younger sibling. "Your sister?"

"Yes, my sister," Worth chided him. "I only have one. Joss will be thrilled to see you. You'll have to find her and reacquaint yourself."

Heath had a sudden vision of a curly-haired hoyden scrambling after both boys every summer. A girl utterly resolute in her intention to drive anyone around her to madness with her constant lectures on a confusing array of topics.

"Of course," he murmured. Not that he wouldn't be dutiful and welcome Will's sister back to London, but he very much doubted Josephine Somerhall had given him a moment's thought since he'd last seen her, especially since Heath hadn't been overly gracious to her in his youth. In fact, he might describe the bulk of his past actions toward Will's little sister as abysmal. With some discomfiture he shoved those recollections aside. He'd certainly grown up since then, and whatever idiocy he'd suffered as a boy had little bearing on the matters at hand.

As if reading his mind, Worth peered at him over the rim of his glass. "So what's your excuse tonight, Boden, really? You're not usually one for balls of any sort."

The footman reappeared, and Heath accepted a glass of whiskey. He took a healthy swallow before he spoke. "As I said, I need a wife."

"Holy God, you're actually serious." Worth's forehead creased. "When did you decide this?"

"When I got home from Liverpool and discovered my housekeeper quit and my valet eloped with my only upstairs maid."

"I'm not following."

"I've managed my family's business for more years than I care to remember. I dug the damn earldom out of a financial hole so deep I'm not sure I ever did find the bottom. My mother is still hiding in Bath, unwilling and unable to face society after what happened with my sister and the aftermath of her broken betrothal. I did what I could to mitigate that indignity—"

"Very admirably," the duke interjected.

"—only to find myself with another sister so determined to elevate her social standing through marriage that I am constantly extracting her from compromising situations. And so are you, if I may be so gauche as to remind you."

Will winced at the last. "Ah, yes, the unfortunate Ascot incident. Please let's forget it."

Heath ran a hand through his hair in suppressed frustration. "Since becoming earl I've had crumbling buildings repaired, leaky roofs replaced, fences mended, hired stewards and workers, and sorted through piles of outstanding taxes and payment schedules. All while still maintaining my business. I simply have no energy left to deal with the domestic aspect of my life, Worth. I need a partner. A pleasant, even-tempered soul who will simply be content with me and the comforts I can provide." He glanced down at the crowds of people.

"You're surveying the prospects."

"You make it sound so mercenary. But yes, I am exploring my options."

The duke snorted. "Well, what you've described to me is a well-trained broodmare," he said. "And I have a stable full of them. I shall ask my wife to select one for you, and you can have it, no strings attached. There's no need to do anything rash."

"That's not funny."

"I wasn't trying to be funny. I was trying to convey that you're selling yourself short."

Heath let his eyes rove over the masses of pretty, pastel-clad women. "I don't think I am," he sighed. "I just want to be happy."

"You won't be happy with a match of convenience. You're too clever and too..." Will struggled for a word. "Passionate about life. You'll be bored to death."

"I like boring," Heath snapped. "For once, boring would be a nice change. What's wrong with wanting a wife who will not go looking to stir up trouble? One who can manage my household, bear my children, and provide pleasing companionship? Is that too much to ask?"

"The difficulties you've encountered in the past were not your fault," the duke protested.

"Not my fault, but my problem. And I'm bone-tired of solving problems," Heath sighed. Four years of family scandal had left him spiraling down into a pit of numbing exhaustion.

"But that doesn't mean—"

"Not all of us are as immune to infamy as you," Heath said. "It just seems to roll right off your back."

"That is because I finally discovered what truly matters to me."

"And you're a duke," Heath muttered.

Worth gave a self-deprecating snort. "Doesn't hurt."

Heath gave his friend a weary smile. He wished things were that easy for him. But Heath had a business to run, the success of which depended on an upstanding image. It also relied on connections and good relations with suppliers and buyers and customers. He simply couldn't afford to ignore how society judged his family.

He drew a deep breath. "Boring," he repeated firmly. "I want boring. I want you to help me find the most boring woman here." Heath scanned the dancers. "What about that one?" He gestured to an attractive brunette standing with a woman who could only be her mother near the edge of the floor.

"Ah, Miss Alice Edget. Daughter of Viscount Edget. Impeccable breeding along with a spotless reputation. A lovely girl, but not known for her, ah, wit." William made a face. "Conversation, I fear, would be rather limited."

"She sounds perfect."

"You can't be serious, Boden."

Heath crossed his arms. "These days, I am always serious."

"I've noticed. You were far more fun when you were merely the son of a soap maker. Inheriting a fancy title has been the ruin of you, you know."

"Are you going to insult me or help me?"

Worth sighed. "Of course I'll help you. But at least wait for another month. There will be more eligible ladies in town by then."

"Introduce me to Miss Edget."

"No."

"No?" Heath repeated more harshly than he'd intended.

"I have been your friend since we were three years old. I cannot in good conscience allow you to consign yourself to a lifetime of regret and mediocrity."

"If you won't do it, I'll find someone who will."

"You'll be asleep before you're halfway through a waltz." Worth stared at him, but Heath refused to look away. "Fine," the duke relented. "But don't say I didn't warn you."

In hindsight, Will had indeed warned him, though Heath would never give him the satisfaction of knowing he'd been right. Miss Edget had been flawlessly polite upon Heath's introduction to her, even if her mother had seemed less enthusiastic than he would have liked. Though that was nothing he hadn't experienced before. Not everyone believed any amount of money could adequately compensate for the fact that his title had been completely accidental or that he depended on the vulgar practice of industry and trade to keep his coffers filled. But Miss Edget had placed her hand on his arm with no hesitation when he'd made his bow, and he'd been encouraged.

"Are you having a nice time tonight, Miss Edget?" Heath asked as she executed the steps with perfect precision.

"I'm having a lovely time, my lord," she replied, even as the music stuttered and shrieked.

"What do you think of the orchestra?" he inquired with a small chuckle, hoping to put her at ease. The musicians were spectacularly inept.

"It's lovely, my lord." She smiled up at him.

Lovely? A herd of tortured donkeys would sound better. Though perhaps she was simply too polite to remark upon it.

"Did you enjoy the supper?" he tried.

"It was lovely, my lord." Her smile flashed again.

Heath hid a frown. "Tell me something about yourself," he prompted.

"Like what?"

Heath flailed for a suggestion. "Do you enjoy travel?"

Miss Edget shuddered, though she recovered with a brave face and another bright smile. "Not overly, my lord. I find it very upsetting to my constitution."

Heath struggled to keep a pleasant smile on his face. Well, that was no good. His potential wife might need to travel from time to time with him. Especially if he expanded his business in America the way he was hoping to.

"That is too bad. I believe you would like Boston very much."

"Is that in Scotland?" she asked, blinking prettily.

"Er, no," he managed.

"Is that where Lady Josephine was?"

"I beg your pardon?"

"My mother told me you are very close with the Duke of Worth."

"Yes. We've been friends for many, many years."

Miss Edget nodded, pleased with his answer. "That's lovely. It must be very advantageous to be friends with a duke."

Heath had never really thought about it like that before. And why were they talking about Worth? Or his sister? "Er..."

"I heard my mother talking about Lady Josephine. She said she lived with savages. Is it true?"

"I'm sorry?" The question was so unexpected that Heath wasn't sure he'd heard properly.

"I heard she lived in strange places." Miss Edget was watching him with round eyes. "With *savages*."

"I can assure you, Lady Josephine did not live with savages. I believe she has resided in Italy for a good number of years." But even as he finished speaking, he realized he had no idea where Joss had really been for the last decade.

"Oh." She nodded. "Are there savages in Italy?"

Heath sighed. "No, Miss Edget, there are no savages in Italy."

Perhaps William had been partly right. Alice Edget might not be exactly what he was looking for, but there were plenty of choices. He was an earl now, and an obscenely wealthy one at that. How hard could it be?

～

Heath had retreated back to the sanctity of the balcony overlooking the ballroom, and was nursing another glass of whiskey. He brooded darkly, examining the results of his efforts these last three hours since he had returned Miss Edget to the care of her mother.

He'd danced with at least a half dozen ladies, some seeming impossibly young, others impossibly jaded. The conversations had ranged from stilted to outright awkward, and Heath had been at a loss as to how to improve upon any of it. Worse, the topic of the Duke of Worth's sister had come up on more than a few occasions, veiled as a casual inquiry, though currents of speculation ran swiftly below each offhand remark. Heath most certainly hadn't come to this ball to be pummeled for information on the return of the prodigal Lady Josephine. He'd come as the Earl of Boden, to interview potential wives.

And he'd failed miserably.

Was there not a woman in London who might possess a modicum of intelligence paired with a pleasant demeanor? He wasn't looking for brilliance, though the ability to have an opinion on at least something would be nice. He didn't require beauty, though a woman with a bit of backbone and confidence in herself certainly appealed. And he wasn't so naïve that he didn't realize his wealth was at the forefront of every whispered conversation between prospective in-laws should he dare ask for a second dance, but the poorly disguised hints about annual allowances were starting to wear.

A subtle disturbance altered the pitch of the crowd in the corner of the ballroom below him, just enough to distract him from his quandary. It was enough to be detected beneath the clamor of the orchestra that seemed to be getting worse as the night went on. Idly Heath scanned the mob, looking for the cause, relieved to be distant from whatever disruption was happening. Someone, at least, had bigger problems than he did. A scandalous waltz danced between lovers, perhaps. The arrival of a man's mistress in the presence of his wife. An argument between two gentlemen over a— Heath's speculation died an abrupt death as he followed the craning necks and darting eyes of the guests below. He froze, his eyes riveted on the scene below him.

Heath had finally found Josephine Somerhall.

Fall in Love with Forever Romance

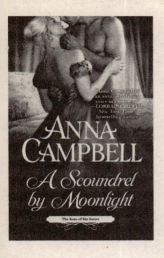

A SCOUNDREL BY MOONLIGHT
by Anna Campbell

Justice. That's all Nell Trim wants—for the countless young women the Marquess of Leath has ruined with his wildly seductive ways. But can she can resist the scoundrel's temptations herself? Check out this fourth sensual historical romance in the Sons of Sin Regency series from bestselling author Anna Campbell!

SINFULLY YOURS
by Cara Elliott

Secret passions are wont to lead a lady into trouble . . . The second rebellious Sloane sister gets her chance at true love in the next Hellions of High Street Regency romance from bestselling author Cara Elliott.

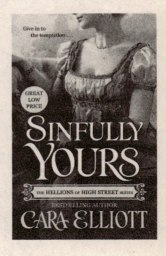

Fall in Love with Forever Romance

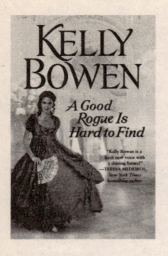

A GOOD ROGUE IS HARD TO FIND
by Kelly Bowen

The rogue's life has been good to William Somerhall, until he moves in with his mother and her paid companion, Miss Jenna Hughes. To keep the eccentric dowager duchess from ruin, he'll have to keep his friends close—and the tempting Miss Hughes closer still. Fans of Sarah MacLean and Tessa Dare will fall in love with the newest book in Kelly Bowen's Lords of Worth series!

WILD HEAT
by Lucy Monroe

The days may be cold, but the nights are red-hot in *USA Today* bestselling author Lucy Monroe's new Northern Fire contemporary romance series. Kitty Grant decides that the best way to heal her broken heart is to come back home. But she gets a shock when she sees how sexy her childhood friend Tack has become. Before she knows it, they're reigniting sparks that could set the whole state of Alaska on fire.

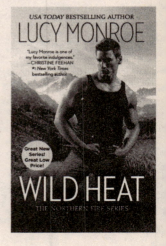

Fall in Love with Forever Romance

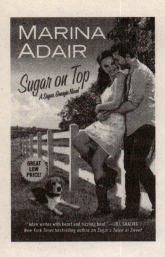

SUGAR ON TOP
by Marina Adair

It's about to get even sweeter in Sugar! When scandal forces Glory Mann to co-chair the Miss Sugar Peach Pageant with sexy single dad Cal MacGraw, sparks fly. Fans of Carly Phillips, Rachel Gibson, and Jill Shalvis will love the latest in the Sugar, Georgia series!

A MATCH MADE ON MAIN STREET
by Olivia Miles

When Anna Madison's high-end restaurant is damaged by a fire, there's only one place she can cook: her sexy ex's diner kitchen. But can they both handle the heat? The second book of the Briar Creek series is "sure to warm any reader's heart" (*RT Book Reviews* on *Mistletoe on Main Street*).

Fall in Love with Forever Romance

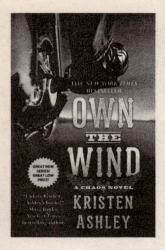
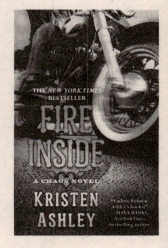